DUKE DARCY'S CASTLE

Also by Syrie James

Historical Romance

Duke Darcy's Castle

Summer of Scandal

Runaway Heiress

Historical Fiction

Jane Austen's First Love

The Missing Manuscript of Jane Austen

The Secret Diaries of Charlotte Brontë

Dracula, My Love

The Lost Memoirs of Jane Austen

Contemporary Romance

Nocturne

Songbird

Propositions

Young Adult Romance

Forbidden

Embolden

DUKE DARCY'S CASTLE

A Dare to Defy Novel

SYRIE JAMES

AVONIMPULSE
An Imprint of HarperCollinsPublishers

Excerpt from *Runaway Heiress* copyright © 2018 by Syrie James.
Excerpt from *Summer of Scandal* copyright © 2018 by Syrie James.

Digital Edition FEBRUARY 2020 ISBN: 978-0-06-284970-0
Print Edition ISBN: 978-0-06-284971-7

Cover photographs © Michael Frost (couple); © Athip_Taechapongsathon/Shutterstock (estate); © Helen Hotson/ Shutterstock (foreground)

FIRST EDITION

20 21 22 23 24   HDC   10 9 8 7 6 5 4 3 2 1

Every great dream begins with a dreamer. Always remember, you have within you the strength, the patience, and the passion to reach for the stars to change the world.

HARRIET TUBMAN

CHAPTER ONE

———————————————————

Patterson Architecture
7 Hatfield Gardens, London

His Royal Highness the Duke of Darcy
St. Gabriel's Mount, Cornwall

July 6, 1894

My dear Lord Darcy,

I hope and trust that you received my wire this morning. Pray allow me to elaborate in this missive, which I am obliged to dictate. Yesterday I suffered the misfortune of being thrown from my horse, resulting in significant injuries to my person. Knowing that you wish to begin improvements to St. Gabriel's Mount posthaste, I felt it necessary to send an associate in my place.

I wish therefore to introduce to you a member of my team, Miss Kathryn Atherton. You will find it highly unusual that I have sent a woman (and an American, at that) to do a man's job! However, Miss Atherton completed her studies at the London School of Art and Architecture, the first woman to do so, and over the past two years has proven herself to be eminently capable of the kind of work you require.

As we discussed in our previous communications, the length of her stay will depend upon the scope of the project. I presume, however, that if she works at her usual speed, three weeks should suffice for her to ascertain your needs, take necessary measurements, undertake initial drawings, and etc., at which point she will return to London, where I will oversee the execution of the final drawings.

I pray that this arrangement meets with your approval. It is a privilege to work with you, Your Grace, on renovations to such an ancient and renowned castle as St. Gabriel's Mount. I look forward, at what I hope will be a not too distant date, to meeting you again in person.

I have the honour to be, Sir, Your Royal Highness's most humble and obedient servant,

George Patterson

Kathryn Atherton finished rereading the letter for the umpteenth time, folded it up, and shoved it into her leather satchel.

No one said this was going to be easy. In fact, nothing about her professional journey had been easy. From the first moment she'd embarked upon her quest to become an architect, she had met with an endless parade of obstacles, prejudice, and heartache.

"You are an heiress, Kathryn," her mother had cried on

too many occasions to count, "from one of the wealthiest families in New York. You will not *embarrass* us by working. And in a man's profession! Whatever are you thinking?"

What Kathryn had been *thinking* was that she'd like to do something special and important with her life. Not just marry an Englishman with a title, as her sisters had done. Not that Lexie and Maddie had been set on marrying noblemen—that had been their mother's wish. But they were both madly in love with their husbands, and Kathryn was happy for them.

Two countesses in the family, however, would have to satisfy their mother's social-climbing ambitions in New York. Kathryn was determined to do as she pleased.

And what pleased *her* was to not marry anyone at all. She had far bigger plans in mind.

As Kathryn made her way up the old, twisting road, the uneven cobblestones made for difficult walking in her high-heeled boots. Holding her long skirts in one hand and her satchel in the other, Kathryn tread carefully, her thoughts returning to the letter.

It rankled that Mr. Patterson had felt the need to call attention to her being a woman, as if women were somehow less capable than men. That might be society's view, but it was hogwash. It was equally provoking that he'd mentioned her being "an American, at that." As if being American were a blemish upon her character. Equally hogwash.

On the other hand, Kathryn reminded herself, even if she didn't appreciate all the wording in the letter, she did have a lot to be grateful for. Mr. Patterson had hired her when no one else would. And he'd sent her on this prestigious assignment. To work on such a well-known castle would be a real feather in her cap.

Pausing briefly to catch her breath, Kathryn gazed up at the ancient edifice looming above her. She could hardly believe she was actually here—at St. Gabriel's Mount, a tiny tidal island at the southern tip of Cornwall. In the shadow of its enormous, celebrated castle, which looked like it belonged more in a fairy tale than real life.

The castle was so *huge* and so . . . well . . . *castle-y*. The sun, hanging low in the sky, cast a golden glow on massive gray stone walls that stood five stories high. The uppermost level was encircled by a low wall, enclosing several other large, ancient buildings topped with towers, turrets, and crenellated battlements replete with arrow slits, indicating its former use as a fortress. The only thing missing was a moat.

Which was an impossibility, of course, since the castle was perched like a majestic, multilayered wedding cake at the crest of a high hill in the center of the island. Approachable, apparently, only via this narrow road that wound upward with a dizzying array of switchbacks.

Kathryn's fingers itched to sketch the scene before her, but she didn't have time for such an indulgence. When the boatman had dropped her off at the island's diminutive harbor, he had urged her to wait until he could find a local man to deliver her to the castle via a horse-drawn cart. Kathryn had declined the kind offer, requesting that said man simply bring up her luggage instead. A brisk walk in the early-evening light had seemed like the perfect antidote to the nine hours she'd spent sitting on the train from London.

She was glad she'd made that choice, even though, after twenty minutes of steady trudging, she was still only halfway up the hill. Hopefully, the duke would forgive her for arriving a bit later than anticipated.

After three years in dirty, congested London, it was a pleasure to be surrounded by the sounds and scents of the sea. Every inhalation of the brisk, salty air was invigorating. The sharp cries of the seagulls circling overhead were a joyous chorus that made her heart sing.

How marvelous it would be, Kathryn thought, to actually live on such a unique island. She'd been told that at low tide, for a few hours twice a day, you could walk from the mainland to St. Gabriel's Mount across a wide stretch of wet sand. At high tide, as it was now, one had to arrive by boat.

The castle grew closer with every step. Kathryn's excitement mounted. All over England now, it was a common practice for members of the upper classes to update and renovate their manor homes to meet modern Victorian standards. A castle presented a particularly interesting challenge.

True, it was just another interior redesign. Not exactly the stuff that dreams were made of. Not *her* dreams, anyway. But it was the only kind of work that Mr. Patterson was willing to trust her with. So far. At least she was getting experience.

Now, if she could just get the Duke of Darcy to trust her with the job she had been sent to do . . .

Kathryn knew very little about the duke, other than what

Mr. Patterson had told her, based on the one time they'd met several years ago. He recalled Lord Darcy as a confirmed bachelor who was witty, generous, and intelligent. "He insisted on paying for dinner for the entire table," Mr. Patterson had commented, "and he ordered the finest wine I have ever tasted."

A promising endorsement, Kathryn thought, for the duke's character. She looked forward to meeting him. At the same time, worry gnawed at her stomach. She had no idea what kind of reception to expect from him.

For one thing, what if he recognized her family name and connection? It was difficult enough to be taken seriously as a woman in her profession. When people found out she was an Atherton heiress, their incredulity increased. They couldn't understand why she wanted to work at all.

There was always the hope that, in this remote corner of Cornwall, the duke wouldn't have heard of her. It was probably a vain hope. Her sisters had both married Cornish earls, after all.

A far bigger worry, however, was that the duke had intended to meet with her boss, not her. What if, like every prospective employer she'd met with after architectural school—other than Mr. Patterson—the duke was opposed to working with a woman? What if he sent her packing?

Kathryn set her teeth with determination. She'd just have to make sure that didn't happen. She had a letter of introduction. She had come a long way and had a job to do. And she was going to do that job better than anyone else, man *or* woman, could do.

Another five minutes' walk brought Kathryn to the top

of the hill, which offered a spectacular view. Behind her, sun sparkled on the bright blue water separating the island from the coast of Cornwall, which wrapped around St. Gabriel's Bay, the charming town of Penzance perched in the distance. In the opposite direction, the vast ocean stretched out in endless glory, with gulls swooping in an azure sky dotted with white clouds.

The castle looked even older and more imposing and picturesque up close than it had from below. It had been built along the incline of the slope, with the main entrance on the third level. A long series of steep, weather-beaten stairs, made from chunks of gray stone and bordered by scrubby green grass, led to an arched front door of heavy oak.

Kathryn hiked up the steps and paused before the door, wondering, as she caught her breath, if she was supposed to knock. The idea of knocking on the door of a castle felt strange somehow. That's when she noticed a wrought iron bell hanging from a nearby post. Grabbing the attached rope, she gave it a vigorous shake. The bell emitted a sonorous clang.

Above the door, the date 1624 had been carved into the stone wall, along with an impressive-looking coat of arms and the name *D'Arcy*—clearly an ancient spelling of the family name which announced its French origins.

Tilting her head back, Kathryn studied the massive iron portcullis overhead, its dangling points a menacing reminder of the days when enemies had to be cut off at the front gates. Those days were long gone. She'd read that for almost three hundred years, St. Gabriel's Mount had served as the home of the Darcy family.

That is, if the resident duke *had* a family. This one, apparently, did not. To think that a bachelor should live in a castle of this vast size. It was incredible!

The sound of a bolt being drawn rent the air. With a loud creak, the heavy front door was pulled open. A man appeared within the door frame.

Kathryn's heart skittered. She had expected to be greeted by a butler or footman. Judging by this man's clothing, he was no servant. He appeared to be in his early thirties. He was broad-shouldered, lean, and well over six feet tall, a good eight inches taller, she guessed, than she was. His black suit was expensively tailored of the finest materials and perfectly fitted to his well-toned body.

She wondered if he could be the duke himself. But a duke would never answer his own door. Would he?

She lifted her gaze. Short dark brown hair and a dark stubble of beard framed a face that was disarmingly handsome. His true complexion, judging by his hands, was as pale as hers, yet his face and neck were suntanned, as if he had spent years in a warmer climate.

Although he hadn't spoken a word, he radiated a crisp, masculine presence, as though all that he saw was his to command. His eyes found hers and lingered. They brimmed with intelligence and were the most striking shade of dark blue she had ever seen. Like the sky at twilight. Or a stormy sea. In a single glance, he seemed to be taking her in and sizing her up, his expression denoting both interest and surprise.

Under his gaze, a jolt of electricity darted through Kathryn's entire being, leaving her uncharacteristically tongue-tied. As she struggled to recover her equilibrium, the man gave her a polite nod.

"Good evening." His voice was deep and authoritative, evoking the dulcet, buttery tones of the British upper class. "I am the Duke of Darcy."

Lance Granville, the tenth Duke of Darcy, gave the woman at the door a brief smile. "It is a pleasure to meet you."

The burgundy felt hat she wore—except for the feathers at the back—was rather masculine in nature. Which was disconcerting because everything else about her was so decidedly feminine. Her eyes, a shimmering aquamarine blue with a hint of green, held his with a look that, although initially hesitant, turned confident and filled with curiosity.

"The pleasure is mine, Your Grace," she replied with a curtsy. "I'm—"

"I know who you are," he interrupted.

It wasn't difficult to figure out. Despite the fact that the past two weeks had been such a whirlwind of unwelcome change, it was a miracle Lance was even standing, much less able to think straight.

Seven days of travel from Barcelona, leaving behind everything he knew and loved. Only to come home to find his late brother's desk heaped with enough mountains of paperwork to sink a battleship.

The funeral, hastily but he hoped tastefully arranged,

was only yesterday. And then this morning, that cryptic telegram had arrived from London, from some architect named George Patterson.

Why on earth Hayward had invited an architect to St. Gabriel's Mount was beyond him. Perhaps his brother had conceived of some pet project, or hoped to renovate one of the tenants' houses? Whatever it was, an architect was apparently on his way—some associate of the said Mr. Patterson.

This comely young woman, however, was obviously not Patterson's associate from London. She must, Lance concluded, be the teacher from the local village who'd written to him, requesting an audience to discuss the school's needs for the upcoming year. A Miss Kerenza Chenoweth, if he remembered correctly.

Her accent took him aback, though. "You're American," he observed.

"I am," his visitor replied.

Strange that the village schoolteacher should be from across the pond. He couldn't help but wonder why she had come so far to teach in this tiny, godforsaken corner of England. He wondered, too, what she was carrying in that oversized leather satchel. Perhaps some outdated schoolbooks that needed replacing?

"Do come in." Lance stepped back to admit her. "Aren't you a day early for our meeting?" he asked as she swept inside. "Or do I have my dates wrong?"

His question seemed to confuse her. "Actually, I'm a couple of hours late, Your Grace, for which I can only apologize. I missed my connection."

"Connection?" His brow wrinkled. She must be referring to one of the ferryboats. "You don't live on the island, then?"

A laugh escaped her lips and she darted him a look, as if trying to decide if he were kidding. "I do not."

Well, then, he thought, she must live in Rosquay. Several servants at the castle also lived in that small town, just a short walk across the causeway from the Mount at low tide.

Shutting the door, Lance studied her in the glow of sunlight slanting in from a nearby window. She was pretty—exceedingly so—with an oval face, a creamy complexion, and curves in all the right places. Mid- to late-twenties, he guessed. Her hair, pulled back beneath the hat that matched her elegant burgundy suit, sparkled like spun gold. How, he wondered, did a schoolteacher afford such a costly outfit?

He was suddenly reminded of a schoolteacher in Istanbul with whom he had enjoyed several steamy days and nights. And hadn't that winsome creature in Naples also been a schoolteacher? Yes, teachers could make delectable . . .

Damn it all to hell. Those days were behind him. Very much against his will, he was the Duke of Darcy now. He could no longer afford to have random flings with enticing young women. Things were expected of him. Things like marriage and the production of an heir and doing whatever was necessary to save his doomed dukedom from the chopping block.

Until a few days ago, Lance had been completely unaware that his brother, after nearly two decades of bad investments and the worst agricultural recession in English history, had been forced to sell all their property in Hampshire. The

London town house and St. Gabriel's Mount were all that
were left now. Both were mortgaged to the hilt. And the
Mount, with its ancient castle, was a parish with a negligible
income.

In an attempt to maintain his style of living and, apparently,
to help out every parishioner with a financial need, Hayward
had borrowed enormous sums. He had also speculated on a
string of bad investments, losing every penny and leaving the
dukedom in excruciating debt. Worse yet, most of the loans
had been refinanced and bundled together with one lender,
and were due in a lump sum in three months.

Three months to somehow get his hands on £68,000, or
he would have no choice but to sell the castle and all its holdings. The dukedom would be a title only, with no property
whatsoever. That was the legacy Lance had inherited. *Thank
you, Hayward. God rest your soul.*

If only his brother had married and had a son, Lance
wouldn't be in this impossible situation. He would still be in
the Royal Navy. Hayward's son would have inherited the title,
his mother could have managed the estate until he came of age,
and the problem would be theirs to solve, not his.

But no. That wouldn't have been an ideal solution, either.
The estate's financial situation was too far gone for a boy and
his mother to have dealt with. The whole thing would have
come crashing down upon their heads, they would have been
forced to sell out, and the dukedom would be in tatters. Now
that *he* had inherited, Lance at least had a chance, however
miniscule, to figure out a solution to this mess.

"What an interesting space." His visitor's voice drew him

from his musings. She was studying the entrance hall and the profusion of ancient weaponry hanging on the walls.

Lance gave himself a quick mental shake. This was no time to be brooding about his financial situation, however dire. He had a schoolteacher to contend with. He had to smile and keep up appearances. It occurred to him that he didn't remember seeing this woman at the funeral yesterday morning—the entire parish had turned out to honor his brother. Lance must have missed her in the crowd. Or perhaps, for some reason, she had been unable to attend.

"The stonework in the vaulted ceiling is remarkable," she added.

"Is it?" She really was quite pretty, he thought. What a shame that she was so buttoned up beneath that high-collared blouse and velvet-trimmed suit jacket. Her whole air, as she stood taking in the room, was prim and proper and extremely professional.

Which was just as it should be, he tersely reminded himself. He needed to get this meeting over with as efficiently as possible, and get back to his paperwork.

"Pray, follow me." He led her through the drawing room and down a connecting passage.

"This isn't a typical castle layout," she commented. "Is there a fortified inner courtyard further on?"

He looked at her. "Have you never been inside the castle?"

She seemed to find this a strange question. "No, I have not."

She must be new to the school, Lance thought, and unfamiliar with the Mount's history. "St. Gabriel's Mount only served as a fortress for a short time. It began as a monastery, a Cornish counterpart of Mont-Saint-Michel in France."

"Oh yes, I read that somewhere. Didn't Queen Elizabeth later give the Mount to a nobleman?"

"Yes, and he sold it to my ancestor, the first Duke of D'Arcy. There have been additions and improvements over the years, and it was a military stronghold at several points in time. But for the most part it has served as a residence."

She nodded in fascination. "Do you know in what period this part of the castle was built?"

He shrugged. "I have no idea." As they proceeded down a labyrinthine corridor, he felt her eyes on him, alive with curiosity. "What is it?"

After a slight hesitation, she admitted, "I just . . . found it most unusual, Your Grace, that you answered the door."

He couldn't help but laugh. "I suppose it is. We are short-staffed today. It came to my attention at breakfast that Hammett, my butler, hasn't taken off more than a half day a month in the past thirty years, which I found appalling. I gave him leave to visit his sick mother for a few days."

"That was kind of you."

"It was the least I could do. But that is only the beginning of my staffing woes. The footman, it seems, has come down with a cold. The housekeeper has a sore knee and moves at a glacial pace. The housemaids are busy freshening up rooms all over the house. Which only left the scullery maid, who was too timid to come upstairs. I therefore insisted that I would take over the task of door-answering today."

"An occupation which you carried off with aplomb, Your Grace."

He laughed again. "Thank you."

Lance ushered her into the study. A dark, hideous excuse for a room, its green walls were hung with oil paintings of the castle as well as several portraits of his brother at various ages. Every surface was cluttered with Hayward's books and assorted knickknacks. Gesturing toward a fraying tapestry chair, Lance sat down behind the desk, a monstrosity that would have been at home in the palace of Louis XVI. "So tell me, do you enjoy what you do?"

She nodded, setting her satchel on the floor as she took her seat opposite him. "Very much. Every day is filled with new challenges."

"I am glad to hear it." Her eyelashes, he couldn't help but notice, were the same golden hue as her hair. His gaze lowered to her nose, which was slender and had the tiniest upward tilt to it, perched over a sweet, rosebud mouth with lips the color of coral. An idle thought possessed him: what would it be like to taste those lips?

Confound it. Keep your mind on the business at hand. "You must be fond of children."

"Children?" She paused. "As a matter of fact, I am fond of children. But . . ." She seemed to be struggling for what to say next.

"I admit, I am surprised to discover you are American. What made you decide to move to England? There must have been plenty of professional opportunities for you in the United States."

She hesitated again, her pale brows wrinkling. "Perhaps not as many as you might think. I came to London to study. I went to college there. I loved it, so when I was offered employment, I stayed."

College? This woman really was a surprise. All the teachers he had known had been educated by governesses or at local schools. "I have never in my life met a woman who attended college."

"Well, then, I will have to introduce you to my sisters." Her eyes twinkled with pride. "All three of us attended Vassar College in New York."

"What an illustrious family. My hat is off to you." Lance leaned back in his chair. "I have always wished to visit New York," he mused, "but never had the opportunity. I served the best years of my life in the Royal Navy, but was deployed exclusively in the waters of the United Kingdom and the Mediterranean Sea."

She stared at him. "I beg your pardon? Did you say . . . the Royal Navy?"

"Yes." He didn't know why she appeared so dumbfounded. "I presumed that you . . . that everyone knew of my service to the Crown?"

"I . . . did not, Your Grace. As I understood it, as heir to the title, you have lived here all your life."

It took a moment, but then he realized what must have caused this misunderstanding. "Can it be that you never met my brother, the ninth duke? Are you unaware that he passed away?"

A small gasp escaped her lips. She shook her head silently.

It was incredible that she didn't know. Everyone in the parish knew. But then, she lived across the bay in Rosquay. "I'm sorry, it seems I did not go far enough in introducing myself." Clapping one hand to his chest, he explained: "I am Lance Granville, the *tenth* Duke of Darcy."

"Oh I see," she managed.

He gestured to one of the portraits of the former duke which hung on the study wall. "My brother, Hayward—my only sibling," he explained, "held the title these past eighteen years since our parents died, while I have had the privilege of serving in Her Majesty's Navy, most recently as captain of the *Defiance*. A fortnight ago I received a wire at a port of call in Spain that my brother had died—the doctor said it was a heart attack. I was obliged to resign my commission and come home straightaway."

"I had no idea. I am so sorry for your loss, Your Grace."

"Thank you."

"I would not have come, had I known." She squirmed in her seat, apparently uncomfortable now. "Would you prefer that I go and return at a later date? Or perhaps not return at all? This must be a difficult time for you."

"No, no. Thank you for your sensitivity, you are very kind. But in truth, I did not know my brother all that well—he was seven years older than me. So . . ." Lance leaned his forearms on the desktop and clasped his hands. "You are here, after all. We may as well get down to business. Pray tell me how I can help you."

She seemed puzzled. "Forgive me, but I believe it is *I* who am here to help *you*."

"Indeed? I don't understand. I thought you were here to . . . I don't know . . . request funds for materials for the coming term?"

"The coming term?" She gave him a quizzical look. "If you are referring to drawing materials, I brought my own with me."

What was she on about? "I'm sorry. Let us begin again." Lance searched through a stack of missives in the overflowing basket on his desk. "I am in receipt of a letter from you, requesting a meeting. Here it is." He quickly perused the document, quoting the relevant sentence: "'I would be most grateful for an audience to discuss the needs of my students in the upcoming school year, et cetera, et cetera. Yours most respectfully, Miss Kerenza Chenoweth, Schoolteacher, St. Gabriel's Mount School.'"

She started in surprise. Then she shook her head. "Your Grace, I didn't write that letter."

"You didn't?"

"No. I am not St. Gabriel's Mount's schoolteacher."

"Then who are you?"

She leaned forward earnestly. "I'm the architect who's been sent from London to remodel your castle."

Chapter Two

Words failed Lance for a long moment. The phrase *remodel your castle* rang in his ears.

"Forgive me," he said at last. "There has clearly been some kind of mistake."

"I'm afraid not. I understand why this is confusing. It was your *brother*, not you, who has been corresponding with my employer and who arranged this meeting today. Mr. Patterson told me he would send a wire this morning, though. I hope you received it?"

"I did." Sifting through his pile of paperwork, Lance found the telegram. "It merely states: 'Deepest regrets. Unable to travel today. My associate K. J. Atherton arriving on afternoon train.'" He set down the telegram. "I had no clue what it was about, presumed I would find out when this Mr. Atherton arrived."

"Yes, well." She cleared her throat. "The 'K. J. Atherton' to whom he refers is not a *Mr.* Atherton, but rather me. Myself. I am Miss Kathryn Jane Atherton."

Kathryn Jane Atherton? "What the bloody hell?" Lance retorted. She didn't flinch at that, but even so he felt a twinge of conscience over the outburst. It was one thing to swear like a sailor on the deck of a turret ship traveling full steam ahead. The Duke of Darcy, on the other hand, had to behave with more dignity. "Pardon my French, Miss Atherton. Nineteen years in the Royal Navy create habits that are difficult to break." Something about the name Atherton sounded vaguely familiar, but he couldn't say why. "I admit I am at sea here. Patterson of London is an architectural firm. Is that not so?"

"It is indeed, Your Grace."

"And you are employed by this firm as . . ." He glanced at the letter again. "Patterson's associate?"

"I am."

"But . . . you are a woman."

"I cannot deny it."

"Did you travel down from London on your own?" he asked, surprised.

"I did. I am twenty-seven years old, Your Grace. I keep no lady's maid and I often travel unaccompanied."

He had never heard of such a thing, for a woman of her stature. But then, it was hardly the most unusual thing about her. "Did I hear correctly? Did you say that *you* are an *architect?*"

She hesitated, then removed an envelope from her satchel and slid it across the desk to him. "Here is a letter from my employer, Mr. Patterson. I hope this will serve both to introduce me and to explain your brother's intentions."

Lance opened the letter and read it through. *Damn it all to bloody hell.* What kind of mess had Hayward gotten him into? And what the hell was Patterson doing, sending a woman? Even if he *had* sent a man, however, Lance wouldn't have been able to hire him. The dukedom didn't have a farthing to renovate the castle.

Still, he was curious to learn what his brother had had in mind. "Your employer seems to hold you in high esteem," he noted.

"I am honored by his confidence in me, Your Grace."

"He says he was thrown from his horse. I hope his injuries are not grave?"

"He suffered a concussion and broke his right leg and hand. Thankfully, the doctors said he will fully recover. But he is on bed rest and will be unable to walk or draw for eight weeks or more."

"I am sorry, but glad to know he will mend in time."

"So am I."

Lance crossed his arms over his chest, determined to get to the bottom of this. "I had no clue that my brother was contemplating making improvements to St. Gabriel's Mount. Can you fill me in as to what changes he was considering?"

"The details were never fully established, Your Grace. But as I understand it, he wished to update the interiors of the rooms which are currently most occupied. He insisted the work must begin without delay."

Lance took that in, trying to comprehend what his brother had been thinking. Why had Hayward wanted to update the castle? And why the rush? Then—like a punch to the gut—it hit him.

While going through the piles of paperwork on Hayward's

desk this past week, Lance had come across a recent appraisal of St. Gabriel's Mount from an estate agent. *Holy hell.* Hayward had intended to sell St. Gabriel's Mount to pay off the outstanding loans. He must have hoped that modernizing and cleaning up the most visible parts of the castle's interior would make it more appealing to a prospective buyer, and increase the value of the property.

Where did Hayward intend to get the money for said renovations? True to form, Lance deduced grimly, Hayward must have intended to have the work done on credit and pay it off after the castle was sold.

The whole idea, however, was lunacy. The debt would be called on December 11, just three months from now. It would be impossible to design and execute any useful modifications to the castle in such a short time. Wouldn't it?

"Miss Atherton," Lance began, "I regret to say that—" He stopped himself. His father, and afterward Hayward, had kept their financial straits a secret from Lance and the family for decades. Lance felt certain . . . at least, he *hoped* . . . that no one, other than the money lenders to whom he owed mountains of cash, knew that the Duke of Darcy was on the ropes and in danger of losing his castle.

It was a painfully humiliating circumstance in which to find himself. Did he want this total stranger to know how badly off the dukedom was? No, he did not.

On the one hand, Lance mused, maybe Hayward did have the right idea. The castle was like a millstone around his neck. If Lance sold it and paid off the debts, he'd be a duke in name only. He'd have no property to maintain. No tenants to oversee. He'd be free to go back to the Royal Navy. Back to the life he loved.

For a fleeting moment, the notion was tempting. But at the same time, it made him feel sick to his stomach. If he sold out, where would his grandmother go? She'd lived here almost the entirety of her life.

More importantly, St. Gabriel's Mount had been the pride of the D'Arcy family for almost three hundred years. He may not like this shabby excuse for a castle, or the idea of being trapped on this far-flung island for the rest of his life. But history had placed him in this position, had made him accountable.

Could he really just give up? Didn't he owe it to his family legacy, to all the as-yet-unborn generations of Darcys, to at least *try* to save her?

There *was* a way out of this. Lance didn't like the idea one bit, but it had been gnawing at the edges of his mind for days, impossible to ignore.

He could marry money.

It wouldn't be easy to find an heiress with a dowry upward of £68,000 these days. But a widow might have that kind of cash. Or he could turn to the American sector.

It bothered him, the idea of marrying for money. He had always been of the mind that if and when people married, they should do so for love. His parents' union had been a love match, after all, and they had been very happy.

A mantle of gloom descended on Lance like a dark cloud, reminding him that his parents' situation had been unusual. For most people of their class, a love match was pure fantasy. He ought to know. *Look how that turned out for you, you poor stupid bastard.*

Money, or the lack of it, had been the primary reason behind most unions for centuries. Aristocrats with impoverished estates married women with money. Poor women married rich men if they could snag one. He was a duke now. His wife would be a duchess. He ought to be able to *snag* anyone he liked.

Whether or not the woman in question would be someone he could stand living with—sharing his bed with—was another matter, and one he didn't care to contemplate. To save St. Gabriel's Mount, however, a sacrifice had to be made. And there was no one to make that sacrifice but him.

Meanwhile, what was he supposed to tell the comely woman sitting so expectantly before him? She'd come a long way down from London for nothing. He was sorry about that, and felt sorry for her. Well, he would just have to be vague and let her down gently.

"Miss Atherton," Lance began again, carefully choosing his words, "I regret to say that while I might be interested in undertaking renovations to St. Gabriel's Mount at some point, it is impossible for me to do so at present."

Kathryn's pulse hammered with frustration. The duke had just fired her. Before she'd even had a chance to show what she could do.

The hardest part was, she couldn't be angry with him. First off, even though he was the Duke of Darcy, one step down from Queen Victoria herself and arguably among the most fortunate men on the planet, he'd just lost his only brother.

Had she known, she never would have come to Cornwall. But she and Mr. Patterson had been working such long hours lately. If there'd been an announcement in the newspaper about the previous duke's death, they hadn't seen it.

Secondly, this was all, quite obviously, coming at the duke out of the blue. He had just been torn from a career in the Royal Navy which he had apparently enjoyed. Judging from the state of the desk in front of him, he'd been saddled with endless paperwork. Not to mention an unexpected meeting with her on a subject he had probably never entertained in his life.

Thirdly . . .

Thirdly, she couldn't be angry with him because . . . well, because he was so incredibly, bone-meltingly handsome.

Kathryn wasn't the type of woman who swooned over a good-looking man, duke or otherwise. But from the moment she'd arrived, every time his dark blue eyes had come into contact with hers, she'd felt a shiver go down her spine and her insides had done this little, inexplicable flippy thing.

And the way he spoke! Since childhood, she had always loved the sound of an English accent. She'd been living in London for years—you would think she'd be inured to its effects by now. *His* voice, however, was so deep and masculine, so soothingly, enchantingly upper crust and lyrical and . . . commanding. Every word that issued from his mouth was like the confident, golden note of a magical lyre. She could sit here and listen to him speak all night, even if he were doing something so prosaic as reading aloud from a dictionary.

Which was absolutely ridiculous. Kathryn would not, could *not*, be attracted to this man. She certainly had no desire to get involved with him—or with any man, for that matter. She had come here in a strictly professional capacity. Whether she ever worked for him or not, she was determined to remain professional.

Which reminded Kathryn that she was here, apparently, on a wild-goose chase.

It wasn't fair. Even if this were no more than the intended interior renovations, working on this project could change everything for her.

Up to now Kathryn had, for the most part, been nothing more than Mr. Patterson's hired hand, executing designs and drawings at the office after her employer met with the clients. This time, though, Mr. Patterson couldn't take credit for her work, since she would be doing it right under the nose of the client himself. *This* would finally give her something to put on her résumé. It could open doors to the next level of architectural achievement, the kind of work she'd been dreaming of doing for years.

She couldn't give up. Not when she'd come all this way with such high hopes.

Why, she wondered, had the duke said no to the project? He hadn't given a reason. She felt certain it had nothing to do with her being an Atherton heiress—he hadn't made that connection, apparently. He had, however, said he *might* be interested in renovating *at some point*. Kathryn grabbed on to that slight chance like a lifeline.

"Lord Darcy," she began, "I understand that you've just suffered a great personal loss and I am so very sorry for it. Your brother set this process in motion, and you have no obligation to proceed. But you implied that you are not totally averse to undertaking renovations to St. Gabriel's Mount someday. Why not now? Clearly this is something your brother felt was important. If you will forgive me for saying so, based on the little I've seen of the castle, it *is* rather in need of an update. I would venture to say it's been at least fifty years since anything was done."

"Possibly longer," he admitted.

"Which means," she went on rapidly, "that the kitchens are out of date. Think how pleased your cook would be with one of the more modern cooking ranges. I'm sure you'll be inviting guests to St. Gabriel's Mount, and if nothing else the rooms could use a new coat of paint and freshly upholstered furnishings. Great strides have been made of late with new kinds of lighting as well. Even in a location as remote as this, with your own generator, you could provide electricity to select rooms with the flip of a switch."

His eyebrows lifted at that with guarded interest. "Wouldn't that be rather costly?"

She loved the oh-so-British-y way he said *rather costly.* "Not as much as you might think." Pausing, Kathryn added, "Is cost a consideration?" From the moment of her arrival, she'd had the vague sense that there might be some problem with the family's finances. The place was so threadbare. "If so, I feel certain Mr. Patterson would be happy to discuss a financial arrangement that would suit you."

"No," he insisted abruptly. "That is to say, there are no financial difficulties, I assure you."

She was glad to hear that. "Very well, then. Is it the timing that's at issue? I presume you have a great deal on your plate just now, Your Grace. We can make this as small an endeavor as you wish, whatever is most convenient for you. What would you say if I took a few days to draw up some sketches with a few suggested improvements?" She gave him a quote for her hourly rate, a modest fee compared to what other architects charged. "If you decide not to proceed, no harm done, that will be the end of it."

He frowned, drumming his fingers on the desktop. "Miss Atherton. I appreciate your enthusiasm. I really do. And I realize that you have come a long way to meet with me. But although St. Gabriel's Mount might admittedly be due for improvements, as I said before, I do not see myself embarking just now on such a project with you."

With you. His last two words seemed to vibrate in the air, a testament to the true reason behind his disinclination. Kathryn held back a sigh. Struggling to sound matter-of-fact, she raised her eyes to meet his. "Is it *me* you object to, then? Do you not wish to work on the project because I'm a woman?"

That appeared to catch him off guard. His cheeks flushed and he looked uncomfortable. "I . . . no . . . I didn't mean . . . that is to say . . . well, in all honesty . . . I have never heard of a female architect. And even if I did wish to renovate, I'm not certain I would feel comfortable . . ." His voice trailed off and he averted his gaze.

And there it was.

The room suddenly felt stiflingly hot. A trickle of perspiration trickled down between Kathryn's breasts, and she cursed her tight stays and heavy jacket. She couldn't count how many times she'd been in this exact same situation. Dismissed out of hand, her potential and abilities entirely discounted, simply because of her gender.

She found herself briefly wishing, and not for the first time, that she'd been born a man. This all would be so much easier. But, she reminded herself, she was proud to be a woman. Proud to be attempting to be the first in her field.

It was difficult to be the first at anything. She'd read that the first woman doctor, some forty years ago, had undergone incredible prejudice to get a foothold in that profession. Female physicians were still fighting the good fight. Well, Kathryn had come this far. *She* wasn't going down without a fight. Somehow, she had to convince this man of what she and women like her were capable of.

"When you think about it," Kathryn returned in a firm tone, "it's rather astonishing that architects have historically been men. By its very nature, the practice requires extensive drawing capabilities, an accomplishment drilled into every well-bred lady from a young age. An excellent imagination is also key—and dare I suggest that many of my gender are in possession of an imagination equal to or greater than men?"

Lord Darcy opened his mouth as if to refute that, then closed it again. "That may be," he finally allowed. "However—I admit, having spent most of my life at sea, I have no experience working with architects—but as I understand it, the profession demands a thorough understanding of engineering. And, I image, a familiarity with building codes and such. Areas which are all strictly under the purview of a man."

"If I may beg to differ, Your Grace," Kathryn replied. "I have studied engineering *and* architecture. I am well up to date on all the latest building codes."

"Is that so?" He looked astonished, but still unconvinced. "Good for you, Miss Atherton. I am impressed. Nevertheless, is it not true that an architect, in discharging his duties, must work closely with construction crews? I have seen any number of building sites and thought them to be dirty, boisterous, and rather dangerous-looking places—hardly the environment for a woman."

"Constructing or remodeling a building can indeed be noisy and filthy, and on occasion even hazardous, Your Grace," Kathryn returned with a smile. "However, over the past two years, I have seen too many such sites to count." She wasn't about to tell him that she'd always had to sneak onto the site to view the progress being made on plans of her own design. That wouldn't exactly help her case. "I'm not afraid of risk. I've stood ankle-deep in debris and exchanged stories with the rowdiest of men on the crew."

"Have you indeed?" Lord Darcy ran a hand through his short, dark hair, studying her. "You amaze me, Miss Atherton, you truly do."

As their gazes touched, Kathryn felt that same absurd electrical jolt sizzle through her body. *Kathryn, stop this. It is so unlike you.* The expression in his eyes was so discerning she felt as if he were attempting to peer into her soul. She quickly averted her gaze, her heart drumming. She didn't *want* him to see into her soul. If he did, he'd know that she was fudging her level of experience a bit.

"Do you actually have a degree in architecture?" he asked.

Oh no. Now the cat would come out of the bag, whether she liked it or not. Kathryn swallowed hard. Well, he deserved to know the truth. She raised her eyes to his again and reluctantly admitted, "Not yet."

"Not yet?" Lord Darcy arched a brow at her.

"I completed the entire two years of coursework at the London School of Art and Architecture and earned the highest marks in my class. But the institution refused to grant me a degree. Because I'm a woman."

He pondered for a moment. "That hardly seems fair."

The injustice still burned in her breast like a wildfire. "Before you ask if I have a license to practice architecture, the answer is also *not yet.* But I will. I just took the RIBA exam."

"What is the RIBA exam?"

"Every practitioner must pass an exam administered by the Royal Institute of British Architects and be approved by the board before being granted a license. I've been studying for it for two years while apprenticing. I get the results next month." She may have been denied the architectural degree she'd earned, but they couldn't deny her a license if she passed the test. And she *would* pass. She had to.

"So," Lord Darcy murmured slowly, "although you represented yourself earlier as an architect, in fact, you are an architectural apprentice with neither a degree nor a license." His tone was now awash with both incredulity and a hint of condescension.

Kathryn wanted to scream with vexation. But of course she couldn't.

"Yes," she responded calmly, "but as for the degree, that is hardly my fault. And I should have my license in four or five weeks. I assure you, I'm very good at what I do."

Kathryn read blatant skepticism in his eyes. This opportunity, she realized desperately, was slipping through her fingers like sand through an hourglass. Well, she decided, pressing her lips together with determination, she would just have to *show* him.

Opening the leather satchel at her feet, Kathryn withdrew a roll of small-scale drawings and stood. "Your Grace, I brought with me a preliminary set of plans for a new building of my own design. May I show you?"

He clearly didn't expect that. Throwing up his hands, he sat back in his chair. "Why not."

Kathryn unfurled the stack of drawings on his desk and propped them open with paperweights. "These are for a new branch of Lloyds of London bank. Mr. Patterson is the lead architect on the building, but I had a vision for it that I couldn't get out of my head, so I drew it up in my spare time."

She had devoted many long hours to these drawings—a set of plans for a grand, unique building in a classic style—everything from elevations to floor plans and inserts with architectural details. They were her best work, and she was proud of them. Even knowing she wouldn't earn a penny from them, Kathryn had hoped they would show Mr. Patterson what she was capable of. She hoped the same would prove true for the Duke of Darcy—that at the very least, they would remove any doubts as to her abilities.

It was difficult to gauge his reaction as he glanced through the drawings. Finally he said, "This is all your original work?"

"Every last bit of it."

"What was Patterson's response?"

"He was complimentary, but said it wasn't quite what the client had in mind." Kathryn let out a little sigh. "Still, I'm glad I did the exercise. It has always been my goal to build something brand-new from the ground up. A great edifice, like a hospital or library or school, that will contribute to the needs of society and long outlive me."

His eyebrows raised at that. It occurred to Kathryn that her statement might have seemed dismissive of the type of work she sought from him, so she quickly added, "At the same time, I also enjoy designing interiors. To work on an ancient castle like St. Gabriel's Mount would be a real thrill for me."

He went quiet for a while. "Miss Atherton. As I mentioned, I have no experience in this arena. But this appears to be very impressive work."

"Thank you." Her heart began to pound with hope.

"I fear, in our discourse, I may have seemed . . . doubtful and treated you with less than the professional respect which you deserve. For that, I hope you will accept my apologies."

"There is no need to apologize, Your Grace." Her breath caught; was he going to say yes?

"However," he said firmly. "This does not change the fact that it was entirely my brother's vision to make improvements to St. Gabriel's Mount, not mine. I'm sorry, but it is not a project I am prepared to take on." He rolled up the drawings.

"You may stay the night, of course, and I will arrange for your transportation to the train station in the morning."

Kathryn's spirits plummeted. She felt like a pricked balloon, all the drive and energy seeping out of her. At the same time, she thought: *It can't be over. I can't go back to London with nothing to show for it. Think. Think. There must be some way to convince him. But how?*

"Now what about your luggage? Did you arrange for it to be delivered to the castle?" Lord Darcy's hand moved toward the bell pull behind his desk, presumably to call a servant.

It occurred to Kathryn that while words and formal drawings hadn't worked, there might be another way. "Your Grace," she interjected, quickly grabbing a sketch pad and pencil from her satchel, "what do you think about this room?"

His hand hovered over the bell pull, then fell to his lap. "I beg your pardon?"

"This is your study, isn't it?" Kathryn got busy with her pencil.

"It was my brother's study." His distaste was obvious in his voice.

"Now it is yours." She continued to draw. "Is this room an environment in which you enjoy working?"

Lord Darcy let go a short, unhappy laugh. "As a matter of fact, I hate this room, Miss Atherton. I hate everything about it."

"I figured as much." She sensed his eyes on her as her pencil flew.

"What are you doing there?" he asked, intrigued.

"Allow me a moment, will you? I'd like to show you something."

CHAPTER THREE

Lance sat back in his chair and waited, his eyes on Miss Atherton.

The clock on the mantel ticked off the minutes as she sketched. From the angle of her notepad he couldn't see what she was drawing, but he could guess—no doubt some altered version of this room, as a last-dash attempt to persuade him.

She was tireless, this woman. Like a dog with a bone. Well, she was barking up the wrong tree. The estate was broke. He couldn't renovate a single room of this castle even if he wished to.

Still, he had to admire her tenacity. Miss Atherton really wanted this, he could tell. It was a pleasure to watch her draw. She made a pretty picture, sitting there by the window with the last rays of the setting sun bringing out the highlights in her golden hair.

Her pencil was flying at lightning speed. He'd observed sailors sketching on deck for nearly two decades, some with real talent, but he didn't think he'd ever seen anyone draw this fast.

Part of him wished he could come up with a reason for her to stay at St. Gabriel's Mount. The last week had been a barrage of visits from creditors, funeral directors, tailors, local parishioners, his land steward, and his solicitor (the last being the least objectionable, since Megowan was a friend). Lance could use a little respite from all that. And he always welcomed the company of a beautiful woman.

This woman was far more than just beautiful. Although they'd only just met, Lance was growing more intrigued by her by the minute.

She was obviously intelligent. She had drive, courage, and initiative. To attempt to be the first female in her line of work—in any line of work, he supposed—presented an enormous challenge. Yet she seemed to have undertaken it without blinking. Despite all obstacles, she didn't appear to be giving up.

Ten more minutes ticked by while he patiently waited. He made a pretense of going through some papers on his desk, but in truth was content to simply drink in the sight of Miss Atherton as she worked. After a few final strokes with her pencil, she stood.

"This is just a rough sketch," she explained, passing him the notebook, "my first thoughts about a possible way we could redesign and reimagine this space."

Lance studied the drawing. It was a furnished room, depicted by a highly skilled hand.

"The study is currently very dark," she noted, "and the furniture is growing threadbare and is oversized for the space. Being that you have just come from life on board a ship, I thought you might enjoy a new look, something closer to your own sensibility."

"A new look," he repeated. It certainly was *new*. The shape and dimensions resembled those of the existing study, but other than that, it was a room he didn't recognize.

"My father owns a shipyard which I visited frequently as a girl. The captain's quarters, I recall, were efficiently designed to make maximum use of a minimum space. My thinking was: brighten it up by painting the walls white. Build in cabinets and drawers to hide things away. Hang new artwork, perhaps of your favorite ports of call. Replace these heavy draperies with shutters which can be fully opened to let in the light. And find smaller, simpler furniture. Possibly custom-made from a shipyard."

Lance was at a loss for words.

Everything she had described was elegantly illustrated in her sketch. It was difficult to believe it was the same room. The cluttered, gilded look was gone, replaced by sleek, streamlined furniture and a nautical theme. Half of the bookshelves had been replaced by modern-looking cabinets and built-in drawers. A ship's wheel hung over the fireplace. A life preserver and the cheerful image of an anchor adorned another wall. A model of a sailboat rested on a small table, a globe on another. The overall effect was light, bright, open, masculine, and . . . very appealing.

"I reimagined this alcove as a sailor's berth," she was saying, "thinking you could use it as a reading space or a place to nap. We could build in a narrow bunk or even hang a hammock."

Lance nodded slowly. Somehow, this woman who had known him for less than an hour had hit upon exactly what he would want to do with this room, without him even knowing it himself.

"I don't know what to say, Miss Atherton," he began, finally finding his voice. "Your ideas are clever and your skill and speed with a pencil is most impressive." Before he could go on, a knock sounded on the study door. "Enter!" he barked.

His gray-haired housekeeper hobbled in. "Forgive me for interrupting, Your Grace." Mrs. Morgan darted a confused look at Miss Atherton, and went on: "A trunk has been delivered. John insists the cart man said it belongs to a lady. I said he was mistaken as you were expecting a gentleman down from London today."

Lance paused, glancing at his guest, who was still standing beside his desk with such hope in her eyes. *The hell with it.*

This woman had come all the way from London and just sketched her heart out for him. She obviously, desperately, wanted this job—perhaps *needed* it for reasons that were as yet unclear to him. He couldn't bear to disappoint her. The estate might be in debt up to its ears, but he had some money of his own put by.

With any luck, he might be able to renovate this place someday. If everything went south, a set of plans might add to the castle's value when he sold it. No matter what happened, it would be fascinating to see what else this woman could dream up.

In the meantime, it was an excuse to keep her around a little while longer.

"Miss Atherton," he announced, "may I introduce to you my housekeeper, Mrs. Morgan? Mrs. Morgan: this is Miss Kathryn Atherton, an architect from London."

Mrs. Morgan's jaw dropped in astonishment. To her credit, she recovered just as quickly as the two women exchanged polite greetings.

"Set a place at dinner for Miss Atherton," Lance directed, "and tell my grandmother that I would appreciate it if she would join us this evening to meet our guest. We will begin with sherry in the drawing room at seven-thirty."

"Very well, Your Grace."

Miss Atherton darted him a questioning look. "Your grandmother?"

"The dowager duchess has occupied the same suite of rooms on the fifth floor for over thirty years," Lance explained. "She generally prefers to take her meals upstairs on a tray. But if I know my grandmother, she will be delighted to make *your* acquaintance." To Mrs. Morgan, he added, "Send up Miss Atherton's luggage straightaway. She will be staying with us about three weeks, I should think."

"Three weeks, Your Grace?" Mrs. Morgan echoed with a curtsy.

"Yes." He glanced back at his guest, whose eyes widened in surprise and delight. "As I recall from your employer's letter, three weeks was the stipulated time required to assess any improvements I might wish make to the castle and complete preliminary drawings. Is that not so, Miss Atherton?"

Kathryn stared out the window, admiring the way the setting sun colored the sky and shimmered across the rise and fall of the deep blue sea.

She had changed out of her traveling clothes into a fresh blouse and a gray silk skirt and jacket, which a maid had kindly pressed for her while Kathryn had unpacked the rest of her clothes.

Turning from the window, Kathryn surveyed her room. It wasn't large, the furnishings were old, and the striped wallpaper had faded to a dingy yellow and brown. But it was comfortable. Its aspect was pleasing. And she was thrilled beyond words that she'd been allowed to stay and work on the drawings for the castle renovation.

The Duke of Darcy had been so adamantly opposed to the project for nearly the entire length of her interview. She couldn't help but be proud of the fact that she'd managed to convince him to proceed. This was all new territory for her, and undeniably exciting.

Lord Darcy had seemed pleased by her suggestions for the study. The full scope of the work wouldn't be determined until after she'd had a complete tour of St. Gabriel's Mount and they'd engaged in further discussion. But based on the little she'd seen, she was already bursting with ideas and could hardly wait to begin.

There was one thing about the job that troubled Kathryn, however, and which could be a problem in the weeks ahead. She was attracted to the duke. *Too* attracted.

It wasn't just that he was good-looking. As a New York City debutante, Kathryn had probably danced with hundreds of men. She had attended classes in London with hundreds more. Many had been just as handsome, in their own way, as the Duke of Darcy.

So why, every time their gazes touched, did she get all tingly inside? *So inconvenient.*

She sensed that he was smart and observant. He was a man in a rare position—a Navy captain who'd been obliged to give up his commission to become a duke. Maybe it was the brief flashes of frustration that she'd noticed a couple of times on his face that had made her feel drawn to him. She'd certainly experienced her fill of that exact same emotion over the years.

She sensed, from his expression a few times when he'd looked at her, that he might be attracted to her as well. Which was even more inconvenient.

This attraction and admiration—mutual or not—could go nowhere. There was no place in Kathryn's life for a relationship with a man.

She hadn't always felt this way. Growing up, although the youngest of three sisters, she'd been the most adventurous and the first to be kissed by a boy (their art instructor's son, at age eight). Kathryn had looked forward to love and marriage, had even been a little envious at Lexie's wedding, wishing that her new husband, Thomas, had a brother.

All that had changed when Kathryn entered architectural school. The only woman in classrooms filled with men, she'd been regarded alternately with suspicion, amusement, and disdain. A few men had asked her out—one had even proposed. But no one had taken her quest seriously. They'd considered it a bit of absurdity that she'd give up when she married, their sense of masculinity seemingly threatened by the idea of a woman joining their ranks, or worse yet, having a wife who worked.

It had become clear to Katherine that if she were to pursue this career, no man would ever marry her. So she would have to choose: marriage or career.

She chose career.

She'd had a brief affair once, while on vacation in Paris. To check a box, so to speak. To satisfy her curiosity about certain . . . things. She had no desire to indulge in another. She had a reputation to maintain. Most importantly, Lord Darcy was her client as well as her employer. Under no circumstances could she get involved with him. She was here to work. And she never mixed business with pleasure.

Should any more tingling occur while in the presence of His Grace, she was simply going to have to ignore it.

A knock sounded on the door. A young redheaded housemaid named Ivy announced that it was seven-thirty and sherry was being served. Kathryn followed her downstairs.

The moment Kathryn entered the drawing room, her eyes were drawn to the duke like a magnet. He was standing by a window, sipping sherry from a crystal goblet. He had changed into formal wear—a gorgeous black dinner jacket with waistcoat and bow tie—and, if possible, looked even more handsome than he had at their earlier meeting.

At the sight of him, the now-familiar sparks started *zinging* again through Kathryn's body. Her heart raced while her mind warned: *Ignore. Ignore. Ignore.*

"Ah, Miss Atherton. We were just speaking about you." The duke gestured to the tiny, elegantly dressed woman who sat on a wingback chair nearby, her snowy hair swept up in a becoming, old-fashioned style.

"Grandmother, may I present Miss Kathryn Atherton? Miss Atherton, this is my grandmother, the Dowager Duchess of Darcy, Honora Granville."

The dowager duchess turned in her seat, her pale blue eyes gleaming with interest as she studied Kathryn. "It is a pleasure to meet you, Miss Atherton."

"The pleasure is mine, Duchess," Kathryn replied with a curtsy. It occurred to her that Lord Darcy's grandmother might be his only close living relative—he'd said his parents had died years ago, and now his only sibling was gone. How sad, she thought, that both of these people were so alone in the world.

The dowager duchess's brow furrowed as she looked up at her. "Atherton," she murmured. "I feel as though I have heard that name before."

Kathryn froze. With all that had happened that afternoon, she'd almost forgotten her desire to remain unrecognized. If the duchess realized that Kathryn was an Atherton heiress, it could change everything. The duke might only see her as a woman with a fortune, instead of an architect. He'd think it nonsensical that she was bothering with a career. Every conversation would come back to that; it almost always did. He might even end their association.

Desperate to redirect the conversation, Kathryn glanced around the room. It was a good-sized chamber with elegant architectural details, but the blue silk wallpaper was faded and the furnishings were in need of refurbishing. "The ceiling and crown moldings in this room are lovely," she commented abruptly. "They are Wedgwood, I believe?"

"Indeed they are," the dowager duchess replied with a proud smile. "One of Wedgwood's earlier commissions. The fifth duke had them installed in 1774. The room itself dates back to the time that St. Gabriel's was a monastery in the tenth century."

"The tenth century!" Relieved to have successfully changed the subject, Kathryn accepted a glass of sherry from the footman and took a sip. It was of fine quality and truly delicious. "In America, we think a place ancient if it's a hundred years old."

The duke laughed. It was a deep, hearty, gloriously masculine sound, and it seemed to resonate through Kathryn's entire being. Their gazes caught and held for a moment. The interest in his sent another shiver up her spine. *Look away. Look away.*

"I understand you are here from London to make alterations to St. Gabriel's Mount, Miss Atherton?" the dowager duchess commented. "Something my grandson Hayward set in motion?"

"Yes," Kathryn replied, grateful for the distraction. "That is my hope."

Her eyes suddenly grew misty. "He was such a lovely man, our Hayward. I miss him dearly."

"I am very sorry for your loss, Duchess," Kathryn replied with sympathy.

"Thank you." Composing her features, the dowager duchess went on, "How marvelous that your firm sent *you*, my dear. It is high time women were given a chance to show what they are capable of in the professions."

"Thank you, Your Grace." It was unusual, Kathryn had discovered, for anyone, man or woman, to be so open-minded about such things—most people still clung to the old ways of thinking. She found it refreshing and pleasant to have an ally.

"I admit, I had no idea Hayward was contemplating anything of this nature," the duchess added.

"Perhaps he intended to surprise you," Kathryn ventured.

Lord Darcy's features hardened at her statement, and he downed a long swig of sherry. Kathryn wondered what was behind his reaction, but had no time to contemplate it, for his grandmother went on:

"Lord knows, something needs to be done with this place. The last time any alterations were made was in 1832, not long after I married the seventh duke and came to live here." Turning to her grandson, she added, "I do hope, Lancelot, that I will finally get new carpets in my room."

Lancelot? That's his first name?

The duke's face reddened at the appellation—but Kathryn smiled to herself. In some ways, he did resemble a knight in shining armor. He had hired her, after all, seemingly against his better judgment—and she had a sneaking suspicion he'd done so not just because he'd liked her drawing of the study, but because he liked *her.*

"Do you require new carpets, Grandmother?" the duke was saying.

"I have been badgering Hayward about it for years."

Kathryn wondered again if the family had financial issues. But earlier, when she'd asked Lord Darcy about it, he had firmly insisted that was not the case. And Mr. Patterson *had* specifically mentioned the former duke's generosity. Maybe, she reasoned, he had simply been parsimonious when it came to home improvements . . . until now. She made a mental note to ask, tomorrow, if the duke had a budget in mind.

"Just promise me you will not touch my conservatory," the dowager duchess went on, turning to Kathryn with an imploring look.

"Your conservatory?" Kathryn asked.

"My husband built me a wonderful sunroom, and it is perfect to this day. I am fond of tropical plants and flowers—all growing things, really."

"I share that enthusiasm," Kathryn confided, "although I admit, I cannot abide cut flowers. A bouquet always make me sad—knowing that the flower's life has been cut short, simply to sit in a vase for someone's brief enjoyment."

"I could not agree more," the dowager duchess responded with a smile.

Dinner was announced. The duchess picked up her cane and took the duke's arm as they proceeded to the dining room, a chamber that was lovely but also decidedly dated.

A massive table that could easily seat a dozen people had been set for three. Fine china, crystal, and silver glistened beneath a chandelier festooned with lit candles and ropes of many-faceted crystals. The footman and a maid stood at attendance, and soon began serving the meal with grace and efficiency. The first course was a fish soup that came with a bottle of white Burgundy.

"My brother was very proud of his wine cellars," the duke

commented. "We have thousands of bottles down there waiting to be consumed."

"Lucky us." Kathryn smiled. The wine was an old vintage and quite delectable.

It had been a long time since she had indulged in a nice glass of Burgundy. Over the past four years, while in school and then working, Kathryn had often been obliged to draw and sketch late into the night. To stay as clearheaded as possible, she had avoided drinking at dinner. That is, when she had bothered to actually take time to eat.

Tonight, Kathryn decided, she needn't restrict herself. She'd had a long day of travel. She wouldn't be working and could retire soon. She deserved a glass of wine or two.

"Miss Atherton," the dowager duchess said as they ate, "my grandson has informed me that you attended architecture school in London."

"I did, Your Grace."

The duchess beamed at her. "You give me hope for the future, my dear. I pray that you and others like you will achieve more than women of my generation ever could."

"That is my hope as well."

"How long have you been interested in architecture, Miss Atherton?" inquired the duke.

"Ever since I was a young girl. I remember we were visiting New York City, and I stared up at the new structures that were ten or fifteen stories high. They seemed to reach the sky. I asked my father, how can a building so tall stand on its own?"

"What did he say?" asked the dowager duchess.

"He said, 'Don't bother your pretty head about that, little girl. It's a man's problem.'"

"And so says every man ever born," the dowager duchess retorted with a frown. "They see us as decorative objects without a thought in our heads, which could not be further from the truth." She raised her glass to Kathryn. "Cheers to you for not listening to him."

"I had no choice," Kathryn responded as they all sipped their wine. "I was too curious. So while my sisters were reading children's books, I asked my teachers for books about buildings and architecture. I just had to find out what made a skyscraper stand."

"How *does* a skyscraper stand?" the duke mused, finishing his soup. "I imagine it has to do with the depth of the foundation?"

"Yes, among other things." Oh, how she loved the cadence of this man's voice. It was like gentle music blended with a ring of authority. Kathryn's gaze landed on his lips as he swallowed. Such beautiful lips. She wondered suddenly what it would be like to kiss those lips. *Dear Lord. Censor that thought.*

"Um," Kathryn continued, polishing off her glass of wine as she struggled to recall what he'd just asked. Something about foundations. "There are many challenges to keep in mind when designing a tall building, from overcoming gravity and wind to ground that is far from solid."

"I never thought of such things," the dowager duchess remarked. "What a fascinating business."

The soup plates were cleared away and the fish course was brought in, poached salmon with cream sauce paired with a very nice Bordeaux. A meat course followed, roast lamb with rosemary potatoes. They continued to eat, exchanging pleasantries about the weather and Kathryn's journey to Cornwall, as another bottle of vintage French wine was uncorked and served. This time, Kathryn asked for just half a glass. She really had better pace herself.

"Miss Atherton." The duke gave her a pondering look as the footman refilled his glass. "Earlier today, you mentioned that you are awaiting the results of the architecture licensing exam. Enlighten me. Are there any licensed women architects in Great Britain?"

"There are not."

"None at all?"

"Not yet, Your Grace."

The duke nodded slowly, taking that in.

"What about the rest of the world?" the dowager duchess inquired. "Are there any women architects anywhere?"

"There are two. Signe Hornborg graduated three years ago from the Helsinki Polytechnic Institute, and earned her degree by special permission. She works for a Finnish architecture firm now. Last year she designed a house that has earned her renown."

"Interesting," the duke commented. "And the second?"

"Louise Blanchard Bethune learned the trade as a draftsman in an architecture firm in Buffalo, New York, before opening her own office with her husband. Four years ago, she was named the first female fellow of the American Institute of Architects."

"New York, you say? Have you met Mrs. Bethune?" he asked.

"I actually applied for a position at the Bethunes' firm.

But Mr. Bethune said it was difficult enough to find clients willing to accept *one* female architect, much less two. Anyway, I wanted a degree."

"Little did you know," the duke pointed out, frowning, "that the school you attended would deny you a diploma."

"Did they?" The dowager duchess appeared incensed. "But that is absurd."

"One of my teachers told me, months after I had started the program of study, that the administration had only admitted me as a sort of private joke. No woman had ever applied before, and they thought it would be amusing to see me fail. To reinforce their belief that women were not smart enough to work in the field. When I finished the program with the highest scores in my class, it caused consternation all around. Even so, the board couldn't bring themselves to admit a woman to their hallowed ranks."

The duchess shook her head in dismay. "I am so sorry. What a difficult road you have traveled to get where you are."

"It has been a challenge."

"Well," the duchess remarked, "two female architects in the world is not very many, but it is a start. I hope that one day soon, you will be the third."

"I second that." The duke raised his glass in a toast.

They all took a drink, and Kathryn beamed. "Thank you." She was starting to feel a little light-headed. How many glasses of wine had she consumed? She'd lost track.

"I applaud you, Lance, for having the foresight to hire Miss Atherton," the dowager duchess averred. "I look forward to seeing the improvements take place."

Lord Darcy colored slightly. "Do not put the cart before the horse, Grandmother. I have not committed to any improvements yet. I have only agreed to discussions and sketches."

"Well, if the sketch you showed me before dinner is any indication of this woman's talent, you would be a fool not to do the project entire."

"Indeed. We shall see." The duke managed a brief smile, then looked away.

It was a reminder for Kathryn of the uncertainty of her situation. She may have convinced him to take this first small step, but she still had a great deal of work ahead of her if she was going to persuade him to act on any of her suggestions.

There was no point in focusing on the negative, though. All great things were achieved one step at a time, and this was no different. She would do her best work and see where it led.

Meanwhile, dinner had been excellent, and so many lovely compliments had been directed her way. Perhaps it was the duchess's ebullient mood that had affected her, but Kathryn felt as if she were floating on a cloud. "Your Graces, you are both too kind."

The plates were cleared away and an inquiry made as to whether the duke or dowager duchess desired a sweets course.

"I have had an excellent sufficiency," the duchess declared. "I am fatigued and wish to retire." She waved her napkin at the footman, who pulled out her chair.

Taking their cues, Kathryn and the duke rose. She was a bit fatigued as well. Well, not so much fatigued as . . . relaxed. More relaxed than she'd felt in ages. It was a luxurious feeling, like a cat lying in the hot sun.

"Good night, Grandmother." The duke kissed the dowager duchess on the cheek.

Giving Kathryn a smile, the duchess added, "I generally take my meals upstairs. But tonight was a rare occasion. It has been a pleasure, Miss Atherton."

"The pleasure was mine." Kathryn curtsied. Unaccountably, she made a slight hash of it. She was an expert at curtsying. What was the problem? "I wish you a good evening, Your Grace."

The dowager duchess swept from the room.

"Would you care for apple Charlotte and Champagne, Your Grace?" the footman inquired as Kathryn and the duke resumed their seats.

"What is your wish, Miss Atherton?" inquired the duke.

"I adore apple Charlotte," Kathryn replied with a wave of her hand. "And I am a great fan of Champagne. Especially with dessert. Champagne has the most energizing effect after a long dinner. But as the duchess said, I have had an *excellent sufficiency*. Another time, perhaps."

"Coffee or tea, Your Grace?" inquired the footman.

"No tea for me," Kathryn insisted, a small chuckle escaping her at her unintentional rhyme. (Why was she chuckling? She never chuckled.)

"That will be all, thank you, John," the duke informed the footman. The table was cleared, leaving Kathryn and Lord Darcy alone for a moment.

"This has been an unusual meal for me," he murmured, gazing at her.

"Oh? How so?" Another rhyme. Kathryn grinned.

"I am accustomed to dining in the officers' mess with a table full of men."

"I hope tonight wasn't too unpleasant."

"On the contrary. It has proven delightful."

"I enjoyed it myself, Your Grace. Lately, it seems like all I do is work, work, work."

"Indeed? That's a shame. No one should work around the clock."

"Sometimes I have no choice. Deadlines, you know."

"There are no deadlines tonight, Miss Atherton."

"That's a relief." Kathryn leaned back in her chair, luxuriating in the soothing warmth that enveloped her entire body. She couldn't remember the last time she'd felt so tranquil and at ease.

Her gaze drifted to the duke's hands. They looked strong and manly, his fingers elegant and tapered. "You've got nice hands," she blurted.

His brows rose.

Her cheeks instantly grew hot. *Did I just say that aloud?* "I mean . . . *you're* nice, and . . . I've got to *hand* it to you." She smiled quickly, struggling to save face. "You weren't expecting me today, but you gave me the job, anyway."

"Ah. Well." The duke shrugged. "In my profession . . . my *former* profession," he amended with a slight frown, "I was routinely obliged to make snap decisions. I suppose it has become second nature to me now."

"It's the opposite for me in my profession. I often take five or six or ten passes at a drawing, obsessing over every detail before I'm happy with it."

"But you are very quick on the draw. I have seen you with a pencil, Miss Atherton. You sketch like the wind."

"Speaking of which. I need to see the rest of the castle. What do you say we start now with a little tour?"

"There is no such thing as a *little* tour, I'm afraid. It's an enormous castle with over two hundred rooms. Fortunately, a great many are locked up and unused. Even so, let's wait until tomorrow to see the relevant parts, when the light is better."

"If you insist, Your Grace."

He stood. "I regret there are no other ladies with whom you can enjoy the rest of the evening, Miss Atherton. However, I can show you to the ladies' parlor if you wish to relax and read. As for me, I am going to indulge in a glass of Irish whiskey."

Kathryn rose, a motion that caused the room to sway a bit. "I wouldn't say no to an Irish whiskey," she confessed. *That was rather forward. What will he think?*

"You drink whiskey?" He sounded surprised, although the notion didn't seem to offend him.

"I do." She loved whiskey. "It would be the perfect topper to that lovely meal."

The duke studied her. "Are you certain? We have both had quite a bit to drink already."

"I can hold my liquor as well as the next man," Kathryn assured him confidently.

The duke smiled at that. "Well, then. Let us repair to the smoking room, shall we?"

Chapter Four

The smoking room was a small but elegant chamber with faded silk-covered walls. Two overstuffed easy chairs stood on either side of the fireplace. A sofa, two end tables, and a beautifully carved cabinet took up most of the remaining space.

Lord Darcy produced a bottle and glasses and poured two shots of whiskey. Kathryn briefly closed her eyes as she drank, enjoying the smooth, velvety texture. "Mmmm. Is this also from your brother's cellars?"

"Yes. He had excellent taste."

"I agree," she commented, taking another sip. "It's the barley."

"Hmm?"

"The Irish use a lot of barley in their whiskey. Gives it that lovely hint of caramel."

"You know your whiskey," Lord Darcy observed, smiling, as he savored his shot.

"It's what all the men drank after hours at London College." Another delicious wave of warmth spread through her.

"I wanted to fit in. So, I drank what they drank. To be 'one of the boys.'"

"One of the boys?" he repeated with a light laugh, as if that were the last thing on earth she could ever be. "Do you smoke as well?" *That* notion seemed to appall him, yet even so he offered: "I think there are cigars somewhere if you'd like one."

"No, thank you. I can't abide smoking."

"Neither can I." He made a face. "My fellow officers often indulged in a pipe after hours. A nasty habit."

The duke held out his hand. Kathryn wondered why. Then she realized he was waiting for her to give him her empty glass. She complied.

"Would you care for a refill?" he asked.

Kathryn's head was starting to spin slightly. She thought it best to decline. "No, thank you." Searching for something to say, she commented, "What a cozy room."

"Cozy?" He snorted. "A tactful way to put it. The size of this room has always been a bone of contention for the men in my family. My father, and later Hayward, were always apologizing to their guests about it being too small."

Kathryn glanced into an adjoining room, which was much larger and contained a massive billiards table. "If you want a bigger gentleman's parlor, just take out this wall and open it up into one room."

"Could we? But . . . this wall has always been here."

"I doubt that."

"What do you mean?"

Kathryn gestured toward the ceiling. "The crown molding is slightly different on this wall and doesn't match up in the corners. And this wall isn't as thick as the others. I think it was added after the main structure was built. Which means it isn't load-bearing."

"What a simple solution to a problem my father complained about all his life," the duke said.

The way he was looking at her was so full of interest and appreciation it did strange things to Kathryn's insides. He was definitely attracted to her, and he wasn't trying to hide it.

She felt the same stir of attraction for him. Heat rose from Kathryn's chest to her face and spread downward to her nether regions. Heat that had nothing to do with the wine or the whiskey.

Kathryn, you are in so much trouble.

It occurred to her that she was alone with the duke in a far corner of the castle, without a single servant in earshot. If he were to come any closer . . . if he were to touch her right now . . . she suspected she would combust into a pool of liquid fire and melt all over the floor.

The connecting door beckoned. Kathryn bolted in that direction, her heart pounding.

The duke followed. Of course he did.

She darted to the farthest corner of the room. Dark oak paneling covered the walls. The billiards table was large and expensive-looking, its oak side panels intricately carved with birds, dolphins, whales, and miscellaneous sea creatures.

"What a charming table," Kathryn stated, trying to look anywhere but at Lord Darcy.

He crossed the room, stopping just a few feet from where she stood. "It was my father's most prized possession."

"I've never seen one with seascapes. My father—" She was about to say that her father had purchased a stunning Italian billiards table for his mansion on Fifth Avenue. But she'd avoided any reference to her father so far, except to say that he owned a ship yard, and wanted to keep it that way. "My father used to play billiards," she finished quickly.

"Do you play?"

"I do."

"Let's play, then." The balls were already racked up and waiting in the center of the table. He procured two cue sticks from a rack and handed her one, along with a cube of chalk. "I've spent a week holed up in this house and would appreciate a little diversion."

Kathryn grabbed the edge of the table, suddenly feeling unsteady on her feet. Maybe she *did* have too much to drink. *You really ought to go to bed. Before you fall flat on your face.* But his smile was so warm and inviting, and he sounded so deeply desirous of her company, Kathryn couldn't refuse.

Accepting the cue stick and chalk, she retorted, "I warn you, I'll do my best to win."

"I would expect nothing less." He took off his coat and hung it over the back of a chair, then removed his tie. "Shall I break?"

Kathryn's heart began to beat erratically. As if he hadn't been attractive enough already. Tieless, in his shirtsleeves, with his tight trousers revealing every angle and curve of his lean hips and muscular legs, he was even more delectable. "Be my guest."

His shirt was white linen and of fine quality. The sleeves were billowy, like a pirate might wear. Its open neck revealed tufts of dark hair beneath the indentation at the base of his throat. *Oh, how she wanted to run her fingers through those tufts of hair. And over those hard thighs.*

Oh, how she wished she would stop thinking these things.

The duke unbuttoned and rolled up his shirtsleeves, revealing muscular forearms that were lightly dusted with the same dark hair. *Holy hell.* It was too much, really. Were she viewing him in the company of a girlfriend or one of her sisters, they would all surely have been comically fanning themselves and pretending to hyperventilate.

But she didn't have any girlfriends or sisters nearby. *No one* was nearby. Except this indecently good-looking, coatless, and tieless man with too much flesh showing, a scenario that broke more rules of propriety than she could count.

How had she gotten herself into this situation? How was she going to get out of it?

"You may wish to remove your jacket," the duke offered matter-of-factly. "I find it is much easier to play in your shirtsleeves."

There was nothing shocking about the suggestion, per se. Kathryn couldn't argue that her jacket was binding. And hot. *So hot.* She was wearing a perfectly decent, modest blouse beneath her jacket. But there was something about the *way* he'd said it, and the look in his eyes *as* he'd said it, that sent a shiver traveling up her spine and made her loath to act upon it.

"A lady dare not disrobe in front of a gentleman," is what issued from her lips. Again, her face burned scarlet with mortification. Clearly, her brain had deserted her.

Grinning, he picked up his cue stick and began chalking

the tip. The act seemed incredibly sensual, although at first she couldn't say why. Kathryn focused her attention on her own cue, slowly rubbing the chalk around the hard, round tip of the stick. The movement caused a warm glow to build inside her pelvic region—an odd reaction, she thought. Until she made the association. *Rubbing. Hard. Round tip.* Gasping, Kathryn let go of the chalk as if it were a ball of fire.

Lord Darcy removed the triangle, leaned over the table, and gracefully took the first shot. A resounding crack rent the air as balls scurried off like cannons, a yellow ball sinking into one of the pockets. "Solids," he claimed.

As he made his way around the table, lining up and sinking several more shots, Kathryn's eyes were glued to the manner in which his back and shoulder muscles worked beneath the fabric of his shirt. And the way his trousers pulled tightly across his buttocks. *Good God in heaven, now I'm looking at his buttocks.*

He missed a shot and gestured to her to play. Kathryn redirected her focus to the game. And to the effort of keeping herself standing upright. Which wasn't as easy as it sounded. Given that her legs were so wobbly. And the fact that the room was growing fuzzy at the edges.

She chose her ball, got in position, and hit away. *Bam.* A striped blue ball sank into a corner pocket. *Yes! I may be slightly drunk, but I still have it.*

"Nice," he commented.

She neatly sank two more balls in succession.

"You said you knew how to play," he accused. "You didn't say you were an ace."

"I said I'd play to win," she fired back. "And I'm not an ace.

Those were easy shots." They had been. Kathryn leaned over the table and lined up another shot, focusing on a striped red. Before she took the shot, however, he moved up close behind her.

"You're going to miss."

"How do you know?"

"Your angle is off." His hand hovered above her right shoulder. "May I?"

He was leaning over her, asking for permission to touch her. She'd been yearning for his touch for hours now, pretty much since the moment she'd arrived at the castle.

She knew she shouldn't allow it.

But who would ever know? Her heart was thumping so hard now she felt as though it might explode. "You may."

His hands gently closed around her shoulders as he readjusted her position. Then the hard length of his body pressed against the back of hers as he reached around with both arms, took hold of her hands, and moved them slightly to correct her aim. His warm breath grazed her ear. "Try it now."

"Now?" He was so close she was conscious of a fresh, delicious scent emanating from his skin, a mix of soap and a woodsy, masculine cologne. "I can't move."

"Forgive me." He stepped back a fraction, releasing her.

She stabbed the cue stick forward, barely nicking the cue ball and completely flubbing the shot. She straightened. Her feet seemed to belong to someone else. "You deliberately distracted me."

"I was only trying to help." The look in his eyes was impish, like molten danger.

"Or trying to make me *miss*. Afraid I might beat you?"

"I have no objection to being beaten. In fact, I'd enjoy it." He sank numerous additional balls until more than half of the table was clear, and then it was her turn. She'd no sooner lined up a shot than he moved in behind her again, his body pressed against hers, his arms around her once more as he readjusted her aim. "Like this," he breathed against her neck.

A riot of sensations cascaded through her. Every nerve in her body seemed to be on edge. Kathryn felt dizzy and more incredibly alive than she'd ever felt in her entire life, and yet it was difficult to think straight.

"Your Grace." Kathryn knew she should remove herself from his grasp but couldn't bring herself to move a muscle. She wanted to add, *Don't*, but she couldn't form the word; it was the antithesis of what she really wanted.

His arms scooped neatly around her now, pulling her even closer to him as his lips nibbled the side of her neck. "Miss Atherton. You intoxicate me."

She felt equally inebriated. Probably because she was. "We shouldn't—" she began.

"I think we *should*." He pressed his mouth against her neck, implanting a trail of kisses that made her gasp and her entire body quiver.

A thought from some far-off place cautioned her as to where this might lead. That she ought to call it off at once. But she didn't want to call it off. Not yet. Everything she was feeling was so wondrous and new.

She had made love to a man once. To Pierre in Paris. But it hadn't been anything like this. Not even close.

Kathryn knew how to satisfy herself. She'd explored, she'd discovered. But that was a solo act enabled by imagination. This was thrillingly real.

And all he was doing was kissing her neck.

His hands glided up to press against the sides of her silk jacket, molding to the curves of her breasts beneath it. She wished now that she *had* taken the garment off. She ached to feel his hands against her own flesh. Such thoughts were wrong, totally wrong. She was working for him! But somehow she didn't care.

One of his hands slid down past her navel, to massage her abdomen through the fabric of her skirt. She gasped at his boldness, but didn't want him to stop. A glow built in that region within her. Moisture gathered in her most private of places. She knew what it meant: that she wanted him. That her body craved more.

Kathryn was starting to feel even more fuzzy around the edges now as he slowly, with utter gentleness, spun her around in his arms to face him. One hand was on the small of her back as the other came up to caress her chin and tilt it upward. Their eyes met silently. She saw the ache of desire in his.

An identical, answering emotion bloomed throughout her entire body. It must have shown in her eyes. Because without another word, his lips came down on hers to claim them.

Lance hadn't invited her to play billiards with the intention of seducing her. He had just thought: a simple, friendly game.

Then things had started heating up between them. Until he hadn't been able to help himself.

He didn't know a thing about this woman, except that she was a talented almost-architect from New York who had studied in London. From the quality and style of her clothing, he guessed she earned a damn good salary.

He liked her. He admired her gumption. And he'd been dying to touch her since the moment they'd met. Every hour in her presence since had only made him want it more.

But she was working for him now, at least for the next few weeks or so. As such, he shouldn't be kissing her. Or touching her. Especially like this.

Damn it, he couldn't think about that now. Not with her body and lips crushed against his, returning his kiss with a fervor that matched his own.

Breaking the kiss, he looked down at her. He had noticed her wavering slightly on her feet a while back. She had seemed like a woman who could hold her liquor, and she'd insisted on that shot of whiskey. But they'd both had a lot to drink. He couldn't be sure she wasn't intoxicated. If so, he didn't want to take advantage of her.

She hadn't offered any resistance, but he needed to make sure she wanted this.

They stood there for a moment, each catching their breath. Her aquamarine eyes glittered as she gazed up at him. He read desire and invitation in their depths. Then she raised up on her tiptoes and planted another firm kiss on his mouth.

Hellcat. He ran his hands up and down her back, slowing

his pace with softer kisses, then teased the seam of her lips, urging them apart until he was able to slip his tongue inside her mouth.

She let out a soft whimper as their tongues sparred and tangled. She tasted of wine and whiskey and something else that was delectable and essentially *her*. His cock was aching hard and he pressed himself against her, wanting her to know what she was doing to him.

Her response was a moan and her arms tightened around him. Her skin and hair smelled like roses, a scent that was an aphrodisiac. They kissed and kissed, running their hands up and down each other's bodies until he felt he might die from the joy of it.

His mind was a fog of desire. Lance had made love to many women. Even as a lowly sailor, women had fawned over him at every port. Since he became an officer, he'd been able to walk into any public house and have his pick of any female in the room. His chosen companion—or companions—had happily invited him home or followed him on board for a night of steamy sex. They had just as happily left the next morning.

What he was feeling now seemed different, somehow, than what he'd experienced with those women.

This encounter had just barely begun. But there was something about this woman that had kept him off-kilter since he'd first set eyes on her. Something he was feeling to the very core of his soul. She was unlike any woman he had ever met.

And she was kissing him with a passion unlike any

woman he had ever kissed before. Every movement of her tongue, every touch of her hands, left him breathless.

He broke off the kiss, gasping for air. Her earlobes invited exploration. Taking one lightly between his lips, he licked and nibbled it, then proceeded down her neck, soon reaching the collar of her blouse. *Damnation.*

He had hoped that if she changed clothes for dinner, she would don more typical evening attire—a gown with a low-cut bodice that would show off some cleavage. Instead, to his disappointment, she had appeared all high-collared and buttoned-up in yet another businesslike suit that was even more conservative than the one she'd arrived in.

He wanted the jacket and blouse gone. And the skirt. He wanted to see her. All of her.

His hands moved to the top button of her jacket. He paused, meeting her gaze, again waiting for her reaction. Giving her a chance to protest. If he saw even the slightest hesitation, he would stop.

But she didn't protest. Her breath was coming hard and fast and her eyes were still filled with open invitation. It was all the invitation he needed. Lance made short shrift of the jacket's buttons and yanked it open. Hastily, she helped him remove her arms from the sleeves. The garment dropped to the floor.

Her blouse was white, probably silk, and looked expensive. Despite his impatience, he didn't want to ruin it. With nimble fingers, he undid the row of pearl buttons which handily ran up the front of the blouse. He undid the cuffs. In seconds, the blouse was gone.

He stopped to take in the creamy expanse of her neck and décolletage above her corset.

Dear God, she was beautiful.

He kissed her again, urgently, then trailed more kisses across her upper chest. Her skin was hot and moist beneath his mouth. Her head fell back now and her back arched, pushing her upper breasts into view. Her pink nipples perched at the edge of her corset, both breasts threatening to burst free of their confines.

His cock was as hard as a rock and straining to burst free of *its* confines. He kissed every inch of her exposed breasts, kissed the cleft where they met, licked the edge of one pink nipple, then swept his tongue down beneath her corset and chemise to tease the hidden treasure to a pert point. She moaned and made a whimpering sound.

He wanted more.

In one smooth motion, Lance lifted her into his arms and laid her faceup on the billiards table, then nimbly climbed up and settled beside her, shoving errant balls out of the way as he drew her into his arms. Her eyes were closed now and her breathing had grown soft and slow. As he kissed her again, he massaged her breasts through her corset.

Time seemed to have lost all meaning. A tiny voice in the far recesses of his mind warned him that he ought to stop. But he couldn't stop. Didn't want to. All he could think about was the fiery need that threatened to consume him and the astonishing woman in his arms.

Ending the kiss, he yanked down the top edge of her corset until one of her nipples popped fully into view. Her breast was full and white and perfectly round, the coral nipple begging to be suckled.

He obliged, running his tongue around the areola and the hard tip. She didn't move, just made a slight, soft sound, something between a sigh and a whimper. It excited him all the more.

He wanted to be inside her. He wanted every stitch of their clothing gone.

Something told him that she wasn't a virgin. He had made love to virgins. They had always been tentative and uncertain. This woman was anything but uncertain. She had met him play for play, every step of the way. Her reactions, though, at certain points in the action, suggested that she didn't have a great deal of experience. Or perhaps whatever experience she *did* have hadn't been particularly good.

He was going to make it good for her. Very, very good.

He didn't have a French letter on him. But there were other ways to protect her.

Lance raised her skirts until he was able to slip his hand beneath them, then slowly massaged his way up her undergarments toward the part where her legs joined. There was usually a slit in the fabric there. Once he touched her in that spot, once his fingers worked their magic, he knew she'd be his.

As his hand inched in that direction, he suddenly noticed that she had grown very still. He raised up to look at her. Her eyes were closed. She wasn't moving a muscle. Her face was relaxed and her breathing was slow and deep.

Lance paused, a wave of guilt washing over him. Was she . . . *asleep?*

She let out a slight snore.

Well, that confirmed it. Lance sighed with regret, then couldn't help but chuckle. He couldn't recall ever being in this situation before. Plenty of women had fallen asleep in his bed *after* sex. But none of them had passed out on him *before* they had completed the act.

He told himself not to take it personally. It was no mark against his sexual prowess—she'd simply had too much to drink. In truth, it was probably better that things hadn't progressed any further. She was going to be working for him for a while. They ought to keep things professional. *Damn it all to hell.*

Rolling off of her, Lance readjusted her corset, smoothed her skirts into place, and slid off the billiards table, pausing until he'd regained mastery of himself.

What now? She made an endearing picture, snoring ever so slightly in between long, even breaths. She looked so relaxed he couldn't bring himself to wake her—even if he *could* wake her, which was in serious doubt.

He needed to get her back to her room and put her to bed. He considered calling a servant, but decided against it. Lance had a feeling that, were Miss Atherton to be aware of the situation, she would be mortified. So he'd deal with it himself and hope that nobody was the wiser.

CHAPTER FIVE

The swoosh of draperies being pulled open awakened Kathryn with a start. Before she opened her eyes, she was aware of a parched mouth and an insistent pounding in her temple.

"Good mornin', miss," announced a cheerful female voice with a Cornish accent.

With difficulty, Kathryn pried open her eyes, squinting against the blast of sunlight that invaded her room. She made out the vague outline of a maid standing a few yards away.

"Would ye care to breakfast in yer room, miss?" the maid inquired. "Or do ye prefer to dine downstairs?"

Kathryn struggled to think. Where was she? Oh yes, St. Gabriel's Mount. Her stomach felt queasy and she couldn't remember the last time she'd had such a blinding headache.

A blanket was pulled up to her chin. Rubbing her eyes to free them of grit, Kathryn glanced at the maid again. She recognized her now. It was the redheaded girl who had brought Kathryn down to dinner the evening before. What was her name? Some kind of flower or plant? Ivy, that was it.

"Just tea and dry toast, Ivy. Nothing else. Thanks. If you'd bring it up, I'd be most appreciative." Kathryn yawned. "I might want to sleep a bit longer."

"Very well, miss." The girl bobbed and left the room, shutting the door softly behind her.

Kathryn closed her eyes again and sank back onto the pillow, wondering why she felt so dreadful. Was it something she ate? She recalled a lovely dinner the evening before with Lord Darcy and the dowager duchess. And afterward . . .

The *afterward* slowly started coming back to her. Kathryn remembered talking with Lord Darcy in the smoking room. Downing a shot of delicious Irish whiskey. He'd looked so handsome in his evening attire. They'd discussed something about tearing down a wall. About opening up the room to include the billiards room.

The billiards room.

Kathryn's pulse stuttered. Something had happened in that room . . . What? They had started playing a game. The duke had adjusted her aim. And then . . . she remembered his arms around her. His warm breath against her neck. All at once she had been in his embrace and . . . they were kissing. A hot and passionate kiss.

Kathryn gasped at the memory and sat up abruptly in bed, an action that made her stomach lurch and her head pound even harder and the blanket fall to her lap. *Oh dear God, she'd kissed him. What happened after that?*

She noticed with sudden horror that she was wearing her

corset instead of a nightgown. Throwing off the blanket, she confirmed that she was also still wearing her skirt and everything else beneath it. She caught sight of her blouse and jacket lying over the back of a nearby chair, and her boots on the floor.

Why hadn't she finished undressing for bed? How had she even gotten back to her room? She couldn't remember.

Panicked, Kathryn held her hands to her forehead. *Think. Think. Why was it so hard to think? Why did it feel like her head was splitting open?*

Slowly but surely, additional images from the evening before began to fill her mind. That first kiss, she realized with growing humiliation, had just been a precursor to a storm.

She blushed as she recalled Lord Darcy's mouth on hers, hot and insistent. The way his hands had roved over her body. The way *her* hands had roved over *his* body. How he had pressed himself against her and she'd felt the proof of his desire.

More memories came into sharp focus: his fingers working at the buttons on her blouse. His mouth on her breasts. His tongue dipping beneath her corset. If her face had been hot before, now it felt as if it were erupting in flames.

Kathryn had a distinct memory of him laying her on top of the billiards table, then stretching out beside her and scooping her into his arms.

Try as she might, she couldn't recall anything after that. *What have I done?*

Had they made love? She had no idea. *Oh God, I hope not.*

Staring down at her state of dress, or rather undress, Kathryn tried to persuade herself that they had not actually . . . done the deed. After all, she was still *mostly* clothed. Had she gotten totally naked, she doubted the duke would have gone to the effort to dress her again.

Leaping out of bed, Kathryn freshened up at her pitcher and basin, then slipped on her blouse and jacket. When Ivy returned with the tea, she'd never know Kathryn had fallen asleep with her clothes on.

She wondered again how she'd gotten back to her room. She prayed that the duke hadn't involved the staff in any way. Were anyone else to find out what she'd done, she'd be even more embarrassed.

Sitting down on the chair, Kathryn put on her shoes. What had happened last night was wrong on so many levels.

It had been one thing to make love with Pierre in Paris. That had been by design. Knowing she would never marry, Kathryn had wanted one sexual experience to understand the mysteries everyone was always talking about. Afterward, they'd gone their separate ways, knowing they'd never see each other again.

Last night was a different thing entirely.

Last night, she had behaved in the most wanton manner with the *Duke of Darcy*. A man who had just hired her to work for him.

Never mix business with pleasure.

She wished she could blame Lord Darcy. Tell herself that he was a cad. That he'd taken advantage of her, made her do things against her will. But it wasn't true.

His behavior, of course, was equally wrong. He had deliberately made advances when they were playing billiards. Everything that had followed was entirely inappropriate.

But she had been a willing party to it all. A sudden image surfaced, of herself standing on her tiptoes and planting a kiss on him. And then eagerly shrugging out of her jacket and helping him take off her blouse. *Gaaaaack!*

Clearly, she hadn't been in her right mind. Clearly *he'd* been right when he'd suggested, before they ventured into the smoking room, that she might have already had too much to drink. She must have been tipsy long before things got so out of hand. Or maybe even been flat-out intoxicated. Yet she'd asked for a whiskey, anyway.

Kathryn couldn't recall ever being intoxicated in her life. A shot or two with the boys had always gone down smoothly, no problem. But then again, it hadn't been preceded by three (or was it four? Five?) glasses of wine.

None of that was an acceptable excuse, however, for what she'd done. Even inebriated as she was, her better judgment should have prevailed.

This morning, she ought to be congratulating herself for landing an assignment which could mean a world of difference to her career. Instead, on her very first evening in this house, she had put the entire project in jeopardy by engaging in a shameless sexual encounter with the duke. *Idiot.*

Kathryn covered her face and groaned into her hands. This was all so totally, incredibly mortifying. Yet at the same time—she couldn't deny it—a tiny part of her was thrilled by the memory. There was no comparison between what had happened in the billiards room to what she'd experienced during her one night with Pierre.

She'd only chosen Pierre because he'd been convenient and available. What had transpired between them had been educational, but there hadn't been any sparks.

Whereas she'd felt sparks from the first moment she'd set eyes on Lord Darcy. Sparks that had turned incendiary when they'd gotten their hands and lips on each other. If things had progressed to their inevitable conclusion . . . which she could only hope and pray they had not . . . she had a feeling the experience would have been . . . incredible.

A discreet knock sounded at the door. Ivy brought in a tray and quickly departed.

Pouring out a cup of tea from the small pot, Kathryn took a grateful sip of the warm, fragrant brew. It felt good going down. A few sips later, she heaved a sigh, trying to figure out her next move.

Obviously, she couldn't stay here. It would be impossible to work with the duke after their illicit liaison. Despite everything she had done to make this job happen, Kathryn thought gloomily, she had no choice but to hand in her resignation and return to London as soon as possible.

It wouldn't be difficult to explain to Mr. Patterson. She would just say that their client, the ninth Duke of Darcy, had passed away. She'd have to pray, however, that Mr. Patterson never, *ever* found out what had occurred last night. It might put her very job in jeopardy.

Meanwhile, how on earth was she going to face the tenth Duke of Darcy, who was undoubtedly waiting for her downstairs?

"It is a dire state of affairs, Darcy."

"Tell me something I don't know." Lance stared at the loan documents on his desk. The sum he owed was enough to crush any man's soul. "How on earth did Hayward let things get so out of hand?"

"It wasn't for want of advice from me, I assure you." Henry Megowan, the estate's solicitor, heaved a sigh from the chair opposite.

Megowan—fair-haired, bespectacled, and sensible—had been Hayward's best friend since their schooldays at Eton and Oxford, and had often spent holidays at St. Gabriel's Mount. Although seven years older than Lance, Megowan had always treated him kindly. As the years passed, the age difference had melted away and become irrelevant. Megowan had eventually opened a practice in Penzance and taken over when the Darcys' former solicitor retired some five years previously.

"Things have been going downhill for years," Megowan continued. "Your brother was a good man with a kind heart—too kind. He didn't have a clue how to invest or manage money, and never turned down a parishioner in need. The more he owed, the more he borrowed. I tried to warn him that he was digging himself into a hole he would never get out of, but he didn't listen." Megowan shook his head. "Have you been down to the village lately?"

"Not since my last visit three years ago."

"You'll find that things have changed a great deal."

"Changed how?"

"There's been no money to pay for repairs for ages. I'm surprised Avery hasn't spoken to you about this."

Avery was the land steward at St. Gabriel's Mount. "I did meet with Avery last week. But I was too distracted by funeral arrangements to pay attention to what he said. I seem to recall something about . . . the school roof?"

Megowan nodded. "It's bad, Lance. It's been leaking for years. They have to catch rainwater in buckets. Just about every building in the village has some kind of maintenance issue. And now there's a problem with the stairs at the quay."

"I used the stairs when I took the ferryboat. They were fine."

"Not the ferryboat quay. The fishermen's quay."

"Bollocks. My tenants must be ready to storm the castle with knives and pitchforks."

"Hopefully, it won't come to that. But I think you had better do something to appease them, and soon. It doesn't have to be a financial outlay."

"What do you suggest, then?"

"Hayward used to engage with the community on a regular basis. I'd say: take a walk down to the village and say hello. Pay a few calls, listen to people's problems, assure them that you will try to make things right."

"How can I make things right, with this ridiculous loan hanging over my head?"

"Maybe you can't. But hopefully a new owner will. You just need to buy yourself some time."

The reminder that in three months Lance might lose this place only served to frustrate him further. "There is no guarantee that whoever buys St. Gabriel's Mount will take any interest in the villagers' problems. I don't want schoolchildren catching their death of cold, or fishermen struggling to disembark with their catch. I have some money of my own. It isn't an enormous sum, but while I'm still here . . . I'm happy to invest, if I can, in these most desperate causes. Get someone out here to bid on the schoolhouse roof, will you? And find out what it will cost to fix the quay steps."

"Will do." Megowan nodded. "That is very generous of you, Darcy. But be advised: it is a drop in the bucket when it comes to healing all the ills in this community."

"It is better than nothing, I hope."

"Yes. And it will be greatly appreciated." Megowan leaned forward and paused, then looked Lance in the eye. "Your Grace . . . May I speak frankly?"

"Isn't that what I pay you to do?"

"I don't mean to criticize. But you have only further complicated matters by hiring this architect you mentioned. Of all times, why on earth you chose to take on such an expense now—"

"I am aware of how crazy it sounds," Lance interrupted. "Believe me, I was adamantly opposed to the whole thing from the start. But you were not here yesterday, Megowan. This woman is an unstoppable force. She wouldn't take no for an answer. And when I saw the kind of work she can do . . ." From his desk drawer, Lance withdrew the sketch Miss Atherton had made and slid it across the desk. "Here's how she proposes to redo this room."

Megowan's sandy eyebrows lifted as he studied it. "A nautical retreat, eh?"

"On the spot, she came up with this vision that is not just new and unique and absolutely smashing, but seems to gaze into my very soul." Lance realized he had invested more passion into the statement than he'd intended.

Megowan looked at him. "She *is* talented," he acknowledged. "But to hire her to renovate the entire castle?"

"Not the entire castle. Just the interiors of a few rooms. And it's just drawings, which I will pay for out of my own pocket."

"What is the point, when you will probably have to sell St. Gabriel's Mount before the year is out, and never get to implement them?"

"The point is: I am intrigued by her. I want to see what else she dreams up."

Megowan regarded him with narrowed eyes. "You like this woman. *That's* what's going on here, isn't it?"

"What? No! Well, yes. I do . . . like her." The memory of his encounter with Miss Atherton the night before swept into Lance's mind. She'd arrived all buttoned up to her chin, the picture of propriety, and then she'd turned out to be such a surprise. In his arms, she'd come alive, become an entirely different woman.

He couldn't forget the fire in her eyes whenever their gazes had touched. The way she'd responded to his kisses and had initiated some of her own. He had all but made love to her on the billiards table. And he'd spent half the night fantasizing about the way that interlude might have concluded, had she not fallen asleep in his arms.

"Lance?"

Lance blinked. Megowan was staring at him, as if waiting for him to answer a question. "Sorry. You were saying?"

"I said: Is that the real reason you hired her? Because you're attracted to her?"

"Of course not," Lance replied defensively. "As you saw, she's a talented woman."

Megowan pursed his lips, unconvinced. "I'm beginning to worry about you, Lance. You are behaving just like your brother, throwing good money after bad."

"I am nothing like Hayward," Lance insisted. "This is a sound investment. If I am obliged to sell the castle, the drawings will be of value to a prospective buyer. And if I'm lucky—if I can find a bride with enough money to pay off this damn loan—I won't have to sell. And some day I might actually be able to renovate this place, after all."

Megowan took that in and nodded thoughtfully. "What are you planning in that direction? To find a wife, I mean?"

"I was thinking of going up to London next week. When it becomes known that the new Duke of Darcy is in town and looking to marry, the ladies will come flocking. Hopefully, one will turn up with the money I require."

The picture of that nameless, faceless woman hovered at the edges of Lance's mind, the prospect so unappealing it made him flinch. He still hated the idea of marrying someone for their money. But he was not the first aristocrat to find himself in this position, and he wouldn't be the last.

"However," Lance went on. Now that he'd met Miss Atherton, he preferred to stick around for a while. "It would be rude to leave St. Gabriel's Mount now, when Miss Atherton's firm has sent her all this way on invitation from my brother," he rationalized. "She's only going to be here for three weeks. I can wait that long before going up to town." At which point, Miss Atherton would be going that way herself. Perhaps they could even share the same train car.

"All right. You're the duke." Megowan shrugged. "It's your money—or lack of it. I will say nothing more."

"You really ought to meet her."

"Meet who?"

"Miss Atherton. Ten minutes in her presence, and you'll think me a little less mad."

"That's not necessary," Megowan insisted.

"Perhaps not. But it would please me just the same." Lance checked his calendar. "Are you free Monday evening?"

"I believe so."

"Join us for dinner."

"Your wish is my command." Megowan smiled and stood. "I will contact the tradesmen you mentioned. Meanwhile, remember what I said about calling on the villagers."

"I will. See you Monday."

They shook hands and Megowan departed. Lance filed the loan documents in a desk drawer, sat back down, and glanced at his pocket watch. It was a quarter past eleven already. What, he wondered, was keeping Miss Atherton?

She hadn't appeared at breakfast. He hoped she wasn't holing herself up in her room, too ashamed to come downstairs after what had happened last night. *If* she even *remembered* what had happened. Or was she absent because she wasn't feeling well? That wouldn't surprise him.

Lance had sensed, early on, that she'd had more to drink than she should. For that reason alone, he ought to have kept his distance. Not to mention that they were involved in a business relationship. But in the heat of the moment, he'd gotten carried away. They both had.

He knew he owed her an apology, and he would give her one. But in truth, Lance could not regret what had taken place. In his mind, they hadn't done anything to be ashamed of. In fact, he looked back on their encounter with real pleasure.

Were they ever to actually finish what they'd started, he suspected that it would prove incandescent. How he would love to have her entirely naked and writhing beneath him. Or settled on top of him, with those lovely breasts in his . . .

Hellfire and damnation. His imagination was going to drive him mad.

A light tap sounded on the study door. "Enter!" Lance commanded, his pulse leaping slightly. Hopefully, the object of his thoughts had finally come downstairs.

She hadn't. Mrs. Morgan hobbled into the room. "Your Grace," she began apologetically. "As Mr. Hammett is away, I am obliged to perform certain of his butlering duties. Even if it gives me no pleasure to do so."

"You begin to alarm me, madam. What is it?"

"You have a visitor."

"A visitor?" That was all? Lance sat up straighter in his chair. "Who? Miss Atherton?"

"No, she has not stirred from her room this morning."

"Is she unwell?"

"I could not say. She ordered tea and toast to be sent up. Nothing more."

"I see." Lance fully comprehended the lady's Spartan breakfast choice. "Pray do not disturb Miss Atherton until she chooses to appear. She . . . had a long journey yesterday."

"Very well, Your Grace."

"Now who is this visitor?"

"Miss Kerenza Chenoweth, the village schoolteacher."

"Oh! Yes." Lance had completely forgotten his appointment with the teacher. "Show her in."

"Before I do," Mrs. Morgan insisted, her voice still rife with apology, "there is something I feel I should mention, Your Grace."

"Yes?" Lance said, striving for patience.

"I didn't want to say anything when you first come home, what with your brother's passing and the funeral to plan. But I fear Miss Chenoweth will bring it up, and the plain truth is you ought to know about it."

"Is this about the schoolhouse roof?" Lance asked. "Because I have just been informed about its condition and I hope to fix it."

"It is not that, Your Grace."

"Then what is it, Mrs. Morgan?"

"It is the Children's Fête."

"The Children's Fête?" Lance repeated, at a loss.

"Years ago, it was an annual summer tradition for the Duke and Duchess of Darcy to host a party on the grounds below St. Gabriel's Mount for children from Rosquay and our own village."

"Was it? I had no idea." But even as Lance said that, a childhood memory began to surface of himself participating in a sack race with a crowd of children.

"I had forgotten all about it myself. But as it happens, the former duke, God rest his soul, decided to resurrect the tradition this summer."

Lance tensed with a sense of foreboding. "When is this Children's Fête supposed to take place, Mrs. Morgan?"

"In a little over three weeks from today, on the thirty-first of July."

"Dear Lord." This was the last thing Lance needed right now. "Can we cancel it?"

Mrs. Morgan looked troubled. "I shouldn't like to think so, Your Grace. Signs have been posted in the village and in Rosquay for months now. Everyone knows about it, and from what I hear, the children are looking forward to it."

"How much would something like this cost?"

"I don't know."

He sighed. "Well, if we do this, it will have to be on a strict budget." Quickly, he added, in what he hoped was a casual tone, "I have a great many expenses just now, you understand. Is this something you can take on and manage, Mrs. Morgan?"

"I . . . I would rather not, Your Grace," she stammered. "I have a great many responsibilities of my own, and no experience whatsoever with such things. The last time a Children's Fête was held here, I was a chambermaid. I wouldn't know where to start."

"Well," Lance admitted ruefully, "I wouldn't know where to start, either."

"What about the dowager duchess? I believe she and your grandfather hosted the parties in their day. Perhaps she'd be willing to take it on."

"An excellent idea, Mrs. Morgan, thank you. I will speak to my grandmother about it. Now, you may show Miss Chenoweth in."

His meeting with the schoolteacher took no more than thirty minutes. A starched-up, tired-looking woman who appeared to be in her late fifties, Miss Chenoweth explained that all their schoolbooks were sadly out of date and gave him a list of books and materials she would be most grateful to acquire for the upcoming year. Lance agreed to comply. *Yet another thing that will come out of my personal savings. Which will be bled dry before I know it.*

Miss Chenoweth then brought up the matter of the schoolhouse roof, which she said was endangering the health of every child in the classroom.

"I will do everything in my power to address the situation," Lance told her.

"Thank you, Your Grace." Her face was the picture of relief. "By the by," she added, rising, "my students have been asking about the Children's Fête. I do hope it will go on as planned?"

"That remains to be seen, Miss Chenoweth. I am looking for someone to take charge of it. Are you interested?"

Her eyes widened in dismay. "That has always been the province of the duke and duchess, Your Grace. I would not think of interfering." Thanking him for his time, she made her excuses and hastily took her leave.

Kathryn's heart pounded with anxiety as she arrived at the duke's study. Thankfully the tea and toast had worked wonders and her headache and stomachache had both eased.

The door was ajar. She rapped purposefully, hoping to get this meeting over with as quickly as possible and be on her way.

Upon hearing the duke's abrupt command, Kathryn entered the room. He sat behind his desk, glancing through paperwork. His black suit pulled across his broad shoulders, emphasizing his muscular frame. His hair looked invitingly tousled. His stubble of beard looked bewitchingly touchable.

Stop it, Kathryn. This is how you got into trouble in the first place.

"Miss Atherton. Good morning." The duke stood, his eyes brightening at the sight of her.

"Good morning, Your Grace," she replied quietly. "Although technically it is only morning for another ten minutes," she added, glancing at the clock on the mantel. "I apologize for coming down at such a late hour."

"Think nothing of it. Yesterday was a long day." He gestured for her to sit opposite him, and resumed his seat.

She sat. "I will be brief. I would like to terminate the agreement we made yesterday, and return to London on the next available train."

Chapter Six

"What?" The duke frowned. "Why?"

Was he going to make her spell it out? "You *know* why," Kathryn responded. "After last night, I can't possibly stay and work for you."

Lord Darcy waved an idle hand. "Don't give last night another thought. Things may have gotten a little out of hand—"

"A *little* out of hand?" she repeated, shame washing over her. "I cannot think back on what . . . occurred without extreme mortification."

"I take full blame for last night, Miss Atherton. Don't beat yourself up about it. These things happen."

"Not to me, they don't. I have never behaved in such a manner in my entire life."

"Which only proves that it was my fault. We both had too much to drink. I believe I can hold my liquor better than you can, and I should have put a stop to things much earlier. Correction, I should never have started *things* in the first place. My behavior was completely out of line. Forgive me."

There was sincere apology in his eyes. It was gratifying to know that he was willing to admit his own culpability in the affair. But even so. "Thank you for your apology. I do forgive you. But I cannot forgive myself. First, for drinking so much, and second, for . . . everything that followed." She took a breath. Finding it hard to look at him, she continued, "The truth is, to be honest . . . I don't actually remember everything that . . . followed."

"Don't you?"

"No." Her cheeks flamed. "Things get foggy after the part where I was . . . um . . . I think . . . lying on the billiards table? I was wondering . . . that is to say . . . how far did things go after that? Did we actually . . . ?"

"No," he interjected, his tone and expression clearly meant to be reassuring. "We most emphatically did not."

"Oh thank goodness." A relieved breath escaped Kathryn's chest. "When I woke up this morning and discovered myself in *dishabille*, I was so worried."

"Nothing much happened after the point which you described. I promise you."

"So, did I . . . pass out? Or . . . ?"

"You fell asleep."

"Oh." Her face grew even hotter. "Well. That must have been . . . awkward."

"I found it rather adorable actually."

"Adorable?" Kathryn wished she could bury her head in a very deep, dark hole and remain there for several weeks.

"You looked quite angelic, fast asleep." His lips twitched, but his eyes were kind.

"How did I . . . get to my room?"

"I carried you there. And put you to bed."

"Oh," she said again. The idea that he had brought her upstairs in his arms while she was passed out cold, and then put her to bed and covered her up, sent a little shiver down her spine. It was such an intimate act she was almost sorry she had missed it.

There you go again. Instantly, Kathryn reprimanded herself for having such a thought. What was wrong with her? She hardly recognized herself.

"I was discreet," the duke was saying. "No one else saw. So, nothing to worry about there."

"Again, thank you. I appreciate your candid account, and that you took pains to keep this quiet. Nonetheless, I still feel that I must leave."

He paused, then let out a disgruntled breath. "Only yesterday, you worked so hard to convince me to embark on renovations to St. Gabriel's Mount. Despite every obstacle I threw at you, you refused to back down. I can only surmise that this project is important to you, Miss Atherton, and possibly to your career. Am I right?"

"Well, yes, but—"

"Do you really wish to give up before we have even begun?"

"No," she burst out. "But after what happened—"

"I repeat: I take full blame. If you insist on feeling culpable, consider it a momentary lapse in judgment. No harm done. No one else need ever know. Let us put it behind us and move forward."

Kathryn hesitated. On the one hand, it was a relief to know that he didn't view her in a negative light after last night. An even bigger relief to understand that no one else would ever learn how foolishly she'd behaved.

On the other hand, his attitude toward their . . . encounter . . . was a bit disquieting. The way he was taking the whole matter in stride, as if this kind of thing happened to him all the time.

Well, maybe it did. He'd spent nineteen years in the Royal Navy, after all. Who knew how many women he'd slept with in all those ports of call? The notion of the duke making love to women all across the Mediterranean sent an unexpected twinge of jealousy spiraling through her, a feeling she didn't much relish. Why should she care how many women he'd bedded? She had no intention of ever *bedding* him herself.

She focused on the decision before her. He might consider it a simple matter to "put it behind them." But would it be that simple for her? Just looking at him across the desk, she felt the same intense tug of attraction that had drawn her to him like a moth to a flame last night.

Well, if she wanted this job—and she did—she was just going to have to work harder at ignoring that flame.

"I can only stay," Kathryn replied, "if we agree that our relationship will be entirely a professional one."

"That goes without saying," he responded.

"Then . . . fine. Let us move forward."

"Excellent. How shall we proceed?"

Kathryn suggested that the duke give her a tour of the premises, after which they could discuss which parts of the castle might benefit from renovation or freshening up. She would then get to work on preliminary sketches, and if he wished to continue, she'd proceed with larger scale ink drawings.

They began with a look at the basements, and were now working their way up to the battlements.

"Except for the servants' quarters and kitchens," Lord Darcy explained as they climbed the staircase that led up from those lower apartments, "the parts of St. Gabriel's Mount currently in use are the main rooms on the third floor, several bedrooms on the fourth and fifth floors, and the chapel on the terrace level. A substantial area, yet a fraction of the castle itself."

Kathryn had already pointed out that the kitchens were in need of updating, and Lord Darcy had agreed, a bit reluctantly, she'd thought. As they arrived on the third level and passed through a shabby hall, Kathryn commented in a gently inquiring tone, "I know you said cost isn't an issue . . ."

"Not at all," Lord Darcy returned smoothly. "Were finances a problem, Hayward would not have engaged the services of your firm."

She was glad to have that point reaffirmed. "Why do you suppose he put off making alterations to St. Gabriel's Mount for so long?"

The duke hesitated, as if carefully choosing his words. "Hayward was a typical bachelor, I think, busy with his own interests. I'm guessing he wasn't interested in decorating and refurbishing."

"Until your grandmother's repeated requests for new carpeting finally made him feel obligated to take action?"

"Something like that."

Kathryn laughed. "Well, whatever the reason, I'm very pleased that he called on Patterson Architecture."

Lord Darcy devoted the next hour and a half to a tour of the main rooms on the third floor. The library was in good shape, but Kathryn felt the dining room and drawing room would both benefit from new wallpaper, lighting fixtures, and furnishings.

"Add that to the list," the duke instructed.

They glanced into a pleasant sunroom filled with orchids and other tropical plants, where the dowager duchess was napping on a chaise longue.

"The conservatory," Lord Darcy whispered. "My grandmother's favorite room."

"It looks perfect to me," Kathryn observed. He agreed.

Farther down the hall, he showed her into a chamber decorated with a feminine flair, its walls covered in pale peach silk and floral-patterned carpets covering the wood floor. A couch, two easy chairs, and a good-sized desk populated the room along with a round table surrounded by six chairs.

"My mother called this the ladies' parlor. She entertained her friends here, played cards, wrote letters, and such. I don't think it's been used much since she died. Most of my grandmother's friends have passed away, and she prefers the conservatory."

"It's beautiful and looks to be in good shape."

"The staff seems to take pains to keep it presentable, perhaps as a tribute to my mother."

"I wouldn't touch a thing."

As they moved along, Kathryn took notes and continued to make suggestions. But even though she found every room of the castle fascinating, at times it was difficult to concentrate on the work at hand. Because her eyes kept darting to the man accompanying her.

Every glance his way still made her heart dance and did strange, flippy things to her insides. She admired the way he carried himself. He strode with such purpose and confidence. She pictured him in her mind, dressed in his regimentals, issuing orders to his men aboard his ship. It was a rather thrilling, handsome image.

"I like your idea of removing this wall and opening these two rooms into one."

The duke's voice snapped her back to attention. He had made a deliberate and tactful point, she suddenly noticed, of bypassing the billiards room, instead taking her into the smoking room again.

The memory of all that had gone on in the adjoining chamber the night before made her cheeks grow warm. *Keep your mind on your work, Kathryn.* She quickly jotted down "Smoking room/Billiards room: remove connecting wall" on her growing to-do list.

Her resolve was tested further when they toured the

fourth floor. The master bedrooms—on the same floor but on the opposite side of the building from the guest room where she was staying—were a His and Hers arrangement with their own dressing rooms and sitting rooms.

"This is my room," Lord Darcy explained as they entered the large, beautifully appointed chamber. "Admittedly, it feels odd to be sleeping here."

Kathryn's gaze fell upon the huge four-poster bed. Her pulse skittered as the image of him stretched out and sleeping there vaulted into her mind. Did he sleep clothed, she wondered, or naked? She immediately drew a mental curtain over the thought.

You have designed dozens of bedchambers. This is simply one more.

Clearing her throat, Kathryn replied, "Why does it feel odd, Your Grace? Because you are accustomed to much smaller quarters?"

The duke shook his head. "It's not that. This was my brother's room. And my father's and grandfather's before that." He glanced around, visibly discomfited. "My brother, God knows why, never got around to getting married. He was a very good-looking man. Women adored him. All he had to do was choose a bride, but he never did. I suppose I am still not used to the idea that it's up to me now to . . ." He broke off.

Kathryn suspected he was thinking about his duty, as the new duke, to marry and produce an heir. The responsibility seemed to weigh heavily on him. "I'm sure you will settle into your position soon enough, Your Grace. Just take things one day at time." The moment she said it, Kathryn felt herself blush. It was a very personal comment to make, and here she was trying so hard to be all business. "As for this room," she added quickly and more matter-of-factly, "it is very nice. Is there anything you wish to change in particular?"

"I haven't given the matter an iota of thought," he reminded her.

"Right. Well. I do have one suggestion. There's only one bathroom on this floor, and it's at the end of the hall."

"And?"

"Today, most houses of this size are designed with en suite water closets in the master suite. If you want to enter the modern age, we should add a water closet—or as we Americans call it, a bathroom—for you and your wife."

"My wife," the duke repeated sharply. With those two words, a dark gloom settled over his features that she couldn't quite decipher.

Kathryn wondered if he resented the idea of being obligated to marry. He'd been a bachelor all his years in the Navy, after all.

"It wouldn't be a difficult modification," she explained quickly. "We could convert one of the master sitting rooms. I promise, you will be very glad of a private chamber with your own plumbed bathtub and toilet. Every new house on Fifth Avenue in New York City features one, if not several."

He frowned, considering it, then gave in with a shrug. "You are the expert, Miss Atherton. Whatever you say."

The fifth and uppermost floor, the duke explained, was primarily devoted to guest bedrooms and suites that hadn't been used in over a hundred years, and was primarily closed off. As such, he only showed her his grandmother's suite.

"Your grandmother was right," Kathryn pointed out. "She does need new carpets. Rather desperately."

That brought a smile back to the duke's lips. "Add that to the list," he said.

They climbed the last flight of stairs and issued outside onto an enormous terrace surrounded by a stone wall, with an expansive view of the sea and coastline. This level also featured two large, ancient stone buildings topped by towers and turrets.

The first building was a thirteenth century chapel. As they stepped inside, Kathryn gasped softly. A quiet feeling of reverence imbued the space. Light filtered through stained glass windows before and aft, casting a colorful glow. A stunning stone altar presided, and a carved mahogany lectern overlooked rows of sturdy pews. The side walls of the nave were hung with countless memorial plaques to departed ancestors, some spelled *D'Arcy*, others spelled in the more modern fashion.

"How incredible," Kathryn gushed. "To think that this is part of your family home, and has been for—how many hundreds of years?"

"Nearly three hundred."

She bit her lip. "I wonder how many of your ancestors have been married and christened here."

Lance didn't respond immediately. "It's interesting to see it through your eyes. I never thought of it as being anything special. It's always just been the family chapel."

Kathryn gave him a look. "Not many people *have* a family chapel, Your Grace."

He chuckled. "You're right. Thank you for that reminder of what a privileged life I have led."

"Even dukes ought to retain a *shred* of humility," Kathryn teased.

He gave her a warm smile, which made butterflies flit in her stomach. *What are you doing?* Kathryn issued a strict mental reminder that she was supposed to be behaving like a professional, not chatting up the duke and making him laugh. Or smile. So . . . warmly.

They agreed that the chapel was another part of the castle that required no improvements. As they exited onto the terrace, Kathryn asked to see the much larger building across the way.

"The great hall?" The duke shook his head. "I won't waste your time. I don't care for that chamber."

"All the more reason for me to see it."

He sighed. "If you insist."

Crossing to the building in question, the duke pushed up a heavy iron latch and swung open the old wooden door. When they stepped within, Kathryn was enveloped by the scent of dank, cold mustiness.

The windows were so covered in grime that they barely let in any light. As her eyes adjusted, she perceived that she was in a large ceremonial chamber, every inch of which was blackened from centuries of soot.

Even so, Kathryn was awestruck as she glanced around.

The ceiling was more than two stories high, enclosed by barrel-vaulted open latticework. Ornate plasterwork carvings ran like a decorative ribbon around the tops of all the walls. Huge plasterwork coats of arms were prominently featured at each end of the room above massive fireplaces.

"This is magnificent," Kathryn exclaimed.

"It's a relic," Lord Darcy disagreed, "from the days of knights and armor. My family never used it."

"Oh! But it should be used. This room should be the showpiece of St. Gabriel's Mount."

"The showpiece?" He glanced at her as if she'd just suggested that they fly to the moon. "How? And for what purpose? It's far too big. It's cold and dark. The floors have been eaten away by insects and wood rot. It's an eyesore."

"All that could be addressed, Your Grace."

He crossed his arms over his chest and stared down at her dubiously. "I'm listening."

"I'd start by washing all the windows and scrubbing the plasterwork. Then I'd repair and refinish the floors. The biggest thing I'd change, though, is the ceiling."

"The ceiling?"

"The latticework is nice, but it's old and cracked, and you can't get access beyond it to clean the ceiling."

He gazed upward. "What would you do?"

"I'd replace the lattice with new, sturdy beams, retaining the same barrel structure but filling in the gaps with plaster and decorative woodwork. That would make the ceiling simple to clean and give the room a new dynamic. This would make an ideal ballroom, and the perfect site to host elegant parties. With a few pieces of well-placed furniture, it could also make a welcoming family parlor."

The duke stared up at the ceiling, as if trying to picture what she was describing, but failing. "Can you draw that?" Before she could respond, he added with a chuckle, "What am I saying? Of course you can."

Lance couldn't help but be inspired by all the suggestions Miss Atherton had made.

St. Gabriel's Mount had always seemed to him an ancient behemoth and crumbling burden that he was glad would never fall on his shoulders to maintain.

By a twist of fate, it had become his. He'd had very little time to get used to the idea of being its caretaker, but the prospect had seemed daunting. And most likely a losing battle.

Now, he was beginning to see the castle in a new light. Miss Atherton's ideas were excellent and at times quite innovative. As they exited the great hall and crossed the terrace, he found himself imagining the possibilities she'd described, and wishing he could find a way to implement them.

"How stunning." Miss Atherton had paused by the stone wall enclosing the terrace to take in the view.

Lance joined her at the wall, leaning on the crenellated stone surface and squinting out at the bright blue water surrounding them. Puffy white clouds dotted an azure sky. Seagulls squawked. The sun felt warm on his face, and the scent of the sea enveloped him like a tonic.

"The sea looks so vast," Miss Atherton commented. "I could almost imagine that it's endless ocean all the way to America. But doesn't France lie just over there?" She gestured with one hand.

"The French coast is only 112 nautical miles away." Without thinking, he added, "What I'd give to be on a ship right now, making a beeline for France."

A frown pulled at her mouth. "You miss it very much, don't you? Being at sea?"

"Yes," he admitted, taking in the castle behind and above them with a wave of his arm. "*This* is all very new to me."

"You said you served in the Navy for nineteen years?"

He nodded. "My father sent me off for training at age thirteen on an old-timber Navy ship moored at Devonport. I was the second son, with no expectation that I'd ever inherit and no aspirations in that direction. After four years of schooling, I signed on for ten years' continuous service."

"How old were you when you made captain?"

"A month shy of thirty-one."

"That's rather young, isn't it?"

"I was lucky. I was taken under the wing of an admiral who was friends with my father, and I moved up the ranks quickly. I had only had command of a ship for a little over a year when I learned that my brother had died."

"It must have been difficult to walk away."

"It feels as though I've lost a limb, Miss Atherton," Lance replied, his eyes fixed again on the horizon.

"I am so sorry." The sympathy in her voice rang true. "Tell me what you loved about it. The Royal Navy, I mean."

"How much time do you have?" Lance laughed lightly. "I loved everything. My crew. My fellow officers. The daily drills. The gleam and polish of a well-ordered ship. The calm of an evening at sea. The nightly yarns told around the table after dinner in the wardroom."

"Nightly yarns?"

"Many officers are accomplished raconteurs. Those who could tell the tallest stories with the most conviction were greatly admired."

She laughed. "How about the food?"

"The food on board could have been better. In port, however—from Spain and France to Egypt and Morocco—it was often quite spectacular."

"I've traveled a bit in the Mediterranean myself. One could spend a lifetime exploring there and never see or taste half of its wonders."

"Exactly." Lance was intrigued to discover that she enjoyed traveling as much as he did.

"When I think of the Royal Navy, I think of wooden ships. And cannons." She gestured toward an ancient black cannon nearby. "I suppose that's all gone now?"

"Entirely gone. We've had to completely replace our war fleet over the past half century. All our ships are metal now, powered by steam, and they carry explosive munitions."

"It's a little sad, isn't it? To know that the age of sail has been banished to the pages of history?"

"Yes, but we shouldn't romanticize it, either. Life on board ship is safer now and far more comfortable for the crew."

"Did you see any action while at sea?"

"No. England hasn't been at war since 1815. Our job was to police the waters of the Mediterranean. It's a point of pride that, even during all these transformations, the Royal Navy has maintained its advantage over all potential rivals."

"'The best guarantee for the peace of the world . . .'" she began.

"'. . . is a supreme British fleet,'" he finished with her, smiling. "Established dogma at the Admiralty. How do you know that slogan?"

"I read a lot." She returned his smile. "Your career—it sounds thrilling. I'm sorry you had to give it up."

"Don't be. Any reasonable person would say that inheriting a dukedom is hardly a cross to bear. I'm fully aware of how lucky I am." If only she knew the truth about the headache he had actually inherited. But he couldn't tell her that. He couldn't tell anyone.

"Life, I think, has a way of leading us places we never expected to go," she said thoughtfully. "You never expected to find yourself master of this place. But St. Gabriel's Mount is magnificent. It's a piece of history." She gestured to the castle towers rising behind them. "I hope you can find some excitement in the notion that this wonderful place is yours to command."

"Mine to command," he repeated, unable to prevent a note of irony from creeping into his voice.

His tone seemed to sadden her. After some hesitation, she replied: "My grandfather used to say, 'The past is behind you. The future is yet to be discovered. Soon, your new path will become the most comfortable direction you could have ever hoped to follow.'"

He processed that and found himself nodding. "Wise words, Miss Atherton. Thank you. I shall keep them in mind."

They retreated to the study, where they went over the to-do list Kathryn had compiled.

"I have to take measurements of all the rooms in question. But it would be helpful if you have drawings from any previous renovations."

"The same thought occurred to me, so I took a look last night." From a cupboard, Lord Darcy procured two sets of drawings and spread them out on his desk. "I found the plans from the improvements my grandmother mentioned, done in 1832. This second set appears to be for alterations made a hundred years before that."

Wishing to study the drawings more closely, Kathryn crossed behind the desk to stand beside him. She instantly realized that the move was a mistake.

All day long, as they'd toured the castle, Kathryn had deliberately maintained a certain distance between herself and the duke. Now, he was standing just a foot away. So close, Kathryn could feel the heat emanating from his body. So close, she could hear the thud of his heartbeat. Or was that her own heart that had begun to pound in her ears?

"These are . . . excellent," Kathryn blurted, focusing on the drawings. "The ink hasn't faded too badly. They'll be a huge help."

"Good."

She stared at his large hands, which were splayed atop

the desk as they studied the plans. *You've got nice hands.*
When she'd uttered those words the night before, she'd had
no idea—yet—of the magic those hands could make as they
played her body like a musical instrument.

"Look," Kathryn said hastily, pointing to one of the drawings dated 1740, which listed the owner's name as *Robert
Granville, Fifth Duke of D'Arcy.* "I saw your name spelled that
way over the front door. I presume it's of French extraction?"

"It is. François Granville, the first Duke of D'Arcy, emi-
grated from Paris in the sixteenth century. Over time, the
apostrophe in our name was deleted."

"It's a shame it was Anglicized. The French spelling is so
much more romantic."

"I should like to think we English aren't *entirely* unro-
mantic." The duke straightened and turned to face her, his
gaze finding hers and lingering.

Kathryn's breath caught. She could lose herself in the
depths of those deep blue eyes. Staring into them was like
being carried aloft by the rush of an ocean wave. Quickly
lowering her own eyes, she found herself staring at his lips.
Another mistake. She couldn't help recalling how those lips
had felt when pressed to hers. Oh, he was good at kissing,
this man.

And not just good at kissing lips.

Her pulse began to beat erratically now as she recalled
the sensation of those lips planting soft kisses along the side
of her neck and throat. Over the crest of her breasts. The
way his tongue had lapped at her nipples, tantalizing them
to peaks.

A warm wanting bloomed in her pelvis. Kathryn suddenly ached to feel his mouth on all those places again.

Stop it stop it stop it. She struggled to recall what they'd been talking about, but failed. She could hear the slight hitch of his breath as his eyes continued to hold hers. Was he thinking what she was thinking? Remembering what she was remembering?

Yes, he was. It was written all over his face.

He wanted to kiss her just as much as she wanted to kiss him.

All it would require was the smallest movement. The smallest look of encouragement. And she felt certain he would take her in his arms again.

CHAPTER SEVEN

"Miss Atherton," the duke said ever so softly.

"Lord Darcy," Kathryn replied just as softly and huskily.

A long moment passed, tension sparking between them like invisible electrical waves. Then the duke cleared his throat and, with what appeared to be extreme reluctance, took a step back.

"I hope you have everything you need to get started?"

Kathryn took a step back as well, engulfed by a rush of disappointment. Struggling to quell her runaway heartbeat, she forced her thoughts back to the matter at hand. "Not everything, Your Grace. There is one more thing I do need."

"What is that?"

"I require a room in which to work, and a table large enough to accommodate my drawings."

"Ah. Of course." He paused, thinking. "There is a table in the ladies' parlor that accommodates a party of six. You will have quiet and privacy there. Will that do?"

"That would be perfect, thank you."

"Set yourself up in that chamber at your convenience. I'll tell Mrs. Morgan to expect to find you there. Feel free to take whatever measurements you require in the castle, Miss Atherton. And do let me know if there's anything else you need."

"Thank you, Your Grace. May I take these?" Kathryn indicated the drawings on his desk.

"Certainly."

After rolling them up, she grabbed her hat and notebook and started for the door.

"Miss Atherton," he called out.

She paused and glanced back at him. "Yes?"

"Don't forget. Dinner begins with sherry in the drawing room at seven-thirty sharp."

Kathryn's cheeks burned as she fled the duke's office. She couldn't believe it. She'd actually hoped that the duke would kiss her again. Hoped he would do far more than kiss her.

Oh! This was entirely unacceptable. She was behaving like a schoolgirl with a ridiculous crush.

Kathryn had a feeling, though, that the duke might have a crush on her as well. She had read the burgeoning desire in his eyes just now.

Apparently, his better judgment had prevailed.

Earlier that day, in that very same room, he had agreed that their association would be entirely professional moving forward. Well, Kathryn chastised herself, she was going to have to get her *own* better judgment in line where it belonged. She was here to do a job, not romance a duke.

Lance frowned at the note in his hands.

> *My dear Lord Darcy,*
>
> *Forgive me for declining your kind invitation to join you for dinner this evening. When I am working, I often keep strange hours and find it easier to dine on my own. I will therefore request that all my meals be brought to me on a tray.*
>
> *Thank you again for your gracious hospitality. I will inform you when my initial sketches are ready for your review.*
>
> *I remain yours truly,*
> *Miss Kathryn Atherton*

Damn it to hell and back. The woman was deliberately staying away from him.

He knew why.

I can only stay if we agree that, moving forward, our relationship will be entirely a professional one.

He had accepted those terms—perhaps foolishly. It was an agreement that he was finding difficult to keep. In his study, when they'd been looking over those old drawings, it had been all he could do not to take her into his arms and kiss her.

He couldn't forget what she'd tasted like. What she'd felt like with her sweet curves pressed against his. He closed his eyes and let the memory wash over him. It was something he would like to experience again. And again.

Even though they shouldn't. At least not now. She was

right; it was a bad idea to get involved with someone with whom you had a business relationship—anyone would tell you that. It could affect the work, could have all sorts of negative, unforeseen repercussions.

She wouldn't be working for him forever, though. Perhaps someday . . .

He frowned. If everything went as planned, he would soon be married. To someone else. Someone with a great deal of cash. So there never would be a *someday* with her.

Lance sighed. One of the reasons he'd agreed to work with her was to have the pleasure of her company while she was staying under his roof. If she deliberately avoided him the entire time, where was the pleasure in that?

Lance dined alone that evening. The following day he spent tediously going through correspondence. Although he looked for Miss Atherton, he never encountered her. Twice, he made a point of visiting the ladies' parlor, hoping to find her at work there, but the room was empty.

"Miss Atherton?" Mrs. Morgan mused that evening when Lance inquired as to the woman's whereabouts. "I hear she spent all morning in the grand hall, Your Grace, doing some kind of work with a tape measure. She was spotted elsewhere this afternoon doing something similar in the dining room, library, and master bedrooms, I believe."

"Thank you, Mrs. Morgan," Lance replied, frustrated that he had missed those chances to observe Miss Atherton at work.

Early the next morning, an erotic dream about Miss Atherton caused him to awaken at dawn with a raging cockstand. He leapt out of bed, frustrated.

There was only one cure for this lunacy, and he knew exactly what it was.

Kathryn was in a small boat, crossing the bay toward St. Gabriel's Mount. A seagull swooped and dove overhead. The sun shone on the sparkling sea, but she couldn't feel its warmth.

She *had* to reach the Mount. Time was of the essence. She couldn't recall why.

All she knew was that the Duke of Darcy needed her. If she didn't get there in time, some terrible calamity might happen.

The oarsman plowed against the current, but every stroke of his oars seemed to keep the Mount even farther off in the distance. All at once, to Kathryn's horror, the oarsman vanished into thin air. She was all alone on the boat. Scrambling to the empty seat, she picked up the oars. The harder she rowed, the less progress she made.

Huge waves began to lap at the boat, rocking it to and fro. Kathryn's heart hammered. She had to get to the island. She couldn't be late! Suddenly, an enormous wave began rushing toward the boat, then flung itself overhead in a towering crest of foaming water. Kathryn tried to scream, but no sound issued from her throat.

Just as the wave was about to engulf the vessel, Kathryn awoke with a start, her skin clammy and her pulse pounding.

Thank God. It was only a dream.

Kathryn hated dreams like those. When they happened, she was always rushing to get somewhere. Often she was trying to catch a train or a coach, or she was late arriving at the docks and her ship was leaving at any moment.

Other times, she was racing across town to get to a meeting or appointment, but every hansom cab was taken, the Underground had shut down, and the crowds on the streets were so thick she had to fight her way through them.

This was the first time she'd ever dreamt of being in a small boat.

Or desperate to reach the Duke of Darcy.

What did it mean? *Nothing,* she reassured herself. *It was just another stupid dream.* At least there had been no sex involved in *this* dream. She'd had several dreams of a sexual nature over the past two nights that she blushed to recall.

Kathryn perceived a dull white light peeking in around the edges of the curtains. The clock announced that it was just after six a.m. So early. But she was too wound up to go back to sleep now.

Instead, Kathryn got up and got dressed. It was the perfect time, she decided, for a walk. She'd get some exercise and then devote the rest of the day to her work.

The sun was low on the horizon as she made her way downstairs and out of the castle, heading for the narrow path she'd discovered on the steep, rocky eastern flank of the Mount. The hard dirt path had been carved out of the granite cliff and meandered back and forth as it wound its way down toward a small, pebbly beach below.

About halfway down the cliff, Kathryn found an old wooden bench, perfectly positioned to enjoy the view. She sat for a moment, drinking in the crisp tang of the salty breeze and the expanse of open sea before her, which stretched out toward the horizon in an endless field of blue. Unable to resist, she took a small notepad and pencil from her skirt pocket and sketched the scene before her.

What a lovely and special place, she thought, not for the first time. How lucky the duke was to live here. How fortunate *she* was, to have been given this opportunity to work on redesigns for the castle, and to enjoy its beauty during her stay.

She and the duke had agreed on a great many proposed changes, some more complex than others. The task before her was extensive.

She had written to Mr. Patterson to inform him of the work she'd undertaken, guessing that it would take the full three weeks he had envisioned, if not longer, and she promised to send him regular updates.

Kathryn had also written to her sisters to explain where she was and what she was doing. She regretted being unable to see Lexie and Maddie while she was in Cornwall. But they lived many miles away, and Kathryn didn't have time to visit family. Maybe, three weeks from now when the project was finished, she could see them on her way back to London.

Three weeks from now. Kathryn felt a little on edge at the notion of residing at St. Gabriel's Mount so long. She told herself it was because she didn't want to impose on the Duke of Darcy's hospitality any longer than necessary. But there was more to it than that, and she knew it.

She felt on edge because her attraction to him refused to wane. And it wasn't just the dreams.

The day before, while taking measurements of the master bedroom for the proposed bathroom addition, Kathryn hadn't been able to resist looking about the chamber. Although she'd seen the room before, she hadn't had a chance to study it, to get a measure of the man.

He kept his room neat as a pin and had few personal items. Just a brush and comb. A shaving set. A bottle of cologne. Despite herself, she'd opened the stopper on the bottle and had breathed in. Aaah. Yes. The same heady, woodsy scent that she'd come to associate with him. On his bedside table she'd spied a copy of *Ivanhoe* that looked well-read. His choice of book had delighted her; it was one of her favorites.

While measuring the master closet, her attention had been drawn to the clothing inside. Several black suits looked brand-new, probably hastily assembled as mourning clothes for his brother. At the back of the closet, she'd spied three Royal Navy uniforms. Kathryn had run her fingers over the heavy, dark blue fabric. The fanciest was a gorgeous, full dress tailcoat with gold buttons and gold epaulettes on the shoulders. On the shelf above was a tricornered cock hat with a feather and insignia.

Her pulse had quickened as she'd imagined the duke attired in such regalia. He would, she had no doubt, make a regal and imposing figure. As soon as the thought crossed her mind, Kathryn had shut the closet door, annoyed and embarrassed.

Now, as she finished her sketch, pocketed it, and continued down the cliff path, Kathryn was equally annoyed with herself. What had she been doing, looking through the Duke of Darcy's closet? What if he had walked in at that moment and found her snooping?

Just then, to her surprise, she spotted the man himself rounding a bend below. Apparently, he'd had the same idea to take an early-morning walk. As he was approaching from the opposite direction, he must have headed down the road on the other side of the castle and circled around.

Kathryn ground to a halt. The duke had almost reached the base of the cliff path by now, but he didn't seem to have noticed her. He was casually dressed in trousers and a loose white shirt. He strode with purpose toward the pebbly beach, then stopped a few yards from the shore.

Kathryn considered what to do. She had managed, quite successfully, to avoid him the day before. She had no wish to encounter him now. On the other hand, if she were to turn and flee up the path, he would surely see her and think her rude.

She didn't want to be rude.

She blew out a conflicted sigh. Should she walk on down? What if he suggested taking a stroll on the beach together? Surely she could manage a few moments in his company without falling prey to her baser desires. Couldn't she? Kathryn was about to call out to him, to alert him to her presence, when the duke did something that made her freeze.

He began taking off his clothes.

In one swift motion, he lifted his shirt over his head and tossed it onto the beach. Then he kicked off his shoes and divested himself of both his trousers and his smalls. He stood there, fully naked, inhaling a long, deep breath as he stretched his arms above his head and stared out to sea.

Kathryn's heart began beating like a drum.

She knew she shouldn't be standing here, staring at him like this. But if she were to call out to him now, it would be so awkward. If she crept back up the hill, he might see her, which would surely embarrass him.

So she shrank back into the shadow of the rocky cliffs and kept watching.

Dear Lord, what a beautiful male specimen. He stood with his back to her. The early-morning sun played over the muscles of his broad back and shoulders. His buttocks looked firm and round. His long, lean legs were muscled as well, and even from this distance she could see that they were lightly dusted with dark hair.

The duke thrust his arms overhead, stretching, then turned so that he was half-facing the cliff. He wasn't looking in her direction, thank goodness.

But she couldn't take her eyes off of him. Her gaze fixed on the beauty of his torso. The dark curls spreading across his upper chest. His tight abdomen. The male . . . appendage . . . which hung down between his legs.

Oh my. In her entire life, Kathryn had only seen one man naked: Pierre. He had been almost as slender as a girl, and his male appendage had not been all that impressive.

Kathryn had, however, spent many pleasant hours studying the classical statues of naked men in Rome, Florence, and Athens. She thought the nude man's form, as idealized by such statuary, to be exquisitely beautiful. Her favorite was Michelangelo's *David*.

Kathryn swallowed hard. Lord Darcy's genitalia was much larger than the *David*'s.

A warmth ignited inside her belly, sparking upward toward the tips of her breasts, and downward to her feminine core.

Close your eyes. You shouldn't be seeing this. But she couldn't look away.

As she watched, the duke bent to touch his toes, then straightened and curved his arms overhead to each side, bending this way and that. It was clearly an exercise routine.

She wondered if he used to do something similar while in the Navy. And whether this was something he did every morning, even now. Glancing up behind her, she noted that only the top most edge of the castle's eastern tower, one of the uninhabited parts of St. Gabriel's Mount, was visible from this location. Which explained why he was exercising here, in a spot he presumed was private and out of view.

Even so, why did he do it naked?

The answer became readily apparent. Turning seaward, he made his way across the pebbly beach to the water's edge. Without hesitation, he walked straight into the ocean until it reached waist height, then plunged headfirst into the waves. A moment later he came up spouting, throwing his head back, and whipping water from his face and hair. With strong, deliberate strokes, he began swimming out to sea.

It was no wonder, Kathryn thought, that his body was so gorgeously muscled, if he regularly indulged in morning swims like this.

This was her exit cue. He was swimming away from the beach. If she made a fast getaway up the path, he wouldn't ever know she'd been here.

Lance plowed through the waves, relishing the feel of the cold water that enveloped his body and enjoying the salty taste of it in his mouth.

It was the first chance he'd had to swim since he'd come home. As a boy, he'd often taken a morning dip. As a trainee in the Navy, a cold plunge in the sea had been part of the required morning routine. He had continued the practice in ports of call across the Mediterranean. The water there had generally been a lot warmer than it was here. But the Gulf Stream that wrapped around Cornwall made for a more temperate climate than anywhere else in England. Something he'd always been grateful for.

The exercise refreshed and invigorated him. As he swam toward the horizon, his mind drifted to the dream he'd had the night before. The one that had prompted this need to dive into frigid water.

Lance didn't always remember his dreams, but this one had been too vivid to forget. He'd been on board the *Defiant*, on the officer recreation deck, engaged with the men in a lively game of deck hockey.

As they'd raced to and fro, slapping at the puck with their sticks, one of the officers had slammed directly into him. Lance had fallen back onto the deck, the breath knocked out of him as the fellow landed on top of him.

But when the officer's cap flew off, it revealed a head of billowing, golden hair. The man on top of him was no man at all. It was Miss Atherton.

The luscious curves of her body had molded against him. She'd gazed down with eyes as blue as topaz. Her lips had hovered above his like a ripe peach that he'd ached to taste.

In the dream, Lance had slid one hand along her backside. Through the coarse fabric of the naval uniform she wore, he'd reveled in the feel of her tiny frame. Her slender back. Her firm derrière.

He had wanted that uniform to disappear. Wanted to rip every shred of clothing from her body and make love to her then and there. Who cared if the entire crew was watching?

He'd reached up to draw her mouth to his. Just as their lips were about to touch, he had awakened, his cock as stiff as a ramrod.

Even now, despite the temperature of the water in which he swam, recalling the dream made him go hard again. He dove under a wave, swimming like there was no tomorrow, anything to get his mind off the dream. And the woman.

It was going to be a long three weeks.

Flipping over onto his back, Lance rested a moment as he gazed back at the island. He noticed a distant female figure hastening up the path toward the castle. Intrigued, he tread water, trying to figure out who it was. It couldn't be his grandmother. She wasn't able to make that climb anymore. The servants would be at work already, and she was too nicely dressed to be a local.

That's when he caught a glimmer of the sun on golden hair, and he recognized her. It was Miss Atherton.

She was heading up the cliff, not down. And she was moving quickly, which was hard to do on that steep path—with her head down, almost as if she were running away from someone or something.

A sudden blush heated his face. Could it be that she had seen him a few minutes ago, exercising on the beach? He shrugged it off with a low chuckle as he continued to tread water.

The notion of her coming upon him, unexpectedly, in the nude, *was* a little embarrassing. But it was also somehow . . . titillating.

He knew what a passionate heart beat beneath those buttoned-up suits she wore. Granted, she'd had a few too many drinks in her the other night. But they had served to liberate the woman inside.

So what if she had seen his naked body? He had nothing to be ashamed of. He was toned, in excellent shape. Perhaps, seeing him naked would make *her* dream about *him*.

Perhaps an erotic dream or two would help loosen up some of those laces of propriety that bound her so tight.

Which, Lance thought as he turned and continued to swim, was something delightful to contemplate.

Chapter Eight

After breakfast, Lance made his way down to the village.

His first stop was the fishermen's dock. Only a few boats were in the harbor, most of the men still out at sea going about their daily catch. Lance inhaled the beloved scents of hemp, rope, old wood, and tar as he studied the steps by the landing. They did seem to require some work. He would see to it that the matter was taken care of.

At the schoolhouse, Lance met with the roofer Megowan had engaged. The man said the situation was grave. A new roof was in order. He agreed to give Lance a bid for the work.

Lance devoted the next hour to visiting his tenants. He'd known these people, in a distant sense, since he was a boy. Over the past two decades, whenever he'd come back on leave to visit his brother, the villagers had been friendly. But Lance had never made a point of actually calling on anyone; that had been Hayward's job.

Now, it was Lance's duty. It was a bit awkward at first. But the more calls he made, the easier it became. Everyone seemed happy to see him. They expressed sorrow for the passing of the former duke, and delight that Lance had taken up residency.

A few people made requests which were easy to accommodate. An elderly woman needed more coal. A young couple begged his permission to hold their wedding in the St. Gabriel's Mount chapel. He said yes, giving them a wedding date a month before his loan was due, when he could be certain that—no matter what the future brought—he'd still be in possession of the castle.

As Lance feared, however, other problems were brought to his attention that wouldn't be so simple to take care of. The schoolhouse wasn't the only roof that leaked. In many houses, mildew was starting to take over the walls. Every cottage needed their chimney swept, and several needed new chimneys.

Lance added these issues to his growing list of financial woes. Where was the money going to come from? As he plodded down the lane that served as the main street of the village, Lance felt as though he carried the weight of Olympus on his shoulders, a stress that had centered in his gut. He fleetingly questioned his decision to let Miss Atherton draw up renovation plans for St. Gabriel's Mount. That project was doomed, anyway, and the timing couldn't be worse.

He had made a commitment to her, however. By God he wasn't going to back away from it now.

As he passed the bakery, Lance noticed a sign in the window advertising the upcoming Children's Fête. Similar signs had been posted in windows of other shops and houses and several villagers had brought up the subject, which had slipped his mind.

"How d' ye do, Yer Grace?" called out the craggy-faced baker from his doorway.

"Nice to see you, Mr. Finch." Lance offered the man his hand. "I hope all is well with you?"

"Very well, thank ye." Finch returned the handshake with a firm, leathery grip. "My three young'uns, they be countin' the days 'til that fête. Right good of ye to do this fer the children, Yer Grace, what with it bein' the former duke's notion and all."

"Of course," Lance replied. "It is important to keep the children happy."

As he climbed the cobblestone road back up to the castle, Lance made a mental note to speak to his grandmother about the matter—the sooner, the better.

The clock had just struck seven. Kathryn was on her way upstairs to her room when she ran into the duke on the halfway landing, on his way down.

"Miss Atherton." He paused, his face lighting up. "There you are."

"Good evening, Your Grace." All day long, Kathryn's mind had drifted treacherously to what she'd seen that morning. The duke naked on the beach. She felt guilty that she'd witnessed him in such a private moment. At the same time, the white-hot memory made her feel a bit weak in the knees.

Kathryn had known she couldn't avoid the duke forever. She'd tried to prepare herself for the moment when she would run into him again, and had convinced herself that she'd be fine. She would simply ignore this absurd crush and operate in the professional capacity that was expected of her.

But ignoring this crush wasn't going to be so easy. Despite herself, seeing him in the flesh again made her heart thump at a more frantic pace. He was dressed for dinner in elegant attire that accentuated his masculine form. *Why did he have to be so incredibly good-looking?*

The appreciative gleam in his eyes as he took her in told her that he found her equally attractive.

"I received your note the other day." His voice was as deep and luscious as clotted cream. "I admit, I was aggrieved about what it communicated."

"Sorry. I just . . . have a lot of work to do. It's best if I keep my nose to the grindstone, so to speak."

"I appreciate your dedication. But no one can or should work every minute. Have you taken any breaks at all?"

"Of course."

"What kind of breaks?"

Kathryn didn't want to mention her walk down to the beach that morning. Hopefully he hadn't noticed her. "I have paused as needed to eat and sleep."

"The rest of the time you have been working?"

"Yes, and I've made excellent progress."

He didn't appear to be appeased. "You cannot continue to work at this pace, Miss Atherton. I will not allow it."

"You will not *allow it?*" She was miffed by his imperious

tone. "I assure you, Lord Darcy, I am accustomed to working long hours."

"Not on my watch. You will take the time to eat proper meals. I will not have you make yourself ill on my account."

"I am not making myself ill," Kathryn insisted. "I—"

"Sherry will be served as usual in the drawing room at seven-thirty," he interjected. "I have invited a guest to dinner: my solicitor, Henry Megowan. I'd like you to meet him. My grandmother is also dining downstairs this evening. I insist that you join us."

I insist? Kathryn bristled. "I hate to disappoint your solicitor and the dowager duchess, but I am not—"

"That is a command, not a request, Miss Atherton."

"This is not a ship in the Royal Navy, Your Grace," Kathryn fired back, "and I am not under your command."

He at first seemed taken aback by her censure. But after reconsidering, he blew out a breath, and replied: "True enough. Forgive me, Miss Atherton. As I said, old habits die hard. Might I be permitted to revise my prior statement?"

She looked him in the eye. "You may."

"Naturally, you are free to choose your own schedule. But you *are* living in my house *and* working for me at present. If you prefer to take breakfast and lunch on your own, be my guest. I would very much appreciate it, however, if you would join me at dinner tonight. And every evening going forward."

Kathryn bit her lip, her annoyance fading. He was trying so hard to be fair and accommodating, which must be difficult for a duke and former naval captain. She considered her options. On the one hand, she *did* have an enormous amount of work ahead of her and she was eager to get going. To preserve her sanity, she still thought it best to stay away from this very appealing gentleman.

On the other hand, she *had* been working nonstop for two days. She was tired. It seemed important to Lord Darcy that they dine together. She wanted to keep this job, and didn't want to risk offending him.

She would just have to find a way to get through a few weeks of dinners with him without her knees turning to jelly.

"Aye-aye, Captain." Kathryn touched her brow in a formal salute. "I'll see you at seven-thirty."

Kathryn hadn't realized how hungry she was until the first course arrived, and she found herself devouring a bowl of delicious lobster bisque soup.

As always, the table was set with elegant formality and everyone was dressed to the nines. Being that this was a professional visit, Kathryn hadn't brought any evening gowns, but she wore her most elegant suit, a dark blue fitted silk enhanced with many tucks and embellishments. She declined the wine, just as she had declined the predinner sherry. On no account could she risk a repeat of what had happened three nights before.

The duke's solicitor, Mr. Megowan, was a pleasant gentleman with intelligent eyes who looked to be about forty years of age. He inquired about the scope of the work upon which Kathryn had embarked and listened with interest as she gave him an overview.

It was a pleasure to see the dowager duchess again, and the feeling seemed to be mutual. The duke seemed equally pleased to have Kathryn's company at the table. The foursome made for a companionable party as they ate and exchanged pleasantries.

When the main course was presented, a roast pork with carrots and savory potatoes, the duke introduced a new subject. "Grandmother, is it true that you and Grandfather used to host an annual summer fête for the children of St. Gabriel's Mount and Rosquay?"

"Yes, we did. Lord, I haven't thought about that in years. It was your grandfather's pride and joy, that fête. A shame your father let the tradition lapse. The children always seemed to enjoy it."

"You haven't heard, then?" the duke replied. "Before he died, Hayward resurrected the notion."

"Did he?" The dowager duchess pursed her lips. "Now that you mention it, I believe Hayward did say something about a Children's Fête. I never thought he'd actually go through with it."

"There are signs up all over the village announcing it. It is scheduled for the end of the month."

Kathryn smiled. "What a lovely idea."

"Yes, tremendous," the duchess agreed, sipping her wine. "I am sure it will be a great success."

"Actually, Grandmother," the duke said casually, "I was hoping that you would chair the thing."

"Me? Oh heavens, no," the duchess drawled. "I am much too old to undertake something like that."

"But surely, since you've hosted the fête before," he insisted, "it would not be too great a challenge to undertake it one more time?"

"You are talking about a party for a hundred children," the duchess retorted. "An event of that magnitude must be planned out to the last detail. It requires a host or hostess with a great deal of energy. I am afraid I am past that now, darling. In any case, it was always more your grandfather's affair than mine."

The duke nodded, clearly disappointed.

"I shouldn't think it would be a problem to cancel it, Darcy," Mr. Megowan offered. "It was your brother's idea, after all. Surely people will understand."

"I hoped the same, until I spoke to people in the village today. Everyone seems to have their hearts set on it."

"Did you ever attend the fête as a boy, Your Grace?" Kathryn asked.

"I did, once," the duke replied. "I must have been very young. I believe there were lawn games. And cake."

"It will be a challenge, Lancelot," the dowager duchess said, "but I feel certain you are up to it."

"Am I?" Lord Darcy didn't look happy about it. "Give me command of a ship, and I am in my element. Ask me to lead three hundred and fifty men in a cutlass drill, do spherical trigonometry, or find my position by the sun or moon with a nautical sextant, and I am your man. But I know absolutely nothing about children, and even less about children's parties."

Kathryn found his honesty and lack of confidence disarming. "Compared to commanding a ship of three hundred and fifty men, Your Grace, hosting a Children's Fête is child's play. Pun intended."

He arched both brows at her. "And you know this . . . how?"

"When I was a girl, my church in Upstate New York held such events every summer. As we grew older, my sisters and I helped host them. We called them children's fairs, not fêtes, but I imagine they are the same thing. When did you say the event is to take place?"

"July thirty-first."

"Well, then, you have three weeks to plan. You're right: you will need cake! Lots of it. Perhaps a few other refreshments and a beverage as well. Your cook can take charge of that. In addition to lawn games you'll need a few other activities, some entertainers, perhaps. And prize ribbons and party favors, of course."

He looked lost now. "Prize ribbons? Party favors?"

"You cannot hope to have a successful children's party without them. The winners of every game and race must be awarded ribbons for first, second, and third place. Not everyone can be a winner, so you want each child to take home a small gift of some kind. Something to set on their bedside table, to look at and remember the day. And the duke who gave it to them."

The duke appeared overwhelmed. "You make it sound so simple. Yet I know it is not."

Mr. Megowan let out a laugh. "Darcy, it's quite clear who ought to be hosting your Children's Fête. She's sitting across from you."

"Now there's a thought." The duke graced Kathryn with a radiant smile. "Would you, Miss Atherton?"

Kathryn didn't know what to say. "Your Grace, there's no guarantee that I'll still be here three weeks from now. Even if I were, I have a mammoth task ahead of me that will take every moment of my time."

"Couldn't you find a moment or two, here or there," Lord Darcy implored, "to at least help me plan this? For the sake of the *children?*" He gave her such a pleading look, and invested the last sentence with such sweet and impish emotion, Kathryn couldn't help but laugh.

"Well. For the sake of the children," she replied, "I suppose I could."

The duke looked as if she had just offered him diamonds of worth beyond measure. "Thank you, Miss Atherton."

Kathryn suddenly realized she'd made yet another blunder. She'd been determined to maintain her distance from him over the coming weeks. Now she'd just offered to assist him in planning a party. She wanted to smack herself.

Dragging her gaze away from the duke, she noticed that Mr. Megowan was studying her with a peculiar look on his face.

"Miss Atherton," the solicitor said slowly, "where did you say you grew up?"

"Upstate New York."

He gave a sharp intake of breath. "I thought, when we were introduced, that I'd heard your name before."

Kathryn's stomach clenched in dismay. *Oh no.*

"Are you at all connected with the Atherton family in

New York City?" he went on. "The banking tycoon—what is his name—Colis Atherton?"

Lance glanced across the table at Miss Atherton.

"Um," she said.

He couldn't account for the uncomfortable look on her face. Megowan had asked a perfectly innocent question.

"Ah—yes!" his grandmother cried, wide-eyed. "I, too, thought your name sounded familiar. Now I know why."

"The Athertons of New York are as rich as the Vanderbilts," Megowan put in. "The daughters are all heiresses."

Miss Atherton seemed to be struggling for a reply. Lance thought he would save her the trouble. "What are you both on about? Our Miss Atherton cannot be related to *that* family. An American heiress would never work for a living. It's preposterous."

"Is it?" His grandmother fixed her eyes on Miss Atherton like a hawk.

Why, Lance wondered, wasn't Miss Atherton negating the idea with a laugh? Instead, she was twisting her linen napkin in her hands as if she were wringing out a towel. Was she afraid they would think less of her, for being unconnected to these famous Athertons?

"I'm sorry if these inquiries have made you uncomfortable, Miss Atherton," Lance said. "I feel certain that your name is quite common in America."

"Actually," she intoned a bit awkwardly, "it's not that common. And the truth is . . . Colis Atherton *is* my father."

Lance stared at her, too astonished for words.

"Then you must be the third heiress?" Mr. Megowan speculated, his eyebrows lifting.

Miss Atherton gave a reluctant, confirming nod.

"I know of your sisters!" his grandmother exclaimed, turning to Lance with enthusiasm. "Perhaps you are unaware, Lance, as you have been away so long at sea. Two of the Atherton heiresses married Cornish noblemen. The Earl of Longford married the eldest daughter. Her fortune, I am told, quite revitalized Polperran House. The Earl of Saunders—heir of the Marquess of Trevelyan, with whom I am somewhat acquainted—married the second daughter." To Miss Atherton she added, "I have not yet had the pleasure to meet the new countesses, as I rarely travel anymore. But everyone in Cornwall knows their stories."

Lance realized he *had* heard the stories. They'd made headlines in any number of newspapers five or six years ago. Two American heiresses who had stolen the hearts of Cornish peers. He recalled, as well, the primary reason for the public's fascination with these women: it was because they each came with a huge dowry.

How huge? He couldn't remember.

"Why did you not say anything about this, Miss Atherton?" Lance asked her in wonderment.

She let out a long sigh. "Because I didn't want to be seen as *That American Heiress*. Which is the way the newspapers and much of society refer to me and my sisters. I worried that if you knew, it would be difficult for you to separate the *heiress* from the *architect*. I wanted to get this job on my own merits."

"And so you did, my dear," his grandmother commended.

"Forgive me if this seems impertinent," Megowan inter-jected, "but if you are an heiress, why are you working at all?"

"A good question," Lance heard himself blurt. "Coming from such a prominent family, Miss Atherton, surely you have no need to pursue a career?"

Miss Atherton frowned, then shot back at him, "Why did you serve in the Royal Navy for nineteen years, Lord Darcy?"

He groped for a reply. "My father sent me up when I was a boy. He insisted that I have a profession."

"But as the second son of a duke, you had no real need to work, did you? When your brother inherited the title, you hadn't yet signed on for continuous service. You could have left the Navy and lived comfortably on a stipend from him for the rest of your life. Couldn't you?"

Lance pondered that. "So I could have, I suppose."

"Yet you stayed," she continued, impassioned, "because committing yourself every single day to an enterprise which you came to love and believe in gave you such immense sat-isfaction, you couldn't imagine life without it. Am I right?"

He nodded slowly. "Your point is taken, Miss Atherton. You are saying that it is the same for you."

"I know my strengths and talents, Lord Darcy. I want to employ them in a real occupation, as men do, where I can make a difference in the world. Someday, I hope to run my own architectural firm, to design great buildings and bring them to life."

"It takes courage to pursue such a dream," his grand-mother declared. "In my day, no young lady born to the manor would ever think of working. I commend you for your bravery."

"Are your parents supportive of your choice?" Megowan asked dubiously.

"No," Miss Atherton admitted. "My mother has been against it from the start. Her goal in life was to have all three of her daughters marry a British nobleman. My sisters granted her wish, albeit not to please her. In my case, she is destined to be disappointed. I am resolved to make my own way in the world, even if it means giving up my fortune."

"Giving it up?" asked Mr. Megowan.

"My father has made it clear that he will only give me a dowry if and when I marry."

"You are a true Modern Woman, Miss Atherton," his grandmother remarked with admiration.

"Indeed you are," Lance agreed. Again, he wondered just how large Miss Atherton's dowry was. His grandmother's next statement answered the question.

"To turn your back on a million dollars is no easy feat, my dear."

Lance started inwardly. *A million dollars?*

That was the size of this woman's fortune. If and when she married, she would get—technically, her *husband* would get—*a million dollars.* The phrase resounded in his brain like lightning inside a can.

He quickly did the math. It was the equivalent of £200,000. An almost unheard of sum.

In a flash, Lance realized that the answer to all his problems was sitting right across the table from him, as if it had been handed to him on a silver platter. Miss Atherton wasn't just an architect in training. She was a million-dollar heiress.

"Now that you both know," Miss Atherton was saying, "I hope it will not make any difference with regard to the work I have undertaken here."

"Of course not," Lance replied. "It makes no difference whatsoever."

But oh yes, it did.

CHAPTER NINE

"The timing is uncanny." As he paced back and forth in the smoking room after dinner, Lance felt as though he were embedding a permanent path in the carpet.

Megowan sat in a chair by the fireplace, nursing a glass of whiskey.

"I had already decided that I must sacrifice myself," Lance went on, "that I had no choice but to marry for money, with no expectation that said marriage could make me happy." Lance whirled in his tracks to face his friend. "And now this chance has been presented to me. A suitable companion—more than suitable, a very *desirable* companion—has landed right on my doorstep."

"The other day, if you had mentioned that her name was Atherton," Megowan put in, "I could have enlightened you as to who she probably was. Everyone knows that Colis Atherton is one of the richest men in America. And everyone who's anyone in Cornwall knows that two of his daughters married earls in this county."

"*I* didn't know. I have been at sea for nearly two decades. I never pay attention to the society papers."

"A million-dollar dowry does not come along very often." The look on Megowan's face reflected his incredulous delight with this turn of events. "Marrying Miss Atherton will solve all your problems in a heartbeat."

"Won't it, though? I can pay off the loans and still have plenty left over to update the castle, to take care of all the problems in the village."

"You'll never have to worry about money again."

"If a fortune-teller had told me two months ago that I would inherit St. Gabriel's Mount and want to marry the daughter of an American banker, I would have laughed in her face." Lance shook his head in disbelief. "Fate takes us strange places, doesn't it?"

"It is a real stroke of luck, Darcy. Although, I mean to say, admittedly, this has all happened rather fast. You only just met a few days ago."

"True. But in that time, I feel as though I have gotten to know her. She is charming, talented, intelligent. And beautiful. You saw all that yourself. And you saw what happened when I brought up the Children's Fête. She had all the right ideas at her fingertips. She would be the ideal person to run any number of similar, future events."

"In short, she would make an ideal duchess."

"She would."

"As long as she is willing to give up this ridiculous career business of hers," Megowan mused.

"That goes without saying," Lance agreed.

"It is an odd choice in any case, isn't it? An American heiress pursuing a profession? And of all things, architecture? What can she be thinking?"

"She is setting herself up to fail. I may have agreed to work with her, but how many other people will? She could be as skilled as Da Vinci and it won't make a bit of difference. Her school of architecture refused to grant her a diploma. I'd bet my last pound that they'll never give her a license."

Megowan nodded. "She is a woman in a man's business. She has chosen to travel an impossible road."

"I'll be doing her a favor by marrying her."

"When do you intend to ask her?"

"I was thinking tomorrow morning."

"So soon?" Megowan looked at him. "I don't mean to play devil's advocate, Darcy. No one knows better than I how desperately you need that money. But I feel I would be remiss if I didn't point out . . ."

"What?"

"Marriage is for life. Shouldn't you take a little more time to get to know her, to make certain she is the one you want before you commit yourself? You still have three months before the loan is due."

"I could have three years, and I wouldn't find a better companion who just *happens* to have the money I require," Lance insisted.

"I don't suppose love is expected to enter the equation?"

"Love?" Lance scoffed. He knew that love existed and thrived in some relationships. His parents had loved each other, after all, and had been very happy. But . . . "For me, love just causes humiliation and heartache. I learned *that* the hard way."

"All that happened a long time ago, Darcy. You might still fall in love again, with a better result. If you give it a chance."

"No. Miss Atherton and I are attracted to each other. That is sufficient."

For Lance's part, that attraction had started at first sight, and had become almost combustible that same night when they had gotten their hands and lips on each other. Try as he might, Lance hadn't been able to stop thinking about their tryst in the billiards room.

Not that he was going to share *that* with his solicitor.

Whatever else the future might hold, Lance knew with certainty that he and Miss Atherton would get along just fine in bed.

"I need a wife and heir, and I need money. I don't need love into the bargain. Miss Atherton will make the perfect bride."

"Well, then, as you say. This chance has fallen in your lap and you had better take it." Megowan sipped his whiskey. "Does she know about your debts?"

"Er . . ." Lance felt a dash of guilt. "She asked about my financial status. I was not exactly truthful."

"An heiress deserves to know what her dowry will be used for. Don't you think?"

"Yes." Lance crossed his arms over his chest and leaned back against the fireplace with a frown. "Were I to bring it up now, though, it would be a bit awkward, I feel. I would have to explain why I lied."

"You said she seems to admire St. Gabriel's Mount?"

"Very much."

"If she understands that her money will save the castle for generations to come, I'm sure she can bring herself to forgive a little white lie."

Lance processed that, then nodded. "I'm sure you're right. There's an old saying my father used to repeat now and again: 'A duke does not ask for a woman's hand. He bestows upon his prospective bride the opportunity to become a duchess.'"

Megowan's mouth quirked into a smile. "And what woman in her right mind would turn down the opportunity to become a duchess, eh?"

Kathryn was deeply engrossed in a preliminary drawing of the study when the butler strode into the parlor where she was working. A reserved, gray-haired gentleman with a staunch air of propriety, she had met Hammett the day before when he'd returned to the castle and resumed his duties.

"Begging your pardon, miss," Hammett intoned politely, "your presence is requested in the drawing room."

Kathryn looked at him in surprise. "Requested by whom?"

"His Grace."

If the duke wanted to see her, why hadn't he simply come here? Kathryn lay down her pencil and stood. "Well, then, I suppose I had better go."

She followed the butler down several long and twisting

corridors to the drawing room—the same elegant chamber where drinks were served every night before dinner.

Kathryn tried hard not to think about what had happened *after* dinner on her first night at the castle.

As she entered the drawing room, however, it was impossible *not* to think about it.

Lord Darcy stood by the fireplace, one arm resting on the mantelpiece, looking sinfully handsome as usual. Despite herself, the sight of him set her stomach aflutter.

He was clean-shaven, his hair impeccably coiffed. He had never appeared less than perfectly dressed, but this morning it appeared as though he had taken extra time with his attire. His black frock coat and trousers looked freshly steamed and pressed, and he wore an elegant brocade vest embroidered with gold threads.

"Miss Atherton."

"Your Grace."

The butler vanished and closed the drawing doors behind him.

Lord Darcy's tone was formal as he gestured toward the settee. "Please, have a seat."

Kathryn sat down. The duke's eyes took her in with an intensity that she found disquieting. Something about the situation felt odd. "Your Grace? Is something wrong?"

"Not at all."

"May I ask why you have summoned me here?"

"You may indeed ask. You are here because I have something to say to you."

Kathryn sat up straighter on the settee, filled with sudden dread. Was he going to fire her? Tell her he'd changed his mind and didn't want to pursue the project, after all? "What is that, Your Grace?"

"As you know," Lord Darcy began, his voice still highly formal, "I inherited my title only recently. With it came certain responsibilities, among which include the duty to marry and continue the family line. I had never thought to marry an American, yet that seems to be done more and more now among the peerage."

Kathryn's entire body tensed as the possible direction of his words occurred to her. *Oh dear God, no.*

"I realize we have only been acquainted a short time," he continued, "but in that time I have become aware of your many attributes and charms, and I believe our union would be an amicable one."

Our union?

"As my duchess, you will have a home here for the rest of your life. I trust this arrangement would not be unwelcome to you. You have professed your admiration for St. Gabriel's Mount. Your sisters live in this county, and it would be possible for you to see them at holidays and such or whenever you like. In conclusion, I have only to impress upon you the sincerity of my proposal, and my hope that you will do me the honor of becoming my wife."

Even though he used the word *hope*, from his expression and tone it was clear he had no doubt of a favorable answer.

Astonishment rendered Kathryn speechless. *This can't*

be happening. It has to be a joke. The whole thing was so un-expected, so ludicrous, and so far from anything Kathryn wanted for herself that amusement began bubbling up inside her chest. Try as she might, she couldn't contain it.

A chuckle escaped her, which turned into a ripple of full-blown laughter. After which, waving her hand as if she were swatting a fly, Kathryn finally managed, "You can't be serious, Your Grace. You really shouldn't tease a girl like that."

The duke's face froze. It was his turn to be at a loss for words. Finally, his voice still ringing with authority, he said, "I assure you, I am entirely in earnest."

Kathryn felt horrible now that she'd laughed. But her lips kept twitching and she still couldn't believe she'd heard right. "Then . . . sorry . . . what did you just say?"

His eyes flashed darkly, as if incredulous that he was being asked to repeat himself. Through tense lips, he replied, "I just asked you to marry me, Miss Atherton."

Dear God, he was serious. The Duke of Darcy actually just proposed marriage to me.

It took Kathryn a few moments to assemble her thoughts. This had happened to her before, sometimes on even briefer acquaintance. On the night of her New York debut, she'd received proposals from two men she knew only by reputation. Three more offers had come in the years that followed. Of course, they'd all just been after her money.

The fact that the Duke of Darcy was offering for her was a bit mystifying. Kathryn couldn't help but wonder at his motivation. He was still standing by the mantelpiece, his features tightening as he waited for her response. A thought occurred to her. Only last night, he had learned she was an heiress. Suddenly, he was asking for her hand. Was it a coincidence? Or . . . ?

"Your Grace. May I ask what prompted this extraordinary offer, after only three days' association?"

"I told you, I am a quick study."

"Is it really *me* you are interested in? Or is it my fortune?"

The duke's face reddened at that. He looked both affronted and offended. After a pause, he said quietly, "Your fortune is most generous, Miss Atherton. Any man who doesn't admit that such an influx of wealth would be welcome is lying. But your dowry is immaterial to me."

Well, that was a relief. If there was one thing Kathryn hated, it was being thought of as a meal ticket. He'd already dismissed the issue when she'd broached it a few days ago, as if money were the last thing on his mind. After all, if finances were a problem, why would the previous Duke of Darcy have invited her firm to remodel the castle?

A very different notion suddenly seized her. Her hand flew to her mouth. "Then what is this? An act of chivalry?"

"Chivalry?" He looked confused.

"After what we . . . *did* . . . in the billiards room the other night . . . did you feel obligated to propose?"

That *really* seemed to take him aback. "My offer," he retorted, "was not precipitated by the events of that evening. And I assure you that *obligation* is the furthest thing from my mind."

"Because just to set the record straight," Kathryn replied, "I was a full participant in what happened that night. Too much wine was involved. And anyway, I'm sure you've done *that*, and far more than *that*, with plenty of women in ports all across the Mediterranean. And you didn't *propose* to any of them, did you?" Kathryn clamped her mouth shut, hardly able to believe she'd said that. Clearly, she was in a state of shock, and needed to get this interview over with as quickly as possible.

To her surprise and further discomfort, the duke's face grew an even deeper shade of scarlet and he appeared to be tongue-tied. A haunted look entered his eyes. Kathryn sensed that her words had inadvertently struck some deep chord within him, perhaps awakened some memory that gave him pain. Maybe he *had* proposed to someone else in the past? If so, it obviously hadn't gone the way he'd hoped. She sought desperately for something else to say. But he saved her the trouble.

"Miss Atherton," he declared, his voice tense and tight, "my prior romantic history has nothing to do with this. Let us stick to the present, shall we? I offer you my hand because I need a wife. I felt a connection to you the moment we met. You've felt it, too. You cannot deny it."

Kathryn nodded slowly. They *did* have chemistry—that was indisputable. "I don't deny it. But—"

"Therefore, my offer. I believe we would get on well together."

All she could figure was that, as the newly minted duke, Lord Darcy felt pressure to marry and produce the obligatory heir. He'd admitted that he was a man given to snap decisions. Kathryn was here and convenient. She was from a renowned

American family, and her sisters had married peers in the same county. It must have seemed natural to him to offer for her.

She knew that almost any woman in the entire Western world would be flattered and thrilled by such an offer from a duke.

Well, she wasn't one of those women.

"Your Grace," Kathryn said, "I am sensible of the honor you bestow upon me by your offer, and I thank you for it. However, I must decline."

"You must *decline?*" he repeated slowly in undisguised surprise. "You do realize that I am offering you the opportunity to become a duchess?"

"I understand that."

"Yet still you decline?"

"I do." Kathryn blew out an impatient breath. She didn't imagine that dukes or Royal Navy officers were accustomed to being refused anything. "I am sorry if that disappoints you. But surely you must know that I cannot possibly marry you."

He looked both astonished and stung. "Why is that?"

"For one thing, no mention of love was made in your matter-of-fact, rather callous proposal," she pointed out passionately. "And how could it? We barely know each other."

"Love can come after marriage," he shot back.

"Not for me, it can't. *If* I ever marry, it will be for love. But all that aside: my focus is on my career. You don't truly wish to have an architect as your wife, do you?"

"Of course not," was his direct reply. "A duchess cannot work in a trade, it would be unseemly."

"Exactly," she began.

Before she could elaborate, he went on: "But surely, in exchange for the honor of becoming a duchess, the highest title in the land for a woman short of the queen herself, you would be happy to give up this idea of a career."

This *idea* of a career? Kathryn stiffened at his comment. "The only title I'm interested in is *architect*," Kathryn said heatedly. "I've worked long and hard to get where I am, and I will never give it up. Not for you, not for anyone. I have no desire to marry."

"Surely you don't mean that."

"Oh, but I do."

He looked incredulous. "You wish to remain unattached all your life? To have no husband? No children?"

"To succeed in my profession, I will need to work twice as hard as any man. I'll have no time for a husband or children. I don't require a family to be happy or content. My career will be my life. My buildings will be my legacy. They will speak for me long after I'm gone."

Lord Darcy shook his head slowly, as if struggling for the proper reply. "You have chosen a very difficult if not impossible road, Miss Atherton. You said yourself, there are only two practicing female architects in the world, and not a single one in the United Kingdom."

"I am aware of the challenges ahead of me. But someone has to be the first. I will persevere. And I *will* succeed." She took a breath. "I'm sorry if by refusing I have offended you in any way. Please understand: it is nothing personal. I'm certain there are hundreds if not thousands of women who would welcome your suit and be happy to be your duchess. I encourage you to seek one out. I am simply not the right wife for you."

"I see," he snapped.

Kathryn stood. "Your Grace. I pray this will not affect our working relationship? I am wholly committed to the project upon which we've embarked. As we agreed recently with regard to that . . . other matter . . . can we put this behind us? Keep our minds on the job and move forward?"

For a long moment he didn't reply, his face dark with anger and a mortification that he tried to hide. At last, he gave her a curt nod and said abruptly, "If that is your wish."

"It is." Kathryn held out her hand to him as a peace offering. "I am willing to pretend we never spoke of this, if you are?"

Again, he hesitated, as if shaking her hand was the last thing on earth he wished to do. Finally he complied, silent, tense, and angry, his eyes elsewhere, his handshake brief but firm.

"Thank you," she said. "I'll get back to work now."

Kathryn fled the room with as much grace as she could muster, dismayed not only by the conversation that had just passed, but by the traitorous spark that had traveled up her arm as their hands had connected.

CHAPTER TEN

Bloody hell.

Lance had walked into that drawing room so sure of himself. Without a doubt in the world that Miss Atherton would say yes to his offer. Yet she had refused him!

It hadn't occurred to Lance for a second that the woman would be so attached to her career that she would turn down a chance to become his duchess. Or anyone's duchess. Or anyone's wife, for that matter.

How could he have misread her so badly?

On the other hand, how could he have known that her view regarding marriage would be completely different from every other woman he had ever met?

Lance was completely, utterly mortified. To think that he had agreed to a work contract that might take another two or three weeks. She would be living under his roof that entire time. What on earth was he going to say to her the next time they met? It would be damned awkward.

He considered terminating their agreement. He could

simply say that after giving the matter more thought, he'd decided he didn't wish to renovate, after all. So what if he'd signed a contract? He could simply pay her off and send her on her way.

But, coming on the heels of her refusing his offer, it would be so obvious he was firing her out of bitterness or spite.

Lance had hired her in good faith. He had made a promise, and he wasn't one to break a promise. Still, the thought of encountering her in a hallway or sitting down to dinner with her every night (whose brilliant idea was *that?*) was anathema to him now.

Following their liaison in the billiards rooms, *she* had avoided his company. Now, Lance was determined to avoid her.

That afternoon, he set out for Falmouth, telling his grandmother that he had business there. The only business he had was walking along the harbor and staring at the boats, interspersed with visits to a series of taverns. He ran into a few retired seamen and a couple of sailors on leave, and passed a few jolly hours in their company. But the whole time, his mind kept drifting back to Miss Atherton, and how mortified he felt.

He tried to tell himself that she was a bitch. A self-centered, ungrateful American who considered herself too important and high and mighty to marry an Englishman. That she didn't deserve his offer in the first place, and that with her refusal, he had made a lucky escape.

But on his second day in Falmouth and his third tankard of ale at the Horse and Feathers, he had to admit to himself that she wasn't a bitch at all. She was an unusual woman, to be sure. But he didn't really think she considered herself above him. She had just chosen a path for herself and was sticking to it. He couldn't fault her for that. In fact, he rather reluctantly admired her for it.

He ought to follow her advice. Find someone else.

There was still about a month left of the London Season. If he put the word out that he was looking, surely one or two candidates, who had the cash he needed and who would be over the moon to become his duchess, could be located and presented to him.

The problem was, he thought with a sigh, he didn't want another candidate.

Now that he'd met her . . . he wanted *her*.

Unluckily, she was the one woman in a million who didn't want *him*.

After two days of feeling sorry for himself, Lance returned home, tired of twiddling his thumbs.

He figured if he was paying Miss Atherton to make drawings, he might as well be around to weigh in on those drawings. Work was about to begin on the schoolhouse roof and the fishermen's quay steps. He ought to be on hand for that as well.

Lance still hadn't made any brilliant conclusions as to how to deal with Miss Atherton. Other than to grow a stiff upper lip and get through it. Which he was grimly determined to do. Meanwhile, he'd put the idea of searching for a wife on the back burner for a couple of weeks, until he had the stomach for it.

He had no sooner entered the castle and started down the hall to his study when he heard his grandmother call out from the conservatory.

"Lance? Is that you?"

He paused in the doorway. "How are you, Grandmother?"

"Fine, thank you." She wore a gardening smock and was watering a row of potted plants. "So you are back, then?" she added rather unnecessarily.

"Just arrived this minute."

"Good. Do you have a moment, dear? I have been wanting to speak to you."

Lance entered the room. Afternoon sun shone in through the mullioned windows, casting a golden glow on potted tropical-looking plants of various species, colors, and sizes, from small flowering things to tree-sized plants with enormous leaves.

"I have always liked this room." He breathed in the pleasant scent that filled the air, a delicate floral perfume mingled with damp earth and bark. It brought back warm, fuzzy memories of chats with his grandmother as a boy.

"It is my favorite room in the castle." As she directed a stream of water onto a plant, she gestured with her free hand toward a nearby chair.

Following her silent directive, he sat. "What is on your mind?"

"Miss Atherton."

That took him by surprise. "What about her?"

"Did you make her an offer of marriage?"

Sudden warmth infused Lance's cheeks. How on earth could she have guessed *that*? "I don't know what you're talking about."

His grandmother fixed him with her pale blue gaze. "I think you do. I think you proposed, and she refused."

"Did she say something to you?" Lance blurted.

"Aha!" His grandmother's eyes flashed. "I knew it! Miss Atherton hasn't said a word about it. I made my own assumptions. I sensed that something was heating up between you two the moment she arrived. Hammett tells me you summoned her to the drawing room a few mornings ago. And then, *whoosh*! Off you scurry to Falmouth for no good reason, with your tail between your legs."

"I had business in Falmouth," he insisted through gritted teeth.

"Of course you did, Lancelot."

"I hate it when you call me that."

"Why? It is your name. And a good name, too. You expected her to snap you up in a heartbeat, I suppose?"

Lance opened his mouth to refute that, then closed it again. She was a crafty woman, Lance had to hand it to her—and she didn't miss much. "Fine, yes. I offered for her. She said no. It was humiliating. Are you happy?"

"No, I am not happy."

"I am a duke! Dukes are supposed to have the right to the bride of their choice. And that bride is supposed to accept with gratitude."

"Who put that idea in your head? Your father? Only another duke would say something so pigheaded."

"Is that why you called me in here? To insult and berate me? If so, I will take my leave." Lance made to get up, but she waved him back into his seat. He sat back with a sigh.

His grandmother put down her watering can and came over to sit in the chair beside him. "You always were impulsive, even as a boy. But to propose marriage to someone you barely know is something even I would have never expected."

Lance frowned. If only he could tell his grandmother about the financial horrors hanging over his head. How close they were to losing St. Gabriel's Mount. But she was eighty-five years old. She had lived in this castle for more than sixty of those years. The thought of being cast adrift, to live who knows where, might be more than she could bear. If he could somehow fix the problem, she need never know.

"I realize that she and I have just met. But I need to marry someone, and from the moment I first saw her . . ." *I wanted to rip her clothes off and shag her.* "I felt drawn to her. I like her."

"I like her as well. She is a remarkable woman. She would make a wonderful addition to this family. But is it really *her* you like, Lance? Or her money?"

Alarm spread through him like a wave. "What do you mean?"

"I may be an old woman, and I may have led a rather sheltered life, but I am not blind or stupid. I am aware that your father had money troubles, which Hayward inherited. I know that Hayward sold the Hampshire estate years ago."

"He did," Lance acknowledged, struggling to keep his voice matter-of-fact.

She looked at him again. "Is our financial situation very bad, Lance?"

Her question evoked a rush of relief. It meant she *wasn't* aware of the true state of affairs. She merely had a *suspicion.* He needn't admit anything. This was a man's problem, and his alone to solve.

He gave one of her hands an affectionate squeeze. "We are doing just fine financially, Grandmother, I assure you." Lance felt a stab of guilt over the lie. "Admittedly, Miss Atherton has a very generous dowry, but my offer was not about her money." Another stab of guilt.

If he was honest with himself, however, although he desperately needed Miss Atherton's fortune, his desire to marry her wasn't *only* about the money. If he didn't have a single financial problem in the world, the fact was that after spending only three days in her presence, Lance had become totally . . . smitten with her. Which lessened his feelings of culpability somewhat.

"I am relieved to hear that. I have been worried."

"Miss Atherton comes from an excellent family," Lance added, with what he hoped was a casual shrug. "I thought we would make a good match."

"A good match?" his grandmother echoed, shaking her head ruefully. "If you have any hope of marrying the woman, I would hope you think of her as more than just a good match."

"What do you mean?"

"When you proposed, Lance, what did you say to her?"

The question made him shift uneasily in his seat. "I don't recall my exact words."

"Let me guess. You probably told her that as the new heir, it is your duty to marry. That although your acquaintance has been short, you find her amiable and charming. That in accepting the great honor of becoming your duchess, she will have the pleasure of living the rest of her life at St. Gabriel's Mount, with the added incentive that she will be near family, as her sisters live in Cornwall."

"I . . . may have said something along those lines," he sputtered. The woman was uncanny. Had she been eavesdropping? "How could you know what I said?"

"Because your grandfather said something akin to those very same words the day he proposed to me." She shook her head. "My dear boy. It is no wonder she refused you."

"*You* didn't refuse Grandfather," Lance pointed out.

"That was sixty years ago. Times have changed. You cannot expect Miss Atherton to respond as other women have in the past, or even as most women would respond today. Miss Atherton is a Modern Woman. She has worked hard to get where she is."

"So she mentioned to me. Very emphatically."

"Cannot you see how important her career is to her? She has already achieved in her field what almost no other woman on earth has ever done. I shouldn't like to see her give up. She is talented and at the very beginning of things, with so much yet to do."

"I see that now." Lance sighed. "I feel like an idiot,

Grandmother. I should never have offered for her in the first place."

"I would not say that. Miss Atherton could still make a proper wife for you."

"What?" Lance glanced at her, puzzled. "I don't understand. You just insisted that Miss Atherton's career is everything to her."

"Yes, I did."

"Then how could she be my wife? A duchess cannot be an architect."

"Why not?"

"Why not?" he sputtered. "You ask *me* this? You know better than anyone what is expected of a duchess. She has duties and responsibilities in the home and the community. She cannot be involved in *trade*."

"Every marriage has problems, Lance. You can also find compromises if you look for them."

"What compromises? *If* she succeeds in her field, which is very much in doubt, she works in London. And I repeat: in *trade*. She would have no alternative but to give it up. Anything else would be impossible."

"Sometimes," his grandmother replied, "I've believed as many as six impossible things before breakfast."

Lance huffed. "Don't quote *Alice's Adventures in Wonderland* at me."

"It's what you need to hear right now. An impossible thing can *become* possible if you want it badly enough. How much do you want to marry this woman, Lance?"

"Very much." The forcefulness of his reply surprised him.

"How hard are you willing to work to win her?"

"I . . . don't know," he admitted. "Anyway, this is a moot point. I've already asked her. She has already refused."

"So you're going to give up, just like that?"

Lance threw up his hands. "What would you have me do?"

"I would have you ask her again. Not today, or tomorrow. But . . . bide your time. Wait for the right moment and ask again."

"Whatever for? I need an heir. She made it clear that she never wants a husband or children."

"*Never* is a strong word, Lance dear. In my experience, it rarely has credence. Although Miss Atherton says that now, she may feel differently in time. You sprang this on her quite suddenly, only three days after meeting her. Give her a chance to get to know you. People change their minds every day."

Lance considered that. Was there really a chance that if he waited and asked again, she might give a different reply? A ripple of hope darted through him.

"All right, then." If there was a chance he could still win her hand, he would take it. This was, Lance decided, a battle now. He felt as though a gauntlet had been thrown. He had severely underestimated his opponent. His first parry had missed its mark, so he must reassess the situation, employ new tactics, and find another way through. "Miss Atherton may have refused me once, but bloody hell, I will not give up. I will find a way to convince her somehow."

"That's the spirit." In a gently worried tone, she added: "When is the last time you wooed a woman, Lance?"

"Wooed a woman?" he echoed. Women had, for the most part, fallen at Lance's feet. He hadn't *wooed* anyone in a very long time. Not since . . .

Lance's thoughts turned to the one woman he had dearly wanted, so many years ago. *Beatrice.* He recalled all the hoops he had jumped through on her behalf, the sacrifices he had made in his attempt to win her heart. And he *had* won, only to have happiness snatched from him in the most humiliating of ways.

"I mean, other than . . . Beatrice." His grandmother's voice snapped his attention back to the present. She was looking at him with sympathy in her pale eyes.

"No," he said abruptly. "I have rarely been obliged to *woo*."

"Well, the time has come to remind yourself how. You can win this woman. Your approach just needs refinement, that's all."

"My approach?" He looked at her. "Pray explain yourself."

"Miss Atherton is from one of the wealthiest families in America. If she were to marry you, she would be obliged to hand over an immense fortune, and no doubt make many other sacrifices as well. I wouldn't make it sound as though *you're* doing *her* a favor by asking for her hand. I would graciously imply the reverse."

Lance pondered that, then nodded. "Point taken." He was suddenly grateful to have his grandmother at hand to offer advice. "What else do you suggest? No doubt she already has every material thing a woman could want. Should

I bring her flowers?" In the past, a fresh bouquet had worked wonders in one port of call or another.

His grandmother gave him a dead-eyed look. "Were you not paying attention, Lancelot?"

"To what?"

"On her first night here, Miss Atherton said she cannot abide cut flowers. She prefers living, growing things."

"Oh. Now that you mention it, I do recall her saying something like that."

"You really must learn to *listen*. What most women appreciate . . . what I think Miss Atherton in particular will appreciate . . . is to be seen and understood. Talk to her, Lancelot. Find out what makes her tick."

"What makes her tick," he repeated. "That will be a challenge. I enjoy talking to Miss Atherton, believe you me. But she spends all her time in that damned parlor, drawing. It was all I could do to persuade her to join us for dinner the other night."

"And yet you did." His grandmother's eyes gleamed, as if she were remembering something from her own past. "You're a smart man, Lance. Find a way to persuade her to take some time off and to spend it with you. Open yourself up to her. Women appreciate a man who isn't afraid to show his vulnerable side."

He made a face. "I am *not* going to cry in front of her."

"I didn't say anything about crying. I said: be vulnerable. There is a difference. Who knows? Maybe, somewhere along the line, you'll discover that you have feelings for her. And that she has feelings for you."

Lance stood up, instantly annoyed. "Is that what this is about?" He felt as though he'd just been duped, blindsided. "You're hoping I'll fall in love with her?"

His grandmother eyed him sharply. "I know you were hurt long ago, my darling boy. But that is no reason not to love again."

"When and if I marry, Grandmother, love will not enter into it."

"Well, then, you are setting yourself up to fail. Trust me on this. If you want to win that young woman's hand, you will first have to win her heart."

Kathryn had been hard at work since early that morning, pausing only to consume the breakfast and lunch that had been brought in on a tray.

Although she had completed several drawings that pleased her, she felt an unfamiliar restlessness that was difficult to define.

Kathryn chalked it up to the unusual circumstances of her situation. She'd never lived at someone else's house before while working for them. And nothing about this job was going the way it was supposed to. Within a few hours of meeting her client, she'd had almost-sex with him on a billiards table and then passed out in his arms. Three days later, her client had proposed. Things like this were not supposed to happen on the job.

Kathryn's refusal had obviously hurt the duke's pride. Shortly thereafter, he'd vanished from the premises. She was aware that Lord Darcy had returned the previous afternoon. No note had arrived, though, demanding her presence at the dinner table, and she had been only too happy to eat dinner on a tray.

They couldn't avoid each other forever, however. Would it be awkward when they next encountered each other? She hoped not. All that mattered to her was the work. At least . . . that's what she kept telling herself.

Unfortunately, her mind was not cooperating on the same level. Last night, she'd dreamt about him again. Another erotic dream.

In the dream, he had appeared in her bedroom, attired in his full naval captain regalia. She had risen from bed, entranced. His eyes had been filled with desire. In seconds, he had removed her nightgown until she stood naked before him.

She hadn't been embarrassed, just filled with yearning for him to take her in his arms. Which he had done without hesitation. Then he'd kissed her. A luscious, delectable kiss from which she'd awakened far too soon, her heart pounding like a runaway train, the region between her legs throbbing.

Kathryn's heart sped up again just thinking about the dream. It was absurd, the places the mind went when one was supposed to be at rest. Why was she lusting after this man? She was here to work for him, that's all!

Heaving an annoyed sigh, Kathryn refocused her attention on the drawing of the main stairwell that lay on the table before her. She'd been working on it for hours, but even though it looked finished, something felt like it was missing. She had no idea what.

Frustrated, she set the drawing aside and moved to the next item on the list: the new master bathroom. She had already sketched out a basic floor plan. Her task now was to determine the most convenient locations for the plumbing fixtures.

Where, Kathryn wondered, should the sink go? Against the north wall? To help her decide, she tried to envision the duke actually using the room.

In her mind, she saw him standing at the sink. In his undergarments. Naked from the waist up. Shaving.

She gave her head a quick mental shake. That was *not* an image she ought to be contemplating. Quickly, she sketched in the sink placement and redirected her thoughts to the placement for the bathtub.

The bathtub.

A new image appeared in Kathryn's brain: the duke stepping out of the bathtub. His well-toned, beautifully proportioned physique wet and gleaming. She knew exactly what he looked like naked. She had observed him on the beach. She had seen his sculpted chest and taut abdomen and lean legs and . . . other things. A shiver traveled up Kathryn's spine at the memory.

Her cheeks flamed and she threw down her pencil. *Why, oh why, did she keep thinking about him naked?*

It was obviously a bad idea to work on the bathroom today. It was nearly one o'clock. Which meant she'd been sitting here working for seven hours straight. She stretched her arms above her head, suddenly feeling as though all the blood in her legs had gone stagnant. She needed to get up and out of this room. To get a bit of fresh air to clear her head.

After neatly arranging her drawing materials on the table, Kathryn hurried to her chamber, donned a hat, and made her way farther upstairs to the upper level.

As she stepped outside, she was greeted by a welcoming sea breeze. Smiling, she crossed the terrace to one of the outcroppings in the battlemented stone wall and stopped beside a pair of ancient cannons. The view was spectacular. Beneath a cobalt canopy dotted with scattered white clouds, the afternoon sun glittered like diamonds on the bright blue sea.

Kathryn closed her eyes, enjoying the feel of the sun on her shoulders, the rush of the wind in her face, and the scent of the sea in the air. For a few minutes, she wanted to stop thinking about the duke and concentrate on how blessed she was to be here, working on such a challenging job in this incredible place.

Her musings were interrupted by a deep, familiar voice.

"Good afternoon."

Kathryn's eyes flicked open with a start as she turned to find the Duke of Darcy striding across the deck toward her.

Chapter Eleven

"Miss Atherton." The duke joined her at the terrace wall. Although he held himself stiffly and rather uncomfortably, his sensational blue eyes gleamed with some undefined emotion. "How nice to see you."

His nearness sent little shock waves rippling through Kathryn's body. Against her will, her stomach began to flutter. "Your Grace. It is . . . nice to see you as well." She struggled to rise above her own discomfort, searched for something else to say. "I understand you . . . had business in Falmouth?"

"I did." He also appeared to be fumbling for words. "But it is good to be back." After a pause: "I am surprised to see you outside. Instead of hard at work at your desk."

"Yes, well," Kathryn replied, unable to prevent the defensive note in her voice, "I've been working since dawn. Since you advocated that I must not toil around the clock, I thought I would take some air." She wasn't about to tell him that said *taking of air* had been necessitated by naked visions of him.

"I was not criticizing," he insisted. "I am delighted to see you out and about. Is the work going well?"

"It is, thank you. In a few days, I should have some preliminary drawings to show you."

"Excellent."

She felt the awkwardness between them easing a bit.

"A lovely day, is it not?" he commented.

"Magnificent."

He hadn't mentioned the proposal—Kathryn was relieved and grateful about that—and she certainly had no intention of bringing it up. In fact, he seemed to have put behind him the anger and mortification he'd felt that day, and instead was determined to make conversation. She was only too happy to follow suit. Anything she could do to help promote a good working relationship.

"This view," Kathryn remarked, "is to die for."

"To die for," he echoed, his tone more contemplative now. "Such an interesting phrase." He glanced at the pair of cannons beside them, then at the row of additional cannons that wrapped around the terrace deck. "It reminds me that men have actually risked their lives fighting to defend this island."

"Have they? Were many battles fought here?"

"There were two famous sieges. The first in 1193, when the Mount was captured on behalf of Prince John in the reign of King Richard I. Another siege took place during the War of the Roses. The Mount held its own against six thousand troops for twenty-three weeks."

"Impressive."

"Thankfully, for the most part, St. Gabriel's Mount has managed to ward off invaders with its threatening façade."

"It *is* an imposing castle. It must have been a thrilling place to grow up."

He considered that. "It was . . . unique, I suppose. But my brother was seven years older. He left for school when I was small. I wasn't allowed to associate with the local children. I only saw my parents for an hour at tea. So whatever time wasn't spent with my nanny or devoted to studies with my tutor, I was obliged to spend pretty much by myself."

Katherine had heard similar reports from men of the upper classes. Her heart went out to him. "That must have been lonely."

"I didn't know any different."

"My sisters and I were also left to ourselves a great deal," Kathryn said, "but we had each other. What did you do with your free time? How did you entertain yourself?"

"Oh, many things. I built model ships, for one."

"Model ships! What happened to them?"

"I don't know. I suppose my brother threw them out."

"What a shame."

"They weren't anything special. Just a youthful hobby. I spent the greater part of my time reading. I used to curl up in a window seat in the library and lose myself in the pages of a book every chance I got."

"I did the same thing as child." Kathryn tried to picture the duke as a young boy, reading, an image that made her smile. Suddenly an idea came to her. "Oh!" she cried.

"Is something wrong?" the duke asked, alarmed.

"No, something is very *right*. What you said just now . . . it made me realize what's missing from my drawing of the castle stairwell. Window seats!"

"Window seats?"

"There are lovely mullioned windows on every landing of the main staircase, and the walls there are a good two feet deep. It's the perfect spot to put built-in nooks that invite the eye, to hold Chinese vases or blooming orchids or a cushion to sit upon and read."

"What a lovely idea. Add that to the list."

"I will." Grabbing her notepad and pencil from her skirt pocket, Kathryn jotted that down. Replacing the tiny book, she gave him a grin. "I'm a great reader myself. I noticed a copy of *Ivanhoe* on your bedside table that looked well-read."

He looked surprised. "You were in my bedroom?"

Heat crept up Kathryn's throat and cheeks. "I . . . was taking measurements for the plans," she explained quickly. "I just happened to notice the book."

"I see. *Ivanhoe* is one of my particular favorites."

"Mine as well. Sir Walter Scott was a genius."

"I agree."

"He invented the version of Robin Hood that we enjoy today. My sisters and I spent much of our time playacting Robin Hood in our garden and the surrounding woods."

"But Robin Hood is a boy's story."

"Not true. It is a universal tale about a legendary, heroic outlaw. Robin Hood is as much a girl's story as a boy's."

"I stand corrected, Miss Atherton." Lord Darcy grinned. "Which part did you play? Let me guess: the heroic outlaw."

She laughed. "Lexie and Maddie and I were a very democratic group. We took turns playing Robin and Maid Marian, and brought all the other members of the merry band to life as well."

"You and your sisters were unusual girls. And if they are anything like you, I'd guess they have grown up to be unusual women."

"I can't tell if that is a compliment or a criticism," Kathryn said, eyes narrowing.

"It was meant a compliment."

"Then I will accept it as such."

"What did you say your sisters' names are again?"

"Lexie, which is short for Alexandra. Maddie is short for Madeleine."

"Do you have a nickname?"

"No. My mother couldn't abide the name Katie or Kathy. So I have always just been Kathryn."

"It's a lovely name." His gaze was warmth mingled with admiration, a look that made Kathryn's heart beat more rapidly again.

The duke was so charming and reflective today. It occurred to her suddenly that the former sense of unease between them had dissipated, like the fluffy parachutes of a dandelion scattering on the breeze. She was immensely enjoying their chat.

"Do you know," he said suddenly, "I haven't thought about this in years, but I used to playact as well, as a child. On this very spot, in fact."

"What did you play?"

"I was a knight laying down my life to defend the Mount. I would load and shoot off every one of these cannons."

"I hope you always saved the day?"

"I did." He laughed. The memory seemed to delight him. "I had another game as well. I was defending the Mount against pirates. They would climb up the walls and I'd fight them off single-handedly with a sword, mortally wounding the captain." He enthusiastically mimed the action as he spoke, swinging an imaginary sword. "My skills and bravery so impressed the remaining band of pirates that they surrendered en masse and begged me to be their new captain."

"Did you accept?"

"Of course. It is every boy's dream, I think, to be a pirate captain."

Kathryn laughed and was about to reply when a sudden gust blew up from the sea, rustling her skirts and tugging her hat from head. "Oh no!"

She and Lord Darcy tried to grab the hat in vain. Her spirits sank as she watched it fly into the airy void beyond the wall, then tumble over and over on the wind on its way out to sea.

"That's gone." Lord Darcy shook his head in dismay.

"Oh well." Kathryn gave a shrug. "It was only a hat. Although, admittedly, it *was* one of my favorites."

He turned to her and said gallantly, "I shall buy you a new one."

"I couldn't let you do that."

"But you must."

"I have other hats, Your Grace. I can replace that one when I return to London."

"Miss Atherton. You lost your hat on my premises. Quite literally, on *my* watch. It is therefore my responsibility to replace it."

He was so adamant, she couldn't refuse. "If you insist."

"I do insist. I further insist that we find a replacement at once. The tide has just gone out. Which gives us a three-hour window to cross the causeway. I imagine there must be at least one millinery shop in Rosquay."

"That sounds nice, but I don't have time to go shopping, Lord Darcy. I have to get back to work."

"The last time I checked, you were working for me. Isn't that correct?"

"It is," Kathryn acknowledged, wavering. She was so enjoying his company, she didn't *really* want it to be over just yet.

"As your employer, I am making it a requirement of your contract that you take every Friday afternoon off." He shot her a grin. "Beginning immediately."

The causeway between St. Gabriel's Mount and Rosquay appeared twice a day with the ebbing of the tide, revealing a wide stretch of golden sand bisected by a raised path made of small stones.

"I am intrigued to learn that you used to build model ships," Miss Atherton commented as they strolled along the path to the mainland.

Lance was pleased that she had agreed to accompany him. It hadn't been easy, approaching her on the terrace just now. But he had squelched his lingering embarrassment and hurt pride, determined to follow his grandmother's advice. *Talk to her, Lancelot. Listen to her. Find out what makes her tick.*

So far, he appeared to be succeeding.

"I had a similar sort of hobby as a little girl," Miss Atherton was saying, "except I built model houses out in the woods."

"What kind of model houses?" Lance asked.

"I made them out of bark, twigs, stones, and moss. I added doors and windows, and furniture and accessories out of scraps of wood and acorn caps."

"Who lived in these houses?"

"Fairies, of course."

"Of course." He glanced at her, admiring the way the sun glimmered on her golden hair. A wayward tendril had escaped its pins. He ached to reach over and brush it off her forehead, had to shove his hand in his pocket to restrain the impulse. "Is that what started you on the path to architecture? Fairy houses?"

"Maybe. In art lessons, when all the other girls were drawing landscapes or flowers or animals, I was always designing houses and other buildings, each one more elaborate than the last. My instructor thought me very odd. But I couldn't help myself. Those were the images that filled my head."

An image filled *his* head of Miss Atherton as a girl, sketching fantastic edifices. It made him smile. "I should love to see those drawings."

"My mother burned them all."

"She didn't!"

"She did. She told me to stop drawing things that were so unladylike. Years later, when I told her that I wanted to be an architect and design real buildings, she was horrified. 'It is *unthinkable* for an heiress to work,' Mother said. 'Moreover, architecture is a man's profession. You are setting yourself up to fail.'"

Setting yourself up to fail. Lance had uttered almost identical words to Megowan when they'd discussed Miss Atherton.

Part of him wished that Miss Atherton *could* achieve the goals she sought. But despite all his grandmother's comments about compromise and believing impossible things before breakfast, Lance still believed she was in for a world of disappointment. If she became his wife, however, she would have a new set of goals, a new purpose. Which would make it easier to accept the truth about the viability of this career she thought she wanted.

All Lance had to do was get her to choose *him*. To accept his hand the next time he asked.

"Perhaps there is some truth in what your mother said," Lance pointed out carefully. "Men hold all the power in the world of architecture. It may take a miracle for them to admit a woman to their ranks."

"Then I will pray for a miracle," Miss Atherton responded. They had reached the mainland now and entered the village of Rosquay, which was lined with quaint shops and houses. She paused and gestured toward the King's Head, an old pub across the street. "Tell me, Your Grace. When you look at that building, what do you see?"

Lance stopped and studied it. "A pub that serves excellent ale."

She laughed. "I'm talking about the building. What do you observe?"

"It is whitewashed and half-timbered."

"Anything else?"

"It has leaded glass windows. A sloping roof. I imagine it is very old."

"An apt description. I expect that is what most people see."

"Do you see it differently?" Lance asked, curious.

She nodded. "I see the foundation beneath the building that holds it up. And the skeleton beneath the plaster, the wood or brick that gives the building definition and shape. In my mind's eye, I am taking it apart and seeing it rebuilt from the ground up."

Lance nodded slowly. "Interesting."

He held back a frown. It was becoming increasingly obvious that architecture was in this woman's blood, and not something she would give up lightly. Well, the battle had just begun. He wasn't going to give up lightly, either.

He spied a millinery shop just down the street, and pointed it out.

As they headed in that direction, she said, "Did you always aspire to go to sea?"

"No. I liked building models, but I had no aspirations, really. My father chose the Navy for me. I despised my first year of training school."

"Why?"

"I was teased and bullied for being the son of a duke. A misery made worse by the untimely death of my parents." He hadn't planned to say that. It was a painful subject he'd never spoken of to anyone other than his brother.

"I'm so sorry." She looked at him. "How did your parents die, if I may ask?"

He'd brought it up; he had no choice but to follow through. "They went on a world tour and died in India of cholera."

"Oh! How awful. How old were you?"

"Fourteen." A feeling of deep discomfort invaded Lance's chest. He never talked about these things. He *didn't like* talking about these things. But she seemed so interested. His grandmother had told him to open up to this woman. Lance forced himself to continue. "I was sitting in class on my training ship, listening to a lecture on nautical astronomy. My commander called me up on deck and informed me that my parents had passed away. 'Keep a stiff upper lip, my dear chap,' the old man said, clapping me on the back. 'Shed a few tears if you must, then get over it. You're in the Royal Navy now. You have a good life ahead of you, boy.'"

"That's quite a speech." Her eyes were full of empathy. "And after all this time, you remember every word of it."

Lance shrugged, trying to shove the memory out of his mind. "It happened a long time ago."

"But I suppose the pain doesn't ever really go away. I can't imagine how difficult that was for you. I am so sorry," she offered again as they walked along.

Her gentle manner was a soothing balm to the ache that filled his chest.

"I had to accept it, or go mad. So I made my peace with it, and looked to the future. I soon changed my mind about the Navy," he added, determined to return to a brighter subject. "I discovered that I not only tolerated my new life, I had actually fallen in love with it."

"I'm glad you found an occupation you loved, Your Grace, and that you were able to enjoy it for so many years."

He paused on the threshold of the millinery shop, turning to her.

"Yes. But we never know in what direction life will lead us, do we?" Here, he thought, was an opportunity to lay the groundwork for the new direction he hoped *she* might come to embrace. "As I have discovered, it is important to be open to the winds of change."

She smiled. "I agree, Your Grace."

He grinned in return. *That went rather well.* Pushing open the shop door, he said: "Let us buy you a hat, shall we?"

Chapter Twelve

The milliner didn't carry the masculine-style hats that Kathryn favored, but she fell in love with a confection of yellow straw decorated with blue ribbons and flowers that Lord Darcy and the clerk both insisted was very becoming.

After making the purchase, Kathryn decided that as long as they had come all the way into Rosquay, she might as well put the time to good use. They called in at several other shops, where she spoke to various craftsmen and artisans about the upcoming renovations at St. Gabriel's Mount, gathering paint and fabric samples that might prove useful.

Every shopkeeper and craftsman in Rosquay was pleased to see the duke and treated him with deference. If said townsfolk addressed her in a more aloof manner, or made it obvious that they didn't want to deal with a woman, Kathryn took it in stride. She'd been dealing with this kind of prejudice for so long her response had become second nature. She simply talked their ears off until she wore them down and they begrudgingly came around to her way of thinking.

In one of the shop windows, Kathryn saw a poster advertising the upcoming Children's Fête.

"Oh," she told the duke. "I've been so focused on the castle renovations, I forgot all about your Children's Fête. Have you made any plans in that regard?"

"Nary a one," he admitted, looking sheepish.

"Well, time's a-wasting. We had better get busy." Passing a draper's shop, Kathryn suggested, "Let's stop in here and buy ribbons."

"What for?"

"You cannot have a Children's Fête without prize ribbons," Kathryn explained again.

After buying rolls of red, blue, and yellow satin ribbon in the width required, they arranged with the postmaster to have them sent to a print shop in Plymouth, where they would be cut into prize lengths and stamped in white ink with the name and date of the event.

As they exited the post office, Kathryn found her gaze darting in the duke's direction, finding pleasure in the simple act of being "out and about" with him, as he'd put it. She congratulated herself on having achieved her goal. All that frenzied attraction and marriage business was behind them. They could now concentrate on *business* business. They were just two people out walking together on a sunny day.

This theory was crushed to dust when Lord Darcy stopped and turned to face her so abruptly that she almost ran into him. "I appreciate your help with this," he said quietly.

He was standing just a foot away. The warmth, gratitude, and depth of feeling in his eyes made Kathryn's heart flutter. His attraction to her was as obvious as the nose on his face. A nose that was perfectly straight and as beautifully proportioned as the best noses on the Roman statues she so adored. It was suddenly difficult to breathe, much less formulate words.

"This is . . . just the tip of the iceberg," Kathryn heard herself say. Her gaze was drawn to the stubble of beard framing his face. "I don't know where I'll find the time, but we have to . . . um. . . ." She wished she could touch his beard and find out if it was as soft as she remembered. "We have to map out what races you'll be holding. And invite people to perform. And . . ." His beard surrounded his lips, which were pink and delectable and begging to be kissed. *Dear Lord, she was thinking about kissing him again. This would never do.* "Oh!" she cried in a desperate attempt to distract herself. "We need giveaways! Is there a toy shop in Rosquay?"

There was no toy shop. The general store had nothing that would serve as a suitable gift for children. "The problem is," Kathryn explained as they left the village, "whatever keepsake you wish to give each child has to be available in a quantity of a hundred or more."

"Maybe we ought to order something from London," Lord Darcy suggested.

"Maybe."

They'd been gone so long that the tide had come back in, requiring them to take a ferryboat back.

The duke sat down beside her, even though they were the only passengers and there was another empty seat. As they crossed the strait, Kathryn was intensely aware of Lord

Darcy's thigh and shoulder resting mere inches from her own. A wave of heat enveloped her that had nothing to do with the summer sun.

When they reached the quay at St. Gabriel's Mount, the duke stepped out of the boat first, then reached down to help Kathryn alight. As his hand grasped hers and he assisted her onto the dock, their eyes met and she felt a *zing* travel up her arm. A *zing* that continued to resonate long after he'd let go of her hand.

There will be no zinging, Kathryn admonished herself.

As they made their way along the dock, she noticed a construction crew at work across the harbor. It pleased her to see that the duke was taking care of things in his community. When they reached the gateway leading into St. Gabriel's Mount village, a small carriage with the duke's family crest was waiting.

"Knowing how anxious you have been to get back to work," the duke told her, "I arranged for my coachman to provide a conveyance up to the castle. It will save us a half hour and a steep hike, as you know."

"Thank you, Your Grace. That was very thoughtful."

Before they could board the vehicle, however, Kathryn's attention was drawn to a pair of little red-haired girls in faded dresses who were racing along the lane, holding aloft small whirligigs on wooden sticks. The girls laughed with delight as they watched the pinwheels spin round and round.

Kathryn halted in her tracks. "May I have a moment, Your Grace? I'd like to speak with those girls." Hailing their attention, she enthused, "Might I see one of your pinwheels?"

The eldest girl, perhaps seven years of age, placed her toy in Kathryn's hand. The article was simple but well-made of brightly colored paper, the furls held in place by a small nail. "May I ask where you got these?"

"My mum made 'em," replied the girl, glancing shyly at the duke.

"Did she indeed?" Kathryn returned the toy to its owner. "What is your name?"

"Rose Penberthy, miss. This be me sister Flora."

Kathryn introduced herself and the duke followed suit. Upon learning who he was, both girls immediately dropped a wide-eyed curtsy.

"Rose," Kathryn said, "I'd like to speak to your mother. Is she home?"

"Yes, miss. Where else would she be?" Giggling, Rose pointed behind her, down the lane that served as St. Gabriel's Mount's main street. "We live in the house w' the red door." With that, the girls raced off.

Lord Darcy darted Kathryn a glance. "I take it you wish to pay Mrs. Penberthy a visit? Something to do with . . . pinwheels?"

"They would make the perfect gift for the Children's Fête. If she'd be willing to make them."

"I am overdue to call on the Penberthys in any case. I didn't have time to stop in the last time I was here." Lord Darcy told his driver to wait, and they proceeded down the lane. "Penberthy is one of the local fishermen. Their eldest daughter, Ivy, is one of my maids."

"I've met Ivy, she's a lovely girl."

Kathryn realized that this was the first time she'd had an opportunity to venture into the village. "What a charming place." The two dozen or so small houses and shops were constructed of gray stone. She couldn't help but notice, however, that although the tiny front gardens were well-kept, some of the buildings looked a bit worse for wear.

Lord Darcy, noting the direction of her gaze, appeared to read her thoughts as well. "The village could use freshening up," he admitted. "Hayward was neglectful in that respect. I am doing what I can. But these things take time."

The front door of the Penberthys' cottage was weather-beaten, its red paint faded and peeling. A woman in a frayed dress sat on the front steps, shelling peas. Two toddlers played in a patch of weedy grass nearby.

The duke removed his hat and bowed politely. "Good afternoon, Mrs. Penberthy."

The woman gasped in recognition, quickly set aside her basket, and rose to give him a curtsy. "Yer Grace."

"Might I introduce a friend of mine, Miss Kathryn Atherton? She is down from London."

The woman dipped another curtsy to Kathryn. "A pleasure to meet you, miss."

"The pleasure is mine," Kathryn returned.

A worried look crossed the woman's face as she asked the duke: "Are ye here t' collect the rent, Yer Grace?"

"The rent? No. I leave such matters to my steward." The duke lowered his voice and inquired in a concerned tone, "Are you in arrears with the rent, Mrs. Penberthy?"

She nodded, her eyes cast down at her scuffed boots. "I'm

ever so sorry, Yer Grace. But Erasmus, he be laid up these past few months with pain in his foot. It's so bad now he can hardly walk. Hasn't took his boat out since May. We've had narry a penny to live on but me girl Ivy's wages, and what I can bring in wi' a bit o' washing. Mr. Avery said as we could have more time to pay, but—"

"And so you shall," the duke replied. "Take all the time you need, madam."

Mrs. Penberthy gave a visible sigh of relief. "Thank ye, Yer Grace."

"However, there is another matter we should like to discuss with you, Mrs. Penberthy." Darcy glanced at Kathryn, signaling her to take over.

"We saw your daughters playing with pinwheels. Rose said you made them yourself."

"What, them whirligigs?" Mrs. Penberthy let go a guffaw as she picked up her basket of peas. "That just be a bit o' fun to make the young'uns smile. Make 'em out of scraps, I do."

"Would you be able to make a hundred of them, Mrs. Penberthy?" Kathryn asked.

"A hundred?" Mrs. Penberthy's mouth fell open and she nearly dropped the basket.

"You would have until the end of the month. They would serve as gifts at the Children's Fête."

"We would pay you, of course," the duke put in, "whatever fee you think reasonable."

"It would be my honor, Yer Grace," Mrs. Penberthy stammered, her eyes lighting up with joy. "But a hundred! I will need supplies . . . paper and sticks and such."

"I'll have Mr. Avery get in touch with you to arrange the terms and so forth. Tell him what you need, and he will forward you an advance to purchase supplies."

"Very well, Yer Grace. Thank ye ever so much."

"No, thank *you*, madam. You are doing us a great service." Lord Darcy made as if to go, then turned back. "May I ask what ails your husband, Mrs. Penberthy? You mentioned his foot. What does the doctor say?"

"Oh," she scoffed, "we can no' afford a doctor, Yer Grace."

"Well, he must see a doctor, ma'am. I will call one out, and I shall be happy to pay his fee."

Kathryn and the duke soon took their leave. At the touch of his hand as he helped her board his carriage, another *zing* of intense awareness shot through her.

Only a lightweight carriage could make the drive up the steep road, and the vehicle only had one passenger seat. They were obliged to sit side by side again.

As the carriage rumbled along, Kathryn's pulse began hammering too rapidly for comfort. She recognized his distinct scent, that intoxicating mix of soap and cologne, which sent her mind careening back to what had happened that night in the billiards room. She was grateful that thoughts were secrets and he could never know what she was thinking.

"That was kind of you," she said, trying to sound matter-of-fact.

"It was your idea to hire the woman to make pinwheels," the duke retorted, "and an excellent notion at that. It appears that the income she earns will be much appreciated."

"I meant it was kind of you to offer to summon a doctor for her husband."

"It seemed to be the right thing to do."

Upon arriving at the castle, they made their way up the stairs together, pausing on the third floor landing.

"Thank you for taking the time to go into the village with me today," he said softly, his eyes finding hers.

"Thank you for my new hat." She untied the bonnet strings and removed it from her head.

"It was my pleasure."

"I had a lovely time," she said, desperate to be on her way, yet wanting the moment to never end.

"As did I."

"Well. I should get back to work."

"So you should." He took one of her hands in his and pressed upon it a gentle kiss. "Will I see you at dinner, Miss Atherton?"

Zing.

Confound it. Here was Kathryn's chance to tell him that she couldn't possibly have dinner with him tonight. They had just spent the entire afternoon together. She really needed to buckle down.

Instead, she heard herself say: "You will."

As he undressed for bed, Lance thought over everything he and Miss Atherton had done since he first ran into her that afternoon on the terrace, to the moment they had said good night after dinner.

She was such a fascinating woman. He had enjoyed every minute of their time together, and every word of the conversations they'd shared. He suspected that she had enjoyed it equally as much.

Which was a good thing. A very good thing.

"Thank you, Woodston," Lance said as he divested himself of his shirt and handed it over to his valet.

A good-looking fellow in his early forties, Woodston had been particularly grief-stricken when Hayward died. And no wonder. The man had attended the former duke for nineteen years.

Although new to this duke business, Lance was accustomed to being waited on. As an officer in the Navy, he'd had his own servant, who in addition to his normal duties, had looked after Lance's cabin, served as his valet, fetched his washing water, and served him at table.

Woodston, Lance had been pleased to discover, was equally as skilled and devoted as the Marine who had last served him in that capacity. Hayward had chosen well.

"I've had the most wonderful day," Lance added.

"Did you, Your Grace?" the valet asked.

"Yes." Lance sat down and removed his boots and stockings. "Miss Atherton and I went into Rosquay. It began as a simple matter to purchase her a new hat. Then she insisted on meeting with some local craftsmen. I worried that they might not take to her because she's a woman. There *was* some initial reluctance at first. But then something remarkable happened."

"What is that, Your Grace?"

"Once the men got over their initial mistrust and started actually listening to what Miss Atherton was saying, it was a different story. She impressed them with her energy and her imagination." Lance chuckled as he stood up and unbuttoned his trousers. "She charmed the socks off of every single one of them."

"Good for her," Woodston commented, taking Lance's pants and hanging them up.

"She did it all on her own as well." Renovation not being a skill in his wheelhouse, Lance had simply stood by, letting her do all the talking. "We now have an army of painters, upholsterers, wall paperers, and wood carvers at my beck and call, ready to bid on the project."

To bid on the project.

The notion gave Lance pause.

The chance that Miss Atherton's drawings would ever actually reach the bidding phase was still a frail ghost of a prospect. It depended entirely on whether or not she would agree to marry him.

When . . . and if . . . he had the nerve to ask her again.

Give her a chance to get to know you. People change their minds every day.

He pictured the moment in his mind. Perhaps he would find her standing at the terrace wall, as he had this afternoon. Or walking on the beach. He would take her hand in his and kiss it and say, *My dearest Miss Atherton, you are all I think about. And all I care about.* She would admit that she had come to feel the same way. He would bend down on one knee then, and ask her to be his wife. *Yes,* she would say, those stunning aquamarine eyes shining. *I will.*

He would cover her face with kisses, then lift her in his arms and take her back to his bedchamber, where, at long last, he would—

"Your Grace?"

Lance looked up, recalling that Woodston was still in the room. Patiently holding out his silk dressing gown. While Lance was standing here daydreaming, wearing nothing but his smalls. His face grew warm as he slid his arms into the garment's sleeves and tied the belt around his waist. "Thank you, Woodston. That will be all."

"Very well, Your Grace. Good night." The valet left the chamber and closed the door.

Alone now, Lance allowed himself to pick up the fantasy where he'd left off.

He would take her back here to his bedchamber, where, at long last . . . he would begin to divest her of every single article of her clothing. Starting with that infernal suit jacket she always wore. He would grab hold of the lapels and rip it open, then do the same to the blouse beneath it, scattering buttons on the floor in his haste to touch and taste her flesh.

Lance's blood began to simmer as he contemplated the sight of her chest. He remembered what it looked like. Her décolletage was an expanse of creamy porcelain skin. The upper part of her breasts curved enticingly above her corset. He remembered exactly how those breasts had felt in his hands. Oh, how he remembered.

Just thinking about it made him grow hard. His breath began to waver as he imagined what would happen next. How he would unhook her skirt and let it slip down until it lay in a pool of fabric at her feet. He would remove her corset next, until she was down to her chemise. And then . . .

What are you doing, Lance? You depraved idiot. Banish all such thoughts from your mind at once.

Lance's pulse and respiration were rioting. His cock was as hard as a rock, aching for release. *Bloody hell to damnation and back.*

He had two choices now. Either climb into bed and finish himself off by hand. Or take an ice-cold bath.

K athryn stood at the mirror above the bathroom sink, removing the last pins from her hair. After all that traipsing through Rosquay in the hot sun, she looked forward to a refreshing bath before going to bed.

What a lovely day it had been. More than lovely. It had proved to be one of the most enjoyable afternoons she'd spent in years.

She started the water running in the tub and then began to undress, unbuttoning and removing her silk blouse. Her skirt followed, then her shoes. She had learned so much about Lord Darcy today. About his childhood pursuits. About his early years at the naval training school. When he had shared the pain he'd suffered over his parents' loss, it had touched her deeply.

Kathryn undid her corset and slipped out of it, then

yanked her chemise over her head, adding them to the other clothing she'd draped over the back of a chair. The duke had grown up to be such a kind and generous man. The kind of man who insisted on replacing lost hats. The kind who fixed things in his community. The kind of man who didn't blink an eyelash when asked to order a hundred pinwheels for the Children's Fête. The kind of man who sent doctors to tend to poor fishermen.

It was all a reflection of his goodness.

She smiled to herself, thinking how much she had come to like the man. She had just untied her drawers, slid them down her legs, and stepped out of them when the door to the bathroom was suddenly and unceremoniously flung open.

Kathryn gasped.

The Duke of Darcy stopped short in the doorway, staring at her, his eyes wide with astonishment.

Chapter Thirteen

Kathryn froze. The bloomers she'd been clutching fell from her hand.

Hadn't she locked the door? Apparently not.

Heat flooded her face and her heart began to pound. All she was wearing were stockings and garters. *Grab your skirt! A towel! Anything!* her mind commanded. Yet she couldn't move a muscle.

Neither could the duke. He stood stock-still before her, barefoot and bare-legged, clad in only his dressing gown.

"Forgive me." His voice sounded strangled as his eyes took in her nearly naked form. "I forgot . . . that we shared this bathroom."

She hadn't forgotten. She'd worried that she might inadvertently run into him here. *That's what locks are for, you fool.* "It's . . . the only bathroom . . . on this floor," she heard herself stammer.

Her brain was still madly urging her to cover herself. But she continued to stand there, unable to budge, her eyes focused on him . . . specifically, on a particular part of his body in the mid-range area.

Kathryn couldn't be certain what he wore beneath his dressing gown, but her guess was . . . nothing. She had seen his naked body. The image of that gorgeous masculine torso and the male appendage she had seen between those legs filled her mind.

That appendage, if she was reading the situation correctly, was a lot larger—and in a very different state—from the time she had observed him on the shore. It was jutting out from his body like a steel rod, tenting the silken fabric of his dressing gown.

"Dear God," he said huskily.

The expression on his face was making her stomach do backflips. She recalled a phrase she'd once read in a book: *a gaze filled with molten desire.* This was the first time she had ever witnessed that kind of gaze in real life. And it was directed *at her.*

It made her feel . . . empowered somehow. He was looking at her as if she were the most beautiful woman he had ever seen. As if he wanted, with every fiber of his being, to sweep her into his arms and kiss her, right there on the spot.

And do far more than kiss her.

All at once, Kathryn couldn't think of anything in the world that she wanted more.

She knew it was wrong. Standing here, naked and staring back at him like this, was equally wrong. She swallowed hard, straining to drum up the nerve to utter the words that would make him leave.

"Um," she managed. "Please . . . shut the door."

"As you wish," the duke replied. But instead of backing away, he strode into the room and closed the door behind him.

Lance's heart pounded like a runaway locomotive as he crossed the room, stopping a few feet away from where she stood.

What he beheld, incredibly, was the very thing he had just been imagining in his room. Miss Atherton was standing in front of him, stark naked except for white stockings and garters. Her hair hung loosely about her shoulders like a wave of golden wheat. And she wasn't doing a thing to cover herself.

His erection, which had never quite gone away, had instantly sprung to life with full force at the sight of her.

Hungrily, he scanned her from head to toe. Her figure was slight but perfect. Her waist was slender. Her thighs and hips were just the right shape and size to balance her breasts. And those breasts . . . they were perfectly round, her nipples pink and luscious. He took in the patch of hair at the apex of her thighs. It was exactly the color he'd imagined—as golden as the hair on her head.

Lance knew, when she'd asked him to shut the door, that she had meant for him to take his leave. But there had been a definite lack of conviction in her voice when she'd said it.

In truth, wild horses couldn't have dragged him away. She stood before him like a nymph in a dream, her chest rising and falling with every erratic breath, her aquamarine eyes glimmering beneath the soft glow of the gas lamps with a hooded look that said, *Take me*.

He had never seen a more beautiful woman. And he was only a man.

Lance didn't hesitate further. In three quick strides, he closed the distance between them, enveloped her in his embrace, and crushed his lips against hers.

All rational thought vanished from Kathryn's mind as his body pressed against hers.

His tongue slipped inside her mouth and indulged in a mating dance with hers. He kissed her forcefully, commandingly, one hand behind her neck, tilting her face up to his, the other hand roaming across her back.

She heard a low moan issue from her throat, heard an answering groan from his. She wound one hand up around his neck, cupped the hard curve of his derrière with her other hand, pulling him closer as they kissed. She could feel the steely length of his erection between them, digging into her abdomen. Desire shot through her like an arrow, piercing to her very core.

Her skin felt like it was on fire. His hand slid up between them to cup and massage her breast. Then he broke the kiss and crouched lower, taking her breast into his mouth. Slowly and gently, he manipulated her nipple with his lips and tongue, producing a sensation so erotic it made her groan with pleasure.

He continued to suckle first one breast, then the other,

causing the place at the center of her womanhood to grow hot and moist. Kathryn arched her back, grateful he was holding on to her or she might have fallen.

"You are so beautiful," he whispered, straightening up again as they both fought for breath. He began planting soft kisses along her throat and the side of her neck, a spot so sensitive that shivers raced down her spine.

Capturing her earlobe between his lips, he nibbled softly. "You have the body of a goddess," he breathed against her ear.

"You are pretty gorgeous yourself," she managed, her voice somewhere between a gasp and a sigh.

He gazed down at her. "You've seen me naked," he said huskily. "Haven't you?"

She stiffened slightly. "What do you—"

"A few days ago. Before my morning swim," he murmured in between leisurely kisses. "I saw you on the cliff. And you saw me. On the beach. Didn't you?"

He paused, silently daring her to deny it. Heat consumed her face.

"Yes," she whispered.

"Did you like what you saw?"

"Yes."

"Would you like to see it again?"

All she could do was nod.

His mouth widened into a grin. He let go of her briefly, just long enough to slide off his dressing gown, which he let fall to the tiled floor. Kathryn couldn't prevent another small gasp. She'd been right. He *was* totally naked beneath it.

The evidence of his arousal poked out at her like a living

thing. Her breath caught in her throat as she stared at it, fascinated by its size and shape. She couldn't help but feel a kind of thrill, knowing that she'd made him feel that way.

Her only experience with lovemaking had fallen so low off the mark. Kathryn was filled with a sudden need to amend that.

She knew it was wicked. She was an unmarried woman. Did it make a difference that he had asked for her hand? No, it did not. She had no intention of marrying this man, and he knew it. Yet it was obvious that he wanted her.

The duke had awakened feelings in her that she had never imagined possible. She liked him. Revered him. With him, she would finally discover what she had missed—what she had been missing for so many years—where the coupling of human beings was concerned.

Sliding her arms around him, Kathryn pulled him back into her embrace.

He let out a growl. His hands roved insistently up and down her back and across her buttocks as his mouth claimed hers again. His hard member was pinned between them, pressing against her belly. He began moving his hips in an erotic motion, rubbing against her, a thrilling indication of what was to come.

She became hazily aware of a thunderous sound from somewhere nearby, like the roaring of a lion or a hundred waterfalls. She had no idea what it was and didn't care. She could think of nothing but him. This.

Flames ignited in Kathryn's veins. Every part of her body felt tender and swollen. A burgeoning want began to build inside her. She wondered if he was going to take her right here, standing up on the bathroom floor. Was it even possible to make love standing up? She was eager to find out.

The thundering sound continued. Like a celebratory chorus inside her brain.

Kathryn didn't want this to ever end. At the same time, she couldn't wait for it to move to the next phase. She yearned to feel his magnificent male appendage in her hand. Just as she lowered her hand in that direction, she became aware of a strange sensation around her feet. Warm water seemed to be rushing around her toes, drenching her stockings.

"What is that?" Kathryn breathed in reluctant confusion.

"Hmmm?" he murmured heedlessly.

Kathryn pulled back slightly from his embrace, enough to identify the source of the problem.

Water was cascading over the edge of the bathtub and raining down onto the floor.

"The bathtub is overflowing."

The words came at Lance out of a fog. He ignored them.

"Wait, stop," he heard her say.

Lance paused, annoyed at this intrusion that was pulling him from a beautiful dream. He glanced in the direction she was pointing.

Bollocks. The bathtub was overflowing.

In a flash she was gone from his embrace, shutting off the tap, and yanking up the stopper. "Don't you have an overflow drain?"

"A what?" he said.

She studied the plumbing, then gave up in frustration. They stood in frozen silence for a moment, the only sound in the room that of the bathwater being sucked down the drain.

"All the new tubs have overflow drains," she said a bit awkwardly. "We really must install one as part of the improvements."

"By all means," Lance heard himself reply. "Add it to the list."

Their eyes met. Merriment began to sparkle in hers. "Aye-aye, Captain." Her lips started twitching.

He felt an answering response build within his own chest. In unison, they both burst out laughing. Laughter overtook them for a good long minute, until he had to wipe moisture from his eyes.

"Well," he said finally. "That was a rather unwelcome interruption to very promising story."

Lance assessed the situation. He was stark naked and still painfully aroused. She was equally nude except for her stockings and garters. Water covered the floor. His dressing gown lay in the middle of it, alongside her bloomers, both totally drenched.

The hell with all that. Splashing his way across the room, he took her back into his arms. "Shall we pick up where we left off?" he asked softly.

She stiffened. And blushed. With that blush, her expression flickered and changed. She seemed to be experiencing sudden doubts about what had just passed between them. And regret.

Damn it all to hell.

Releasing her, Lance grabbed a large towel from a shelf and handed it to her. She wrapped it around her body, tucking it in over the tops of her breasts. "I promised myself this would never happen," she said slowly, lamentably. "We agreed to keep things strictly businesslike between us."

"Absolutely right. I don't know what got into me." Lance took a breath, then grabbed a towel as well and wrapped it around his waist. *Down, boy.* "Well, in all honesty, I *do* know *exactly* what got into me. You were standing there naked as a jaybird. Looking absolutely ravishing. And the look in your eyes was . . . beckoning."

Her cheeks turned crimson now. "My eyes were not beckoning."

"They were. Admit it: you wanted this, too."

"I did *not* want this." But her tone betrayed that she was lying.

"'The lady doth protest too much, methinks.'"

"Don't quote Shakespeare at me," she hissed.

"You don't like Shakespeare?"

"Of course I love Shakespeare! Anyone with an ounce of sense loves Shakespeare! But *this* . . . should not have happened." She looked hopelessly, adorably self-conscious and confused.

It might be perverse, but Lance found himself actually enjoying her discomfort and this exchange. "Perhaps it shouldn't have. But you looked into my eyes. You read my intention. You could have covered yourself up and backed away, but you didn't. Instead, when I took you in my arms and kissed you, you kissed me back. Thoroughly and with obvious enjoyment."

She opened her mouth as if to deny that, then closed it. Her hands came up to cover her face. "All right, fine, I admit it. I *did* want you to . . . kiss me. And . . ." Her voice trailed off. Lowering her hands again, she bit her lip in obvious frustration. "But I shouldn't have allowed it and I definitely shouldn't have participated in it. I just . . . got carried away again."

"As did I. But my intentions were honorable," Lance pointed out. He knew this wasn't the time or the place for another proposal, but he wanted her to understand that he wasn't a rake or a cad. "I *did* ask you to marry me. My wishes remain unchanged."

He realized he'd made her feel even more uncomfortable now, and wished he hadn't said that.

"I'm sorry," she responded. "My wishes also remain unchanged."

A brief wave of disappointment washed over him. Which was absurd. What the hell had he been expecting? That one afternoon together and a bit of naked fondling was all it would take to get her to rethink everything and be his bride?

It was going to take a *lot* more than that, and Lance knew it. Unfortunately, he didn't know exactly *what* it was going to take, or if his quest was even possible. But their interlude just now served to reinforce in his mind how *right* they were for each other.

With a sigh, she said, "I don't know how I can continue working here if this sort of thing is going to keep happening."

Lance didn't want to put any restrictions on this *thing* that kept happening. He had a feeling that, were they ever to actually make love, she would finally understand how incredible it could be between them. Maybe then she'd be willing to reassess her priorities, to see just how important her career really was to her.

He damn well wasn't going to give up. Not until he had *made* her see.

Meanwhile, it was necessary to say something; otherwise she might walk away, quit this job, and he'd lose this opportunity to try to win her hand. "It won't keep happening. It's all back to aboveboard and professional from here on out." He touched his forehead in a quick salute. "You have my solemn promise."

"You made the same promise the day after I arrived, and look where it got us."

"I swear to you, that during the term in which you are working as my architect—"

"During the term?" she repeated. "Wait a minute—"

He held up a hand to silence her. "You will not be working for me forever. I don't wish to make promises I may later regret. Therefore, I repeat: during the term in which you are working as my architect, relations between us will remain strictly professional, unless . . ."

"There are no conditions under which the term *unless* would be remotely acceptable, Your Grace."

"Unless *you* initiate something more," Lance finished. There. It was a promise he wished he hadn't had to make—but it kept things open-ended. The ball was in her court now.

She fell silent as if considering the matter. Then, straightening her shoulders, she spoke with as much dignity as could be mustered for a woman who was standing in a flooded bathroom wearing almost nothing but a towel. "That *is* acceptable. Since the scenario you describe will never happen."

I wouldn't bet on that. Lance bowed with a dramatic flourish of one arm. "As my lady commands."

Her nightclothes hung on a nearby hook. She slipped into her dressing gown, then gathered up her other garments from the chair where they lay. "We had best ring for a servant to mop this up, Your Grace."

He ached to touch her again, but restrained himself. "After such intimacies," he said softly, "it feels foolish to address each other in such a formal manner. Call me Lance."

She looked conflicted. "What will the servants think? What will your grandmother think?"

"Call me Lance in private, then."

She gave him an almost imperceptible shrug. "All right." She tested it out. "Lance."

He grinned. "And may I call you Kathryn?"

"You may," she said, slipping past him and heading for the bathroom door. Turning back, she added with an impish smile: "But only in private."

CHAPTER FOURTEEN

A week passed. Kathryn spent the better part of her time working. Often, she toiled until one or two in the morning, determined that every drawing be as perfect as humanly possible.

Every few days, she met with the duke to discuss her progress. He seemed to be pleased with what she was accomplishing.

Kathryn allowed herself only a few reprieves from this busy work schedule.

She carved out time, as promised, to help Lance plan the upcoming Children's Fête. After putting together a list of activities and lawn games, they enlisted Mrs. Morgan's help to gather the supplies and met with the cook to create the menu.

Kathryn maintained a correspondence with her sisters, enjoying reading about the details of their lives. She indulged in a few walks with Lance, down to the beach and into the village of St. Gabriel's Mount. They took in the sea view from the bench on the cliff path, which Lance admitted had been his favorite spot to indulge in contemplation ever since he was a child.

Every evening, they dined together. On several occasions his grandmother joined them, adding her spice and vinegar to their conversations. They learned that Mr. Penberthy—the ailing fisherman to whom Lance had sent a doctor—had been diagnosed with a fractured foot, which thankfully would mend with proper care and time.

Kathryn found herself especially looking forward to those evenings when she and the duke dined alone. She had come to enjoy and value his company more than she could have anticipated.

He wanted to hear about her life growing up in New York. In return, he shared tales of his career in the Royal Navy and yarns that his shipmates had spun, some of which had her laughing far into the night.

She found that sometimes she got her best ideas during these breaks. When she went back to work, she felt invigorated and refreshed.

The duke kept his promise. No more untoward behavior occurred. Whenever he and Kathryn were together, he behaved in a perfectly professional manner, and so did she.

He didn't bring up the subject of marriage again, for which she was grateful. As Kathryn worked on the plans, though, whenever she thought of Lance living here, in the rooms *she* was designing, with his future bride—some perfectly nice and beautiful woman who would be delighted to be his duchess—the idea rankled more than it should.

Despite their determinedly upright behavior, a new kind of vibration hung in the air. An unspoken hint of intimacy that was fed every time they called each other by their first names.

It was subtly different from the sexual tension that had simmered between them when they first met. Now, they had openly acknowledged their sexual attraction. They had agreed that it was inappropriate and promised to hold it at bay. Now, whenever Kathryn caught the duke eyeing her hungrily, there was no wondering what was going on in his mind. She knew what it meant. What he wanted. And what she was missing by refusing to allow it.

Part of her wished she could just give in. Let herself experience exactly what *she'd* wanted to experience that night in the bathroom, when she'd been nearly naked in his arms.

We are both responsible adults, she would tell herself. *We are both unattached. We want each other. Would it be so wrong if I gave in and made love to him?*

Yes, it would be wrong.

She had work to do. And she would focus on that work if it killed her.

Lance awakened to the caw of a seagull. He rose, dressed, and traipsed down to the beach for his morning plunge.

As he began swimming out to sea, he glanced over his shoulder to see if Kathryn might have followed him down here, as she had that morning two weeks ago. To his disappointment, she hadn't.

A week had passed since the bathtub debacle, as he liked to think of it. They'd been getting on famously. There had been no more hanky-panky. He was keeping his end of the bargain, even though it hadn't been easy.

And he was making progress.

Lance had taken her down to the village again and showed her the schoolhouse. Laying the foundation for all the good they could undertake in the community with her fortune at play. They had engaged in lively conversations while out walking and every night at dinner. All day long, he had found himself looking forward to those dinners, when he had the pleasure of her company.

It turned out they had many things in common, in addition to their shared enthusiasm for reading. They both loved to travel. Each had seen a great deal of the world—him in his service to the Crown, her on holidays with her family. They both enjoyed playing cards. They also had a shared appreciation of music.

"I loved attending the symphony in New York City," Kathryn had enthused a few evenings before. "And in London, my guilty pleasure is to treat myself to a Royal Philharmonic Society concert."

"Never consider a concert a guilty pleasure," Lance had admonished her with a grin. "On board ship, I grew so tired of the hornpipe and harmonica I taught myself to play the violin."

"You taught yourself? How is that even possible?"

"It is not easy, and not recommended," Lance had admitted ruefully. "I did manage to find a few instructors in diverse ports of call who corrected critical deficiencies in my playing. But for the most part, I was obliged to learn what I could from books and by diligent practice."

"That must have been difficult."

"It was probably the reason it took me five years to become even halfway proficient."

"I adore the violin. I would love to hear you play some time."

"It has been a while since I took up the instrument. I fear I would be rusty." But Lance had stored away that piece of information, thinking it might come in handy someday.

If only he could ask for her hand again now and have the matter settled, Lance thought as his arms bit through the waves.

When, he wondered, was the right time to come clean about his financial situation? Before he asked her? Or after? He hoped Kathryn's career might not seem so important to her when compared to the loss of a nine-hundred-year-old castle and the island it stood on. Did he dare tell her now?

No. It was still too soon to risk it. No matter how he tried to spin it, he still feared that if he told her now, she'd think her fortune was the only reason he wanted her. Which was not the case. At least not anymore.

It may have started out that way. But he had gotten to know her on a whole new level. There was far more to the woman than a beautiful face and figure and a dowry the size of Manhattan. She was a fascinating person. If he married her, he would have a wife he cared for forever.

Would she accept him the next time he asked? That was

the million-dollar question. The question that teased at the corners of his mind and ate away at his gut. The question that would remain unanswered until the day he felt sure of her. Sure that she wanted him so much that she would be willing to give up her career to be his duchess.

Then he would admit to the financial mess his brother had left him. The desperate situation in which he had been placed. The secret his father and brother had kept for decades. A secret even *he* hadn't known about until he'd inherited the title. A secret he'd been too embarrassed to tell anyone, even his own grandmother.

Then Lance would get down on his knees and beg her forgiveness for keeping it from her.

Then, and only then, could he be reasonably sure that she'd forgive him for not telling her in the first place.

Lance returned to his chamber to find his valet ready and waiting to help him dress.

"That was a bracing swim," Lance said as he put on his trousers.

"Your brother was also fond of a morning swim," Woodston commented, holding up a newly pressed shirt.

"Was he?" Lance slipped into the garment. "I had no idea."

"The habit began a few years after he inherited the title. As I recall, the inspiration came from you, Your Grace."

"From me? How is that possible? I barely knew Hayward. We saw each other so rarely."

"Yes, but you exchanged letters, I believe? He said that in your correspondence, you had mentioned your own practice of taking a daily plunge. He decided to try it, and grew enamored of it."

"Well, what do you know," Lance said, surprised.

He buttoned up his shirt, then donned the waistcoat Woodston had selected. Lance wished he knew more about his brother. This man had probably learned a great deal about him, Lance realized. If only he knew what questions to ask.

A very different subject was taking up his mind at the moment, however. Lance glanced at his valet. The man seemed savvy and observant. It wasn't the done thing for a duke to solicit advice from a servant. But Woodston had worked here for nearly two decades. And Lance had often received good input from the Marine who'd attended him in the Navy.

"Woodston, I have a question for you."

"Your Grace?"

"When you want to impress a woman, what do you usually do?"

Woodston hesitated, his mouth dropping open slightly as he turned to retrieve the coat he had laid out over a nearby chair. "Ladies generally enjoy bouquets of flowers, I believe," he said finally.

"This particular woman doesn't like cut flowers." Lance put on the coat.

"Is there anything of which Miss Atherton *is* particularly fond?"

Lance froze. "I didn't say this was about Miss Atherton."

"Forgive me, Your Grace. I just presumed."

"Did you now." Lance shrugged off his annoyance. He was right: the man *was* shrewd. "Well, what if it *is* Miss Atherton?" he retorted grumpily, buttoning the coat. "She has been working hard and I wish to do something to thank her."

"Well, Your Grace," Woodston answered, "I return to my previous question. Has Miss Atherton ever mentioned something she especially likes? Something she misses or wishes you might do? If you go out of your way to give her or do for her that *very thing*, it would be very endearing."

Lance stared at him. The answer to his dilemma instantly sprang to mind.

"Woodston, thank you. You are a genius."

K athryn put down her pencil and rubbed her eyes. It was not quite eleven o'clock in the morning, but already she was tired. For days, she'd been burning the candle at both ends and getting very little sleep. But it was worth it. The progress she'd made was gratifying.

She had completed architectural plans and decorative sketches for almost all of the rooms they had discussed improving, including the great hall with its elaborate new ceiling. She still had more work to do, but she was getting close to the finish line. If the duke were to implement even half of these changes, it would be an exciting project.

Taking another sip of cold coffee, Kathryn glanced over the plan for the fourth floor to make sure she hadn't missed anything. This drawing had received the least attention, as the only improvement was to be new carpets in the dowager duchess's suite.

As Kathryn glanced at the drawing now, something didn't feel right.

She pulled out one of the elevations of the castle and studied it. Hmmm. Something *definitely* was off. A suspicion began to simmer in Kathryn's mind. She found the set of plans from the renovation sixty years ago and compared the drawings of the unoccupied wing on the fourth floor. What she saw made her gasp.

Kathryn rolled up several drawings, took them to the terrace level, and stared at the eastern wall of the castle. *Just as I thought.* She spent a few minutes in the unused wing on the fourth floor, but couldn't test her theory as all the doors were locked. Weeks ago, when she'd drawn up her own plan of this wing, she'd gone by the measurements in the old drawings, since no new work was to be done here. But she now realized there was an anomaly she couldn't account for.

It was most intriguing. Kathryn needed to speak with the duke at once. Where, she wondered, might she find him at this hour? She headed downstairs and was moving in the direction of his study when the sound of music caught her ears.

Someone was playing the violin.

Whoever was playing was an artist with great talent. She recognized the song: Brahms's *Violin Sonata No. 3.* The music was plaintive, tantalizing, beautiful. Lance had mentioned that he played the violin. Was it him?

She followed the music, finally locating its source. It was coming from the smoking room, just a few doors down from the ladies' parlor where she always worked. Kathryn paused in the doorway and peeked in.

It *was* Lance. He was standing by a window, eyes closed, a violin in his caress. He appeared to be lost in the pleasure of the music.

Kathryn stood stock-still, afraid to make a sound lest she disturb him. She had heard untold numbers of concerts in her life, but only a few violin solos by masters of the instrument. The Duke of Darcy might not be of their caliber, but he was a player of great skill. He would have lit up the stage as a soloist in a professional company.

The sweet melody swept her away, its lilting notes carrying her to a place of enchantment. She couldn't remember the last time she'd heard music that had affected her so.

When the song ended, the duke noticed her standing in the doorway. "Kathryn. Forgive me. I hope my playing did not disturb you?"

"Not at all," she said, entering the room. "In fact, I was looking for you when I heard the music. That was just beautiful."

"You are very kind."

"I'm not trying to be kind. You have a gift, Lance. I could listen to music like that all day long."

He seemed highly pleased by her compliments. "If my playing gave you a moment of pleasure, then I am glad." He set down the violin and said in a more serious tone, "You said you were looking for me?"

"Yes. This is going to sound strange, but . . . I was studying the plans I drew up, and I found a discrepancy."

"What kind of discrepancy?"

She gestured with the drawings in her hand. "May I show you?"

"Please." He indicated a table nearby, where Kathryn unfurled the plans.

"This is an elevation of the castle's east wall," Kathryn explained. "Note that there are ten windows on each floor." Placing two other drawings atop the first, she continued, "Here's the fourth floor of the castle. The drawing on the left is from the last renovation. On the right is my new one. Check out the east wing, which has been shuttered off for years. The old drawing shows five bedrooms with two windows each, which makes perfect sense. But I only drew four bedrooms. Because when I scouted that corridor, I only counted four doors."

"What does that mean?" Lance asked, puzzled.

"I suspect a change was made on that floor sometime over the last sixty years. Maybe one of the rooms was enlarged and the unneeded door removed. Or there might be another room that's unreachable from the hallway."

He arched a brow. "Are you saying the castle might have a secret room?"

"It's entirely possible."

"How fascinating. Let us go find out if you are right."

Lance rang for Mrs. Morgan and asked to borrow her set of keys. She explained which ones would open the rooms in the unoccupied wing on the fourth floor. Kathryn's heart thrummed with excitement as she and Lance hurried upstairs. Halfway down the corridor in question, they paused in an area where several large family portraits were hanging.

"The space between the doors is much wider here than anywhere else," Kathryn pointed out.

Lance unlocked the adjoining rooms and they glanced within. Average in size, they were ancient, unused bedrooms, the furniture draped with white dust covers. "These rooms are not nearly wide enough to fill in all that space in the hall."

"Just as I suspected," Kathryn said, nodding. "Which means there must be another room in between these two. A room that someone wanted to keep hidden. So the door was removed and the wall filled in and painted over."

"If that's true, why has no one ever noticed it before?" Lance asked as they returned to the hall and studied that section of wall.

"I suppose because this part of the castle hasn't been used for decades. If anyone were to come up here, these paintings were hung as a clever distraction."

"But who would go to the trouble of creating a secret room? And why?"

"A good question. Maybe it's the hiding place for your family's secret treasure," Kathryn suggested playfully.

"Wouldn't that be nice." Lance's tone held an unexpected hint of wistfulness, which he quickly shook off. Pacing off the number of steps between the two nearest doors, he stopped at the center. Lance peeked behind the painting hanging there, inviting Kathryn to look as well. "I see no trace of a door."

"That just means they did an excellent job of covering it up."

"There must be another way in," Lance murmured, "through one of the adjacent rooms."

They entered the room to the left. Kathryn laughed, enjoying the mystery of their hunt. "I've never looked for a secret treasure room before."

"Neither have I," he responded with a conspiratorial grin.

To their mutual disappointment, however, the wall facing the proper direction was just a solid wall. Although they checked behind paintings and moved aside furniture, there was no sign of a hidden door into another chamber.

"Let's try the other room," Kathryn suggested.

At first, it didn't seem as though the second room was going to provide a solution, either. Two large bookcases built of solid oak stood against the wall in question.

"Well, that's that, I suppose," Lance muttered.

"Wait." Kathryn studied one of the bookcases. "I think there's a seam in the wall here. This bookcase might be a hidden door." She pressed on the right-hand edge of the bookcase. Nothing happened. Moving her hand lower, she pressed again, harder, in several more locations.

There was a soft *clicking* sound.

And the bookcase began to move.

CHAPTER FIFTEEN

The bookcase swung open a few inches toward them, then paused.

"I think we found our way in," Kathryn said in wonder.

"Allow me. I will ensure that whatever awaits inside is safe." Lance pulled open the bookcase door and issued through it. After a pause, he returned and gestured for her to follow. "It's fine. Come in."

Kathryn entered the room and stopped. She hadn't really been expecting a room full of treasure, but what did meet her eyes was so prosaic that she couldn't help feeling a bit disappointed.

It was simply a bedroom. Admittedly, a beautifully appointed bedroom that had been updated more recently than any of the other rooms on this floor, or in the entire castle, for that matter.

A large four-poster bed was topped by a turquoise satin comforter trimmed in gold braid. Carved mahogany furniture stood side by side with ornate pieces from the Louis XIV period. The walls were covered in brocaded silk and hung with oil paintings of travel scenes from the Continent. Old volumes of classic literature filled a tall bookcase, and small but expensive-looking knickknacks and marble and bronze sculptures were scattered throughout the room.

"What is this?" Lance uttered in a puzzled tone.

"A very nice bedroom," Kathryn observed, "far *too* nice to be used for guests. It looks more like someone's private retreat."

"But who? A room this elegant . . . with all these *objets d'art* . . . it could only have belonged to my father, or possibly . . ." He crossed to a small writing desk. It was covered with an elegant leather desk set embossed in gold with the initials *HJM*. "These are my brother's initials: Hayward Jerome Granville."

"Your brother." Kathryn nodded. "That makes sense."

"Does it?" Lance shook his head, bewildered. "I don't understand. My brother had the entire castle at his disposal. Why would he go to the effort and expense of hiding a room like this behind a secret door?"

"Maybe he wanted a place where he could be by himself, unobserved and uninterrupted by the servants."

"When I want privacy, I simply lock my door or tell the servants not to disturb me. No. This is something else."

"Maybe," Kathryn suggested, "he had lovers he met with secretly?"

"That still makes no sense. Hayward was lord of the manor and an unmarried man. He could have slept with any woman he wanted at any time. Why the need for secrecy? I fail to see why . . ." His voice trailed off, his attention drawn to the art objects in the room. Lance's eyebrows lifted as if a new thought had occurred to him.

Kathryn followed the direction of the duke's gaze. The marble and bronze sculptures in the room, she noticed, were all of nude men—depictions of Greek gods and Olympians. Two of the oil paintings on the walls were also of nude or scantily clad Greek gods.

An orange and black vase, which she suspected might be ancient and extremely valuable, depicted naked Greek athletes on a long distance run.

Kathryn couldn't prevent a small gasp. At the same moment, Lance uttered an oath. And not a mild one. He was staring at a small framed photograph resting on the bedside table.

Kathryn crossed to him and studied the photograph in his hand. It was a picture of two young men, perhaps thirty years of age, dressed in their formal best and artfully posed in a relaxed and affectionate embrace. She recognized one of the men, from his portraits in the study, as Hayward Granville.

The other man was his valet.

"Dear God," Lance muttered, aghast. "Can it be? My brother? And . . . *Woodston?*" He slapped the photograph facedown on the bedside table and sank onto the edge of the bed, momentarily speechless.

"Your brother preferred the company of men," Kathryn realized, nodding in comprehension. The notion, although surprising, didn't shock or appall her.

Lance, however, *did* seem shocked—not so much by the truth her statement contained, but more by her having made it. "I am astonished that you are even acquainted with such things, Kathryn."

"I'm not a naïve ingénue," Kathryn shot back. "I have a cousin in New York with similar inclinations. I have known about it and loved him all my life. And don't forget, I spent two years at architectural school in the company of a great many men, some of whom had the same proclivities."

"And you knew about it . . . how?"

"You would be amazed at the confidences men share over a glass of whiskey, with anyone who is handy and willing to listen," she told him.

Lance nodded grimly. "I, too, have been privy to confidences from my shipmates over a glass of whiskey or ale. But *never* on *this* subject. *This*," he said, taking in the room around them with a sweep of his hand, "is a crime in this country, Kathryn. Just thirty years ago it was a hanging offense. It is still punishable by imprisonment."

"Sadly, it is not much different in America," Kathryn acknowledged.

Lance heaved a sigh and closed his eyes briefly, as if hoping that could somehow make their discovery go away. "No wonder Hayward never married. Life must have been hell for him. And I never knew . . ."

He looked so distraught it made Kathryn's heart ache. Setting down the drawings she'd been carrying, she sat beside him on the edge of the bed, wishing she could comfort him somehow. "His life must have been difficult, that's true. But if you think about it, your brother was fortunate."

"Fortunate? How so? To be forced to keep such a secret

all his days?" His blue eyes were filled with pain and sympathy. "To be so miserable and ashamed of his love that he had to hide it from the world?"

"Even if he had to hide it, because he lived here and could afford to build this room, at least he was able to *experience* love. Or so I would like to assume. *That* was a gift."

Lance took that in. "I suppose you are right."

"I'd like to think your brother wasn't entirely miserable. That he did find happiness, if not every minute of every day, at least during the hours he spent here."

Lance turned to her, his anguish fading. "Thank you for that insight. You have been a great help. I will try to remember him that way."

"I'm glad." They were seated side by side on the edge of the bed. As Kathryn gazed into the blue depths of Lance's eyes, her heart seized with a rush of overpowering affection. "We cannot help who we love," she heard herself say.

Time seemed to stand still as her words hung in the air between them.

Kathryn felt a blush heat her cheeks. It was an innocent comment, but she'd said it with such a depth of emotion it almost sounded as if she were admitting that *she* loved *him*. Which was not the case. Was it?

"No," he murmured. "We cannot help who we love." He was looking at her with such undisguised affection and desire it made Kathryn's blood race.

"I made a promise a while back," he added huskily, leaning in so close that their noses were almost touching, "that I would very much like to break."

"Oh?" Kathryn's reply was more a rush of air than a word. "What promise . . . was that?"

"I promised I wouldn't kiss you or touch you again . . ." Belying his words, he lifted one hand to gently cup her face. "Unless *you* wanted it." His voice was as soft and deep as a promise.

Kathryn swallowed hard. For the life of her, she couldn't remember why she had insisted upon that promise. All she could think about was his nearness, and the drumbeat of her heart in her ears, and the fact that his lips were just inches from her own.

It had been so long since she'd felt his mouth on hers. She'd been thinking about this, dreaming about this, for weeks now. She'd told herself it was wrong. But *was* it really wrong?

Who would ever know?

"I want it," she whispered.

So saying, she slipped her hands up around his neck and pressed her lips to his.

Lance ignited, her mouth on his like a torch setting flame to dry embers. He returned the kiss with all the passion that had been building, unsatisfied, inside him for weeks.

Holding her head with one hand, he slid his tongue between her lips, melting into the heat of her mouth.

As the kiss intensified, his arms possessed her, molding her against his body. He felt her own hands roaming his back and shoulders, returning the embrace.

In one swift motion he turned, propelling them back onto the bed, rolling with her in his arms until they landed on their sides, the kiss unbroken and still steaming hot.

With one hand, he cupped her breast, massaging it through her clothing. Far too much clothing. Even sans jacket, her blouse and corset were in the way. He was too impatient to remove them, though.

Every time they had been together, his fingers had yearned to touch her most private of places, the spot he knew would make her come apart at the seams. Nothing was going to stop him this time.

Still kissing her, he gathered up her skirt to her waist, sliding one hand up the soft, smooth fabric of the bloomers that covered the slope of her thigh, inching toward the apex of her legs. Every pair of bloomers he had contended with, in ports across the Mediterranean, had a slit there.

He reached his goal, only to find a solid seam of fabric. Lance paused, breaking the kiss. "What the hell?"

"What's wrong?" she asked breathlessly.

"I want to touch you *here*," he said gruffly, running his fingers over the cleft of her sex through the thin layer of cotton.

"You . . . *are* . . . touching me," she managed.

"I want to feel *you*. All of you. With nothing in between." He felt and saw her thighs quiver at his touch. "I was expecting an opening in your drawers."

"This is the . . . new fashion," she replied in between gasps. "They aren't making drawers . . . open there . . . anymore."

"Damn the British garment industry and their advancements," Lance drawled. "And leave it to you to have the newest fashions." His gaze lit on the drawstring at her waist. Yanking on the ties, he unfastened the garment, then grabbed hold of it and pulled it down.

She lifted her hips, helping him, until her bloomers reached her knees.

Greedily, he took in the sight laid out before him like a feast. His cock, already as hard as a rock, grew even harder. He wanted to plow into her, to feel the moist heat of her wrapping around him, to ride her until they both came in a white-hot wave.

But his own needs would have to wait. He wanted to pleasure her first.

Lance's hand resumed its former activity, this time with flesh against flesh. He began gently. Teasing her with his fingertips. Like plucking at the strings of a violin. Feeling for the nub at the core of her.

She moaned and writhed beneath his touch. "Lance . . ."

"You like that?" he asked softly.

"Yesssss."

He slipped a finger inside her, crooking it at just the right angle, moving it the way he knew would evoke the most pleasure.

"Please . . ." she murmured. "Don't stop."

"I won't stop. I promise. Not until you come apart beneath my hand." *That* was a promise he didn't mind making. And keeping.

His hand moved back to that nub as he increased the pace of his ministrations. He was playing a concerto now that rose and swelled as he worked her, a sweet rhythm that was accompanied and punctuated by the vibration of her thighs.

Lance watched her face as she rode his hand. She was a thing of beauty. Willingly giving herself up to him. Possessed by a power beyond herself. It thrilled him to see her this way. To see what she was like when she allowed herself to succumb to her carnal urges, to lose control.

She was breathing hard now. Making little sounds low in her throat that were a cross between a chirp, a gasp, and a moan. It was like music to his ears. He knew she was close. Leaning down, he captured her mouth with his again, kissing her deeply. Her hands wrapped up around his neck and held on tight.

She cried out into his mouth as the wave took her. He felt her body tense and her thighs started quaking even more fiercely, an eruption that went on for what felt like minutes.

He was so aroused by the taste and the feel and the sound of her, he felt as though he might explode at the same moment. But he held himself in check. Better things were yet in store.

Lance smoothed the golden hair off her forehead, kissing her there, then gazing down at her. Her cheeks were rosy and a lazy smile played at her mouth.

"Did my lady enjoy that?"

"You know I did." Her languid tone and the sated look in her eyes told him just how much she had enjoyed it.

"You make the most delightful chirping sounds when you get excited," he teased.

That made her blush. "I don't chirp."

"You do," he said, grinning.

She gazed down at his crotch. Covering his aching member with her hand, she began massaging it. "Let's see if I can make *you* chirp now."

Lance couldn't prevent a gasp. "Wait." Once again, he didn't have a sheath on him. *Maybe I ought to start carrying one in my pocket.* But he wasn't about to turn down her offer. First, though, he wanted to know what he was dealing with.

Gazing into her lovely aquamarine eyes, he asked softly, "Have you ever done this before?"

"Once."

She didn't seem to want to divulge more, and he didn't want to ask. "All right." His heart pounded like a drum as her hand continued its attentions. He wasn't sure how long he'd last if she kept that up. "But first, what do you say we get rid of all these clothes?"

Kathryn's skirts were up around her waist. Her bloomers were below her knees. Her hand was on the duke's private parts. It was the most unladylike position in which she'd ever found herself, and she didn't care one whit.

A wanton frenzy seemed to have come over. She had enjoyed every millisecond of what they'd just done. She could hardly wait for what they were going to do next. When she had pleasured herself in the past, it had been satisfying, but it hadn't come close to the intensity of what she'd just experienced beneath the hand of this man.

Feeling his intense gaze on her as he'd worked that magic

with his fingers had heightened her sense of arousal to the nth degree. Now, seeing the evidence of his own arousal straining for attention just served to renew her feelings of want.

She wanted him to fill the void that suddenly existed inside her, in a place she hadn't known could have a void.

"Aye-aye, Captain," Kathryn said, smiling. As she reached for the buttons on the duke's pants, a sound filtered in at the edge of her mind.

She paused. Was it footsteps approaching? If so, it didn't matter. They were in a secret room. Behind a secret door.

Looking up, however, she realized they had left the bookcase door standing wide open.

"Dear God." The duke froze beside her. "Someone is coming."

CHAPTER SIXTEEN

In a panic, Kathryn pulled up her bloomers and retied them. Lance slid off the bed and helped her to her feet.

She quickly settled her skirts back in place and tried to smooth her hair. Lance darted across the room, grabbed the roll of architectural drawings, and flicked them open, casually holding them up to hide his . . . mid-section.

Just then, Woodston walked in with a bucket, a mop, and a basket of cleaning supplies.

Catching sight of the two of them, he screeched in surprise and lost his grip on everything he was carrying. The basket flipped upside down, scattering towels, sponges, and rags in all directions. The mop and bucket landed with a clatter, gushing soapy water across the floor.

"Dear me, Woodston," Lance stated with abject calm, as if finding them in this room were an everyday occurrence, "pray forgive us if we startled you."

"Your . . . Your Grace," Woodston stammered, his face

turning beet red as he stared at each of them in turn, then at
the mess on the floor.

"I admit, it is quite a shock to *me* to see you carrying a
bucket and mop," Lance went on. "Surely that is a maid's
duty?"

"Um . . . yes, Your Grace . . . But, well . . . I . . . I . . ."
Woodston began uncertainly.

"Never mind, I think I understand," Lance said with a
wave of his hand. "I take it this rather remarkable room belonged to Hayward. My brother's secret study, if you will.
He liked to steal away and read here on his own, I suppose.
Clearly you were in his confidence, my good man, since you
have come to clean it?"

Woodston glanced around wildly, his eyes coming to rest
on the bedside table. Noticing that the incriminating photograph was lying facedown, his features relaxed a notch. "I . . .
er . . . Yes. His Grace did tell me about his . . . about this
room. It is just as you said, his secret study. He didn't want
anyone else on the staff to know about it, so I agreed to clean
it for him. After his death, I've been keeping it up as a sort of
a . . . tribute to him."

"Just as I thought. I cannot think of anything more
worthy, Woodston." The duke clapped the valet on the
back. "Please keep up the practice. A secret is a secret,
Woodston. I will say nothing of this to anyone. I think we
were finished here in any case. Miss Atherton has scads of
work on her plate." Turning to Kathryn, he gestured to the
door. "Shall we?"

"That was a close call," Lance said when he and Kathryn had reached the relative privacy of the parlor where she worked. Closing the door behind them, he added with amusement, "We seem to have a habit of being interrupted whenever we find ourselves *in flagrante delicto*."

"And it always seems to culminate with water being spilled all over the floor."

They shared a laugh. Lance crossed to where she stood and slid his arms around her waist. "What do you say, if later tonight we continue what we started . . . but this time do it properly, in my bed?"

Kathryn stiffened slightly in his arms. "I don't think that's a good idea."

"It felt like an excellent idea a few minutes ago," he replied softly, leaning in to kiss her neck.

But before he could plant the kiss, she drew back, gently removing herself from his embrace. "Lance. I know that I . . . initiated what just happened. I know I said I wanted it. And I *did*. It was wonderful. *You* were wonderful."

"The pleasure was mutual, believe me."

"Well, I don't know how mutual it was. I mean, you didn't . . ." She blushed, and seemed unable to complete the statement. "The thing is," she rushed on, "what I'm trying to say is . . . I'll be returning to London soon. And you'll be here, running your dukedom and looking for your ducal bride."

"Yes, about that." Lance moved in close again, until their bodies were almost touching. He gazed down at her. Was this the time? Should he ask her now? He weighed the words in his mind. *How would you feel about becoming my ducal bride?* "Kathryn," he began.

She touched a finger to his lips, silencing him. "Let's not spoil it, Lance." She kissed him sweetly. "What happened just now doesn't change anything. I have work to do. And I had better get back to it."

Three days crawled by. Three days in which Lance only caught glimpses of Kathryn in the hallways or whenever he stopped in to take a look at whatever she was working on.

Three days in which she remained holed up in that damned parlor of hers, refusing to come down to dinner, and politely declining every invitation Lance issued in her direction.

Lance paced back and forth in the drawing room, brooding. Morning sunlight filled the room, but his mood was as dark as night. He had done everything he could think of to win the woman's heart. He'd walked with her. He'd talked with her. He'd played the violin for her. He'd told her things about himself that he'd never shared with anyone.

Their search for and discovery of his brother's secret room had brought them even closer together, forging a connection so strong he had almost popped the question again moments later. What more could he do? Was he the only one who felt something in this relationship?

For the past three days, he'd felt so ostracized he'd worried that he had only imagined her regard for him, that her fevered responses to his sexual advances had never happened. But they *had* happened. And he knew as surely as he knew the sun would rise tomorrow that whatever this was between them, *she* felt it, too. She wanted him as much as he wanted her.

She was just too attached to her damned career to allow herself to even imagine a future without it.

What was he going to do about that?

Lance heaved a sigh as he marched toward the wall of windows and then turned, striding back in the opposite direction. He'd been telling himself that the only way they could marry was if she gave up her career. It was what society demanded. It was only thing that had made sense to him at the time.

But maybe it was time to rethink that. Did he really care what society thought? Lance hadn't ever expected to take over this dukedom. But dukes were supposed to be able to do whatever they wanted, weren't they?

Maybe his grandmother was right. Maybe he *would* have to compromise.

Lance mulled that over as he paced, wondering just how much compromise he was willing to make. And what kind of compromise *she* might be willing to make.

After another few minutes of tromping back and forth, Lance arrived at an intriguing conclusion. He smiled to himself as the plan formed in his mind. *Yes. That might work.* Why hadn't he thought of it before?

Surely, after all the time he and Kathryn had spent in each other's company, and all the intimacies they had shared, she'd be more open to the idea of marriage *now* than she had been the first time he'd asked, when they'd barely known each other. This time, if he asked with this new offer in place, he felt there was a good chance she'd accept.

He didn't want to trick her into marriage, though. That had never been his intention. He'd put off telling her about his financial situation before now because he hadn't wanted to stack the deck against himself. He'd wanted her to *want him*, before risking the truth.

His grandmother's warning rang once again in his ears:

Open yourself up to her. Women appreciate a man who isn't afraid to show his vulnerable side.

Maybe he should just get it over with. Tell her about his debts up front. He'd considered the situation too embarrassing to reveal. But maybe it might actually raise her sympathies, help her to see the good she could do with her fortune. If she understood the whole, horrendous state of affairs, maybe she'd *want* to help him. To stand at his side. To be his bride. To save the castle for future generations, as well as the village that came with it.

Yes, he decided. That was the proper course of action. He had put this off long enough. This time, he'd do it right.

He would go to her. Make her take a break. Then escort her to his favorite bench on the cliff path. He would let her know in advance what she was getting into, signing up for. Then he would get down on one knee and ask for her hand.

Kathryn lay down her pen on the table and leaned back in her chair. Her head was pounding. It felt as if her brain cells were being attacked by armies of tiny knives. And she was so incredibly exhausted.

She gave in to a yawn, briefly closing her eyes.

It had been three days since her wild encounter with Lance in his brother's secret room. It was the billiards room and the bathroom all over again, except this time they'd gone even further. She had never been so aroused in her life, or so . . . satisfied.

The duke's own state of arousal had been all too evident. If Woodston hadn't walked in when he did, Kathryn felt certain that she and Lance would have completed the act.

Thank goodness we didn't. At least, that's what Kathryn had been telling herself for the past seventy-two hours. But another voice in her head, equally as loud as the first, was lamenting that she had missed an opportunity to finally discover what lovemaking was truly about.

She suspected that what she and Lance had shared in their earlier encounters had just been the first course—an absolutely delicious first course, to be sure, but nonetheless just a preliminary taste—of an epic feast that was still waiting to be enjoyed. In the secret room, although *she* might have had *dessert*, she had a feeling it was just a sample of the delectable dessert that she and Lance would experience were they ever to make love all the way to its inevitable conclusion.

Kathryn covered her eyes with her hands, unable to believe she was even thinking about this. *Again.* It seemed to be the only thing she *had* thought about for weeks now. Her attraction to the duke was obviously too powerful to resist. Were they ever to find themselves alone again, she wasn't sure she'd be able to restrain herself from following the same impulse that had led her to kiss him the other day.

Kathryn thought about Lance all the time, wishing she

were with him. She loved talking to him about just about anything. Loved the look in his eyes when he gazed at her, especially when he didn't think she was looking. Her knees wilted whenever he was near. Her entire body pulsed whenever he touched her. And she wanted him to do so much more than *touch* her.

These were feelings, she believed, that should be reserved for a husband and wife. But Kathryn had no desire to be a wife! She certainly could never be the wife of the Duke of Darcy. He needed a woman who would be happy to play duchess at St. Gabriel's Mount and raise a passel of children. He'd made it clear, the day he'd proposed, that to be his duchess she'd have to give up her career. And she couldn't do that. She just couldn't.

Kathryn only had one course of action open to her, and she knew it. She must finish this job as quickly as possible and leave this place. Which was why she'd applied herself to the task with such diligence and ferocity the past few days, working day and night, only pausing when absolutely necessary to eat or sleep. The way she figured it, in a few more days she'd be completely done. She could present all her drawings, obtain Lance's approval, and return to town.

Kathryn removed her hands from her eyes and let go a sigh. A few more days. She could get through a few more days. She had to.

Despite the pounding in her head.

And the fact that her throat felt scratchy.

A sudden cough erupted from her chest that took over for a good long minute. *Damn it.* She picked up her pen and stared down at the drawing on the table before her. The lines of ink seemed to be swimming before her eyes. Strange.

A chill came over her, which was even stranger, considering that it was early afternoon and a warm summer day. She shivered and wrapped her arms around herself, wishing she'd brought her shawl down to the parlor with her.

She suddenly realized that someone was approaching. She knew the cadence of that determined footfall. It was Lance.

A flush rose to her cheeks at the thought of seeing him again. A reminder that her body's response was in complete contrast to the dictates of her mind. She forced herself to remain calm. She was going to finish this job. And then she was going to go home.

A sharp rap drew her attention to the open doorway, where the duke had stopped and was looking in at her.

"Kathryn? Might I come in?"

"Of course."

He strode toward the mantelpiece, where he paused with a distracted air. Then, seemingly rethinking his position, he crossed to her and stopped by the table where she was sitting. "How are you?" For some reason, he looked nervous.

"Fine." Kathryn struggled not to shiver. "And you? I hope you are well?"

"I am," he replied in a clipped tone. Clasping his hands behind his back, he regarded her intently. "Let's go for a walk."

"I, um . . . I don't have time."

"Make the time. Please. This is important. I have something I wish to say to you."

Kathryn struggled to focus on his face. But the image before her began to grow cloudy, as if she were looking through a lens covered with gauze. He continued to speak, but his words didn't connect into patterns that made any sense. All at once, the room started spinning and tilting sideways.

She noted a startled look on the duke's face, and then all the light was sucked out of the room and everything went black.

Chapter Seventeen

"She has a high fever, Your Grace," the physician explained in hushed tones in the hallway outside Kathryn's bedroom. "I suspect a chest infection."

"Is it dangerous?" Worry seeped into Lance's bones. "Will she recover?"

"That remains to be seen. One never knows with this kind of thing. Let us hope that bed rest and medicine will do the trick."

The doctor left several bottles of medication with instructions about how to administer the next required doses, and advice as to how her temperature might be controlled. He departed with a promise to return the next day, and to come at once should an emergency arise.

Lance returned to Kathryn's bedroom, where Ivy was arranging the medicine bottles on the bedside table. Kathryn lay in bed beneath a light quilt, her face flushed and bathed in perspiration. Her hair was also damp and spread across the pillow like a golden wave.

He silently cursed himself. He'd been aware of the long hours she was working. She'd always had a tendency to work too hard, but now she'd pushed herself beyond any acceptable limit.

He could guess why. After their encounter in the secret room, she'd probably been so upset with the professional boundaries she had passed she'd decided to burn the midnight oil and return to London. Now she was lying here as sick as a dog.

And for what? To produce drawings for a renovation that might never happen? *This is my fault. All my fault.*

"I'd be happy to sit with her, Yer Grace," Ivy said. "I've got six younger brothers and sisters, and I've took care of 'em all at one time or another when they was sick."

"Thank you, Ivy, but I will take care of Miss Atherton myself."

"*Yerself*, Yer Grace?" Ivy was astonished.

"Myself," he repeated. He wasn't going to leave Kathryn's care to anyone who might botch it up.

"But you're *the duke*, Yer Grace. Dukes never . . ."

"Dukes never *what*? Dirty their hands? Do any actual work? Lower themselves to take care of the sick? You forget that I spent nineteen years in the Royal Navy. I have seen illness in every imaginable form. I've spent hour upon hour belowdecks in the infirmary, observing the ship doctor's methods. I assure you, I am equal to this task."

Ivy nodded slowly, her expression overtaken by an internal struggle over some other issue. The look in her eyes clued him in as to the possible problem.

"Don't worry, Ivy. I am aware that this means I shall be left alone with our patient," Lance stated calmly. "But there is no impropriety here. I will simply care for her. And sleep in that chair." He gestured to an easy chair nearby.

Doubt lingered in Ivy's eyes, which made Lance frown with impatience. "Look, I am the duke. This is my house. What I say, goes. I am going to take care of this woman, end of discussion. If you value your position in this household, you will wipe that look off your face this instant. There are some aspects of her care, I realize, where I will require help. I will let you or another member of the staff know when I require that assistance. Now bring me a pot of tea, two cups, an empty glass, and a washcloth. And fill that pitcher with fresh water."

"Very well, Yer Grace." Ivy made a swift curtsy before exiting the chamber.

Lance sank down onto the chair by Kathryn's bedside, clasping his hands together as he studied her prone form. Her breathing was raspy, and when she swallowed in her sleep, her face contorted with pain.

"I'm so sorry," Lance said softly. He was fairly certain that she wasn't conscious, but felt the need to speak to her, anyway. "I should have stopped you. I should have insisted that you put down that damn pen and pencil and join me for dinner every night as we did before. I should have insisted that you take breaks every afternoon and get a full night's sleep every night." He hung his head. "But you kept turning me away. I thought you didn't want my company anymore. I didn't want to force you. So I left you to your own devices. A huge mistake."

He had been so focused on his own problems, his own worries—the need to save St. Gabriel's Mount, the need to get her to agree to marry him—that he hadn't really thought about *her* needs.

You're not going to die on my watch, my lovely. I promise you that.

For the next two days straight, Lance kept up a vigil at Kathryn's bedside, taking catnaps in the easy chair and hastily downing meals Ivy brought up on a tray.

His grandmother stopped in several times to offer sympathy and express concern. "I wish I could do something," she said helplessly, "but tending to the ill has never been my strong suit. I prefer to trust these things to nurses and physicians."

Kathryn slept almost the entire time and continued to be feverish and wracked by coughing fits. There were certain bodily functions which, for propriety's sake, he felt were best handled by his female staff. But he did everything else himself.

He followed all the doctor's instructions. He applied cool compresses to Kathryn's brow. When it was time for her medicine, and whenever she awoke and begged for water, Lance gently raised her head and fed her the requisite potion, pausing between sips to make sure she didn't choke.

On one such occasion, her eyes fluttered open and she said feverishly, "Where am I?"

"At St. Gabriel's Mount," he replied, offering her medicine on a spoon. "Swallow this, Kathryn."

She obediently swallowed, then murmured hazily, "What's wrong with me? Am I ill?"

"Yes, but you will get well," Lance insisted, gently laying her back upon the pillow.

She fell asleep so swiftly he wasn't sure she'd actually ever been awake.

Although she was oblivious to his presence, Lance read aloud to her from *Ivanhoe*—the chapters featuring Robin Hood, which she'd said were her favorites. He played violin concertos, and—although her eyes remained closed—he could swear a smile crossed her face. He talked to her, even though he knew she wasn't hearing a word he said, sharing stories from his days on board ship.

The doctor came twice. On each visit, he pronounced the patient no better, but thankfully no worse. The news did nothing to allay Lance's fears.

When dawn broke on the third morning, Lance was so exhausted he could barely stand. Kathryn was still no better. What if, despite all his protestations to the contrary, she were to perish from this illness? He couldn't bear it. But were that to happen, he was not the only person who would suffer.

He needed to tell her family.

Lance sent word via telegram to the Countess of Longford and the Countess of Saunders, informing them of their sister's illness, and requesting that they make haste to St. Gabriel's Mount.

Both women immediately replied by wire and arrived later that same afternoon with their maids, having traveled together from their Cornish estates.

Although Kathryn still slumbered on, her fever broke just hours before her sisters came, and the doctor pronounced the patient at last on the road to recovery. Lance was relieved to be able to greet the countesses with this news upon their arrival.

After spending an hour or so with Lance in Kathryn's room, quizzing him about their sister's state of health, and satisfying themselves that she was not at death's door, the newcomers turned to him with gratitude in their eyes.

"We cannot thank you enough for all you've done for our little sister," said Lady Longford.

"We are *eternally* grateful," agreed Lady Saunders, "and so glad you wired us, Your Grace."

"Please, call me Darcy."

With all three sisters in the same room, it was evident how much they resembled each other. All three were beautiful, with the same slender figures and peaches-and-cream complexions. Their most distinguishing feature was their hair color. Lady Saunders's was a lustrous brown. Lady Longford's was more reddish in tone. Both were a contrast to Kathryn's golden locks, which her sisters said were inherited from their father.

"Kathryn fell ill while working for me," Lance told them with chagrin. "Working too many hours, I might add. I blame myself for that."

"Please don't blame yourself," remarked Lady Saunders. "All her life, Kathryn has been prone to working compulsively at the expense of other pursuits, as well as her health."

"Once, when we were children and on holiday at the

beach, all the rest of us were swimming and picnicking," Lady Longford interjected, "but Kathryn was so focused on the sandcastle she was building she never stopped to go in the ocean or to eat."

"She kept working on that sandcastle all day long until the sun went down," Lady Saunders added.

"It must have been an impressive sandcastle." Lance felt himself wavering a bit on his feet, and realized he looked forward to sitting down.

"Oh, it was. But she got the most ferocious sunburn."

"And the next morning," Lady Saunders said, "when she saw that it had all been washed away by the tide, she cried her eyes out."

"Her first year at Vassar College, she went without sleep for three days straight in order to finish a paper for our History class."

"Her fever lasted a week that time. She was utterly done in."

"I see that *you*, my dear Darcy, are absolutely done in yourself," Lady Longford said pointedly.

"I am fine." Lance shrugged.

"How much sleep have you gotten the past two days?" she asked.

"Not much," he admitted. "I have rarely left this room."

"Well, we can take it from here," said Lady Saunders. "You must go to bed, Lord Darcy. We can't have you getting sick, too."

Although Lance maintained that he would rather not leave his patient's side, the sisters were adamant that he leave matters in their hands. Too spent to protest further, he gave in and took himself off to his own chamber, where he threw himself onto his bed fully clothed and fell instantly asleep.

"My my *my*," Lexie said.

"My my *my* is right," Maddie agreed.

Kathryn had awakened two days ago from what she learned had been a dangerous fever, to find her sisters sitting by her bedside. She'd been as shocked to discover she'd been ill as she had been by her sisters' presence.

Eventually, a few hazy memories of her bedridden days had surfaced. Kathryn vaguely recalled the duke feeding her medicine at one point. And that violin music had accompanied her feverish wanderings. She presumed the duke had been responsible for that, too. He had stopped by her room several times a day after she'd awakened to say hello and to make sure she was all right. The dowager duchess had come, too, expressing her wishes that Kathryn would soon be well.

This morning, Kathryn's cough almost gone and, feeling significantly better, she had at last been allowed to leave her bed.

She and her sisters were sitting in the conservatory, surrounded by tropical plants and flowers. Lexie and Maddie weren't looking at the plants, though. Nor did they seem to be interested in the sea view outside the windows.

Their blue eyes were focused exclusively on *her*. And huge, knowing smiles were plastered on their faces.

"Why on earth are you both looking at me like that?" Kathryn asked.

"How are we looking at you?" Lexie replied innocently, exchanging a glance with Maddie.

"As if you know some deep dark secret that's making you perversely happy."

"I have no idea what you mean," Maddie commented, a sly edge to her voice.

"Nor do I." The buttercup yellow silk of Lexie's frock rustled as she settled it about her legs.

"Then why do you both keep saying, 'My my my'? What's that about?"

"Well," Lexie said mischievously, "it's just that there's something . . . different about you from the last time we saw you."

"I should think so. I was sick. Apparently, very sick."

"I'm not talking about that."

"We've seen you sick plenty of times." Maddie leaned forward in her chair. "But you're on the mend now, and there's a sort of . . . *air* about you that we've never seen before."

"An *air*?" Kathryn repeated, puzzled.

Lexie nodded. "A distracted air."

"When we talk to you, your mind doesn't seem to be focused on the conversation," Maddie put in. "It's like you drift off somewhere else."

"You should understand that better than anyone, Maddie," Kathryn insisted. "When you're thinking about whatever book you're writing, your attention wanders all over the place and sometimes you appear almost comatose. In my case, I've probably been thinking about the architectural project I'm working on."

"I don't think it's that." Maddie toyed with the lace trimming on her blue skirt.

"When you drift off, you get this . . . *look* on your face," Lexie agreed.

"What kind of look?"

"A dreamy look," Maddie explained.

"A *very* dreamy look," Lexie agreed. "A look that nobody gets when they're thinking about *architecture*."

"It's the kind of look Lexie gets whenever Thomas walks in the room."

"The same look Maddie gets whenever Charles's name is even mentioned."

"Except in your case," Maddie told Kathryn, "we don't even have to mention the duke's name—you seem to be thinking about him all the time, anyway."

"The duke?" Kathryn suddenly felt hot under the collar of her silk dressing gown. "That's ridiculous. I don't think about the duke all the time." Which was a complete lie. "Especially in any way that would make me drift off dreamily." Another lie.

"Oh come now, you can't fool us, we're your sisters." Lexie gave her a direct look. "We've known you since the day you were born. It's perfectly obvious to us that you're head over heels in love with Lord Darcy."

"I am *not* in love with him!" Drat them for being so observant. But she *wasn't* in love with him. Was she? "I have simply been drawing up architectural plans for the man's castle."

"Then why do your cheeks go pink every time he walks into the room?" Maddie asked.

"Why do your eyes light up like the candles on a Christmas tree every time he speaks?" Lexie said.

"You hang on his every word."

"You look at him like you want to eat him up."

"I don't look at Lance that way!" Kathryn protested.

"Lance?" Lexie's eyebrows lifted knowingly. "So, you're on a first name basis with him now?"

"We already knew that," Maddie scoffed with a wave of her hand. "*He* calls you Kathryn."

Kathryn wanted to scream. "We just call each other that in private."

"*In private?*" her sisters echoed suggestively, in unison.

"You've kissed him, haven't you?" Excitement reigned in Maddie's voice.

"No!" Kathryn cried. Then, feeling guilty, she retracted the lie. "All right, we *have* kissed. A few times. And . . . more than kissed. But . . ."

"I told you!" Maddie gave Lexie a triumphant smile.

"Have you slept with him?" Lexie asked.

"No!" Kathryn insisted. *Although we've done almost everything but.* She wasn't quite ready to admit how close she and Lance had come to making love.

"But you've kissed," Lexie mused with delight, "and *more than kissed.* This is wonderful!"

"It's about time you found someone who's worthy of you," Maddie agreed.

"I haven't *found* anyone. I—"

"Oh, but you have, sister dear," Lexie cried with enthusiasm. "Whether you're ready to admit it or not, the Duke of Darcy is the man for you."

"He's absolutely gorgeous. And he's smart and kind and incredibly sweet."

"And caring and thoughtful. And clearly besotted with *you*."

Kathryn gasped and shook her head. "He is not *besotted* with me!"

"He is," Lexie retorted. "It's all over his face every time he looks at you. It's like you hung the moon."

"He took care of you all by himself for two days straight," Maddie pointed out. "What *man* would do that for anyone? Much less a *duke*?"

"A duke who's madly in love with our sister, that's who," Lexie agreed.

"But . . . no," Kathryn objected. "He can't be in love with me."

"He is," Maddie maintained. "And if we're reading the signals right, we think he's going to ask you to marry him."

"He already asked," Kathryn burst out without thinking,

"What?" Lexie and Maddie exclaimed at the same moment, staring at her.

Kathryn wanted to bite her tongue off. "Three days after I got here," she reluctantly confessed, "he called me into the drawing room and proposed."

Her sisters exchanged another look, signaling their surprise and delight.

"What did you say?" Lexie asked.

"I said no! I'm his architect! I had only known him three days!"

"He must *really* be smitten with you to propose so quickly," Maddie said, placing one hand dramatically to her chest.

Lexie's brow creased. "Unless . . . what is his financial status?"

"It's not about my money," Kathryn assured her. "He's made that perfectly clear. He's just a new duke who needs a wife, and I guess he . . . likes me."

"Well, then." Lexie smiled. "The only question is: what will you say when he asks again?"

"He won't ask. And if he does, I'll say no again."

"Why?" Maddie asked.

"Because he's a duke! His bride will be a duchess. Which is something I can never be."

"Yes, you could," Lexie insisted.

"No, I couldn't." Kathryn toyed distractedly with the silk belt of her dressing gown, her mind suddenly full of all the steamy interludes that she and Lance had shared. The way she'd melted every time he'd held her in his arms. If she married him, she'd share his bed for the rest of her life. And they could do . . . more of that. Much more.

But she couldn't marry him.

"He needs a wife," Kathryn went on, "who will be content to stay home and give him babies and run the castle and host events in the community. I am not that person! I have a career. And a duchess can't work outside the home. You *know* that. It just isn't done."

"We figured you'd say that," Lexie responded softly. "And we understand your situation, we truly do. You've worked so hard to get where you are."

"But, Kathryn," Maddie said, "it was unheard of for an English countess to write and publish novels until Charles broke the mold and allowed it. We've gotten to know Lord Darcy a bit. He seems to be a very forward-thinking man. Maybe you won't have to give up your career entirely. Maybe he won't mind if you design or renovate the occasional building."

"The occasional building? Do you hear what you're saying? I don't want to give up my career *at all*."

"We don't always get what we want, Kathryn," Lexie said. "You might have to give it up in any case. Have you considered that?"

"What do you mean?"

"Architecture is a man's world," Maddie contended. "As a single woman, no matter how brilliant you are or how hard you work, there's no guarantee you'll succeed. But if you were to marry a man as prominent as the Duke of Darcy, it would open so many doors."

"You'll have access to people at the top levels of society," Lexie agreed. "It may be unheard of *now* for a duchess to work, but you could be the one to change that. And trust me: being the wife of an English aristocrat—if he's a man you adore—is a *wonderful* life."

Kathryn heaved a sigh. "I know you're saying all this because you love me. And because you want me to experience the kind of happiness you both have found."

"Yes!" her sisters cried.

"But, Maddie: you write quietly at home. Lexie: you teach at the village school and take no remuneration for it. Your work meshes with your duties as wives and mothers and countesses. It'd be totally different for me. My job is in London. Even if I gave it up and took work occasionally, I'd have to travel to job sites and sometimes stay for weeks. I'd keep hours that are impossible for a wife and mother, not to mention a duchess."

"That's where you're wrong," Maddie instructed, shaking her head. "Have you learned nothing this week, Kathryn?"

"No one should work such long hours," Lexie told her. "It's unhealthy. You need to find balance in your life. Make time for yourself and for the people you care about. Otherwise—"

"Ladies?"

The duke strolled into the room. Kathryn's heart stood still as she took in his tall, lanky frame and handsome face. He was carrying a large potted orchid covered in exquisite purple blooms. Taking in the scene before him with a warm smile, he added:

"I hope I am not interrupting?"

CHAPTER EIGHTEEN

Lance glanced at Kathryn and her sisters, aware of a silent discord permeating the room. "I *have* interrupted something, haven't I?"

"We were just talking about . . . architecture," Kathryn responded.

"Well, that is something you know a great deal about." Studying her, he added, "You are looking better today."

"I feel better, thank you. And thank you again for taking care of me the way you did. It went far beyond the bounds of duty. I will be forever grateful."

"It was hardly a duty, Kathryn. It was my pleasure. You had us all worried there for a while." He held up the orchid plant he was carrying. "I recall you saying that you don't like cut flowers, so I sent for something . . . potted. I hope this will add a bit of cheer to your day."

"Thank you." Kathryn smiled up at him, her face glowing, "It's beautiful. I love it."

As Lance set the potted plant on a small table beside her, he noticed the countesses squirming in their seats. He also noted the covert glances that both women directed toward their younger sister, as if saying, *I told you so.* He wondered what that was about.

"And now," he went on, turning his attention back to Kathryn, "related to that topic: I have come to tell you that I've decided to cancel the Children's Fête."

"What?" Kathryn stared up at him in obvious dismay. "Why are you canceling it?"

"I think it best. I know you've put in a great deal of effort in planning the affair—"

"We planned it *together*," she interrupted.

"Yes, which makes me aware of how much additional effort will be required to actually host the thing. I do not feel qualified to run a fête for a hundred children on my own. In view of your illness, I cannot possibly allow you to take it on yourself."

"But the fête has been advertised for months," Kathryn pointed out. "I'm told the children are so looking forward to it. By now all the food must have been ordered, and Mrs. Penberthy has made a hundred pinwheels. You can't cancel because of me."

"You have not fully recovered your strength," Lance insisted. "Even if you had, I won't take the risk. Such an endeavor might occasion a relapse."

"When is the fête supposed to take palace?" asked Alexandra.

"Monday," Lance replied.

"That's only three days away. I'd be happy to stay and

help," she offered. "Thomas will understand. I can have the nanny bring Tommy down for the day. He's five years old now, the ideal age to enjoy such festivities."

"I think Emily is too young for a fête," Madeleine mused, "but I can stay, too. The three of us can run it together. Four, if you are willing to assist, Lord Darcy."

Kathryn clasped her hands together with apparent joy. "Oh! Thank you, that would be wonderful."

Lance hesitated. "That is a generous offer, ladies. But are you certain?"

"Absolutely," Alexandra answered.

"We were quite the team when we ran the children's fairs at our church back in Poughkeepsie," Madeleine claimed.

"This will be so much fun," Kathryn declared.

They looked so enthusiastic Lance couldn't help but laugh.

Everyone said it was the best Children's Fête that St. Gabriel's Mount had ever seen.

Although there hadn't been a fête for decades, many members of the community had long memories. Some recalled bringing their children to a fête or attending one as children themselves. This year's event, they declared, eclipsed them all.

The day dawned bright and beautiful with nary a cloud in the sky. Kathryn regained her strength just in time to play her part. She and her sisters had a wonderful time playing hosts, with Lance assisting every step of the way. After a busy morning setting everything up with the help of the servants and volunteers from the village, the festivities began with a bang at twelve noon, low tide making it possible for the residents of Rosquay to walk across the causeway.

As anticipated, more than a hundred children, most with their parents in tow, descended bright-eyed and bushy-tailed at the wide grassy area at the base of the Mount, where tables were laden with cakes, biscuits, lemonade, and punch. A multitude of game stations had been set up, including such favorites as ring toss, horseshoes, lawn bowling, and beanbag throw. Kathryn and her sisters also introduced a new American game to the British crowd, pin the tail on the donkey, which proved to be a great success.

A strolling balloon artist created animals and a conjurer entertained the children under a canopy, followed by a Punch and Judy puppet show which had the youngsters laughing into stitches.

The lawn games were the crowning glory of the day, with much screaming of encouragement from parents and friends who watched from the sidelines.

As the three-legged race was about to start, Kathryn noticed a small boy hovering uncertainly, despondent because he didn't have a partner.

Lance strode up to the youngster and offered to be his partner. The boy's eyes lit with delight. Kathryn's heart caught as she watched Lance tie the calf of his long, lean leg to the boy's much shorter one, and then scramble with him to the finish line, earning a blue ribbon.

The winners of each event held on to their ribbons as though they were made of gold. The small prizes Kathryn and the duke had selected for the games were well-received. And the pinwheels, much to Mrs. Penberthy's credit, were a hit. When the colorful toys were distributed at the end of the afternoon, the children ran off with glee, watching them whirl round and round.

Kathryn gave a sigh of contentment as the crowd began to depart. Some drifted back to their homes in the neighboring village, others made for the harbor where an army of small boats had gathered to return the visitors across the water to Rosquay. "That went marvelously well, I thought."

"It couldn't have gone better," agreed the dowager duchess, smiling as she leaned upon her cane. "You all outdid yourselves."

Maddie wiped her brow with the back of her hand, taking in the bright blue sea lapping at the nearby shore. "It was great fun. And what a spectacular setting for a fête."

"Tommy loved every minute of it." Lexie lifted up her golden-haired son and hugged him. "Didn't you, sweet pea?"

"I got a whirligig!" cried Tommy exuberantly, squirming until his mother let him down so he could race away with delight.

"You ladies were like human dynamos," Lance pronounced, pausing to direct a servant to pack up the pins from the lawn bowling set. "I don't believe any of you have ever stopped moving since dawn. You have earned my eternal gratitude. And a well-deserved rest."

The duke put his footman in charge of the remainder of the cleanup duties. Insisting that Kathryn, her sisters, and his grandmother return to the castle and put their feet up, he arranged for a carriage to transport them up the hill. Kathryn was only too happy to accept a ride. Her sisters said they preferred to walk.

As Lexie and Maddie began their ascent to the castle, Kathryn paused to observe Lance conversing with the lad with whom he'd run the three-legged race. The happiness on both their faces was a joy to behold.

"He is a good man, my grandson."

Kathryn turned to find the dowager duchess standing beside her, watching as the duke shook hands with the boy, then sent him off to his waiting parents with a kind smile.

"He is, indeed," Kathryn acknowledged.

"He will make a good father. And a good husband to the right woman. For all that he had his heart broken at such a young age."

Kathryn eyed the duchess curiously. On the day Lance proposed, she'd suspected that he might have offered for a woman's hand before, but hadn't known for certain that he'd suffered heartbreak.

The carriage rolled up at that moment, and Kathryn and the dowager duchess took their seats. As it rumbled off along the cobblestones, Kathryn said, "I didn't realize the duke had ever been in love."

"Oh yes," the duchess told Kathryn in a confidential tone. "As a young man, just twenty years of age, Lance fell head over heels in love with a girl he met on leave in Portsmouth. Her name was Beatrice. Her father owned a small shop. Lance asked her to marry him and she said yes."

"What happened?"

"He couldn't afford to marry on a midshipman's pay, and

his brother refused to raise his allowance. So Lance invested what little money he had in what turned out to be a risky venture. He lost every penny. When Beatrice found out, she broke off their engagement and refused to speak to him again. She said she couldn't marry a man who couldn't manage his money."

"Oh, that's horrible."

"He has suffered so much. First, in losing his parents at such a young age. Then he lost the woman he adored. Now he has lost his only brother. I have often wondered if, in his mind, love has become so entangled with loss that he is afraid to commit his heart."

"If that's true, it's a great shame."

The duchess turned her pale blue gaze on Kathryn. "I hope you will not subject yourself to the same fate, Miss Atherton."

"Me? What do you mean?"

"Forgive me for speaking candidly. At my age, I feel it my duty to share what I have seen and learned with those younger than myself. And what I think, Miss Atherton, is that you have the same fear of commitment as my grandson."

"I'm not afraid of commitment," Kathryn bristled.

"Perhaps not, my dear, when it comes to your career. And may I say, I applaud all that you have achieved in that corner of your life. Yet I get the feeling that you *are* afraid of something quite different: that if you give your heart to a man, you might lose yourself."

The observation hit so close to home Kathryn found herself at first unable to reply. Finally, she said, "I suppose that is true, Your Grace. It is yet another reason why I am determined to never marry."

"Never say *never*," the dowager duchess replied. "Where there is a will, there is a way." In a thoughtful tone, she added, "I cannot help but hope that in this modern world of ours, it will one day be possible to be both a professional woman *and* a wife."

The next afternoon, Kathryn found herself and Lance standing on the dock at St. Gabriel's Mount's harbor, saying goodbye to her sisters and Lexie's son, Tommy.

"Thank you so much for coming," Lance said, "and for all your help during your sister's illness and with the fête."

"Thank *you* for reaching out to us," Lexie replied. "Our sister means the world to us."

"So I noticed," he returned with a smile.

"I hope we will not be strangers going forward, Lord Darcy," Lexie added. "Thomas and I would love to have you visit us at Polperran House."

"Charles and I would be delighted to welcome you to our home as well," Maddie told him. "Anytime."

"Kind invitations, thank you." Lance extended a hand to little Tommy. "It was a pleasure to meet you, young man."

"And you as well, Your Grace," Tommy replied, returning the handshake with all the grace of a well-trained future earl.

Tears started in Kathryn's eyes as she gave Tommy an affectionate squeeze, and then hugged both of her sisters in turn, admitting how much she was going to miss them.

"*Marry him,*" Maddie whispered in Kathryn's ear.

"Follow your *heart*, not your head," Lexie hissed in a low tone.

A tearful laugh bubbled up from Kathryn's throat as her family climbed into the small boat and it sailed off toward the mainland.

Follow your heart, not your head. It was the opposite of the advice one usually gave.

And it wouldn't be easy advice to follow. Since Kathryn didn't have a clue what her heart really wanted anymore.

L ance leaned on the edge of the wall on the upper terrace, gazing out at the expanse of dark blue sea. The light of a full moon danced on the water like a spray of sparkling diamonds. Waves crashed in a lulling ebb and flow against the beach and rocky cliffs below.

He had always thought these to be delightful sights and soothing sounds. Tonight, they brought him no joy.

Nervous energy infused his body. It had been eleven days since he and Kathryn had spent any quality time alone together. It had felt like the longest eleven days of his life. Since the moment he'd walked into that parlor intending to bare his soul, she'd either been deathly ill or sequestered with her sisters or surrounded by crowds of people.

Yesterday, she'd worked so tirelessly at the fête. No matter where he'd been or what he'd been doing, he'd found himself seeking a glimpse of her. Feasting on the vision of her slender form in her white summer gown, her blond hair curling about her face beneath her flowered bonnet. He hadn't been able to take his eyes off of her as she'd whisked from one task to another, so sweet and charming with the children, managing everything with such capable efficiency.

It was as if she'd been born to the task. Born to be a duchess. *His* duchess.

He craved a private moment with her. To bring up the subject that was foremost on his mind. But she'd spent all afternoon in her parlor making final touches to her drawings. They had dined with his grandmother, after which, to his disappointment, Kathryn had pronounced herself tired and retreated up to her room.

He'd agreed to meet with her in the morning for one final discussion about the work she'd been hired to do. For all he knew, she might be planning to return to London tomorrow. Which meant this might be her last night at the Mount.

The idea of her leaving, of never seeing her again, pierced his chest with a pain so searing he almost choked.

He should have found a way to get her alone earlier that day. Somewhere, anywhere—he should have thrown caution to the wind and gotten down on one knee and asked for her hand. Taken the risk.

Only one day left. He was running out of time.

Kathryn moved to her bedroom window, intending to shut the drapes, when she caught sight of a lone figure on the terrace below.

Lance.

Although she couldn't see his expression from this distance, the sight of him standing there all by himself, leaning against that wall, his head hung low, gave her pause. He looked so . . . sad. And frustrated. And lonely.

The same way that she was feeling.

He straightened suddenly, then headed across the flagstones on his way back to the castle. It was late, almost eleven o'clock. He was probably heading for his rooms to turn in for the night.

Kathryn had retreated upstairs with the same intention. But seeing him like that, so vexed and dejected, made her heart hurt. Was it possible that he'd been thinking about her? Missing being with her, just as she missed being with him?

She closed the drapes and wandered idly in her chamber, lost in thought.

Follow your heart, not your head, Lexie had said.

Kathryn's head was telling her to be smart. Be sane and pragmatic. She had a plan for herself. She needed to go back to London. Back to her job.

Back to your lonely little life.

Where had *that* thought come from?

Kathryn had never considered herself lonely before. Or thought of her life as *little*. Her work was not just her pride; it gave her deep, primal joy. It fulfilled the creative yearnings that danced in her soul. She had been alone for years, but she'd never been lonely. Had she?

Maybe she hadn't *realized* she'd been lonely . . . until she met Lance.

And fell in love with him.

The truth hurtled into Kathryn's mind with the strength

of a thunderbolt, piercing through the armor she'd so carefully built around herself.

I do love him. She couldn't help but gasp as the newfound knowledge rang within her with the clarity of a bell. She had been falling in love with Lance ever since the first day she arrived at St. Gabriel's Mount.

He was an extraordinary man. He was the kind of man who would nurse a sick woman for two days and nights, and bring her potted orchids because she disliked cut flowers. The kind of man who cared about his tenants and the needs of his community, who treated children to festivals and ran three-legged races with a partner-less boy.

He was the kind of man who had earned her deepest admiration and respect.

And her love.

How did Lance feel about her? He certainly hadn't loved her when he'd proposed. But a lot had happened since then. They had grown closer every day as they'd opened up to each other and become more . . . involved. After they'd left the secret room, he had started to say something, but she had cut him off. Not ready to hear it.

He is clearly besotted with you. It's all over his face every time he looks at you. It's like you hung the moon.

Were her sisters right? Was Lance in love with her as well? He had never said the words, but that didn't mean it wasn't possible.

Marry him, Maddie had insisted. Could she marry the Duke of Darcy?

For a moment, Kathryn indulged the notion. Imagined

herself as his wife. Living out the rest of her days here at St. Gabriel's Mount. Raising a family together. Their children would be as good-looking, vivacious, and intelligent as their father—forces to be reckoned with. Lance would make a wonderful companion. And an incredible lover.

It was a tempting scenario. More than tempting. Part of her craved it, more deeply than she could have ever anticipated.

A rush of melancholy quickly followed. There was still no answer to the conundrum that stood between them. Kathryn had chosen her life with her eyes wide open. She still wanted that life.

But, she thought. Maybe, just maybe, it was possible to follow *both* one's head and one's heart at the same time. At least for one night.

She'd been fighting for weeks to retain a professional distance from the duke, a battle she had lost several times. But other than the presentation she intended to give in the morning, she had finished her job here. Which meant that, technically, she wasn't his employee anymore.

She'd be leaving soon. Tomorrow, perhaps. But that didn't mean she had to leave without experiencing one last night of pleasure with the man she loved. Discovering the rapture that she knew would follow if she gave in to the desperate longing for *him* that was invading every pore of her body.

One last taste of him, that's all she could allow herself. One last memory to carry with her forever.

Was it fair to him, though? If Lance truly loved her, was it wrong to offer herself to him on such terms?

There was only one way to find out.

CHAPTER NINETEEN

Lance lay in bed, staring at the ceiling.

The moon was so beautiful he'd left the curtains open. Now, he wondered if that had been a mistake. The bright light beaming in through the mullioned windows cast an intriguing pattern on the carpets. But it was keeping him awake.

Not that he would have been able to sleep tonight, anyway.

His thoughts were too full of Kathryn for any hope of slumber. The scintillating conversations they had shared over the past few weeks played over and over in his mind. He kept seeing the spark in her eyes that had enlivened every reveal of whatever drawing she'd been working on, recalling the laughter they had shared over their many games of cards. Lance had never enjoyed the company of a woman more, or so completely.

Another image invaded his mind: the last time he'd held her in his arms. In his brother's secret room. The way she had called out in ecstasy as he'd brought her to climax. The memory tightened his gut and made him grow hard. Oh, how he wanted her. Now, this instant. If only . . .

A light rap sounded at his bedroom door. Lance frowned in annoyance. Who could it be at this hour? One of the servants, no doubt. What problem required his attention now?

He got out of bed. "A moment," he barked, slipping into his dressing gown and tightening the belt around his waist. He answered the door, expecting Hammett or Woodston. "Yes?"

To his shock, Kathryn stood before him. She wore a sleeveless white nightgown. And nothing else. Her long golden locks curled softly around her shoulders. She didn't say a word, just stood there, gazing at him.

For a moment, Lance was too dumbfounded to move or speak. His cock, however, had other ideas. Already hard just from thinking about her, it leapt to even more prominent life at the sight of her.

Her nightgown clung to her upper body, accentuating the curves of her breasts, which rose and fell erratically with her every breath. The points of her nipples were visible through the thin fabric. Her lips were parted slightly and her eyes, as they bore into his, held a tentative yet heated look. A look that silently telegraphed her uncertainty, just as it told him exactly what she was doing here. And what she wanted.

The same thing that *he* wanted. And had been wanting for weeks.

Lance took hold of her wrist and pulled her into the room, then slammed the door behind them.

In another swift movement, he backed her up against the door, took her in his arms, and kissed her. Instantly, she was kissing him back. The feel of her mouth on his sent a volley of fire racing through his veins.

He kissed her hard, his tongue parting the seam of her lips, invading and tangling with her own tongue. She tasted like warm, sweet heaven. Like silk and a prayer.

He kissed her and kissed her, venting the depth of the desire that had been consuming him for weeks. She met him kiss for kiss, wordlessly communicating a similar need and desire. A moan escaped her throat. He'd never heard a more arousing sound. An answering groan issued from somewhere deep within him.

Her arms wrapped up around his neck, pulling him even closer until his body was so tight against hers he could feel every inhalation she took, feel the heat of her through the thin layer of clothing that separated them.

Breaking the kiss, he whispered huskily against her mouth, "Are you really here? Or is this a dream?"

"I'm really here," she replied, her breath fanning his lips, her eyes lifting, a bit shyly now, to meet his. "I wasn't sure if I should . . . wasn't sure if you'd want to . . ."

"Oh, I want to," Lance assured her. His cock was trapped between them, pressing against her belly. He moved slightly, reminding her of its presence. "*Feel* how much I want to." Cradling her face in one hand, he added, "For weeks, I have longed for this. For *you*. I have thought of nothing but you."

"It's been the same for me." She paused, then whispered: "Do you have . . . protection?"

A practical question. It made him smile. He admired her for asking. And being so up front about it. "I do."

"Good." Her face, bathed in a swash of moonlight, was angelic in its beauty.

He kissed her again, long and hard and deep, until they were both panting for breath. Running one hand up and down the side of her body, he smoothed his fingers over the tantalizing curve of one breast, the most delectable thing he had ever felt. Grabbing hold of her nightgown with both hands, he huskily commanded, "Take this off."

She complied, helping him raise the garment over her head and letting it drop to the floor, until she stood in perfect nudity before him.

He took a sharp, uneven breath, drinking her in. Her skin was almost luminescent in the moonlight's glow. Her breasts were round and succulent, begging for his touch. The golden thatch at the apex of her shapely thighs was like a beacon, calling him home.

His blood ran hot and wild. "You are so beautiful," he managed. His voice was so low and deep it didn't sound like his own.

Lance made short work of his robe and smalls, kicking them aside. Then he took her in his arms again, one hand cupping her naked breast, the other holding him against her as his mouth claimed hers.

"You undo me, Kathryn," he whispered in between kisses. "I want you so much."

"I want you, too," she echoed, her breath coming in unsteady gasps. "But, Lance . . . if we do this—"

"Hush," Lance commanded, gazing down into her eyes. "There is no *if*, Kathryn. Not anymore." With that, he swept her up into his arms and carried her to his bed.

Kathryn had imagined this so many times it was hard to believe it was actually happening. That she and Lance were naked, in his bed, and his hands and mouth were everywhere.

He was kissing her as if he couldn't get enough of her. She was kissing him back with equal abandon. Their bodies were wrapped in an embrace so tight it was impossible to know where she began and he ended. She clung to him, flesh against flesh, reveling in the taste and feel of him.

She loved the smooth slope of his back, the slight indentation at his waist, the way the curve of his buttocks felt under her palm.

She loved running her hands along the angles of his face and jaw, loved his stubble of beard. She loved the soft pliancy of his lips and the way they parted beneath her fingertips. She loved the way he grabbed her hand and captured each finger in his mouth, sucking on one after the other, as if they were lollipops.

She loved threading her fingers through his short dark hair. She loved how it felt when his fingers tangled through her own hair as he brought her head closer for yet another kiss.

He was making love to her breast now. He lapped at one

nipple, his tongue circling the areola as if it were the most delicious thing he'd ever tasted, a sensation that sent titillating electric shocks shooting through her entire body.

Moving to her other breast, he drew the entire crest into his mouth and suckled it. Kathryn gasped. Deep in her feminine core, she grew hot and wet with need.

"Lance . . ." she murmured. In the back of her mind, she was hazily aware that there was something she was supposed to say. Something she had to make him understand. But she couldn't remember what it was. Her mind was reeling, lost in the pleasure of what he was doing to her and how it felt.

He left her breasts and imprinted her abdomen with soft, damp kisses as he made his way lower still. Kathryn took a shaky breath. She had an idea of what might be coming next. She had heard about it, had never been quite certain she believed it.

Sure enough, he was parting her legs with his hands as he settled his body into the space between them, his mouth pausing directly at the juncture of her thighs.

"Lance . . . ?" she breathed again, a question this time.

"Have you never experienced *this*, my darling?" His voice was low and sultry as he licked at her most private of places.

She gasped and nearly leapt off the bed. All she could do was to shake her head.

A soft, wolfish chuckle reached her ears. "Prepare yourself to be delighted."

His tongue began flicking against the folds of her womanhood. A ragged breath escaped her. *Dear God. It felt amazing.*

He kept up the attention with increasing pressure and rapidity. Kathryn writhed on the bed. This was so different from the time he had pleasured her there with his hand, or what it felt like when she pleasured herself. This was warm and wet and molten, the moisture from his mouth and tongue heightening the sensations that were building deep inside her.

Her thighs began to quiver as if an earthquake were rocking them at their very foundations. Her womb tightened and her entire body tensed.

Kathryn heard low, ecstatic moans, followed by sharper, more staccato exclamations, and was only vaguely aware that they were issuing from her own throat. Her breathing grew faster and faster until she was panting.

A crescendo rose within her, demanding release. And then suddenly her back was arching off the bed, a thousand cymbals were crashing in her head, and she was leaping off a peak, breaking apart into tiny fragments of light and sound and air.

It took a long, lazy moment for Kathryn to return to earth. She lay there, as if wrapped in golden gauze, waiting for her breathing to slow and her wits to recover.

Lance gently nuzzled her thighs and kissed his way back up to her abdomen. Sliding his body up over hers, he lay on top of her, cradling himself between her legs with his erect staff wedged between them.

"You," he murmured, "are the most stunning thing I have ever seen." The look in his eyes was filled with tender, unguarded affection.

Kathryn's heart twisted. "I like you, too." She wanted to

say so much more. She wanted to say, *I love you.* But that would only complicate things.

Now that she had come down from the heights of ecstasy and could think again, Kathryn remembered what it was she'd wanted to ask him. She'd wanted to make sure he was okay with making love to her, knowing that it would be this one time, and one time only. That she still couldn't be his wife.

It was a little late to bring *that* up now, though. They were naked and sweaty and they had already *been* making love since the moment he'd pulled her into his room with that hungry look in his eyes.

The full act had yet to be completed. She wasn't about to deny him that—or deny herself for that matter. It was what she'd come here for. He was aching for it—that was physically obvious. The hard length of his manhood was pressing like a hot promise against the folds of her womanhood.

But there were so many things she was still curious about. So many things she wanted to experience. And she wanted to experience them with him.

"Before we finish this, though," Kathryn added, nudging him with her hand in a silent request to move off of her, "I want to . . . *explore* a little more."

"Do you now." He grinned and immediately obliged, sliding off and stretching out beside her on the bed. "What kind of exploring did you have in mind?"

Kathryn boldly reached down and took his erection in her hand. To her delight, his staff twitched in her grasp like a sentient being. It was rock hard, and the short, surprised gasp he emitted was extremely gratifying.

He placed one hand over hers, then silently demonstrated the motion he craved. Under his guidance, Kathryn moved her hand up and down, excited by the way his breath caught as his own excitement built.

As she continued the motion, his blue eyes bored into hers, glittering darkly, conveying a wealth of emotions—from desire and need to a seemingly desperate struggle to maintain control.

His Adam's apple moved as he swallowed, took a breath, and finally stopped her hand. "I want to be inside you." His voice was rough.

"I want that, too. But not yet."

He darted her an inquiring glance. "More exploring?"

She nodded, a slow smile parting her lips. Then, bending down over that stunning male appendage, she ran her tongue over its erect tip.

Yet another thing she had read about. And had always wanted to try.

He gave another gasp.

Holding him in her hand, Kathryn swirled her tongue around him, fascinated by the way his member moved in response. Then she took him into her mouth, giving him the same attention he'd given her fingers earlier, treating him as if he were *her* own personal lollipop.

From the sounds he was making, Kathryn guessed that he liked what she was doing.

She loved the feel of him, loved the sound of his altered breathing, the way his hands clutched her head as if to hold it there in some silent plea to continue.

Then he stopped her again. "I can't hold out much longer," he admitted gruffly.

He reached into the drawer of his bedside table and retrieved a small paper envelope. Kathryn recognized it: it was the packaging for a French letter.

As he slid the condom over his shaft, Kathryn watched, captivated, and grateful that he was prepared. At the same time, for some perverse reason, it also prickled a bit. Was it common practice for dukes and former sea captains to keep sheaths in their bedside tables for all the women they made love to?

She pushed the thought from her mind. He was thirty-two years old, and his sexual history was none of her business. She was just here for one night of pleasure, after all, and she was lucky that no unexpected repercussions would ensue from their coupling.

He stretched out beside her again, half covering her body as he captured her mouth in his, returning his hand to her feminine folds that were still moist from his attentions. Soon, she was aching again with need. She moaned, and so did he, and he nestled between her thighs and poised himself at her entry.

"I'll try to be gentle," he murmured.

And he was. He entered her slowly, an inch at a time, as if aware that it might have been a long time since her last experience. "Are you all right?"

She nodded. It hurt, but not as much as she remembered. When he pressed in farther, she gripped his buttocks, urging him on. She was in no mood for stopping. He slid fully into her and she welcomed the friction. Soon, pain turned into pleasure. Their bodies were one, moving in unison like a machine.

It was wondrous. It was heaven.

And there was one more thing she wanted to try.

"Roll over," she said.

"Hmmm?"

"I want to be on top."

He paused, then let out another low chuckle. "As my lady commands." Wrapping one arm tightly around her, the other gripping her derrière, he rolled them over, keeping their bodies joined together until he lay flat on his back.

"That was a neat trick," she said, smiling.

Kathryn slid her knees up and adjusted her hips, raising herself on both hands until she was straddling him, all the while reveling in the feel of him still nestled deep inside her.

He raised himself up slightly, too, shoving two pillows behind his head and upper back before settling back against them. She quickly understood why. At this new angle, her breasts were just inches from his mouth.

"Ride me," he invited.

"That was my plan." As she began to move on top of him, Kathryn found her own tempo, which seemed to meld perfectly with his.

He held on to her waist with both hands. Taking one of her breasts in his mouth, he suckled it again with obvious pleasure. As she rode him, faster and faster, she heard him breathing harder and faster, matching her own rapid rate of respiration.

"I adore you, my darling," he whispered against her breast.

My darling. No one had ever called her that before. She loved the sound of it. "I adore you," she whispered, overwhelmed by the thrill of their union, as every sense in her body built once more to the ever-closer brink of rapture.

As she hurtled over the edge again, sparks filling her universe, she heard him cry out, felt his spasms within her as his own ecstasy overtook him.

This, Lance thought, must be what heaven was like.

Kathryn was lying in his arms. They had both fallen asleep after their epic encounter. Lance relished the feeling of her head pillowed against his shoulder and the gentle rise and fall of her chest as she slumbered.

Their lovemaking had been everything he'd imagined it would be—no, if he were honest, it had been far *beyond* anything he could have imagined. This woman was incredible. She knew what she wanted and she had boldly gone after it. He had been only too happy to be the recipient of her desires.

With closed eyes he tilted his head slightly downward, kissing her soft golden tresses as one hand relished the slender curves of her back.

Oh, how I love her.

The words leapt into Lance's mind with the force of a typhoon, taking him by complete surprise. The phrase repeated itself with the same vehement force:

Oh, how I love her.

Dear Lord, was it true? How had that happened?

Lance had promised himself he would never love again. That love only brought pain.

And yet, from the moment he'd first set eyes on Kathryn, he had felt a powerful attraction to her. In the days that followed, as they'd gotten to know each other, that attraction had slowly but surely grown into something very real and deep and profound.

He had already known for a while that he didn't want Kathryn Atherton as his wife just because he needed her fortune. That he wanted her because he liked and admired *her*. But he hadn't realized that he also *needed* her. That he couldn't imagine life without her.

Because he loved her with all his heart.

Lance's pulse began thundering so loudly in his chest he feared it might wake her.

Did she love him back?

Kathryn had just given herself to him freely, without asking anything in return. But he believed he had seen the workings of her heart in her eyes. Had heard it in her moans. Had felt it with every kiss, every touch of her hands and lips.

She did love him. He *knew* it.

Now, he thought, his pulse still racing. He should ask her to marry him now. If she loved him, she'd be open to his new ideas about how to make it work between them. And she'd say yes.

It was an unconventional moment to propose, perhaps—not the romantic setting he had envisioned. But on the other hand, it could not be more appropriate. She was lying naked beside him. And he wanted her naked in his bed where he could make love to her every single night for the rest of their lives.

A tiny voice piped up in the back of his head: *You haven't told her you need her fortune.*

Lance's gut tensed. How could he bring up his money problems now? They didn't have a stitch of clothing on and had just made mad, passionate love. This was hardly the time for a discussion about finances.

That discussion would have to come later. In the morning. When they were fully dressed and he could take her, hand in hand, to his favorite bench overlooking the sea. He would sit her down and pour out his heart and explain it all.

Now he would pour his heart out about a very different matter. And he would make this woman his.

CHAPTER TWENTY

Kathryn wanted to memorize this moment. To remember every single thing about it.

The way her cheek rested upon Lance's shoulder. The way his naked body felt against hers. The way his chest hair tickled her chin. The sound of his breathing. The moisture on his skin. A liquid, molten substance that had mingled from two bodies into one, as if binding them together.

The way their lovemaking had bound them together just an hour or two ago.

She would take the memory of this moment with her when she left. Something to look back on all the rest of her days.

Lance moved beneath her. So he was awake, too. Rolling to his side, he turned her in his arms to face her, his head resting on the next pillow, half a foot away. His eyes blinked open.

"Kathryn," he said softly. "Will you marry me?"

She stared at him, panic rising in her throat. Why was

he asking her this again? And why now? "Lance. I've already given you my answer."

"I was hoping you would give me a different answer this time."

"You know I can't." Kathryn sighed. "If you were expecting that just because we made love, I would give up everything to marry you . . ."

"I expect nothing of the kind." He caressed her cheek with the back of one hand. "Correct me if I'm wrong—but as much as you love your career, I think you care about me as well. Don't you?"

Kathryn swallowed hard. "Yes, I do care about you."

He gently brushed a lock of hair off her forehead. "I care about you, too. I love you, Kathryn."

He was gazing at her with a look that could only be described as adoring. Kathryn's heart turned over. *He loved her? Dear God, he loved her?* "I love you, too, Lance," she admitted, which brought a gratified smile to his lips. "But—"

"If you could continue in the profession you love," he interrupted, "would you marry me?"

The question stymied her. "I . . . suppose I might," she conceded. "But—"

"Then I'm sure we can work something out."

"How? Duchesses can't be architects."

"Why not?"

She couldn't believe he was asking *her* this. "Because, I don't know, it's against some long-written rule. You said so yourself. What I do is considered trade. People would frown upon it."

"Let them frown."

"Are you serious?"

He nodded. "You may have turned me down once, but I couldn't give up. Kathryn: you're the only woman I can imagine myself married to. I want to spend the rest of my life with you, raise a family with you. If the only way you'll have me is to share me with your career, then so be it."

Kathryn could hardly believe he was saying these things. "How would it work? My job is in London."

"Then we'll live in London part of the year."

"Do you mean it?"

"St. Gabriel's Mount is home, but we don't have to reside here every minute. I have a house in town for a reason. When you need to be in town, we shall go to town. Hopefully, you can bring work back here sometimes. When you need to do architecture-y things, you'll do them. That is not to say, however, that you won't do *duchess-y* things as well." As he spoke, his hand slid down to cup her breast, then began to roll her nipple between his thumb and fingertips.

"Oh?" Kathryn replied breathlessly, her blood stirring again. "And what . . . *duchess-y* things would those be?"

"I need an heir. And a spare or two would be nice." His voice was husky. "I will *definitely* need your assistance with that."

She couldn't suppress a little laugh. Was this possible? Could it really work out, after all? Had he really just said *I love you?*

"We will have nannies and governesses to help with the children," Lance went on, "and a staff to run the castle.

The community will only need your attention from time to time. If you wish to take on architectural projects, *if* you can manage it without making yourself sick again, then I have nothing against it."

"But . . . what will people think?"

"I don't care what people think. I'm the Duke of Darcy. I haven't been a duke very long, but from what I've seen, whatever a duke says, goes. If I say that my wife can work, and by God I will say it, then the world will just have to accept that."

It was music to Kathryn's ears.

She had vowed to never marry. But that vow had been made long before she met and fell in love with the Duke of Darcy.

And before he fell in love with her.

"Say yes, my lady," Lance commanded, leaning in close and touching his nose affectionately against hers. "Say yes, and do me the honor of becoming my wife."

"Yes," Kathryn answered, her heart soaring. "Yes! I will."

A beaming smile took over his face. He kissed her.

And then his roving hands started doing indescribable things to her again. With a deep sigh, Kathryn melted into his embrace, blinded by joy, her senses reeling with the promise of a future that seemed too perfect to be true.

Lance rose to consciousness from the fog of sleep, aware that his bedchamber was filled with morning light.

He stretched luxuriously, recalling the events of the night before.

The lovemaking that had gone on until dawn.

Kathryn had been a revelation, each encounter better and more satisfying than the last. It was no wonder he was still so tired. If he'd gotten two hours of sleep, he was lucky.

He was lucky for another reason—the luckiest bastard in the world, in fact. Kathryn had consented to be his wife! Joy shot through him, permeating his every pore.

He reached for his partner, only to find the other side of the bed empty. He sat up. Where had she gone? And why?

His eyes took in a small square of paper lying upon her pillow. He snatched it up. A message had been scrawled across it in pencil:

> *I thought it best for propriety's sake that I return to my own bed. Didn't want to wake you.*

Below that, a simple heart had been drawn.

Lance smiled to himself. He supposed it was better that she *had* gone. Stolen away before the maid arrived with his morning tray. No one else knew that they were engaged to be married. Even when that fact was made public, he didn't want word to get out that they'd slept together before their nuptials.

He wanted everything to be proper and aboveboard from this moment on.

Which reminded him: although she had accepted his hand, there was still something they needed to discuss. As soon as possible.

When he'd finished his morning ablutions and was

dressed and ready to meet the day, Lance was about to ask Woodston if he knew where Miss Atherton was, when Mrs. Morgan knocked and announced that his solicitor was waiting for him downstairs.

Lance cursed aloud. Why had he agreed to meet with Megowan this morning, of all times? But then, he thought as he hastened down to his study, maybe the timing was fortuitous. He had good news to share, after all.

His talk with Kathryn would just have to wait a bit longer.

Kathryn hummed as she tucked her blouse into her lavender linen skirt.

Her mind was full of all that had happened the night before. The hours she had spent in Lance's arms felt so magical and unreal it almost seemed as if she had dreamt it all.

Was she, in fact, truly engaged to marry the Duke of Darcy? Had he truly said he loved her? And given his blessing to her working, even while being his duchess?

Yes! *She was. He had.* It was all true.

Kathryn felt giddy with excitement. Her sisters would be thrilled when they heard the news. She could hear Lexie's voice in her mind already: *I told you he was besotted with you.*

Her sisters were right, too, about the duke being forward-thinking. Her future seemed to stretch before her like a golden road, full of possibilities. They would live in London part of the time, and part of the time they'd live here. She'd be an architect and she'd also do *duchess-y* things. It was all going to work out perfectly.

Happiness thrummed through her as she dashed down the stairs, eager to talk to Lance. On the way to the breakfast room, she decided to check his study, just in case he was there.

As she made her way down the corridor, Kathryn heard voices coming from the study. Lance was talking to his solicitor, Mr. Megowan.

"Now I'll have all the money I need to pay off the debts," Lance was saying.

Debts? What debts? Kathryn wondered as she approached.

"When will the marriage take place?" asked Mr. Megowan.

Kathryn ground to a halt a few feet from the door to the study. Were they talking about *her* marriage to Lance? She knew she shouldn't be eavesdropping, but her feet wouldn't move.

"I don't know," Lance replied. "It depends on how quickly I can get Kathryn to agree to hold the ceremony. It would be convenient for us both to have it here at the Mount, since her sisters live in Cornwall. But she might insist on New York. Either way, I presume she'll want to have her parents involved. That will take time. Hopefully, I can get it done in the next month or two. Which still gives me some leeway to move the funds to my bank before the loan is due in December."

Kathryn's blood turned to ice in her veins. *What loan?*

It seemed that Lance was in debt with an outstanding loan. A fact he had failed to mention.

"Will you get hold of her entire fortune at once, do you think?" Mr. Megowan asked.

"I'll make it clear to her father that, at the very least, I require £68,000 up front."

Kathryn could hardly breathe. *Sixty-eight thousand pounds? That's how much he owes? Why? To whom?*

Was it a debt he'd piled up during his years in the Navy? Or a debt he'd inherited? Or both? Did it matter, really?

"She's agreed, then, to the way her fortune will be spent?" Mr. Megowan asked.

"I haven't brought that up yet. But I will."

Mr. Megowan chuckled. "You see? I told you that when push came to shove, she'd give up this absurd notion of a career in favor of becoming a duchess."

"She might still be able to take on a job here or there, Megowan. At least I told her as much. I'm sure I can persuade someone to let her draw something once in a while."

Kathryn felt the bottom drop out of her stomach. She wanted to throw up. She felt as if her heart had just been torn, alive and beating, from her chest.

The hallway began to spin. She spun around with it and traipsed back the way she had come, her mind in a whirl.

All the kisses they'd shared. Their night of passionate lovemaking. All that talk about letting her pursue her career. About loving her. About wanting to spend the rest of his life with her. They were just words. Words he had employed to get her to agree to marry him.

It had all been a ruse. And she had fallen for it—fallen for *him*—hook, line, and sinker.

He had never intended for her to work at all. And he didn't care about her one whit.

All this time, he'd just wanted her for her money.

Kathryn found Hammett and told him she was leaving that morning and returning to London.

"Would you be so good as to send a man up to my room in half an hour to collect my trunk, and have it sent to the train station in Rosquay?" she asked.

"Very well, miss," Hammett replied.

It took twenty minutes to pack her clothes and other belongings. The tide was out, which meant she could walk across the causeway and catch the next train.

Hurrying back downstairs, Kathryn paused at the door to the conservatory. The dowager duchess was asleep on the chaise longue. A good thing; Kathryn wasn't up for the conversation that would inevitably follow. She tiptoed in and propped up the thank-you note she had hastily penned.

Then she headed for the study, where she found Lance working at his desk, this time alone.

"Kathryn!" His face lit up and he stood. "How beautiful you look this morning."

"Don't waste your time on flattery, Your Grace," Kathryn replied stonily, stopping just inside the door, a roll of drawings in her arms. "It won't work anymore."

"I beg your pardon?" He stared at her. "Why are we back to formal address? What's wrong?"

A pang of sadness stabbed through her chest, an emotion so unwelcome she forced herself to ignore it, focusing instead on the anger that fueled her. "I overheard you and your guest chatting a few minutes ago."

His face flushed beet red. He seemed to be at a loss for words. "Oh," was all he managed.

"I can see why you zeroed in on me. With a £68,000 debt hanging over your head, you couldn't marry just any old heiress. You needed a million-dollar heiress."

"Kathryn. I was going to tell you."

"Were you? When? After we were married? When it would be too late for me to object, because you had control over my money?"

"I intended to tell you—and to propose to you again—the last time I walked into the parlor, when you passed out cold on the floor. We haven't had a moment alone since then. And last night . . . it didn't seem the time nor the place to bring it up."

"You should have told me the *first* time you asked me to marry you! And you've had plenty of opportunities since then."

"You're right. I'm—"

"What I don't understand," Kathryn interjected heatedly, "is why your brother sent for an architect in the first place, when he obviously didn't have the funds to remodel this castle."

"He . . . must have intended to borrow the money. I think he was hoping that some improvements would increase castle's value, if he had to sell," Lance admitted.

"I see," Kathryn snapped. "But you figured you'd never need to sell, didn't you? You'd marry me and my fortune would take care of everything."

"Kathryn," he pleaded, his face still scarlet. "I—"

"It was all a grand seduction, wasn't it? I have to give you credit, Your Grace. You're a good actor. You played the violin for me, you brought me potted orchids. You had me in the palm of your hand, believing that you loved me. Insisting that you didn't mind if I worked. But it was all a lie. All you ever wanted was my money."

"That's not true." There was a note of desperation in his voice. "It may have started out that way. But, Kathryn: I genuinely fell in love with you."

"How can I believe anything you're saying? When I first came here, you told me you didn't have any financial issues. When I asked about it again, you stuck to that story. Both times, you lied to my face."

"I'm sorry. That was . . . a mistake. Please, let me explain. About the loan, about the problems that I—"

"I heard all I needed to hear, standing in that corridor." Kathryn blinked back the tears that threatened behind her eyes, steeling herself to remain strong. Crossing the room, she plunked the roll of drawings onto his desk. "Here are the plans I drew up. I'm sure there are plenty of other heiresses with generous dowries who'd be happy to become your duchess. With a little luck, you'll land one before that loan is due, and have enough money left over to fix up the castle. Everything can go ahead just as you planned. It just won't involve me."

With that, she turned for the door.

"Wait!" he called out. "Where are you going?"

"Back to London. Where I belong." Kathryn threw the comment over her shoulder as she flung herself from the room.

CHAPTER TWENTY-ONE

Kathryn sank down onto the sofa, hot tears pricking her eyes. The train journey from Cornwall to London had been exhausting.

She'd considered stopping to visit Maddie and Lexie on the way north, but had rejected the idea. She needed time alone to deal with her anger and grief. Instead, she'd written them each a long letter on the train, which she'd posted from Victoria Station.

With a sorrowful sigh, Kathryn took in the room in which she sat. Charles and Maddie's town house on Grosvenor Street had been her London home for several years now. This drawing room had always felt so warm and welcoming.

Tonight, it felt cold and empty. Other than the servants who kept the house running, Kathryn was the only resident. The rooms, all beautifully decorated in the modern style, had once seemed charming. Now they just reminded her of how much more charming she'd found the rooms of the ancient castle at St. Gabriel's Mount.

And how much she had loved its resident duke.

Loved, past tense, being the operative word. Was it possible to hate someone with whom one had just, that same morning, been deeply in love? If so, that was the emotion she was feeling now. Hate mixed with fury and a deep, throbbing ache that permeated her soul.

A tear slid down Kathryn's cheek, then a sob tore from her throat. She gave in to the anguish and allowed herself a good, long cry.

How could she have been so blind? How could she have not realized that he was just after her money? There had been several red flags. His concerns about hiring her for renovations in the first place. The somewhat dilapidated state of the castle. The community in obvious need of repairs. The fact that he never *had* said a word about her fortune, except when she'd brought it up.

All the other men who had asked for her hand had been up front about it. They had offered her what they'd considered to be a good life in exchange for that million-dollar prize. Lance, on the other hand, had avoided the topic entirely. After *lying* about it. Which made him so much worse than the others. He had deliberately set out to seduce her to acquire her fortune.

Lance had won her by stealth.

He had succeeded all too well. He'd stolen her heart.

And then had broken it.

The sobs wracking Kathryn's body continued for some minutes longer. When at last they subsided, she grabbed her handkerchief, dried her eyes, and blew her nose.

Well, she thought grimly, her heart might be broken. But she wouldn't let it defeat her. She would pick up the pieces and get back to work.

At least she still had work. And it was work that she loved.

Lance sat on the hard wooden bench in the chapel at St. Gabriel's Mount, every molecule of his body tense with frustration.

Kathryn had only been gone a day, and already the hallways of the castle rang hollow without her.

He had rarely ever visited this chapel. It was a place for prayer and penance. It was too late now for prayer, but he had a lot of penance to do, and he knew it.

The door opened and his grandmother ventured in. She made her way down the aisle, then sat down beside him. "What happened?" she asked.

He told her. About the financial mess he'd inherited. How close they were to losing the castle. The reasons why he had kept it from her. What had occurred with Kathryn—everything except the lovemaking part. He admitted, though, that he'd fallen in love with her. And he explained why she had left.

His grandmother listened with a grim expression, only issuing the occasional question or remark.

When he'd finished, she nodded slowly. "I'm sorry, my boy, that all of this has fallen on your shoulders. And sorry you felt you couldn't share it. But I understand why you were reluctant to say anything. And why Hayward couldn't bring himself to tell me, either."

"Do you?"

"You were both trying to protect me. I had an inkling, though, even if Hayward would never admit to it. Any more than he would admit to his other great secret."

Lance glanced at her. "What other great secret?" he asked carefully.

She paused. "Never mind. I shouldn't have said anything."

Should *he* say anything? It seemed that she knew already. "Are you referring to him and Woodston?"

Her white eyebrows lifted. "What do you know about him and Woodston?"

"I know they had a secret room on the fourth floor."

She smiled. "Yes, they did."

"How long have you known?"

"About Hayward? Darling, I've suspected since he was five years old. And I've been certain for decades."

"But you never let on?"

"Some things," his grandmother replied, "are better off left unsaid."

They sat in silence for a while. At length, she heaved a heavy sigh. "About St. Gabriel's Mount: don't worry about me, Lancelot. Whatever happens, I shall survive." She turned to him then, her pale blue eyes flashing. "Regarding Miss Atherton, however. I hope you realize that you have behaved like a complete and utter idiot."

He couldn't argue with that. "I know."

"You should have told her about your debts at the start."

"I know," he said again. "I handled everything wrong."

"You certainly did, you foolish boy."

Lance cursed inwardly. "For years, I've been telling myself that love only brings pain. It has proven so again. This time, though, I have no one but myself to blame. This pain is my own damn fault."

His grandmother gave him a hard stare. "So you really do love her?"

"I do." He probably *had* loved Kathryn, he realized, since that first night when he'd almost ravished her on the billiards table. Before he knew she had a penny to her name.

"Do you still want her?"

"*Of course* I still want her. But it's too late. I've ruined any chance I might have had with her."

"Have you?"

"What do you mean?"

"I mean: is it really too late?"

"She's gone, Grandmother. She left."

"Then go get her back."

He shook his head. "She won't have me now. She thinks I only wanted her for her money."

"But you don't?"

"No! All debts aside, forget about the fate of the castle, even if Kathryn didn't have a farthing, I'd still want her. But I lied to her. She doesn't trust me. And I don't blame her."

"Trust, when broken, isn't easy to repair. But it *can* be done."

"How?"

"I cannot tell you how. You're a very intelligent man,

Lance. I'm sure you can figure it out." She patted his knee, then stood. "I will leave you with this thought: if you truly love her, and you think there is a chance that she still loves you, then it would be a disservice to you both to give up now. Go to her, Lance. Mend what you have broken."

With that, she left the chapel.

Lance sat in silence for a long while, brooding over the mess he'd made of everything, his grandmother's words playing over and over in his mind.

Go to her, Lance. Mend what you have broken.

Was there a chance his grandmother was right? Was it possible that maybe, just maybe, it wasn't too late?

He loved Kathryn. As of yesterday morning, he knew that she'd been in love with him. There must be a way to make up for what he'd done. To let Kathryn know how sorry he was. To try to fix it somehow.

He didn't know how he would achieve it yet, but he'd be damned if he was going to sit here feeling sorry for himself a second longer. He had always prided himself on being a man of action. He had to do something.

Time, he felt, was of the essence.

Go to her, Lance.

That's exactly what he would do. He would go to London. Without delay.

"This just arrived for you in the morning post, Miss Atherton," the butler said, entering the breakfast room with a letter on a silver salver.

Kathryn thanked him and set down her coffee cup. Her pulse jumped as she noted the return address on the envelope. It was from the Royal Institute of British Architects. It must be about the RIBA exam she'd taken so many weeks ago.

Tearing open the envelope, Kathryn found two pieces of paper inside. She read the first page.

> *Dear Miss Atherton,*
>
> *Enclosed please find your results on the recent RIBA examination.*
>
> *Although you passed the exam, we regret to inform you that the Royal Institute of British Architects is and always has been an all-male organization, and it is against institute policy to grant a license to a woman.*
>
> *We thank you for your interest in the Royal Institute of British Architects, and wish you all the best in your future endeavours.*
>
> *Sincerely,*
> *H. G. Atwater*
> *Acting RIBA Secretary*

Kathryn stared at the letter in shock. She read it through again, then a third time.

Against institute policy to grant a license to a woman?

Couldn't they have told her that up front, before she went to all the months and months of effort studying for the exam, and then taking it?

Flipping to the second page of the letter, she noted that it was a breakdown of her marks on the various parts of the exam. A quick perusal confirmed that she had done very well. Her total score, printed at the bottom of the page, was 98%.

Kathryn dropped the missive onto the breakfast table as if it were a hot potato. Ninety-eight percent! And yet *still*, they were denying her a license to practice architecture. Reserving that right exclusively for men.

The indignity and injustice of it burned like fire in her blood. Even though a queen sat on the throne of England, and had ruled the land longer than any monarch in its history, for the most part men had ruled the world throughout time—and they obviously had no intention of changing that.

It was totally unfair. Unacceptable. Kathryn had to talk to somebody about this, throw herself on their mercy, beg if necessary to make the RIBA board reconsider.

There was only one person she could think of who might help her.

George Patterson's bushy dark eyebrows raised in surprise at the sight of her as Kathryn strode into his spacious office at his architectural firm, making sure to leave the door ajar.

"Miss Atherton!"

He was seated by the window in a wheeled chair, still recovering from the injuries he'd sustained over a month ago. His right arm and hand were in a cast and sling. One leg was encased in a cast. "I had no idea you were back in town," he added. For some reason, Kathryn thought she detected a note of dismay in his voice.

"I finished the work at St. Gabriel's Mount and returned

last night," Kathryn admitted as she approached him. "Just this morning I received word from the RIBA that, although I passed their exam with a score of ninety-eight percent, they are refusing to grant me a license."

"Is that so? I'm sorry."

"What more am I supposed to do to prove myself? To show that I'm qualified?" Kathryn paced back and forth before him, frustrated. "They claim it 'goes against institute policy' to give a license to a woman, but that's ridiculous."

"I did try to warn you that this might happen." There was a nervous edge to his voice, and his eyes darted covertly to a set of architectural drawings spread open atop his desk.

Curious, Kathryn moved in that direction. "Yes, but I earned a nearly perfect score. Doesn't that count for anything?"

"It should. But you are an anomaly, my dear. My guess is, they never expected you to pass. When you did, they obviously didn't know what to do with you."

She glanced down at the plans on his desk, recognizing them at once. Her heart went cold.

They were *her* plans for the new Lloyds Bank building. *Her* original design—the ones she had drawn up at home on her own time, as an example of her work. They were stamped with the word *FINAL*. And they had George Patterson's signature at the bottom of them.

Kathryn's mouth fell open and her stomach dropped for the second time in as many days. She whirled to face her employer as yet another awful truth suddenly became clear to her. "That's why you hired me, isn't it?"

"Pardon me?" Mr. Patterson squirmed in his wheeled chair.

"You only took me on because you knew I'd be cheap labor. Working my fingers to the bone, year after year, giving you great drawings and ideas which you could claim as your own."

A guilty look dashed across Patterson's face, but he quickly masked it and raised his good hand in a placating gesture. "There is no reason to get upset."

"This is *my* design for Lloyds Bank. You said it 'wasn't what the client had in mind.'"

"Which I believed at the time. But as you know, I have been incapacitated. So I decided to let them take a look at it."

"With *your name* all over it, instead of mine!"

"This is no different than anything else you have drawn for me since you entered my employ."

"It's entirely different!" Kathryn seethed. "Up to now, I was working for hire. Whatever I designed was yours, that was understood. I drew *these* on my own time, and you stole them without my knowledge or permission."

He sighed. "Be realistic, Miss Atherton. Lloyds Bank would never build a structure designed by a woman, even if you did have a license—which the RIBA board has refused to give you. You should be happy with this turn of events."

"*Happy?*"

"Yes, because something you envisioned is actually going to be *built*. If it's your salary that is at issue, I will see that you get a raise."

"I want more than a raise, Mr. Patterson." Fury and indignation gave Kathryn the courage to ask for what she was due. "I want to be acknowledged and valued for my contributions. Either you tell Lloyds Bank that the design was mine, and give me credit for all the work I do going forward, or I quit."

She stared straight at him, heart pounding, waiting for his reply.

Patterson shrugged. "I will be sorry to see you go, my dear. But if that is your decision, I accept it."

White-hot panic surged through Kathryn's chest. *Dear God, what have I done? Is it truly over, just like that?*

Apparently, it was. Mr. Patterson dismissed her with a wave of his hand.

Kathryn turned toward the open door of his office, still too stunned to take the first step.

Just then, the front desk clerk strode in and announced, "I beg your pardon, Mr. Patterson. A gentleman is here to see you. He says he's the Duke of Darcy, and he's come from Cornwall."

Kathryn gaped in astonishment as Lance strode in.

He was impeccably attired, his long legs, chiseled features, and magnetic presence taking instant command of the room.

"Patterson," he declared, his tone clipped and his eyes as cold as ice.

Kathryn's mind whirred. What was *he* doing here? And why was the look on his face so dark and thunderous? Had he overheard her discussion with Mr. Patterson? He well could have; the door had been wide open.

If so, he knew she'd just lost her job. Mortification rose

like firelight from Kathryn's chest to heat her face. *That* ought to make him happy. He'd never expected her to succeed.

Lance's gaze fell on her now. "Miss Atherton."

"Lord Darcy," she replied stonily. Giving him only the briefest of glances, she swept past him and out of the room.

"**W**hat the hell, Patterson?"

Lance had arrived in London late the night before, armed with Kathryn's address in Grosvenor Street, which Hammett had noted from the tags on her luggage before she left St. Gabriel's Mount. When he'd called there, the butler had explained that Kathryn had gone to the office to meet with her employer.

Now, as Lance stood over Patterson's wheeled chair, it was all he could do not to punch the man in his smug, florid face.

"I have retained the services of your firm for a month," Lance spat out. "Miss Atherton has performed her work with dedication and impeccable skill. You must have known she would, or you wouldn't have sent her to Cornwall in your place. Isn't that right?"

"It is indeed, Your Grace," Patterson replied. "And might I say what an honor it is to meet you in—"

"So what is this I hear," Lance interrupted venomously, "that you took credit for *her* design for a new bank building?"

"Well, er, Your Grace," Patterson sputtered, "that is to say, I had no—"

Lance stopped him with a raised hand. "Don't give me excuses, sir. I heard what I heard. You stole her design, then took the easy route out and let her go. Which makes you one of the greatest blackguards I have ever met."

"Now see here, Lord Darcy," Patterson said, his face turning an even deeper shade of red.

"Take care, Patterson. My family has friends in high places. A word from me could put you out of business in half a minute."

Patterson went quiet at that, casting his beady eyes to the floor.

"You mentioned something about her being refused a license? What is that about? I know she was awaiting the results of an exam."

"She . . . she received her score on the RIBA exam this morning."

"And?"

"Er. Um. Well." Patterson cleared his throat. "That is to say, I have not seen the results myself, but as I understand it, she earned . . ." His voice dropped until it was almost inaudible. "Ninety-eight percent."

"Ninety-eight percent?" Lance echoed. He wasn't a bit surprised.

Patterson nodded ever so slightly, deliberately avoiding Lance's gaze.

"And yet," Lance added slowly, incredulously, "they won't give her a license?"

"Apparently not."

Lance crossed his arms over his chest, his jaw tightening with anger. "Who heads up the RIBA board? Do you know how to reach him?"

"I do, Your Grace."

"Good. Because you're going to give me his name and contact information. And a few other names as well."

W*hy on earth did I open my mouth?*

As the hansom cab rattled along the London street, Kathryn leaned back against the seat with stunned regret. What had possessed her to say those things to Mr. Patterson? What had made her think that she was *due* anything? That *she* could make demands?

She'd been lucky to have a job at all. With a few choice words, she'd thrown that job away.

Now, she had nothing. Absolutely nothing. No job. No architectural degree. No license. And no prospects of ever getting such. It had taken many long months to find a firm that would even hire her. Without Patterson for a reference, she might never find work again.

As if it wasn't bad enough that she'd lost everything, Lance had to be there to witness it! Which made her humiliation complete.

What was Lance doing in town, anyway? He must have come, Kathryn reasoned, to find another prospective bride. As long as he was here, he probably figured he might as well meet with Mr. Patterson about the renovations to St. Gabriel's Mount.

The timing couldn't have been worse. She imagined the two men laughing together after she'd left. Confirming what a fool she'd been, trying to make her way in a man's profession.

Oh, how she despised Mr. Patterson. He was a thief and a cad.

The Duke of Darcy was no better. He was a thief of hearts.

Despite herself, she couldn't stop thinking about the moment when Lance had held her in his arms and said, *I love you, Kathryn.*

Tears burned behind Kathryn's eyes as she struggled to wipe the image from her mind. It had felt so real when he'd said it. She felt like such a fool for saying it back.

The tears broke free and began streaming down her face. After a moment, Kathryn wiped them away and swallowed a sob. She wouldn't allow self-pity to consume her again.

She reflected on everything she'd said to Lance, and was glad she had given him a piece of her mind.

On second thought, she was glad she'd stood up for herself with Mr. Patterson, too. What she'd said had been the truth. It had needed to be said.

Mr. Patterson had stolen her plans for Lloyds Bank and passed them off as his own. He'd been paying her peanuts, raking in good money off of her hard work for years, and taking all the credit. How could she have continued to work for a man like that?

So what if Mr. Patterson wouldn't give her a reference? Kathryn had done excellent work for many of his clients over the past two years. He may have put his name on those drawings, but her originals were stored at the office, dated and signed by her.

She also had her originals of the Lloyds Bank drawings.

She could show them to clients to try to prove the work had been hers. Hopefully, someone would believe her and be willing to give her a reference.

If not, she would just start from scratch. She'd done it before. She would pound the pavement again, visit every single architectural firm in London, including the ones that had turned her down two years ago, this time with a stack of new drawings in her portfolio.

If nothing turned up in London, she could try the smaller cities in England. She'd go back to New York if she had to. A building boom was going on in New York City. Kathryn had remained in London after university because she loved it and because it was closer to her sisters. She'd never actually tried to find a job in her own country. Maybe it was time she did.

It wouldn't be easy. It might take a long time. But somewhere out there, a job was waiting for her. And she was going to make it happen.

In the meantime, to hell with Mr. Patterson.

And the Duke of Darcy.

Chapter Twenty-Two

Lance strode into the private room at his club. The eight men he'd invited were assembled around the table, waiting.

Eight men whom he had never met in his life. Lance had dashed off notes to each of them earlier that afternoon, requesting that they meet him that evening at eight o'clock. Short notice, he knew. But he also guessed that these men wouldn't miss an opportunity to meet with the new duke in town.

He'd been right.

Dukes had power. He'd held a similar kind of power as a captain in the Royal Navy. But people, he'd discovered, treated dukes with even more deference. As if they walked on water. As if they were somehow more important and more worthy than other people, simply by the station of their birth.

It was a ridiculous notion. But tonight, he was going to put that notion to good use.

Lance stopped by the empty chair at the head of the table.

All eight men rose in unison. The mustachioed, gray-haired gentleman to his right held out his hand and introduced himself.

Lance made his way around the table, greeting each man in turn. When the introductions were complete, he returned to the head of the table and sat down.

Everyone resumed their seats and fixed him with intent gazes.

"I am sure I speak for all of us, Your Grace," said the man to his right with a smile, "when I say that we are all very pleased to be here, and honored to make your acquaintance. But might I inquire as to what occasioned this rather unexpected meeting?"

"You may indeed inquire," Lance replied with a terse smile. "We are here to discuss Miss Kathryn Atherton."

The meeting, Lance thought with satisfaction at breakfast the next morning, had gone well. Extremely well. He had every reason to expect that his demands would be met, and in a timely fashion. With that taken care of, he could return to Cornwall.

Lance deeply regretted that his original intent in coming to town—to see Kathryn, to explain and apologize—had not been achieved. Or even come close.

When he'd walked in on her and George Patterson the morning before, she'd stormed out with barely a word. His attempts to call on her at Grosvenor Street had failed. She refused to see him.

It tore at his heart to think about it, but she must hate him now.

Lance hoped that what he'd done last night might help mitigate some of that anger. At least it should make her life a bit easier.

Well, Grandmother, I tried. He had no illusions anymore that he and Kathryn could ever go back to what they once were. That she'd ever want to see him again. Much less love him or want to marry him. He knew *that* was off the table for good.

He was still in debt up to his eyeballs. He had still lied to her about it. It wasn't something he could fix with a meeting. It would take a magic wand.

But perhaps, just perhaps, his intervention would help pave the way for her to achieve a few of those dreams and goals that were so important to her. He hoped she would find her happiness. *That* would make *him* happy. And it would have to be enough.

He was about to ring for Woodston to inform him that it was time to pack when a letter arrived. The engraved notepaper announced that it was from a Lady Carnarvon with a Mayfair address. Yet another person he had never met in his life.

My dear Lord Darcy,

 I have only just spoken to my dear friend Prudence Fowlington, whose husband Reginald, the President of Lloyds Bank, informed her of your presence in Town. Might I presume, my dear Duke, that—being an unattached gentleman recently come into a title—you might be seeking a wife?

Lord Carnarvon and I are hosting a small soirée at eight o'clock this evening. It would give us the greatest pleasure if you would attend. Although the Season is nearly over, there will be several eligible young ladies present, including one to whom I should particularly like to introduce you—Miss Imogen Russell, an heiress from Cincinnati with a sizeable fortune.

I look forward to your favorable reply by afternoon post, and do hope to see you this evening.

With all due respect, I remain,
Lady Constance Carnarvon

Lance tossed the letter onto the table, his spirits sinking. The invitation didn't surprise him. An unmarried duke was always in demand. Why, though, had Lady Carnarvon specifically mentioned a debutante with a fortune?

Was it possible that she had a hunch about the debts weighing him down? He hoped not. Hopefully, it was just standard *modus operandi*. Every peer in possession of a great house needed money these days, after all. Mentioning an heiress's worth was understood to be part of the game. A title in exchange for a whole lot of American cash.

A month ago, he had intended to come up to town seeking just such a bride.

The idea of marrying someone for her money turned his stomach now.

Lance just wanted to go home. Back to St. Gabriel's

Mount. Where he would bury his sorrows in a stiff glass of whiskey.

But, he realized, St. Gabriel's Mount wouldn't *be* his home much longer if he did that. It wouldn't be his grandmother's home, either. Or the home of any future member of the Darcy family. Should his line actually continue, that is. Which at the moment was in grave doubt.

If he did nothing, the castle and all its holdings would be seized by moneylenders. And end up in someone else's hands.

Lance took up the letter and read it again. An heiress from Cincinnati. With a sizeable fortune. He heaved a sigh. The family legacy was in his hands. He had sworn to do his duty by it.

He supposed he ought to meet her.

It was a soirée like all the other soirées Lance had attended over the years, whenever he had been on leave and had time to kill in town. A drawing room filled with overdressed people who were drinking too much and laughing too loudly.

Upon his arrival, Lady Carnarvon had descended on him, taken him by the arm, and introduced him to Miss Imogen Russell, the diminutive daughter of a Cincinnati merchant who had made his fortune in dry goods.

Miss Russell was reasonably pretty, but so young (she'd celebrated her eighteenth birthday just days before) that he felt like a lecher for even considering her as a prospective bride, and so slight she looked as if she might blow away in a strong wind. She was dressed to the nines in a pale pink gown studded with gemstones, a gown Lady Carnarvon assured him had been designed by Frederick Worth of Paris.

Lance had heard of Worth and understood this to be not just a fashion statement, but a testament to the size of the young lady's fortune. Which, Her Ladyship hastened to murmur in his ear, was *half a million dollars.*

Half a million. Half the size of Kathryn's dowry, but still enough to pay off Lance's debts and then some. If he married this slip of a woman, he would save St. Gabriel's Mount.

He made an attempt at conversation with her, but it was stilted and awkward. Although she was sweet and eager to please, they seemed to have nothing in common. Her father, the exact opposite in demeanor, was brash and coarse and so effusive that Lance couldn't get a word in edgewise. After listening to Donald Russell drone on for thirty minutes about the details of his dry goods business, Lance felt as if he could open up such a company himself.

One thing Lance learned, however, did pique his interest. Russell had come to England not just to find a titled husband for his daughter. He also wanted to buy property.

"A real nice estate," Russell said, puffing on his cigar, "that we can visit when we come to England to see our daughter. One of those old-timey manor houses, you get my meaning, with towers and turrets and whatnot. My wife, see, she's always fancied the idea of living in some place that looks like a castle."

Lance glanced over at Miss Russell, who was chatting in a corner with another debutante. He could never marry her.

Or anyone like her. If he couldn't have Kathryn, he realized, he didn't want to marry at all.

He would rather sell out, pay off his debts, find a small home for his grandmother . . . and go back to sea.

Turning to Donald Russell, Lance said: "What would your wife think, sir, about living in an *actual* castle?"

It had been a very productive two days.

Yesterday morning, Kathryn had gone back to Patterson's offices. The clerk and secretary had been the only people present. They had both been unable to look her in the eye, and seemed to feel sorry for her for being fired. Kathryn told them she was there to pick up her things, and had silently gone about her business. Which was to collect every single drawing she had done over the past two years. She'd then cleared out her desk and disappeared from the premises.

The rest of the afternoon Kathryn had spent at home, going over the list of London architectural firms she'd created during her original job search two years ago. She would have to visit each one to see if they were still in existence, and if the same men were in charge.

Kathryn added to the list by studying advertisements in the newspaper and noting stories about new buildings going up and the firms that had designed them.

Today, Kathryn had worked on her curriculum vitae (the British term for *résumé*) and a letter of inquiry that she would adapt for each firm she was applying to. It was important to get the wording right. If only she was a man, she mused, this would all be so much easier. It occurred to her that she could try using just her first initials in her correspondence. Prospective employers would look at *K. J. Atherton* without prejudice and assume she was a man. It would level the playing field.

A knock on her bedroom door interrupted her thoughts.

Kathryn glanced at the clock, surprised to discover that it was almost dinnertime. She was even more surprised to find the butler at her door, holding a silver salver with three letters which had just arrived. She sat down to read them.

The first letter was from the Royal Institute of British Architects.

> *Dear Miss Atherton,*
>
> *Congratulations! We are pleased to inform you that, based on your recent score on the RIBA examination, the board has voted unanimously to admit you to the Royal Institute of British Architects and grant you a license to practice architecture.*
>
> *The official documents will be sent in a separate post. Welcome to the RIBA. We wish you all the best in your future endeavours.*
>
> *Sincerely,*
> *H. G. Atwater*
> *Acting RIBA Secretary*

Kathryn's jaw dropped. She let out a shriek and leapt to her feet, unable to believe her eyes. She was in! She had a license!

Excitement drummed through her as she ripped open the second envelope, which, she noticed, was from the London School of Art and Architecture.

In almost identical terms it announced that, after further consideration, based on her successful completion of the university coursework two years previously, the school board had voted to grant her a degree in architectural studies.

Kathryn jumped up and down, unable to prevent another shriek.

Someone knocked again at the door, this time a maid come to inquire if she was all right. Kathryn assured the maid that she was fine; she'd just had some very good news.

"I got my license!" Kathryn cried, waving the letters with glee. "I got my degree!"

The maid—who had only been working there a few weeks, and had no idea what Kathryn was talking about—looked at her as if she were mad. "Very well, miss," said she with a curtsy, departing as swiftly as she'd come.

The third letter was, incredibly, from Mr. Patterson. He explained that after having given the matter further thought, he had decided to add Kathryn's name as the official designer on the Lloyds Bank project. He went on to extend to her an offer of employment as an architect at a significantly higher salary than she'd been earning previously.

Kathryn stared at the three missives, utterly astonished.

What had brought all this about? How was it possible that her former employer and both of these institutions were doing an about-face at the exact same time, offering what they had previously and so emphatically denied?

Was it simply good fortune? The universe at last granting what she had worked so hard to achieve? Kathryn frowned. She doubted it. It seemed far too coincidental to just be fate or some cosmic reward. Something else about all this didn't feel quite right, although she couldn't put her finger on it.

Before she had time to process the matter further, Kathryn's attention was caught by the sound of an arriving carriage in the street below. Darting to the window, she saw Maddie descending from a conveyance emblazoned with the Saunders coat of arms.

Kathryn smiled. Maddie had wired to say that she and Charles were coming up to London today, as he had a meeting with some lord or another about one of his inventions. Although Kathryn was still mystified as to the reason behind the news she'd just received, she was eager to share it with Maddie.

Hurrying downstairs with her letters, Kathryn met her sister in the front hall and threw herself into her arms.

"Maddie! I'm so glad you're here."

"When I got the letter you wrote on the train, I just had to come," Maddie exclaimed, returning the embrace. "You sounded so heartbroken. I wanted to be with you."

"A lot has happened since I wrote that letter," Kathryn admitted as their hug ended. "But first, where is Charles?"

"He insisted on being dropped off at Lord and Lady Carnarvon's house on the way from the station," Maddie explained. "Of course, that meant I was obliged to have tea with Lady Carnarvon and listen to all the latest gossip." Maddie studied Kathryn's face. "You look much happier than I anticipated. Has something happened?"

"It has." Kathryn waved the letters as she led Maddie into the drawing room. "You will never guess what I've just learned by the evening post."

"Then you must tell me."

Kathryn filled Maddie in about her exam results and the turnaround from the earlier letters of denial she'd received. "I have my degree *and* my license!"

"Kathryn, that's wonderful!" Unaccountably, Maddie didn't look the least bit surprised.

"Not only that," Kathryn added. "I haven't had a chance to tell you, but Mr. Patterson fired me two days ago when I dared to ask for credit on the Lloyds Bank building design. Now he's offered me my job back with full credit and a raise. Can you believe it?"

Maddie patted the sofa and they sat down beside each other. "Yes. I can."

"You can what?"

"I can believe it. Kathryn . . . I didn't expect it to happen so quickly, but I knew this was going to happen."

Kathryn stared at her. "How could you know?"

"Lady Carnarvon told me just now that she'd heard from her friend Lydia Benson, the wife of Sir Sidney Benson, head of the RIBA Board, that Lord Darcy organized a meeting two nights ago with him, all the members of the board, the headmaster of the London School of Art and Architecture, and the president of Lloyds Bank, and insisted that they give you your due."

"What?" Kathryn was dumbfounded. But even though this news came as a shock, she realized she should have guessed that Lance had been involved somehow. He'd been in town, after all. And he was a duke. It was the only logical explanation for this rapid and universal turn of events. "Lance did that . . . for me?"

"He did."

Kathryn knew she ought to be grateful. She had everything she'd ever wanted. Her degree, her license, even her name on the plans of a prestigious new building. She also had her job back—not as an apprentice, but as a full-fledged architect.

Knowing that Lance had been behind all this, however, somehow tainted the pleasure of her achievement. She blew out a beleaguered breath. "So this only happened because of *him*."

"Don't be silly. Lord Darcy simply used his ducal power and influence to make those idiotic men finally do the right thing. *You* are the one who put in the years of hard work to get here, Kathryn. You deserve this on your own merit."

Kathryn frowned. "I don't know . . ."

Maddie gave a sigh that sounded like affection mixed with exasperation. After a moment, she took one of Kathryn's hands in hers. "Kathryn: do you remember when I wrote my first book?"

"Of course I do. It's a wonderful novel."

"Do you also remember that I had no one to show it to? Not a single contact in the literary world. I had asked for Father's help, but he laughed at the idea of me becoming a novelist, and Mother always said it was unseemly. If Charles hadn't spoken to his friend at my publishing house, I might never have been published."

Kathryn could see where her sister was going with this. "So you're saying . . ."

"I'm saying that sometimes, no matter how hard we work to achieve something, we still need a little boost from someone else to open the right door to make that final step possible. Lord Darcy just helped open a door. *You're* the one who earned the right to walk through it."

Kathryn nodded reluctantly. "I guess you're right." Why, then, didn't she feel more happy about this? "I don't understand why he did it, though."

"Isn't it obvious? The man *loves you*."

"No, he doesn't. He only said he loved me to get me to marry him."

"Kathryn. I know you feel he betrayed you by keeping mum about his debts. But I bet it almost killed him to keep that information from you. Do you know why he owes so much money?"

"I didn't ask."

"Lady Carnarvon heard it on good authority—even though the dukedom has kept it tightly under wraps for years—that St. Gabriel's Mount is mortgaged up to its eyeballs. Lord Darcy inherited the entire debt from his feckless brother."

"Oh." Kathryn had presumed that Lance must have inherited some of the debt, but she'd also supposed that part might have been due to his own financial mismanagement or reckless spending.

"The situation is so bad Lady Carnarvon thinks the duke is in grave danger of losing the castle."

"Oh no." Kathryn's heart caught. It hadn't occurred to her that Lance might actually lose the castle. "Why didn't he tell me?" But even as she voiced the question, she recalled something the dowager duchess had mentioned, and the answer came to her. "Wait—I think I know why. He didn't tell me because he was too embarrassed." Kathryn told Maddie about Lance's first love, who broke off their engagement because of his debts and perceived financial mismanagement.

"That explains a lot. Darcy was probably terrified that he'd lose your respect—*and* any chance at winning your hand and heart—if you knew."

Kathryn pondered that. Had she known about Lance's immense debts, would she have thought less of him? No, she decided; she would have felt sorry for him. But would she have seen him as a marriage prospect?

She'd seen the need in the community. She'd fallen in love with the castle. *And fallen in love with the man.* Had she known all the facts, might she have been willing to marry him so that her fortune could help save St. Gabriel's Mount?

Maybe I would have. If he truly loved me. Now, she would never know.

"He may have lied about that one thing," Maddie went on. "But I met Lord Darcy. I believe he is a man of honor. And a gentleman. He didn't have to hire you to work on St. Gabriel's Mount—God knows he couldn't afford it—but he did, before he knew you were an heiress. I think he did it out of the goodness of his heart, because he wanted to give you the opportunity."

Kathryn sighed. "I never thought of it that way. But this doesn't really change anything. He still just wanted to marry me for my money."

"I don't think that's true. He stayed by your bedside for forty-eight hours, nursing you back to health when you could have died. Yes, he needs your fortune to save his family home. Maybe that was part of his draw to you in the beginning. But I think somewhere along the way, he lost his heart to you."

Kathryn's mind was in a turmoil. "That's exactly what Lance said: *'It may have started out that way. But I genuinely fell in love with you.'* I didn't believe him."

"He was telling you the truth."

"But I overheard him talking to his solicitor. It was clear, from what he said, that after I married him, he never intended for me to work at all."

"Actions speak louder than words, Kathryn. When Darcy called that meeting the other night, he had nothing personally to gain from it. He went out of his way to make sure that you could achieve your career goals. Because he's proud of you. Because he loves you."

Kathryn's chest felt so tight she could hardly breathe. Everything Maddie was saying rang true. "Do you really think so?"

"I *know* so! You love him, too, don't you?"

"I do," Kathryn admitted, her voice barely a whisper. "I do love him."

"Then get your priorities straight, sister dear. For years,

you've been pouring everything you have into one bucket: your career path. Now it's time to stop and take a breath. Working yourself to death isn't the answer. You need time off, too. If anyone understands that, it's me. I've learned to force myself not only to take breaks from my writing, but to carve out specific time for things other than work. When you make time for the people you love, it shows you care about them. And trust me, you'll be happier and more creative as a result."

Kathryn found herself nodding. Whenever she'd taken breaks to be with Lance, it had always replenished her energy. And during those times she'd gotten some of her best ideas. "I've been so blind. You're right, Maddie. About all of it."

"If you love him, if you want him, then go to him, Kathryn. Before it's too late. Because if you want to save St. Gabriel's Mount, you're going to have to act fast."

"Why?"

"According to Lady Carnarvon, Lord Darcy is about to sell St. Gabriel's Mount to some rich businessman from Cincinnati to use as a vacation home. And he's heading down to Cornwall tomorrow to look at the place."

Chapter Twenty-Three

The train journey took the usual nine hours, but felt more like nine weeks.

As Lance hiked up the cobbled road in the fading light of evening, he wondered how many times he had left to make this trek. It was always something he'd looked forward to after a long sea or train voyage—this walk up to the castle on the Mount.

Most home owners with the means drew up to their front doors in a carriage. But how prosaic was that? To live in a castle atop a hill—*that* was far more interesting. And what better way to arrive than on foot?

Grimly, Lance thought about the meeting that would soon take place here. When Russell arrived to see if he wanted to buy the castle. Lance had given him a detailed description of the property and its history, and Russell had sounded extremely interested. *Champing at the bit* would be a more apt term.

The idea of selling St. Gabriel's Mount to that loud-mouthed American turned Lance's stomach. But these days, not many people had the kind of cash that Russell did. Lance had to sell to someone. It might as well be Russell.

If Russell liked it, and they could agree on a fair price, Lance would turn matters over to Megowan to handle the paperwork. The estate had already been appraised. Lance was fairly certain that after the sale, even after all his debts had been paid, there would be enough left over to buy a small house somewhere for his grandmother.

Lance hoped, when he returned to the Royal Naval office and made his appeal, they would reinstate him at his former rank. There was no guarantee, though. Another man had already taken over the helm of the *Defiant*. It might be years before Lance could be assigned command of another vessel—there weren't that many to go around. But he could settle for a lesser rank for a while, until "his ship came in," as the saying went.

Fixing his gaze again on the monolithic castle looming above him, Lance heaved a sigh. He would miss this place. When he first came back, he hadn't been enamored of the idea of being stuck on land for the rest of his life. He'd felt trapped. He'd worried that he'd get restless and fidgety.

But he had come to like it. To actually . . . prefer it.

Being on land, land that was *yours*, especially at a place like St. Gabriel's Mount, came with distinct advantages. Yes, the place was old and outdated and parts of it were drafty and crumbling. Yes, you were cut off from the mainland most of the time by the tides.

But you always knew where you were. Your bed didn't rock and roll with the whims of the sea. The food was consistently good. There was something satisfying about living in a property that had been in the family for hundreds of years and would long outlive you. And the views from every vantage point were indisputably spectacular.

As he trudged up the hill, he found himself imagining Kathryn standing beside him at the drawing room window as they took in that spectacular view. His mind drifted further, picturing her at the dinner table, talking and laughing over all the events of the day. He saw her in his bed, in his arms, as they made passionate love.

Damn it all to hell. Stop thinking about it. It's never going to happen.

A wave of disappointment surged through Lance's chest. He hadn't just lost Kathryn. He was losing St. Gabriel's Mount as well. It had been entrusted to his care. And he had failed. Failed his family. Failed to live up to what had been expected of him.

It's not your fault, he tried to tell himself. *You inherited the place encumbered by so much debt it was impossible to save.*

But he knew that was only partially true. He *could* save it. All he had to do was marry Miss Imogen Russell. Or someone like her.

All at once, it was difficult to breathe. It had nothing to do with the exertion of hiking up the steep road. He couldn't breathe because the idea of marrying anyone other than Kathryn Atherton was like shoving his lungs and heart into a vise and squeezing it tight.

If only there were some other solution to this conundrum he faced. . . . But there wasn't.

So. If all went well, he would soon be shaking Donald Russell's hand and sealing the deal to sell St. Gabriel's Mount.

End of story.

Kathryn played with the handle of her satchel, her stomach tied up in knots.

She had dropped everything, packed a bag, and taken the 6 a.m. train out of Victoria Station, hoping against hope that she would arrive at St. Gabriel's Mount before the American who was reportedly interested in buying it. A Mr. Russell, if Maddie had her facts straight.

As the train rumbled along the track, every mile bringing her closer to Cornwall, Kathryn's nervous anticipation grew.

She had known Lance owed an enormous sum of money. But it had never occurred to her that it would come to this. That he would actually sell that beautiful castle and the island it stood on.

The evening before, when those letters had arrived— when she'd held her future in her hands and it was everything she'd ever dreamed of—something about it hadn't felt right. Not just because of the incredible coincidence of it all. It was something else she hadn't been able to decipher.

Now she knew what it was.

Although she had finally jumped over all the major hurdles that had been an impediment to her career, the achievement didn't have the same meaning it might once have held. Because now, she was in love with Lance Granville, the Duke of Darcy.

Now, she knew she could never be truly, completely happy unless she could share her life and achievements with him.

Maddie had been right. In her quest to become an architect, Kathryn had focused so hard on the prize that she had, literally, almost worked herself to death. In reward, her employer had dumped her after stealing her best work.

She would never make that mistake again. Yes, she still loved what she did, but she wanted a full life. A balanced life. And Kathryn couldn't imagine her life without Lance in it.

There must be a way to compromise. To fulfill her professional dreams and become his wife, too.

She wanted to spend all the rest of her days with Lance, living wherever he was living—whether it was in his castle or on the moon. She wanted Lance to talk to, to make love to, to share every moment with. She wanted to have his children, sons and daughters who would bring them both joy and carry on the line of Darcys.

But as sure as Kathryn was of her love for him and what *she* wanted, she couldn't be certain he still felt the same way.

He had said he loved her. But even so, she worried that maybe, after losing out on Kathryn's fortune, he'd decided that he preferred to sell the castle, after all, so he could go back to sea. He had often expressed how much he missed his life in the Royal Navy.

Or—even if he did regret selling the castle—maybe he'd

come to the realization that marrying Kathryn would have been a mistake. Just because he had advocated for her career, it didn't mean he truly wished to have a wife who worked. It was still possible that what he'd said that night in bed really *had* just been words to convince her to marry him. And after being caught in the lie, he had used his ducal trump card on her behalf to ease his conscience.

Either of those two scenarios stung. But the second one stung most painfully of all. Kathryn hoped and prayed that neither of them was true. Because marrying Lance, being loved by Lance, was what she wanted more than anything in the world.

The moment the train arrived at the station at Rosquay, Kathryn leapt out and ran all the way to the quay. The small ferryboat was docked in its usual spot. To her dismay, no boatman was sitting in it or lingering nearby.

Where, Kathryn wondered, would a bored sailor go on a hot summer afternoon? She spied the King's Head pub down the street and, on a hunch, took off in that direction.

Pushing open the door of the ancient building, Kathryn ventured inside. A half dozen crusty old men were seated at the bar, chatting over pints of beer. She didn't recognize any of them. Even so, she walked up to them and, struggling to catch her breath, said, "Gentlemen, can you tell me where I might find the boatman to take me to St. Gabriel's Mount?"

"That'd be me," one of the men replied, lifting his cap to reveal a shock of white hair.

"My good sir, I require a ride to the island at once. Can you oblige me?"

He nodded. "Soon as I finish my beer, milady." He took a gulp, then returned to his conversation with the other men.

Kathryn wanted to scream in frustration. "I am in a hurry, sir. I really must reach the island at once."

"Oh aye?" returned the man, eyeing her as he took another gulp. "And what business ye got there 'at can't wait another two minutes? Do the castle be on fire?" He grinned at his mates, who all exchanged a loud guffaw.

"It might as well be, if I don't hurry," Kathryn insisted anxiously.

Her tone seemed to get his attention. He finished off the rest of his glass, wiped the foam from his mouth with the back of his hand, and stood. "Well, then, we'd best get a move on, hadn't we?"

Ten minutes later, Kathryn was seated in the man's small boat, heading toward the island beneath swooping seagulls and a hazy summer sky. Although the oarsman plowed hard against the current, it felt as though they were crawling across the sea at a snail's pace, the castle exasperatingly out of reach in the distance.

The scene felt familiar somehow. Kathryn suddenly recalled the nightmare she'd had a few days after arriving at St. Gabriel's Mount. When she'd been in a boat, desperate to reach the Mount to prevent some terrible calamity from happening to the Duke of Darcy.

She was living that nightmare in real life at this very moment.

Kathryn's heart pounded with frustration. The Darcy legacy was about to end up in the hands of some American businessman, just so his wife could vacation in a castle a few weeks out of the year. Kathryn couldn't bear to see that happen. Not if her fortune could save it.

But she had an even more important reason to reach the Duke of Darcy.

She had to tell him that she loved him.

Lance trod down the cliff path, then sank onto the wooden bench and stared out to sea.

Sadness seemed to fill every pore of his body. The thought that no Darcy would ever again set foot inside St. Gabriel's Mount, or ever walk down this much-loved path, was so painful he couldn't even contemplate it.

As bad as that was, though, it wasn't close to the worst of it. Lance had lost something that, to him, was far more precious than the castle or this island. The woman he loved had slipped through his fingers. And there wasn't a damn thing he could do about it now.

Lance picked a blade of grass from the weedy patch at his feet and shred it between his fingertips, trying to picture the future that lay ahead of him. His life at sea. Aboard a steel ship, surrounded by men. Stopping at different ports of call. Giving orders. Or taking them. Leading drills. Polishing guns.

He hadn't found that life lonely or monotonous before. But he suspected that he would now. He suspected that every night for the rest of his life, he would go to bed with an aching hole in his heart. The same way his heart ached at this very moment.

Every moment of every day he would think about *her*. Wondering where she was. What she was doing.

He couldn't help but wonder that now. Was she at home? Had Patterson offered her her job back, as he'd promised? Had she heard from London College? Had the RIBA contacted her? He hoped, by now, that she knew she had the certifications she'd earned. And that they'd bring her the success and joy she deserved.

He hoped, too, that she'd never find out he was behind it. That had been one more thing he'd insisted upon. He didn't want credit or thanks. He just wanted her to be happy.

A sound caught his attention. A rustling. Was it grass in the wind? No, the grass at his feet was moving almost noiselessly. This sounded more like the rustling of . . . skirts in the wind.

Turning, Lance saw Kathryn making her way down the cliff path in his direction. He froze in utter shock. What was *she* doing here?

She was wearing an elegantly tailored burgundy suit—the same one, he recalled, that she'd worn the first time they'd met. Her golden hair was drawn up beneath a felt hat that looked more masculine than feminine.

But there was nothing masculine about this woman. She was the most feminine creature he had ever seen.

Lance stood and started up the path toward her, his pulse racing. Unsure what to expect.

"Lance," she said, stopping a few feet away from him. Her aquamarine eyes were filled with apprehension.

"Kathryn." He breathed her name like a prayer. He

wanted to ask what had brought her here. To pour out his heart. Tell her how he felt about her. But his mouth had gone dry and he couldn't find the words.

"Please tell me you haven't signed anything yet."

"Signed anything?"

"I heard that you're planning to sell St. Gabriel's Mount."

"Oh. Yes, I am. I'm expecting a visit from a prospective buyer tomorrow."

"Tomorrow?" She sighed in relief. "Don't sell it, Lance. Please."

He didn't dare to let himself hope what that might mean. "I don't have much choice, I'm afraid."

"Yes, you do. Marry me, and you can save it."

Lance's heart skittered. Had his ears deceived him? Had she truly just asked him to marry her?

"You've asked me twice," she went on. "Now *I'm* asking *you*. That is, if you still want me?"

"Of course I want you!" Lance burst out. He took two giant strides and swept her into his arms, both incredulous and ashamed. "But . . . Kathryn, I don't deserve this. After what I did—I should have told you—"

"I understand why you didn't. Your grandmother told me about Beatrice."

He took that in. "Still, I should have come clean about my debts long ago."

"They're not *your* debts, Lance. They're your family's debts. Now they're *our debts*."

Our debts. Lance's heart turned over at her words. She

said them so naturally, as if taking on this burden were something that had already become a part of her. The weight that had been crushing Lance for so many long weeks seemed to magically lift from his shoulders. "Do you truly mean it?"

"I do. We'll see this through together. You can have my fortune, all of it. Pay off the loans, renovate the castle, take care of the village, whatever you wish. The money is yours. *I'm* yours, if you'll have me."

"Then . . . yes. Yes. Thank you, my love! *Yes!*" He kissed her deeply, a silent declaration of all that he was feeling. Her arms wrapped around him and drew him even closer as their kiss became more impassioned. At length, she pulled away slightly, catching her breath as she gazed up at him.

"I think that's the first time you've called me *my love*. I like the sound of it."

"I shall remember to say it as often as possible in future. I love you, Kathryn. I love you with all my heart."

"And I love you."

Her words spread joy through his every vein, warming him to the core. "I believe," he said softly, after kissing her again, "I have loved you since the moment you first appeared at my castle door, so eager to be my architect."

"Ah yes. About that." She took a breath. "I wanted to thank you for what you did in London. I know that I have my degree and license now—and my job back, if I want it— because of you."

"Who told you?" Lance frowned. "That was supposed to be kept in confidence."

"There shouldn't be any more secrets between us, Lance."

He paused, then nodded. "You're right. I just didn't want you to feel any obligation to me."

"I know." She hesitated. "I also know that, despite having my credentials . . . as your duchess, society will expect me to behave a certain way. I hope . . . you'll keep an open mind about that?"

He stared down at her. "I told you before, I am fully on board. I wouldn't dream of you giving up your career."

"I wasn't sure you really meant it. I heard what you said to Mr. Megowan."

"What did I say?"

"You said, 'She might still be able to take on a job here or there. At least I told her as much. I'm sure I can persuade someone to let her draw something once in a while.'"

Lance winced. "Forgive me for my poor choice of words. But I meant no disrespect by that remark, Kathryn. You are so talented, but you have a difficult road ahead of you. I can help open doors. And this only works, I believe, if there is compromise on both our parts."

"Yes," she agreed. "Compromise."

"I understand that you may have to put in long hours from time to time. But not *all the time*. If you marry me, you won't be able to work at the same pace you are accustomed to."

Kathryn nodded. "I understand that now, too. I've learned something since I came to St. Gabriel's Mount."

"That you chirp when you get excited?"

She blushed. "Not just that. I've learned that life shouldn't *be* all about work. We have to make time to play as well. And to be with the ones we love. You and our children will always be my top priority. I promise."

"I'm so glad to hear that." He caressed her face with his palm. "At the same time, I will be proud to be married to the first female architect in Britain. Who also *happens* to be a duchess. You can create a new tradition, Kathryn. Instead of raising money for new hospitals and schools, you can *design* new hospitals and schools."

"That would be a dream come true. You really won't mind?"

"Your dreams are my dreams, my darling."

Kathryn met his gaze, beaming. "Speaking of which—I was thinking. After we pay off the loans, if we invest the rest of my fortune and live off the interest, I won't need income from my work. So if I do manage to earn a pound or two, I could do the *duchess-y* thing and donate the money to charitable projects. It might be the first time such a thing has been done, but—"

Lance—thrilled by the notion—kissed her again. "There is a first time for everything, my darling. You and I will write the new rules."

EPILOGUE

Two Months Later

Their wedding day was resplendent with a crisp autumn breeze and a fresh wind off the coast.

Kathryn's mother and father sailed over from New York for the occasion. Maddie and Lexie were matrons of honor, of course. Henry Megowan served as a groomsman, along with Lance's first lieutenant from the *Defiant*, who managed to secure leave from the Navy.

The ceremony was held in the chapel at St. Gabriel's Mount. Kathryn wore the white lace gown and veil that Maddie had worn at her wedding in Cornwall, a fabulous creation by Worth which only required slight alterations to fit and meet the changes in fashion over the intervening years.

Lance wore his Royal Navy dress uniform, a sword belted at his side, and atop his head a traditional cocked hat from the days of the age of sail. Kathryn thought her heart might burst with pride at the sight of him as she walked down the aisle on her father's arm.

"You look every bit as dashing in that uniform as I always imagined you would," Kathryn whispered in his ear, after the clergyman pronounced them man and wife and they had kissed to seal their vows.

"And you look more beautiful in that gown than I could have ever imagined," Lance murmured in return, his eyes blazing admiringly.

As they left the chapel hand in hand and emerged onto the sunlit terrace, Kathryn asked Lance, "I hope you've made peace, my dearest, with the idea of being retired from your life at sea?"

"I have," Lance replied, drawing her into his arms for another kiss. "I have no desire to go back. Only forward to the life we will build together."

Kathryn smiled into his dark blue eyes, never ceasing to be astonished by and grateful for the affection she saw written there.

The celebratory breakfast was held in the great hall. Kathryn still hoped to someday redo the hall's ceiling, but in the meantime, she had supervised a master cleanup and had the walls coated with fresh white paint until they gleamed. Garlands of flowers hung from the rafters and adorned the tables, imbuing the room with their sweet scent. Musicians played lively music as everyone dined and chatted and danced and laughed.

"Welcome to the family, Kathryn," the dowager duchess said, beaming beneath an enormous hat. "You look radiant today."

"It is the happiest day of my life, Your Grace," Kathryn admitted.

"Oh, stop with that Your Grace nonsense," the duchess insisted. "Henceforth you will call me Grandmother."

"Yes, Grandmother." Kathryn kissed her on the cheek, thrilled and grateful to have such a dear person in her life.

Kathryn's mother hadn't stopped beaming since she'd set foot in the castle a week before.

"You know how proud I am of your sisters," Josephine Atherton said as she took in the festivities with a smile. "Alexandra is a countess. Madeleine, when her husband inherits, will be a marchioness. But *you*, Kathryn, have out distanced them both. You are a duchess!"

"That was never my aim nor my ambition," Kathryn replied, "but if my being a duchess makes you happy, Mother, then I'm glad."

"Oh, it makes me more than happy, my dear. I have it on good authority that when Mrs. Astor read about your engagement in the New York papers, she gasped in shock, dressed immediately, and arrived uninvited at the door of Ward McAllister, the only person alive who owns her confidence. Just think of it: the Duke of Darcy! And to live here at St. Gabriel's Mount! Of course, your father and I have already been on Mrs. Astor's list of Four Hundred ever since Alexandra married, but this raises our level of prestige to the highest ranks. Now she must include us *forever*."

Kathryn had declined the job offer from Mr. Patterson, deciding she'd rather risk operating on her own in a freelance capacity than continue in the employment of a man who had so readily stolen her work. To her delight, she had discovered that there was a great deal of work much closer to home, which would allow her to spend more time with Lance.

They had agreed to put off the renovations to the castle

for a while, preferring instead to update the buildings in the village, a project which Lance had turned over entirely to Kathryn. And that was just the beginning. With the Lloyds Bank building and all the projects of the past two years on her résumé, further aided by Lance's growing contacts in the community, Kathryn had already taken meetings with prospective clients in Rosquay and Falmouth, and had been signed to design a new house in Penzance in the coming year.

When they were at last in the privacy of the master bed-chamber later that night, and Kathryn was snuggled into her new husband's embrace after making love, Kathryn said, "Lance. There is something I have been meaning to ask you."

"Yes, my love?"

"Oh, how I adore it when you call me that."

He smiled and kissed her. A kiss that lingered and continued for several delectable minutes.

"I can't think when you kiss me," she said breathlessly.

"Then don't think." His eyes glittered as his hand roved up to cup her breast. "Just feel."

"But I'm curious about something," Kathryn said, her body tingling with desire all over again. "That night in London . . . what did you say to all those men at your club?"

"Do you really want to talk about that *now*?" he asked as he kissed the sensitive skin at the side of her throat.

"The fact that they all capitulated at the drop of a hat. I've often worried that you . . . paid them off."

Lance stopped kissing her neck and looked at her. "Paid them off? Not at all. It would never have occurred to me."

"Then how did you convince them?"

"I told them you were incredibly smart and talented, you had done the work, and you'd earned it. I said it was almost the twentieth century and time to let a woman into the fold."

"That's it?"

"Well, I may have waved my ducal power about just *a bit*."

Kathryn laughed as she drew a fingertip along the seam of his lips. Oh, how she loved those lips. "I'm relieved to know that money wasn't involved. But dismayed that you had to bully them into it."

"What fun is there in being a duke if you can't put the position to good use?" He grinned, then added: "Trust me, if you hadn't been qualified, my title wouldn't have helped. You have changed history, my darling. You are the first woman architect in Great Britain. And I couldn't be more proud." He kissed her again as his hands continued their exploring.

"I couldn't have done it without you," Kathryn said, struggling to maintain her wits, despite the sparks that were igniting everywhere he touched. "Dukes are like gods. People will jump through hoops to make your every wish happen."

"Would you jump through a hoop for me, my love?" His voice was deep and sultry as he moved on top of her.

"I would," Kathryn replied with a gasp.

"Good to know," he said softly. "But in this case, I would rather be the one . . . taking the plunge."

And all thought vanished from Kathryn's mind as she gave herself over to the pleasure of making love to the man she adored.

Acknowledgments

A heartfelt thank you to Lucia Macro, Asanté Simons, Brittani DiMare, and everyone at Avon for all your hard work preparing this novel for publication. I'm especially grateful to Guido Caroti, who designed my cover, which I think is absolutely stunning!

Thank you so much, Tamar Rydzinski, for your helpful notes. I so appreciate you and all that you do on my behalf.

A big thank you to Laurel Ann Nattress, for pointing out the little things that required tweaking with regard to nineteenth-century British customs and manners. Your input was invaluable.

A huge thank you to my dear late husband, Bill, who was a big supporter of my writing, and was very excited about this book in particular. I will miss him forever, with every breath I take.

And to my readers: I couldn't do this without you. Writing is my love and my life. Thank you so much for your support!

My greatest pleasure in writing the Dare to Defy series has been the opportunity to create motivated characters who must struggle to achieve their dreams and aspirations, since they go against society's dictates at the time.

For *Duke Darcy's Castle*, the third book in the series, I immediately seized upon architecture as my heroine's professional goal. Being an architectural enthusiast myself, I was appalled to learn how few female architects there were in the world at the time this story takes place—and that nearly all had been refused admission to architectural schools and societies.

In real life, the first woman to be admitted to Britain's Royal Institute of British Architects was Ethel Charles in 1898. After training as an architect at a private firm, in 1893 she applied to the Architectural Association School of Architecture, but as a woman, was refused entry. Ethel completed part of the course at another school, receiving distinctions. After passing the RIBA examination, despite opposition from many members, Ethel was finally granted membership. She faced discrimination in the workplace, and was forced to concentrate on modest housing projects.

Louise Blanchard Bethune, as noted in this novel, was the first American woman known to have worked as a professional architect. Mary Gannon and Alice Hands graduated from the New York School of Applied Design for Women in 1892, and later opened an architectural firm focusing on low-cost residential housing. Several other American women, including Fay Kellogg and Mary Rockwell Hook, traveled to Paris hoping to study at the École des Beaux-Arts, but suffered from discrimination after sitting for examinations, and were refused admission. In spite of this, Kellogg went on to design hundreds of buildings in the New York area, and Hook designed a school in Kentucky and a number of buildings in Kansas City, employing innovative architectural techniques. Julia Morgan was the first woman to receive a degree in architecture from the École des Beaux-Arts (1901), and the first woman architect licensed in California. Morgan completed over 700 projects, including Hearst Castle in San Simeon.

When it came to my hero, Lord Darcy, I was excited by the idea of a man in a career transition, who had never expected to inherit a dukedom. At first, when I envisioned Lance in the Royal Navy, my head was full of images of wooden ships and the Age of Sail. I was fascinated to learn about the enormous changes that had taken place in the Royal Navy during the nineteenth century.

A very special aspect of this novel, for me, is the location.

St. Gabriel's Mount is based on the real life St. Michael's Mount in southern Cornwall, which I visited a few years ago. As I strolled across the causeway to the island at low tide and spent the day exploring the nooks and crannies of the castle and grounds, I fell in love with the place. I will never forget the sweeping views from the upper terrace, the majesty of the ancient castle with its towers and turrets and rows of cannons, the crash of the waves on the rocks below, and the invigorating scent of the sea air. The remote location seemed like the ideal setting for a steamy romance. I hope you enjoyed the result!

Don't miss the beginning of the
amazing Dare to Defy series!

Keep reading for a look at the very first
book in the series,

RUNAWAY HEIRESS!

Runaway Heiress

Chapter One

London, England
May 8, 1888

"One first-class ticket for Liverpool, please." Alexandra Atherton managed a smile for the ticket agent behind the window.

"One way or return?"

"One way." Alexandra anxiously made her way across the busy train station, hardly able to believe she was doing this: running away, dressed in her maid's old clothes, bound for Liverpool and the steamship that would take her home.

Her escape, she knew, would cause something of a scandal. Over the past few years, whenever her name or one of her sisters' names had cropped up in the press, it was always followed by "the American heiress," or "the daughter of multimillionaire banking tycoon Colis Atherton." As if they were not actual people in their own right.

Alexandra hated to feed the gossip, but after last night, what choice did she have?

She had left a note explaining where she'd gone and why, which her maid Fiona was to "accidentally discover" later that afternoon. By then, it would be too late for her mother to prevent Alexandra from sailing. She just prayed that upon her reaching Liverpool, a berth would be available aboard the *Maritime*.

The train platform was alive with the clamor of movement and conversation. Gentlemen in black frock coats and ladies in elaborate plumed hats darted to and fro, checking the printed timetables, studying the large clock hanging from the rafters, purchasing apples from a vendor and papers from the newsstand. As Alexandra wove through the crowd, she heard a high-pitched voice at her elbow:

"Got a penny for a poor orphan?"

She paused. Before her stood a raggedly dressed, dirty little girl. Alexandra's heart went out to the creature, who gazed up at her with wide eyes, her hair all in a tangle.

Alexandra wondered how a penny could possibly be of any help to a child in such need. Withdrawing her coin purse from her reticule, she offered the child a shilling. "Here you go, little one." Suddenly, more children in similarly dirty clothing appeared and crowded around her.

"Mine!" cried a boy.

"No, mine!" cried another.

A grubby fist flashed out and snatched the shilling from Alexandra's grasp. She couldn't tell if it was the first girl who took it or one of the boys; indeed, she wasn't entirely sure *what* happened next. All Alexandra knew was that multitudes of small, filthy hands were striking at her as young voices erupted in raucous shouts. Her coin purse was suddenly wrenched from her grasp, and a second later her handbag was gone.

"Wait! Give it back!" Alexandra cried as the flock of children fled. "Help! Stop those children! They've stolen my bag!"

No one made any move to help her. Alexandra pushed her way through the crowd, racing after the children, but the ragamuffin band vanished as quickly as it had appeared. At the end of the platform, she stopped to catch her breath. The whole incident, she saw now, had been cleverly played, the efforts of a pack of urchins who preyed on unsuspecting travelers.

She searched for a policeman (what did they call them here? Bobbies?), but realized that even if one materialized, she couldn't report the theft. She was dressed as a servant, in the act of running away.

Alexandra stood rooted to the spot, overwhelmed by a crushing sense of horror and disappointment as the depths of her predicament became clear to her. Her handbag was gone. It had held all her money as well as her train ticket. She hadn't been able to take anything else with her, and now had nothing left except the clothes on her back. Clearly, there would be no trip to Liverpool today, and no voyage to New York.

Tears stung Alexandra's eyes as she made her way back through the train station. What should she do now?

She considered the English girls she'd met over the past five weeks of the London Season, but realized they'd be no help. Not a single one had responded to Alexandra's attempts at friendship. They'd seemed to consider Alexandra too outgoing, too outspoken, and had eyed her with reserved and stony suspicion, as if she were there to deliberately steal away all the best men. The matrons Alexandra had met had all befriended her mother. Nor could she seek refuge from Rose Parker, a debutante from Chicago who'd landed her titled man the year before and was now the most miserable human being in creation, entirely under the thumb of her husband.

As Alexandra exited through the train station's high Doric portico, she wiped tears away. It was over. It was all over. Unless she wanted to starve on the street like the poor, ragged, toothless woman selling apples at the curb, Alexandra had no alternative but to go back to Brown's Hotel with her tail between her legs.

Even though it would spell her doom.

Even though her mother would surely lock Alexandra in their suite again until she agreed to marry Lord Shrewsbury.

Well, Alexandra told herself as she hailed one of the waiting hansom cabs and climbed aboard, her ruse hadn't worked this time. She would just have to think of something new and try again in a few days for another ship.

"Brown's Hotel," she instructed the cabbie through the trapdoor near the rear of the roof.

"That'll be a shilling." The man's tone conveyed his distrust of such a shabby customer.

Alexandra peered up at him through the tiny window behind her. "Sir, I've been the victim of a robbery. My handbag and all my money were stolen. I'll see to it, however, that you are paid upon arrival."

"Cash in advance, Yank, or there's no ride."

"Sir, my name is Alexandra Atherton. My father is a mul-timillionaire. If you will please take me to Brown's Hotel, I assure you that my mother will pay my fare."

"And who's your mother? America's first lady?" A brief, contemptuous laugh escaped his mouth. "There's plenty of folk who'll be happy to pay in advance, girl. Go on, step down."

Cheeks flaming, Alexandra climbed down from the vehicle. She tried every cab in sight, but it was always the same story: no fare, no ride. Alexandra was incensed and hu-miliated. She was an *heiress*. She'd attended college! She'd been the belle of the ball at numerous events of the London Season. Yet she was being treated harshly, simply due to the clothing she wore.

Alexandra realized she'd have to walk. How many miles lay between Euston Station and Brown's Hotel? She had no idea. During the cab ride that morning, she'd been so ab-sorbed in her thoughts she hadn't paid attention to their route.

Pausing at a corner, Alexandra asked a shoeshine man how to get to Brown's Hotel. His instructions were long-winded and delivered in a thick cockney accent. She was able to gather, though, that it was a journey of about two miles. Following his gesticulations, she began walking south.

It was a gray, cloudy spring morning with the threat of rain. Although Alexandra had always enjoyed long walks in the countryside growing up, she'd never been enamored of strolling in a city. The sidewalks of London were jammed with men and women rushing about their business, and the streets were clogged with traffic. Horse-drawn carriages of every size and description jockeyed for position with hansom cabs, men on high-wheel bicycles, and buses topped with crowds of people. The air, heavy with soot and smoke, was further befouled by the stench of horse dung and urine that covered the street and lay piled up in heaps at the curb. A boy of twelve or thirteen dodged among the vehicles, struggling to scoop the excrement into a bucket, but it was a futile battle.

Alexandra waited for an opening in the traffic, then raised her skirts and picked her way across the street. Thank goodness she'd worn her oldest, sturdiest pair of walking boots, the only shoes she possessed that wouldn't have looked out of place with the plain black cotton dress she wore. Even so, by the time she reached the opposite curb, she had to scrape off the filth that clung to her soles.

She plodded on, past a street locksmith's stall, a man towing a barrel organ on wheels, and a fancy wares dealer selling porcelain ornaments from a wheelbarrow. Sandwich-board men crowded the curb, wearing signs proclaiming such slogans as TRY DR. CLARKE'S TONIC AND HAIR RESTORER and DRINK COLA: IT QUENCHES THE THIRST AS NOTHING ELSE WILL.

Twice more, she stopped to ask for directions. Eventually, a clock on a bank building told Alexandra she'd been walking for two and a half hours, and she began to wonder if she'd made a wrong turn. She should have reached Brown's Hotel by now. At the very least, she should recognize something of the neighborhood. But nothing looked familiar. Instead of elegant white houses, she saw rows of redbrick buildings and streets lined with shops and pubs.

"Fresh muffins!" shouted a woman in a cheap dress and dirty apron who was selling bread and pastries beneath a makeshift tarp.

The aroma of freshly baked goods made Alexandra's mouth water. She hadn't eaten anything since dinner the night before, having planned to purchase something at the station. Although she'd never bought food off a city street cart in her life, she would have been happy to do so now, if only she had the money.

Alexandra's feet were beginning to hurt, and she was growing tired. She was more alarmed, however, by the darkening clouds and increasing chill in the air. Shivering, she noticed a chimney sweep leaning against a wall and approached him. "Is Brown's Hotel nearby?"

"Brown's Hotel?" The sweep scratched his head beneath his cap. "Well now, miss, if you're headed for Brown's Hotel, you'd best take a cab. It's a good three or four mile from here, and looks like rain any minute."

Alexandra's spirits fell. Three or four miles! Clearly, she'd wandered very far out of her way. "I have to walk," she replied with resignation. "Can you please point me in the right direction?"

He barked out a few instructions, then indicated an alley just up the street. "You can cut through that lane beyond the Horse 'n' Hound; it'll save you ten minutes."

Alexandra thanked him, and they moved off in opposite directions.

She turned into the narrow, refuse-strewn alley, and was

halfway down it when a big man in a rough coat and cap emerged from a doorway and stopped directly in front of her.

"Well, well, well, what's the hurry, lassie?" he called out in a thickly accented voice which was slurred from drink.

A foul stench emanated from his body. Alexandra wrinkled her nose, more irritated than afraid of this unexpected disturbance. "I've already been robbed once this morning," she declared flatly as she attempted to dodge around the man. "I have nothing left to give you."

He grabbed her forcefully by the arm, grinding her to a halt. "I wouldn't say nothing, lassie." With beady eyes, he studied her slowly from head to toe, then back up again, giving her a leer that exposed a mouthful of rotten teeth.

Alexandra's pulse now quickened with apprehension. "Please, let me go."

"Not until you gives us a kiss." He pressed his free hand to her back and yanked her against his chest.

"Don't!" Panic surged through her as she turned her face away, struggling to break free.

The man persisted, pressing fleshy lips against her neck. He reeked so strongly that Alexandra felt bile rise in her throat. Her arms were trapped, so she kicked at him, landing a good one against his shin. He roared in pain and fury. Still gripping her upper arm, he raised his other hand as if to slap her, when all at once the skies opened up and unleashed a sudden, cold, and very heavy rain.

Her attacker started in surprise, the unexpected downpour causing him to loosen his grip. Alexandra took advantage of the reprieve to free herself and fled back down the alley. The pelting rain came so fast and furious that, in seconds, she was wet through.

At the lane's end, Alexandra burst onto the sidewalk—and plowed directly into someone. She heard the sound of breaking glass, glimpsed a man's startled face. Spinning in a half circle, she staggered backward into the street.

What occurred next came all in a whirl: the clatter of hooves. A horse's whinny. The sight of a vehicle bearing down on her. The world tilting as she dodged sideways. A sharp pain in her head.

And then she knew no more.

"**B**loody hell!"

Thomas Carlyle stared at his recent purchase, now smashed to bits on the sidewalk, the victim of a collision with a woman who'd raced out of the alley.

As he stood there, pelted by freezing rain, he saw the woman careen into the street, directly into the path of an oncoming vehicle. He gasped in horror as the woman stumbled and fell to the ground, where she lay unmoving as the horse and carriage thundered past, narrowly missing her.

Was she dead? He hoped not—the carriage didn't appear to have touched her. A few people hurried by, huddled beneath their cloaks and umbrellas, paying no attention to the prone figure lying in the muck and mud.

He ought to do the same.

This is not your affair, an inner voice warned. He was cold and wet. He had work to do. He shouldn't get involved. But another, stronger voice insisted, *This is partly your fault*. If she—whoever she was—had not run smack into him, she might not have stumbled backward into the road.

Thomas spied a carriage rapidly headed in the young woman's direction. She could be crushed in the next instant. With no time for further deliberation, he darted into the street and scooped her up. Once he regained the safety of the curb, he stared down at the limp form in his arms, rain dotting his spectacles as he noted several things in rapid succession:

She was young and slender with long limbs and a pale complexion. Her black dress and worn boots marked her as a member of the working class. The bodice of that dress pulled tight across an ample bosom—a sight mere inches from his eyes, and from which he had difficulty averting his gaze.

Those breasts, he saw now, were moving gently up and down. *Thank heavens*. She was breathing. She was alive. But what on earth had happened to cause her to run full tilt like that out of the alley, without looking where she was going?

Thomas peered down the alley from which she'd emerged. No one was there. He glanced back at the street to determine if she had dropped a handbag or any other item which might help identify her, but he saw nothing other than the sodden, trampled remains of a straw hat.

The rain was coming down in buckets, rapidly washing away the street muck that had clung to the young woman's hair and clothes. What was he supposed to do now? He considered dropping her off at the Horse and Hound, in the hope that someone would take pity on her. But no, that wouldn't be gentlemanly. Besides, she might need medical attention. He had no idea, though, if there was a doctor's surgery in the neighborhood.

He couldn't just stand there holding her in the pouring rain. He lived a block away. It seemed best to bring her there and let Mrs. Gill take over.

When he arrived at the redbrick town house, unable to reach the key in his pocket, Thomas gave the dark green door a few solid kicks. "Mrs. Gill! A little help, please!"

A moment later the door was flung open. His Irish landlady, her graying hair half-hidden beneath a white cap, was all astonishment. "Mr. Carlyle! What on earth?"

"This young woman fell in the street," Thomas explained as he brushed past Mrs. Gill into the compact foyer. "She was nearly run over by a carriage and appears to be unconscious. Pray, allow me to bring her into your parlor."

"Of course," Mrs. Gill cried, skirts rustling as she bustled after him. "The poor thing! Who is she?"

"I have no idea. Forgive me," Thomas added as they entered the small, overstuffed room, where a fire was blazing in the hearth. "We are both drenched through and dripping all over your carpets."

"Just you stand by the fire and wait, Mr. Carlyle. I'll fetch towels and blankets before you set her down." Mrs. Gill disappeared into the back room.

Thomas moved to the hearth, grateful for its flickering warmth as he made a more comprehensive study of the woman in his arms. She looked to be in her early twenties, a few years younger than himself. She was pretty, her oval face and delicate features reminiscent of Romney's early paintings of Emma Hart. Her hair, too wet to determine its true shade, had come loose and hung in waves to her waist.

He guessed her to be a shopgirl or seamstress, or perhaps a servant on her day off. As he gazed down at the lovely yet helpless form he was holding against his body, Thomas felt an unexpected spark of interest and compassion. He hoped she was going to be all right.

"Here we are." Mrs. Gill returned, her arms full of cottony fabric. She draped several towels over the sofa, and Thomas laid the insensible young woman down.

She was starting to shiver now, and so was he. Mrs. Gill removed the girl's gloves and dabbed at her with a towel, then tucked a blanket over her, while Thomas dried off his own face and hair and wiped his spectacles clean.

"You'd best take off that wet coat, Mr. Carlyle," Mrs. Gill advised, "lest you catch a chill."

He obliged, shrugging out of the sodden garment, which she took and hung over the fire screen. "Now what? Shall I fetch a doctor?"

"Let's give her a minute. She's young and healthy-looking, no doubt she'll wake up soon enough. A doctor would cost a pretty penny, which you and I can ill afford."

Thomas flinched at this assessment. He had never told Mrs. Gill—nor any of his clients in town, for that matter— who he really was. If anyone knew, he would be treated differently; he certainly wouldn't be able to stay here any longer, or to continue his work. But what she'd said was true. His finances *were* in a bad way. Ever since he was a child and aware of such things, he'd had the vague impression that money, for his family, was a problem. Now that he was twenty-eight years old and faced with all the sordid facts, his sense of mortification over the situation was acute.

A soft moan issued from the direction of the sofa, interrupting his thoughts. Glancing over, he saw that the young woman was moving restlessly beneath the blanket—hopefully, a sign that she would soon wake up.

Keep reading for a look at

SUMMER OF SCANDAL,

book 2 in the Dare to Defy series!

SUMMER OF SCANDAL

CHAPTER ONE

Bolton, Cornwall, England
June 21, 1889

The brisk wind bit Madeleine Atherton's cheeks as she stepped down from the train. Cornwall might be known for its temperate climate, but it felt more like November than June. At least the rain had stopped—for the moment.

The rural station at Bolton was much smaller than Madeleine had remembered. Just a redbrick building that resembled a cottage, with a single wooden bench facing the tracks. The platform was empty. Beyond the station stretched a single street lined with small houses and shops. Beyond that, wide green meadows were bisected by a narrow road as far as the eye could see. There was no sign of an approaching carriage.

Where was Alexandra?

Madeleine had spent the entire seven-hour train ride from London thinking about this moment, how wonderful it would be to see her sister again, and how happy Alexandra would be that Madeleine had dared to come. But no one was here to meet her.

Madeline pulled her velvet cloak more closely about her, worried. She had sent a wire yesterday to inform her sister of her plans. *I'm stealing away*, she had written, *just like you did last year*. Well, *stealing* wasn't exactly the right word. She had simply left a note, packed a trunk, donned her best green traveling suit, and slipped out of Brown's Hotel early that morning while her mother was sleeping.

As the second of three daughters of one of the richest men in the United States, Madeleine understood that she was expected to make an exceptional match. The quest for a titled husband might be her mother's ambition, to further the family's standing in New York society, but Madeleine had agreed to give it a try. It had worked out so well for her sister, after all. Alexandra had fallen madly in love with Thomas Carlyle, the seventh Earl of Longford, and was now happily married and a countess.

Madeleine wasn't actually opposed to the man her mother was urging her to marry. In fact, she rather liked him. The problem was, unlike most of the girls unleashed on the London Season, Madeleine wasn't a wide-eyed, immature debutante. She was twenty-four years old. She was a college graduate. This was her second Season in London, taking into account last year's half Season, when she'd hastily crossed the Atlantic to take part after Alexandra's impromptu exit.

And Madeleine had specific goals in mind.

Like her sister, Madeleine wanted love to figure into the equation in any match she made. And not just *any* love. Madeleine wanted a man who adored and respected her, but who also understood her and would be supportive of her dreams.

Was Lord Oakley that man? She wasn't certain.

Her abrupt departure from town would no doubt enrage her mother, but Madeleine desperately needed a few weeks away to clear her head. She had a life-altering decision to make. And she needed her sister's advice.

"Is this everything, then?" The query from a mustachioed porter broke into her thoughts. He and another man had deposited Madeleine's trunk and two bags onto the platform.

"Yes, thank you so much." Madeleine tipped both men, who touched their caps in thanks.

She was trying to decide what to do when she caught sight of an approaching carriage on the horizon. *Thank goodness. Alexandra was coming at last!*

Just then, from another car farther along the train, a tall, well-dressed gentleman descended, carrying a leather satchel. Madeleine's breath caught in her throat.

It was Charles Grayson, the Earl of Saunders. The best friend of her sister's husband.

A man she had no desire to see, much less speak to.

But he had already spotted her. His eyes widened in surprise as he closed the distance between them, then greeted her with a bow. "Miss Atherton!"

Madeleine gave him a terse smile and a dutiful curtsy. "Lord Saunders."

"I had no idea you were on this train." His voice was just as deep as she'd remembered, just as cultured and refined. He regarded her with calm detachment and a hint of something like curiosity, as if unsure where he stood with her or what to make of her. "I spotted you last month at the Fitzhughs' ball," he added, "and another time at the races. But each time I sought you out, you seemed to disappear."

"Did I? I'm sorry," Madeleine replied noncommittally. There was a good reason he hadn't connected with her on either of those occasions. She'd gone out of her way to avoid him.

Looking around, he asked, "Did you travel alone?"

"Yes." She knew it wasn't the "done thing" for a woman to travel by train unaccompanied, but she'd had little choice in the matter. She and her mother were sharing the same lady's maid while in England, and Madeleine couldn't very well have robbed her mother of her only servant. She silently dared Lord Saunders to reprove her. But he only said:

"So did I. My man Evans came up yesterday with most of my things. But why have you left the Season? I pray you are in good health?"

"I'm fine, thank you."

A cloud of steam emanated from beneath the great locomotive, and the smokestack belched a dark, filthy blast.

"I hope you are not here to see your sister?" he further prodded.

His expression and tone sparked another dash of worry within her. "Why do you say that?"

"Because I received a wire from Longford yesterday morning. He and his wife and sisters are away at Bath."

"Oh!" Madeleine's spirits sank. "Then Alexandra never received my telegram." What a fool she'd been to leave

London on such short notice, without waiting for a reply! But it had never occurred to her that her sister wouldn't be home. Alexandra was seven months pregnant, and had said she intended to remain at home until her child was born.

A new thought worried her. "People go to Bath for their health, don't they? Do you know if my sister's all right?"

"I haven't heard otherwise. Bath is also a popular holiday destination."

Madeleine wished she felt more reassured. The train whistle blew, a bell clanged, and the huge wheels began to turn. With a rhythmic *chug-chug-chug*, the locomotive moved out of the station. Leaving Madeleine alone on the platform with Lord Saunders.

"Do you know how long my sister and Lord Longford intend to be away?" she asked.

"A fortnight, I believe."

Two weeks! Madeleine's mind worked on the problem. If she could learn where Alexandra was staying in Bath and contact her, maybe her sister would return earlier. Assuming—praying—that she was all right. If not, Madeleine would go to Bath. In the meantime, she could wait at the Longfords' estate, Polperran House. The carriage she'd noticed earlier was making its approach.

"Well," Madeleine observed, "it looks as though the staff at Polperran House opened my telegram, and have sent a coach for me."

"I am afraid that is my coach, Miss Atherton," Saunders pointed out.

Indeed, as the coach—a smart equipage, painted red and

black, with large glass windows—drew up, Madeleine recognized the Trevelyan coat of arms and the coronet of a British marquess emblazoned on the side.

"I see."

"Please, do not distress yourself." Saunders's smile was polite. "It would be my honor to escort you to Trevelyan Manor. You will be most welcome to stay there until Longford and his family return from Bath."

"Thank you, but no," Madeleine replied quickly. She had no desire to spend time with this man, nor to stay at his family's estate. "I would not wish to impose."

"It would be no imposition, I assure you."

"I appreciate the offer, my lord. But I would rather find a way to get myself to Polperran House and remain there, while I send word to my sister."

He nodded. "In that case, pray allow me to offer you a ride thither."

Madeleine considered. It was a two-hour drive from Bolton Station to Polperran House. She could try to find a cab, but she knew it would not greatly inconvenience Lord Saunders to do her this favor. Although she'd never been to Trevelyan Manor, Alexandra had told her that it was situated near the coast some five miles beyond Polperran House, which was more or less on the way.

Still. Did she want to be cooped up in a carriage with this man for such a long period of time? It was bad enough that she'd traveled unaccompanied all the way from London. But to ride in a closed carriage with a man to whom she wasn't related or engaged? An Atherton girl, her mother would insist, did not behave that way.

Noticing her hesitation, Saunders added: "There are no more trains today. Your only alternative is to take shelter at the Inn at Bolton—and I would not wish my worst enemy to stay at that establishment, nor even have a meal there. Unless you are absolutely famished?"

"I had something to eat on the train," Madeleine admitted.

"Well, then?" He quirked an eyebrow. His eyes, she noticed, were an arresting shade of hazel. As he looked at her, it seemed as though he was working hard to take the measure of her, as if she were a problem that needed to be solved. Despite herself, she felt a ripple of sudden interest run the entire length of her body from her head to her toes.

Don't let him charm you, Madeleine.

She'd spent the past two months at endless balls and parties, subjected to the calculating scrutiny of every fortune-hunting bachelor in London. She'd learned to grin and bear it, and, after meeting Lord Oakley, to actually enjoy it. But Lord Saunders's gaze made her feel self-conscious somehow. And . . . rattled.

A low rumble of thunder rent the air, recalling her attention to her predicament. Raindrops began to patter against the pavement. It was quite apparent that no one was coming for her. It seemed she had little alternative but to accept his offer.

Madeleine swallowed a sigh. "Thank you. I'd very much appreciate a ride to Polperran House."

"Excellent."

Lord Saunders directed two porters to load Madeleine's luggage onto the back of the carriage. As the men struggled under the weight of her trunk, Saunders asked her, "What have you got in here? Bricks?"

"Books."

He eyed her with amusement as the coachman secured the trunks and covered them with a tarpaulin. "Did you bring an entire library?"

"Not quite." She'd only packed two dozen or so of her favorite novels in with her clothes. All the other books she'd brought from New York, she'd been obliged to leave at Brown's Hotel. In truth, she felt a bit bereft without them. But, she reminded herself, this was a short trip. She'd be back in London in a few weeks.

"May I assist with your satchel?" Saunders gestured toward the tapestry bag Madeleine carried.

Instinctively, she clasped the carryall to her chest, feeling the weight of the precious cargo within. "No, thank you."

He smiled agreeably, then offered his gloved hand to help her board. She took it. His grip was strong and firm, and once again, she felt a sizzle of sparks dance up her arm. *Drat the man for being so charming.*

She climbed inside, withdrawing her hand and settling on the forward-facing upholstered seat. Saunders took the seat opposite. As the carriage pulled out of the station, rain began pouring down in earnest. Saunders removed his top hat and set it down beside him. Madeleine dared a glance at him across the carriage.

She had to admit, he was very good-looking. His nose wasn't perfect, but its slight bend gave it character. His cheekbones were, well, high. His curly hair looked soft and was a lovely shade of dark caramel brown. His three-piece suit was perfectly tailored to his broad shoulders, trim waist, and long legs. It was too much, really. No wonder the debutantes had called him "swoon-worthy."

Madeleine had no intention of swooning before any man, however. Especially this one. No matter what the other ladies had said about him, as they tittered and gossiped behind their fans.

"It is a shame that he makes such infrequent appearances during the Season, and is so skittish about settling down," one of her acquaintances had intoned breathlessly at a dinner party. "He is still young, just a year shy of thirty, and he will one day inherit the title of Marquess of Trevelyan. The way he flirts! Why, he almost married an American heiress a few years ago! Thank goodness *that* did not come to pass."

Madeleine knew all about *that* scandalous affair. It was the reason she disliked him.

"So," Saunders quipped, breaking into her reverie as his eyes lifted to hers, "have you run away from town as your sister did?"

His voice held a teasing lilt to it. Madeleine realized she'd been caught staring and in embarrassment looked away, the question setting her on the defensive. "No! I haven't run away. I have merely taken . . . a small break."

"In the middle of the Season? How unusual. What

prompted your departure? Other than a sudden impulse to visit your sister?"

"What prompted yours?" she challenged.

His smile fled. After a pause, he replied: "My father is unwell."

"Oh!" Madeleine had only met Lord Trevelyan briefly, the summer before, but had the impression that he was well-liked and respected in the community. "I'm so sorry."

"He has been ill on and off for years, but never this se-riously. It is why my parents remained in the country this Season. The physician and my mother are very concerned."

"I'm very sorry," Madeleine said again. "I do hope he re-covers fully and quickly."

"Thank you."

Saunders sat in worried silence as the carriage rumbled along, rain beating against the windows. Madeleine felt bad that she'd deflected his question with one of her own. Hoping to fix her mistake and lighten the mood, she said, "You asked my purpose in coming to Cornwall."

He replaced his frown with a look of genuine interest. "I did."

"I've come because I've had an offer of marriage."

"Congratulations! Who is the lucky gentleman?"

"The Marquess of Oakley, eldest son of the Duke of Courtenay."

"Ah! I know him well."

"Do you?"

"We roomed together for a year at Oxford. Philip is an excellent fellow."

Madeleine hesitated. "Yes, he is."

"You sound uncertain."

"I don't mean to. I'm honored by his proposal." Lord Oakley was handsome, upright, intelligent, thoughtful. Everything Madeleine wanted in a husband. Her mother was thrilled with the match, and Madeleine knew that where titles were concerned, she couldn't do better than the eldest son of a duke. "But it's a big decision," she added.

"Indeed it is."

"He's gone off on a tour of the Continent, so I have time to consider the matter. I didn't want to accept until I'd discussed it with my sister."

"I understand why. The Countess of Longford is a paragon among women. I should very much like to consult with her myself before making a decision, were I a woman."

The comment made Madeleine's hackles rise again. "Were you a *woman*?"

Her tone seemed to take him aback. "Er . . . Yes."

Madeleine reminded herself to see the humor in the situation. He was, after all, a man. Most men viewed the world as though it were their exclusive dominion, convinced that women were a weaker, less worthy, less intelligent gender. "Are you saying that a man can only turn to another *man* for advice? That you would never seek a woman's counsel on any matter?"

"I . . . did not say that."

"Yet you implied it."

"Forgive me, Miss Atherton. That was not my intention."

"If you think about it carefully, you will see that what you said was condescension, thinly veiled."

He nodded solemnly as he considered her remark. "Perhaps it was. Again, forgive me. I see that I shall have to mind my *p*'s and *q*'s with you."

"*P*'s and *q*'s. That is such an interesting expression."

"It is, isn't it? Now that I said it, I realize I have no idea what it actually means."

"It's thought to be a schoolroom phrase," Madeleine told him. "When pupils were taught to write the alphabet, they were reminded to place the letters in the proper order. *P* comes before *Q*."

"That makes sense."

"There are two other theories, though, that I recall."

"Please enlighten me."

"One is that it's short for 'mind your *pleases* and *thank-yous*'"—the latter of which sounds a bit like the letter *Q*. My favorite insists that the phrase derives from English pubs of the seventeenth century, when bartenders were obliged to keep an eye on the *pints* and *quarts* their patrons consumed."

Saunders chuckled. "How on earth did you come to know all that, Miss Atherton?"

"I had a rather remarkable English professor in my second year at Vassar."

He paused. "Ah, yes. Your sister mentioned that you just graduated from college. May I congratulate you on your accomplishment?"

"Thank you."

He cocked his head slightly, regarding her with what appeared to be a mixture of esteem and curiosity. "I find you most unusual, Miss Atherton."

"Do you? Why?"

"Your father is one of the wealthiest men in America. You have no need to work. Yet you chose to attend university."

"Every member of the peerage goes to college," she pointed out, "and you don't engage in a profession."

His brows furrowed at that and he seemed perturbed. After a moment, he commented, "Yes, but that's different."

"Why is it different? Why shouldn't I educate myself? Because I'm a woman?"

An awkward laugh escaped him now and he seemed incapable of a reply.

Madeleine leaned forward in her seat, passion fueling her words. "Women are just as smart as men, my lord, and sometimes smarter. We are equally as capable. We can do anything men can do."

He studied her. "Is that so? Anything?"

"Anything. Women are doctors and surgeons now—highly skilled ones. And we have women lawyers now in America."

"So I have heard," he admitted. "But you must admit, there are *some* limits as to what women can do."

"Name one."

"Well, for example, a woman could not dig ditches."

"Give me a shovel, and I will prove you wrong."

His eyes twinkled. "Something tells me you would. All right, then. A woman could not be a police officer."

"Why not?"

"She does not have the physical prowess the job requires."

"I beg to differ. You'd be surprised how strong a woman can be, my lord, when the circumstances demand it."

He took that in, seemingly considering it, but shook his head. "I do not see it. In the same vein, a woman could never serve in the military or go to war."

"Untrue!" Madeleine protested. "Absolutely untrue."

"How so?" He pointed a finger at her. "And pray do not use Joan of Arc as an example. She was an anomaly."

"Joan of Arc was not an anomaly. Women have served in combat since the dawn of history!"

"Have they? Who?"

"Chinese General Fu Hao, for instance, a woman, led thousands of people into battle in the thirteenth century BCE, and defeated the Shang. In the eleventh century CE, Matilda of Tuscany, an accomplished archer, commanded armies to defend the pope and made kings kneel before her. In our American Civil War, hundreds of women concealed their gender so they could fight alongside their Union and Confederate counterparts. And that's barely scratching the surface of the—"

"Truce! Truce!" Lord Saunders laughed again and raised his hands in defeat. "I stand corrected. This is clearly a subject which you have studied and I have not."

"Given the opportunity, women can accomplish great things, Lord Saunders. And one day—I hope to see it in my lifetime—we *will* have that opportunity. When we have the vote, men like you will be obliged to accept us as your equals." She paused, conscious that she'd put a somewhat negative emphasis on the words *men like you*, and worried that she'd gone a bit too far. After all, she *was* a guest in his carriage, and beyond expressing doubts about women's physical capabilities, he hadn't said anything too terribly chauvinistic.

He went quiet for a moment as he stared at her. "Miss Atherton, since the first time we met, I have had the sense that you do not like me very much."

"Oh, my dislike for you began long before we met, Lord Saunders." The words tumbled from Madeleine's mouth before she had a chance to stop them. She stifled a gasp at their brazenness, instantly regretting them. "Forgive me, I should not have said that."

"No, I appreciate honesty, Miss Atherton," was his astonished reply. "But pray tell me, what did I ever do to give you offense, before we had even met?"

Don't miss out on Syrie James's critically acclaimed historical fiction books!

ABOUT THE AUTHOR

SYRIE JAMES is the *USA Today* and Amazon bestselling author of thirteen novels of historical, contemporary, and young adult fiction and romance. Her books have hit many Best of the Year lists, been designated as *Library Journal* Editor's Picks, and won numerous accolades and awards, including Best New Fiction by *Regency World Magazine* (the international bestseller *The Lost Memoirs of Jane Austen*), Barnes & Noble's "Romantic Read of the Week," Best Novel of the Year by *Suspense Magazine*, Best Snowbound Romance by Bookbub (*Nocturne*), and the national Audiobook Audie Award for Romance (*The Secret Diaries of Charlotte Bronte*, also named a Great Group Read by the Women's National Book Association).

Los Angeles Magazine dubbed Syrie the "queen of nineteenth century re-imaginings," and her books have been published in twenty-one languages. A member of the Writer's Guild of America, Syrie is also an established screenwriter and playwright who makes her home in Los Angeles. An admitted Anglophile, Syrie has addressed audiences across the U.S., in Canada, and the British Isles. Learn more about Syrie and her books at www.syriejames.com